I0775513

Permafrosts
Emeraude Port
Oakbury
Stormair
Emerald Woods
Mirefield
Grey Shoal Ocean
Sagebrush Forest
Brookhill
Ardenas
Whitebridge
Greenmills
Bridgebarrow
Western Desolates
Arden Forest
Winding Steppes
Flatlands
The Wastes
Twisted Woods
Yearning Sea

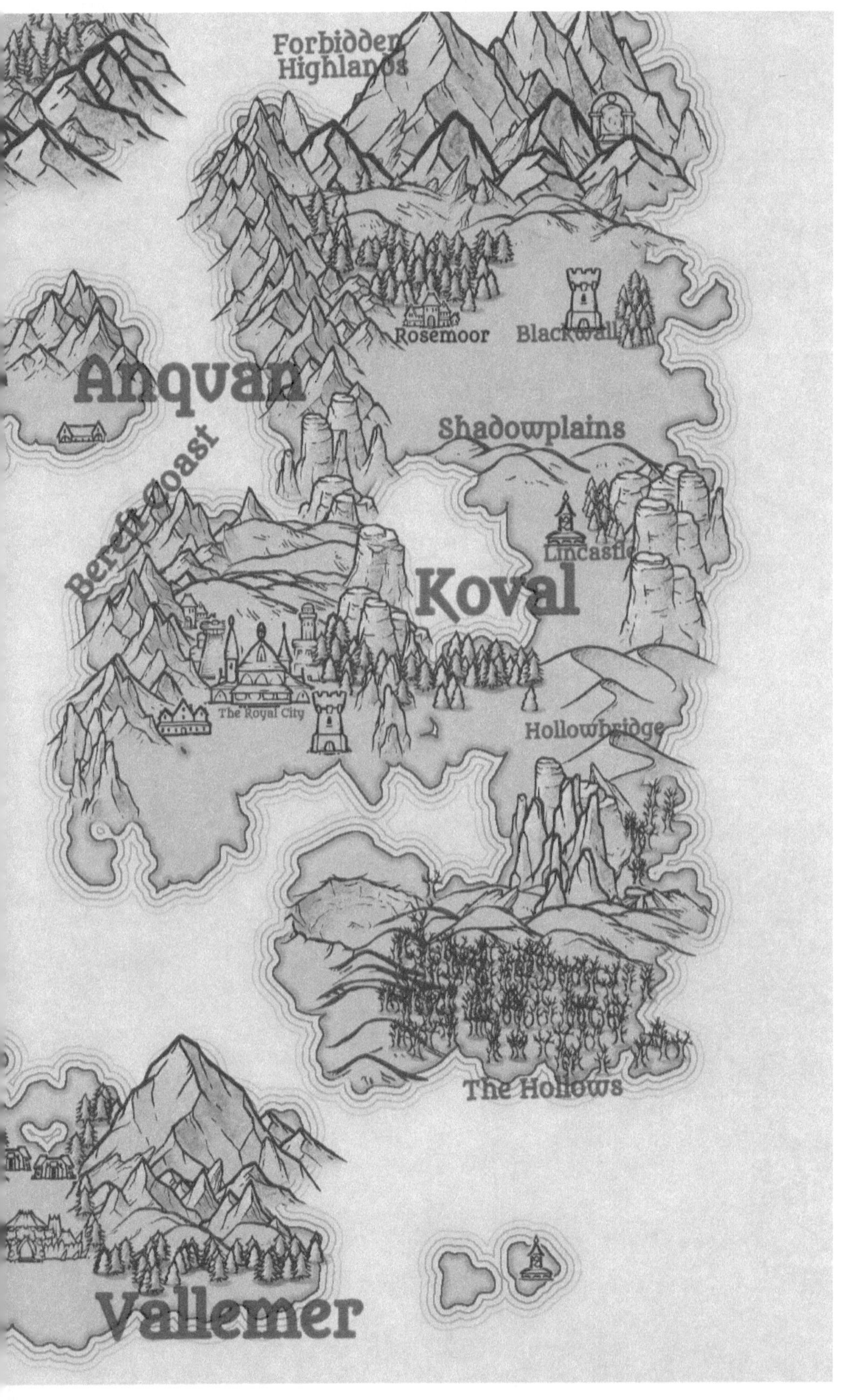

Forbidden Highlands
Rosemoor
Blackwall
Anqvar
Bereft Coast
Shadowplains
Koval
Lincastle
The Royal City
Hollowbridge
The Hollows
Vallemer

LAMENT OF THE WOLF

BOOK TWO OF A DREAMER'S MISFORTUNE

C. A. FARRAN

LAMENT of the WOLF

C. A. FARRAN

CONTENT WARNING

This story contains content that might be troubling to some readers, including, but not limited to, depictions of and references to death, harm against children, references to sexual assault, graphic depictions of violence, and sexual content.

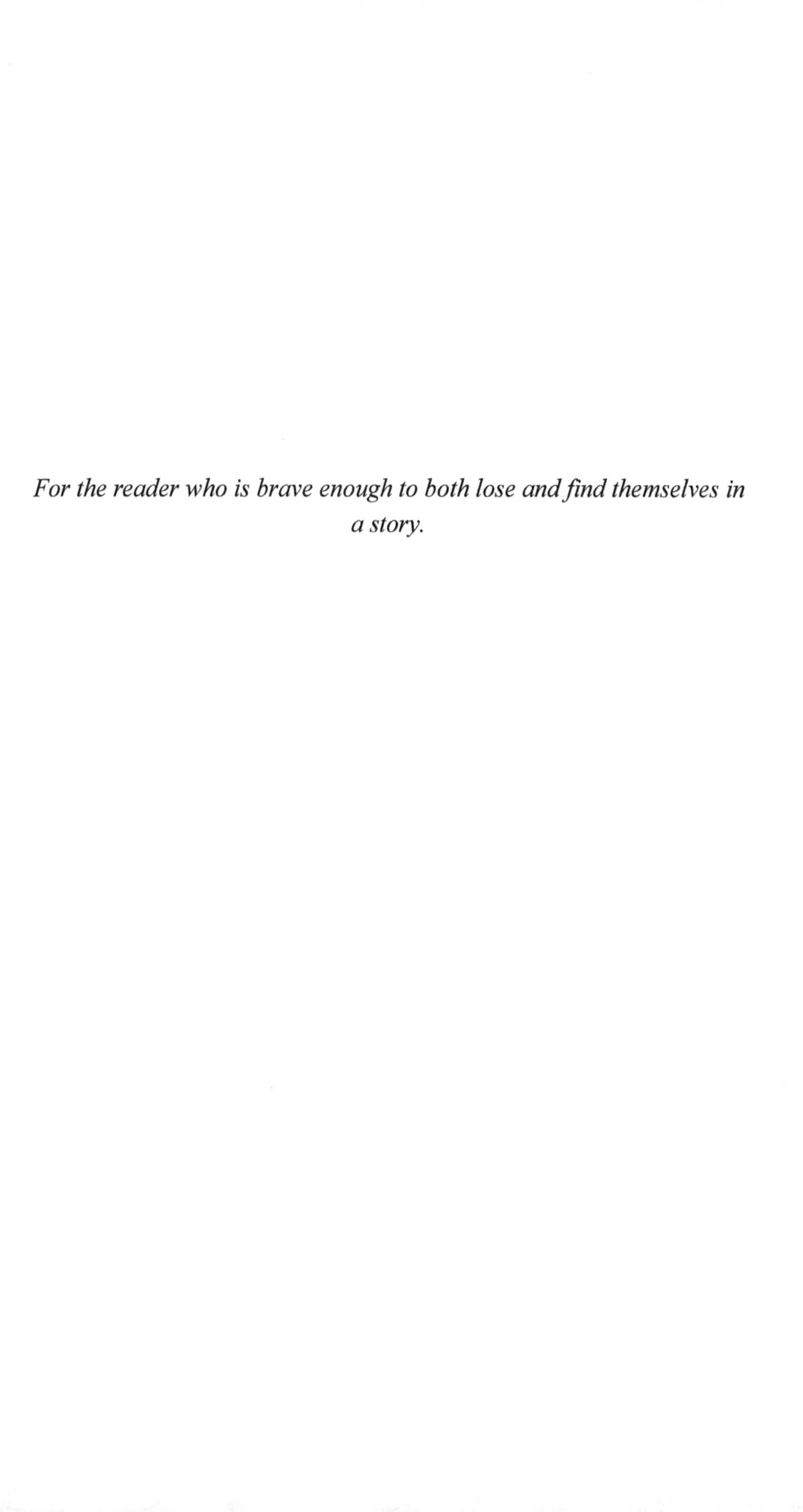

For the reader who is brave enough to both lose and find themselves in a story.

DEMETRIA

$\mathcal{A}$ warm hand gripped Demetria's throat, choking a gasp from her lips. Her eyes fluttered open, and darkness surrounded her, smothering her with the unforgiving truth: this was no dream, and she was at the mercy of her assailant. Dizzying fear threatened to paralyze her, but a distant reminder echoed in the back of her mind.

She was not helpless.

Demetria felt for the blade beneath her pillow as the last of the air squeezed from her lungs. Her fingers closed around the familiar grooves specially hewn for her grasp. Hooking the curved hilt of her knife around her attacker's wrist, she twisted and pried her neck free. Blessed air flooded her chest as she rolled away and fell off her bed, landing in a tangled heap of blankets. She leapt to her feet and tripped over the coverlets as she brandished her blade.

Her eyes adjusted. A broad form stalked toward her. He had the element of surprise, but there was one thing he hadn't accounted for.

Demetria knew every corner of her bedroom.

She dove for her chamberpot. It was empty and only used when she was too ill or too lazy to find her way to the latrine. But she swung true, and the metallic clang of brass hitting her attacker's skull was downright gorgeous.

Fighting a grin, she clambered across her mahogany linen chest, the one she always left jutting out at an odd angle. She'd slammed a toe on more than one occasion in the dark, yet never tucked it in so she wouldn't trip on it again.

When her assailant caught his foot on the edge, he grunted.

Demetria laughed, picking up a bottle of ink from her writing table and throwing it toward the sound. The tinkle of glass breaking and a long-suffering groan filled the air.

A balmy breeze fluttered through Demetria's sheer white curtains, and silvery moonlight slashed across the black pool on the marble floor.

"I'm not cleaning that up," a familiar voice called out.

Demetria turned the key of her oil lamp, filling her room with warm light. Her bedclothes lay in a tangled mess on the floor and her wood chest sat crooked in the center of the room. Ruslan stood rubbing the side of his head with his large hand, eyes narrowed at her. Specks of black painted the side of his face, jaw, and disappeared into the grey of his hair. Demetria might have felt bad if she didn't catch the glimmer of pride in his honey-brown eyes.

"You cheated," he said matter-of-factly.

"I did not! You said the purpose of these exercises was to keep me ready for a fight." Demetria glanced around the room. Her sketches she'd pinned to the wall above her writing desk fluttered in the breeze from the open window. Images of monsters and heroes from the stories her mother used to tell. Her blankets still lay in a twisted heap on the floor, and the black ink now reached the tips of her toes. She wiggled them, reveling in the slick oily substance that could have been her blood had this been real and not practice.

Ruslan frowned, creasing the deep lines of his bronze face. He looked down his straight nose in disapproval, but the intended effect was lost on her. For an aged warrior who now spent most of his time barking orders, Ruslan still had the strong features of the man who starred in many of her daydreams as a child. If Demetria had known at the tender age of eight that her father's most trusted captain and her pretend husband would spend his time training her, she would have swooned. Now, she knew he was a pain in the ass.

"Had I been a demon or a blood-feeder, you would have been dead." Ruslan indulged Demetria's preference for training to fight the monsters from her mother's stories. Almost as if he sensed she needed to keep that part of her alive, even if it was silly. That, and it was easier to imagine killing a monster than killing a person. "And I'd prefer you use your weapon rather than your bedpan next time."

"Anything can be either a weapon or a liability depending on who wields it," Demetria said, echoing him from lessons prior. She tucked her arms behind her back in a mocking posture of respect. "And don't sully my triumph. It's unsportsmanlike."

Ruslan huffed a laugh, rolling his wide shoulders. "Next time, I won't go easy on you. I expect you dressed for training by the eighth bell." He strode across the room, pausing at her door. "You did well, Princess."

SUMMER IN KOVAL was as hot as the blazing Netherworld. Sunlight streamed through the window, assaulting Demetria with the reminder it was time to meet Ruslan for training. No doubt he'd push her hard as payback for their simulation. He'd grown more intent on her progress lately, and suggested they employ more creative maneuvers to aid her readiness. Demetria still wasn't certain what exactly his goal was. Besides stealing her sleep.

Stretching, her gaze fell to the portrait her parents had commissioned on her tenth name day. She'd insisted on playing with Evander that morning, despite knowing the artist was arriving to render her portrait to canvas. She'd returned with not a moment to spare, covered in mud, her hair a mess from the wind. Her mother let her sit, filthy and all, for her portrait, just as she was. With her new ivory gown streaked with brown and green grass stains, she'd sat poised as if she were the very picture of decorum. The artist even captured the gleam of mischief in her dark eyes, the smears of dark mud against her light-umber skin, and the sticks peeking out from her tangled black hair.

Demetria ran her hand over her sweaty face. She should have risen before the dawn and convinced Ruslan to complete her training beneath cool shadows. But she didn't regret the extra sleep. What was the point in a month-long reprieve from her studies if she didn't sleep past the seventh bell?

A sharp squeak sounded from the corner. Demetria turned to find the new maid, Maya, trembling by the bookcase, feather duster quivering in her hand. She hadn't even realized she was in the room, which soured her previous achievement. She wouldn't tell Ruslan the maid snuck up on her.

"Were you summoned?" Demetria asked as gently as possible. She didn't appreciate servants in her room while she slept, a preference her parents always respected and enforced. But things were different since her brother ascended the throne.

"Apologies, your majesty." The girl bowed, and the duster slipped from her grasp. She quickly snatched it up. "I was only—I was sent to tidy your chambers." Her pale face bloomed red with shame.

Zaire must have been in one of his moods again to leave this girl a quivering mess.

Demetria flung the heavy covers back, eager to get her training over with so she might find Evander and pester him to take her riding. He wouldn't take much convincing. A bit of flattery always made his fair skin burn brighter than his red hair.

Her feet found the smooth marble floor, and she shuffled her way over to her dressing partition. She grabbed her training leathers from their mounted hook, yawning as she pulled them into place.

One day, she'd tell her brother she'd rather study art. Sketching was her preferred medium, but there was so much she didn't know. So much to learn. They were in the capital. There were dozens of artists she could apprentice under. Each time she broached the topic of attending the university when she came of age, it never ended favorably. She knew better than to ask again. For the time being.

It warranted another discussion, but not today. Today would be pleasant, despite the infernal heat.

"Again."

"I'm tired. Someone broke into my room and rearranged my furniture."

Ruslan barked out a laugh. "Your chambers are abysmal. If you were one of my soldiers, I'd have you on latrine duty for keeping your quarters in such a state."

Demetria wiped the sweat from her brow and grinned. "I'll have you know I designed my space with purpose. There's order to the chaos. If I wanted it tidy, it would be."

Ruslan's brow furrowed, though amusement won out over his features. "The day you clean up your own messes, Princess, is the day I dance the Kovalian Madrigal."

A sharp laugh burst from Demetria's chest at the image of large, cantankerous Ruslan waving scarves around as he swayed his hips. Tidying her room would be worth it.

Demetria lifted her gaze to the valley sprawling before the Silent Mountains. Soon, daisies would pepper the land. She used to run her hands over their delicate, white petals on her way to the place Evander called "Mermaid Rock." Perhaps they could find that waterfall again. As children, they used to sneak away and build little houses out of leaves and twigs to leave on Mermaid Rock. She'd heard a story of little winged creatures befriending a girl who built them a home and brought them honey and sweets. Demetria had become obsessed with discovering the truth of this tale, and Evander followed along. They'd sit for hours, listening to the steady rush of the water and waiting for magic that never came. She kept meaning to return, if for no other reason than to see if the houses they built still stood.

"Princess?" Ruslan's voice broke through her thoughts. He eyed her with concern. "Are you well?"

"I'm merely picturing you dancing the Madrigal."

"Show me an effective combination instead of a simple parry and retreat, and I'll think about it."

Demetria lifted her sword, bracing for the next attack.

Sweaty and sore, Demetria limped her way to the kitchen. The staff bustled in a blur of commotion. Her brother was hosting some sort of luncheon for visiting nobles.

She didn't merit an invitation.

The long wooden counters overflowed with spiced pork, plump purple grapes still on the vine, buttered asparagus, and more wines than Demetria thought they even had in the cellar. Rolling her eyes, she snagged a honeyed roll leftover from breakfast.

The head cook, Gaspard, gave her an affectionate smile even as she pilfered his kitchen. The heat flushed his generous cheeks.

"You know," he began in the rolling softness of his Anquanian accent, "I could have whipped up something fresh for you."

Demetria licked the sugar off her thumb, frowning at the salty taste of her sweat. "I wouldn't trouble you so. Not when my brother seems determined to have a feast for every meal."

Gaspard wiped his hands on a towel. "There's not a culinary challenge I could not meet." As he spoke, he shot a conspiratorial smile her way.

Demetria grinned around a large bite of her roll, sweet glaze filling her mouth. She mumbled a goodbye and set out for the back gardens. Past the fluted marble columns and the rows of hedges, until she found Evander pruning the rose bushes. He wore a ridiculous wide-brimmed hat that shielded most of his neck, apart from the line of skin above his collar, already reddened from the sun. His arms were thick beneath his white tunic, and the material rippled with every movement.

Demetria took another bite and watched him. He'd long outgrown his gangly limbs and filled out in a way she found curious. Others had surely noticed his transition into manhood.

Demetria snorted. *Manhood.*

Evander turned, tucking his garden shears into his belt and pulling his gloves off. "Ruslan let you out early?" He wiped the sweat from his reddened forehead. An endearing flush claimed his cheeks, and if it was possible, he'd sprouted even more freckles across his elegant nose. Demetria wanted to count them, just to make sure.

"More like we began training early. He actually bombarded me in my chambers while I still slept!"

Evander laughed, tipping the ridiculous hat with the movement. "He's only been threatening to do so for months."

One of Zaire's guards, Bastian, strolled by, offering a wave and a warm smile. Bastian was fun to talk to, if one didn't mind everyone knowing their secrets. He was a notorious gossip, which made him one of Demetria's favorites. How else would she know Guardsman Calum was courting Lord Baltham's oldest son?

But right now, the only person she wanted to speak with stood before her, mopping sweat from his neck. Demetria took a step closer and pulled Evander's hat over his face. "Oh, hush. Tell me you can duck out now. It's boiling and gardening is boring."

Evander pushed his hat off his head so it dangled by the leather cord around his neck. His flaming head of hair glinted in the midday sun, and a soft smile dimpled his cheeks.

Demetria took another bite of her honeyed roll and ignored the warmth that lit in her belly.

Evander shoved his gloves in his pocket and grabbed her hand, pulling her deeper into the gardens. Labor roughened his palm, but his hold was gentle, as always. Although normally she led, and he followed. He guided her past the rows of blush-pink peonies. Their thick scent swallowed her as the garden grew wilder.

The portion open to the public was well-kempt and pristine. But the deeper they went, the more untamed it became. Purple crocuses still adorned the path, growing at random in wild patches. This was once her mother's favorite part of the garden. High walls of vines offered privacy their lives could scarcely promise. A forgotten statue of an ancient paragon stood sentry. Demetria couldn't recall its name, but she remembered the chip in its outstretched hands. As a child, she used to hold the hands of the nameless paragon and pretend she was a goddess, too.

Evander steered them toward the overgrown hyacinths, and the fresh scent of spring itself enveloped her like a forgotten dream. Rich shades of lavender, blue, pink, and white surrounded them like a citadel of safety.

Evander halted and spun to face her. The open expression of hope on his face made something stutter in her chest.

"Demetria," he began.

She leaned forward as if pulled by the sound of her name on his lips.

"Your brother—"

Like the bucket of piss she dumped on a nasty guard when he made her favorite footman cry—shock doused her nerves.

"Zaire? You brought me here to talk about Zaire?" Demetria yanked her hand from his grasp. What else could this excursion have signified? Of course, Evander took her somewhere private to complain about her brother.

Evander's face fell. "He's getting worse."

Demetria threw her arms out to the side, pacing the space of the private garden. "His moods are nothing new. He's a right tit, and you know it. Remember when he put a snake in your sleeping roll? Knowing full well you'd piss your pants in fright—"

"Demetria!" Evander grabbed her by the shoulders, turning her to face him. He slowly let his hands fall. "This is serious. I'm not speaking of a bout of anger or a prank. Zaire is becoming…" His gaze fell to the ground, and his throat bobbed. "Your brother is dangerous."

Demetria narrowed her eyes, crossing her arms so he wouldn't notice her hands shaking. "You're speaking treason, Evander."

"I'm not the only one. People are angry and scared. They won't tolerate a ruler who sells their family to work in the mines at every indiscretion."

"The mines are barely in use anymore. My parents put an end to that practice—"

"No, Demetria." Evander ran a hand over his face. "Zaire has created incentives for assigning indentures. He's all but pushed for land wars and the ones who suffer aren't the lords squabbling over titles."

Demetria exhaled a sharp breath. Zaire wouldn't do that. He was a lot of things. Stubborn, callous, harsh. But he was also her brother. Her brother who assigned his advisor and Captain of the Guard to train her. To make her strong. Someone who cared that much for family couldn't possibly tear other families apart, could they?

"There must be some mistake..." Demetria sagged on the stone bench, staring at the overgrown blades of grass caressing her boots.

"Why do you think he assigned Ruslan to you? He's made you a target with how many enemies he's garnered. He knows of the unrest in Koval. But he won't do anything about it."

Demetria's head swam with impossible thoughts. Had things really gotten so bad while she failed to notice? The urge to argue swelled, to tell Evander he was mistaken, and Zaire couldn't be all he said. But the impulse quickly dissolved as memories of the frightened staff, of the way whispers would cease when she drew near, drifted into her mind. How laughable it must have been, watching her parade around without a care in the world.

Evander crouched in front of her, staring up at her with a solemn expression. He gently took her fists, running his thumbs over her knuckles. He even had freckles on the backs of his hands. "We've tried to make our voices heard, but Zaire continues to ignore us. There's a rally this day. A call to end drafted labor in the mines. To demand only volunteers."

Demetria's head snapped up. "You're petitioning my brother?"

"It's the only way. If enough of us speak out, he can't ignore us. He can't silence us, and he'll have to listen. Especially before his well-respected audience today." The meeting with the lords—the banquet Gaspard was prepping. They meant to humiliate Zaire. Evander's eyes searched her face. Was he searching for permission? Support? How many times had he followed her blindly into all of her petty schemes? He'd always trusted her and had her back.

She trusted him, too.

Demetria cupped his jaw, running her thumb along the scar she gave him when she threw a rock at his face. Back when her temper was a fierce little beast. He'd cried and bled and swore he wasn't mad, but every time she saw that scar, something tugged in her chest.

"I'll speak with my brother."

"You don't have to—"

"Yes, I do. He'll listen to me."

Evander's brow furrowed, and he laced his fingers with hers, holding her hand against his face.

Zaire would listen to reason, she was sure of it.

WHEN DEMETRIA WAS NINE, she broke Zaire's favorite toy—a glass globe reflecting every country of the world when the light refracted through it. It glimmered in the sun, shapes dancing along the walls. She was never allowed to play with it, so when he went riding, she snuck into his room. Her parents never permitted her such things. She was always liable to break something precious, whether by accident or in a fit of rage. She couldn't help the smooth glass dome slipping from her hands and shattering on the floor. The fear and guilt, the weight of disappointing him when he returned from his riding lesson.

This felt a lot like that.

Demetria tugged on her dusty rose gown, gauzy fabric fluttering under her touch. Her hands still bore faint ink stains from her nighttime drawing sessions she couldn't scrub clean, but she'd attempted to tame her wild hair into a low twist at the nape of her neck. Zaire hated it when she looked a mess, so this was a calculated maneuver before broaching the uncomfortable discussion.

She glanced around the council room. Light from the picture window flooded the space, and the soft breeze carried the humid scent of summer into the room. She loved the circular table made from the trunk of a giant olive tree. Upon its surface sat the map of the world. The parchment had faded with age and still had the rip in the corner from when she tried to play marauders with Evander. She ran her fingers over the aged map, and it crinkled beneath her touch. The trade routes between Ardenas and Koval were clearly labeled, and a few markers sat atop Vallemer. Curious. Vallemer was an independent nation, wasn't it?

The doors creaked open, a soft sound of warning. Demetria lifted her gaze to find her brother, King Zaire, standing in the open doorway.

Concern etched his face, deepening his seemingly permanent frown. Sweat beaded his deep golden skin, and no crown graced his head. He wasn't the type to wear ornate royal garbs when he wasn't holding court. And instead of his mantle, he wore a simple military jacket of crimson and gold. He appeared more like a general than a king. Stepping into the room, he left the doors open and approached Demetria with an air of caution—as if he could sense something was amiss.

"Were you hoping I'd changed my mind?" Zaire's deep voice reminded her of their father, but there was something off about it. It was cold where their father was always warm. He eyed her dress. "You'll be utterly bored. I'm doing you a favor."

Of course, he thought she wished to attend the luncheon.

"Not at all. I wished to speak with you."

"What about?" He arched a dark brow and ran his hand over his thick black hair. "You haven't even addressed me properly."

Demetria's mouth quirked. It was an old game they used to play when he was a conniving shit who refused to play with her unless she swore fealty.

With an exaggerated curtsy, she murmured, "Your grace."

He nodded and braced his hands on the table. "Speak. I'm listening."

She hesitated. It would be best to handle this delicately. To slowly weave her thoughts into a larger conversation so he didn't feel attacked.

"Demetria, I have important matters to attend to and I still need to prepare—"

"I hear rumors of unrest."

His gloved hands tightened, the leather creaking in the silence between them. "Rumors."

Demetria wiped her sweaty hands on her fine gown. "Zaire, is it true you've reopened the mines? That more and more indentures are forced to work?"

Zaire leveled her with a punishing glare that ghosted a shiver down her neck. But he said nothing.

His silence told her everything.

"I know things haven't been easy, and you've been forced to make a lot of decisions at a time we should have spent grieving." They'd both lost their parents, but Zaire had lost his autonomy. Demetria couldn't imagine the pressure he'd been under, and it hurt to think she hadn't recognized his struggles. But she was here now. She could help him correct the course of their kingdom. "You'd earn a lot of goodwill if you listen to the people. Show them you care. A slight gesture, a show of good faith while we figure out a way to help everyone prosper."

Zaire's dark gaze bore into her, a fierce rage burning in his eyes before they dulled, a cool distance clouding over. "This is your council for me?"

Demetria nodded. She knew her brother would see reason. He loved their kingdom just as much as she did. "It is, and I can help you. I can speak to some groups on your behalf, let them know you're working on a plan—"

"Yes, how valuable your insight is. Tell me, would you suggest I draw them a pretty picture? Fund the country with scribbles?"

Heat flushed her cheeks. "That's not funny."

"No, of course it isn't. What's funny is a child coming into my council chamber and telling me how to run my kingdom. You know nothing of what you speak, and yet you command me with such authority."

Demetria clenched her fists. He was angry and lashing out. It was nothing new, but she wasn't backing down, not this time. She would have this difficult conversation with her brother, no matter how he insulted her. She would endeavor to remain calm. "Zaire, your kingdom is on the verge of civil war. Your people are unhappy. This should matter to you. What are you, but their voice?"

Astonishment dawned on Zaire's features before it quickly melted into anger. "And I wonder, dear sister, where you get your information from."

Something mysteriously close to shame burned in her gut. Yes, Evander brought this to her attention, but her brother's paranoia left no room for this explanation. "It's not information. There's no plot against you. Your people want to be heard and they deserve it. You owe them an audience."

"I owe them nothing more than what I already give."

The force of his anger rumbled through her as Demetria tried to slow the rapid pace of her pulse.

"You're more than this," she whispered. "You're more than whatever this desperation is. What do you lose by listening? Are you any less a king if you offer your ear to your kingdom?"

Zaire studied her with a furrowed brow, calculating. "You know nothing of what it means to rule. I've protected you from these harsh truths—let you languish like a leech in our court. I haven't pressed you for marriage. I haven't even forced you to be productive, and not so you can turn around and stab me in the back."

"Stab you in the—I'm trying to help you even if you are too stupid to realize it."

His hand flew so swiftly she scarcely had time to witness. But the crack it made against her cheek and the force of the blow sent her staggering with tears burning behind her eyes. Warm pain bloomed across her cheekbone, and her left eye pulsed. A glimmer of shock stole across his features before he schooled them into a harsh expression. She glared at him, ignoring the sting smarting her cheek. She drew strength from the pain as it drowned out the force of his accusations. "Even the servants fear you. You've become a tyrant, and if you aren't careful, they'll drag you off the throne."

"I can see I've been too lenient, wishing to shield you. I won't make that mistake again." Zaire grabbed her by the elbow and yanked her toward the doors of the throne room. He thrust her onto the dais and sat on his throne, clenching and unclenching his fists on the armrests.

Demetria glanced around, her stomach rolling.

The Kovalian throne room was a place she rarely visited anymore. Crimson drapes, golden steps, and the very walls shimmered with flecks of gold. When her parents were alive, they threw extravagant parties and balls. The annual masquerade hadn't felt the same in years. There was once a time when being in this room was a wonder. A chance for Demetria to feel like the princess her birthright claimed her as.

Now, all she felt was the fear gripping her chest and shallowing her breath.

Dozens of guards poured in as if they'd been expecting to be summoned. In they filed with the rhythmic pounding of their boots against the carpeted floor.

"I wanted to leave you out of this, sister." Zaire waved to the guards stationed at the door. "Bring them in."

Voices carried into the room as the doors opened. People flooded in, some battered and bleeding, some weeping. Bastian, the guard who once made her laugh so hard she cried, dragged a man by the arm, pulling him from the middle of the throng to stand before Demetria at the foot of the dais. As the crowd parted to let them through, her heart sank. Pale skin and freckles, a flame of red hair, and crystal blue eyes stared up at her.

Evander.

His eye swelled behind purplish bruising and his mouth bled, but when he took one look at Demetria, his gaze trailing her tender cheek, his expression turned murderous.

Zaire's voice rang out, and a fearful hush settled over the crowd. "We have a traitor in our midst. One who dares commit treason in my very castle."

Demetria turned back to her brother, but there was nothing on his face she recognized.

"I have received grave reports. I took pity on the one responsible, thinking he couldn't possibly understand the danger of his actions." Zaire's lip curled in a snarl. "But when he tried to turn my own sister against me, he went too far."

Demetria's legs went numb. "Evander never—"

"Don't lie!" The force of Zaire's bellow silenced the throne room. "You think I don't have eyes and ears within the walls of my own castle? You disappeared into the gardens with Evander, and return spouting treasonous insults?" His expression smoothed into a false calm—the sort of calm that rumbled before a storm. "I have known of his little gathering for weeks. Do not insult my intelligence again, sister."

Demetria trembled, her knees threatening to buckle. "You can't be serious. Zaire, this is Evander. You've known him since he was a baby. Father taught him to ride alongside you." Bile rose in her throat, and her vision blurred. This couldn't be happening. This couldn't be real. She would awaken in her bed and begin her training with Ruslan and pester Evander in the gardens.

Zaire stood, and the quiet rage he wore was the most terrifying expression that had ever graced his features. "Gather your strength and harden your stomach. We can't afford such sentiments. He is a danger to our peaceful rule. He chose to live as a traitor, so shall he die like one, too."

Demetria blinked and staggered toward Evander like she could shield him from her brother's rage. Evander yanked his arms free of Bastian, hands outstretched as if needing to grasp her. She flung herself into his embrace and finally, the tears rolled down her cheeks. He pulled back to wipe them away.

"Don't cry," he whispered. "It'll be okay."

Demetria shook her head. Nothing would be okay. Not today, not ever again.

"Evander… I'm—I'm sorry."

A soft smile lit up his face, one of relief. "Don't be. You're strong and brave. I've always admired that about you. I've always—" His voice stalled. He pressed his forehead to hers, and his familiar scent of summer earth enveloped her.

Demetria swallowed against a throat thickened by grief. Why hadn't they spent the day in the forest searching for Mermaid Rock?

A harsh grip on her shoulders yanked her back. "No," she cried, trying to hold Evander one last time.

Bastian pressed a rough hand to Evander's shoulder, dropping him to his knees, and refusing to look at Demetria.

Zaire wouldn't order it now, would he?

The sharp clang of a sword freed from its scabbard rang out.

"Wait!"

She met Evander's eyes, though she found no fear. Only warmth.

The blade sliced through the air, through skin and tendons, and muscles and bones. A strangled scream filled Demetria's ears. She wanted to close her eyes, but she couldn't. She wanted to remember how he looked in the gardens, not this. Never this. But she couldn't look away as steel met flesh over and over. The strength fled her body, leaving her cold and shaking. Blood. There was so much blood. The last few ligaments in the side of Evander's neck barely held his head to his shoulders as his body slumped forward. Crimson seeped into the floor and blended with the carpets.

Demetria fell to her knees, a sob escaping her chest.

She would never hear his laugh or see the way his blush traveled up his neck and across the tips of his ears.

Evander was gone.

CHAPTER ONE

DACIANA

$\mathcal{D}$aciana was no stranger to darkened forests—when the last few rays of the sun bled from the horizon and gave way to night. She suffered no fear or mistrust of darkness. She was a child of the moon, and even when her change wasn't imminent, every instinct in her body rejoiced at the black sky. The creeping shadows held no malice, only a warm whisper calling out to her.

Welcome home.

The journey from Koval back to Ardenas was swift without the presence of her companions. Their absence was an ache she keenly felt, but this was something she must do on her own. It was tempting to delay the inevitable, to travel back alongside Lark and claim a few more weeks of her company. But a smaller merchant vessel left the port days before Lark and Gavriel arranged their own transport.

Each day that passed, she missed them more. Alistair, with his incessant need to disagree with every little thing she said. Langford with his impossibly kind heart and quick mind. And Lark, *skies,* she missed that girl. The way they understood each other with a mere glance.

She even missed Gavriel. Were it not for him and his assured presence, she wouldn't have left Lark.

And Hugo…

She slipped a hand into her pocket, closing her fingers around the small stone she'd taken from his burial rite. A burial that held no body to mourn.

Picking up speed, she wended through the dark forest, a canopy of leaves keeping the stars from view. She didn't need their light anyway. The moon's arc had thickened, and the promise of the change whispered along her bones.

Just a few more days. That was more than enough time.

She'd reach the village of Mirefield, an insignificant spot on a map where the cattle outnumbered the people, long before dawn. It wasn't a place Alistair liked to venture. Without the promise of work or a decent tavern, the village was all but useless in his eyes. But nestled in the forest, away from the heavy foot traffic of travelers and traders, it seemed as good a place as any for a hunter to visit in search of monsters. Beasts weren't as picky with their victims as Alistair was with his travel routes.

She'd ask around and follow the stories. Of monsters slain by the girl wearing a red cloak.

Kenna.

Her name clanged around her head, echoing with the force of a blow. The last time they'd crossed paths, she'd barely had the strength to walk away. Kenna's mere presence was enough to set every nerve alight. Raw and exposed.

Kenna's pendant hung heavily around Daciana's neck, mocking her for the faint echo in her heart.

It was madness to seek Kenna now. A risk, the worth she'd been debating this entire trek.

But if the veil fell, and monsters overran the world, the least she could do was offer fair warning.

"RED CLOAK? Yeah, I saw the hunter," said a broad-shouldered man, face and neck reddened from working in the sun. Instead of a tavern,

the local inn housed a modest dining room fit for Daciana's purposes. The patrons were chatty, as she expected. A slip of coin loosened even the tightest of lips. "Not two days ago she came by. No one's paid any notice to the contract we posted, and the guard up north is useless." He spat on the floor.

"What was the contract for?"

He hesitated, his heavy brow furrowing. "Something we never took issue with before. We had an understanding. The creature only attacked those disrespecting the land."

Daciana could guess the true name of this beast. Leśniks were guardians—protectors of nature, with a nasty streak for those who failed to honor the ground they tread.

"We called it The Keeper," the ruddy-faced farmer said. "But once the little 'uns started going missing, we knew it was no longer punishing destruction, but mischief. Can't let anyone wander into the forest alone. Not 'til the hunter comes back to show us proof and collect her payment."

"Where does it dwell?" Daciana peered into his bloodshot eyes.

"You a hunter, too?"

"Something like that."

The farmer shrugged. "Don't much care who faces the beast, so long as the deed is done and my yield doesn't suffer."

FOLLOWING HIS DIRECTIONS, Daciana made her way into another dark forest. Morning hinted its approach from the horizon, but it was lost amongst the trees.

She slipped under the shroud of branches laden with leaves, moving silently across the forest floor. Her muscles twitched, jittery energy buzzing across her skin at each step that drew her closer to Kenna. Images of her deep-set brown eyes, crinkled with amusement, filled her mind. Other images sprang to the forefront of her memory. Pale skin painted with moonlight, a soft press of her full lips to hers, light dancing in her eyes at promises made…

Daciana shook her head to clear her thoughts. This wasn't about a life stolen, a wish not granted. This was duty. If the world fell, they'd need all the allies they could get.

Dawn insisted its stretch across the sky, bold light filtering through canopies of dense trees, and bright beams cutting across the moss covered ground. She was getting closer. The unmistakable pull of predator to hunter sang in her veins. As it had all those years ago.

The scent of burning leaves hit her first. Someone was close.

Daciana's blood roared in her ears, drowning out all sounds of the forest. She didn't need to hear the creatures that rustled in the underbrush; the ones that dug into the earth to find storage for winter; the wind rushing through the outstretched wings of the sparrow that soared from tree to tree. She felt their presence, as assuredly as her own heartbeat.

She edged toward the thicket and peered into the clearing.

A small figure wearing a crimson cloak sat perched atop a fallen tree. Beams of light softly kissed her pale skin, casting her in an effulgent glow. The freckles across her nose and cheeks were more pronounced than Daciana remembered.

Kenna.

As if hearing her thoughts, Kenna's head snapped up, dark bangs falling in her eyes. The knife she'd been lazily whittling a thick branch with instantly flipped to a defensive hold.

This wasn't how Daciana wanted their initial meeting to go—creeping up on an armed hunter and waiting in the shrubberies like a common beast. If she were more like Alistair, she could have strolled in, quick words cutting from her tongue as she regarded the hunter with little more than vague amusement.

If she'd been like Lark, she'd have sprinted into the clearing and thrown her arms around her. The former Reaper wore her heart for all to see in a show of courage Daciana still couldn't fathom.

If she'd been like Langford, she'd have called her name, giving her the chance to run away if she didn't wish to see her.

But Kenna would never run.

Daciana cleared her throat and stepped out from the cover of the forest. To stand as she was, before the girl who haunted her dreams.

Kenna's perfect face regarded her with shock, before the side of her mouth quirked in a tight smile. She placed the stick on her lap, sheathing her knife. "Well, I can't say I saw this coming."

Daciana grabbed the pendant encircling her neck, yanking it free of her hair she'd chosen to plait down her back in a thick braid. She glanced at it, mountains and shimmering sky sitting in her palm, before she tossed it to Kenna.

Snatching it from the air, Kenna's eyes never left Daciana's face. "You came all this way to deliver this?"

Daciana took slow deliberate steps before sitting across from her. Kenna's lone pack and weapons lay on the earth at her feet, and the fire she'd built quietly crackled. It wasn't like the campfires Daciana had with Alistair and their crew, where the flames danced high and sparks of embers shot into the night sky. This was lonely. There was no merriment, no air of camaraderie. She'd seen Kenna dig holes to conceal her fire many times. The second air channel she'd tunneled into the earth, feeding the flame and obscuring it.

"I came to warn you," Daciana finally said, wetting her lips, "about what's coming."

Kenna leaned closer. "What's coming?"

Before Daciana could answer, a soft whistle carried on the wind. There was no melody to it, just a sustained note of warning. Kenna examined the pendant in her palm before she closed her fist, yanking her short sword free from its sheath.

"Hold that thought," she said, angling her sword to her ready stance and studying the spaces between the trees.

Daciana pulled her sword from the sheath on her back. The thick hilt was a familiar weight in her grasp. "The Leśnik?" It should be quick work between the two of them, provided the forest didn't answer its call. If it did, even the roots beneath their feet weren't to be trusted.

The ground shook—a steady approach trembling the surrounding trees. Kenna grinned, the eager face of a hunter in her element, before she took off for the nearest branch. She swung herself up and climbed. The years hadn't dulled her agility.

A shadowy figure swept between the trees, appearing and disappearing, but its height was massive. Almost as if a giant tree stalked them.

Definitely a Leśnik.

Daciana circled her wrist, swinging her sword to loosen her muscles for a fight. Not that she'd face this alone. Kenna wasn't gone. She was waiting. Hunting.

That would make Daciana the bait. Not ideal, but she could adapt.

A great *crash* shook the camp as the creature charged into the clearing. It stilled, and its intent gaze sent her skin crawling. Towering at twice her height, the giant forest spirit was adorned with moss and leaves, its mottled green skin textured like the bark of a tree. It let out a screech and barrelled toward her. Daciana leapt at the last moment, swiping it back with her sword.

The ground split beneath her boots, roots shooting up and seizing her. They wound around her ankles, squeezing hard enough she heard something *pop*. Pain flared in her ankle. Gritting her teeth, she hacked the roots to bits and spun just in time to come face-to-face with the keeper of the forest. Long strands of moss hung from its jaw like a beard, and its humanoid face twisted with rage. Black eyes peered into her own, and there was no mercy in their depths.

It was a shame when killing felt like an unanswered question of 'is it necessary?' Fortunately, she had her answer this time.

Raising her sword, she readied to strike—

Kenna dropped from above, landing on its shoulders and driving her sword deep into its chest. She yanked her sword out and plunged in deep again, her lovely face twisted into a triumphant snarl. The Leśnik clawed at the intrusion, but she yielded nothing and sank her blade again and again, until finally the creature dropped to his knees. Kenna still sat astride its shoulders, a full head taller than Daciana, before she slid down and kicked the beast to the earth. Without wasting a moment, she sliced off one of the Leśnik's clawed hands, its fingers like gnarled branches, and stuffed it into a sack. The rest of the body sank into the earth, roots wrapping around it, as if reclaiming their own.

"Won't be long now. At least it'll feed the trees for a season." Kenna wiped her sweaty forehead. A faint blush had bloomed across her pale cheeks. "Apologies for the interruption. You were saying? Something you wanted to warn me of. Hopefully, not this guy." She kicked at the mound as it rapidly became one with the earth. "Otherwise he stole your purpose."

Daciana ran her gaze over the girl she sailed across the ocean to find—the one she'd abandoned the others for. The one she tried to forget. Her slight form had taken on new edges, firm muscles replacing the softness Daciana had trailed her fingers over countless times.

Daciana realized she had yet to answer the question. Turning her thoughts to the task at hand, to the reason she'd sought Kenna out, she cleared her throat. "The fall of the world."

Kenna narrowed her eyes, staring at her with a look Daciana knew all too well. Her mind was always puzzling. "Well, don't leave me in suspense. What in the blazing nethers happened?"

CHAPTER TWO

LARK

A familiar throne room stretched before her. Archways of gold curved above, lining the vestibules along the sides of the great hall. Harsh light filtered through the giant windows at the head of the room.

Lark's footsteps echoed against the polished marble floors, her heart hammering in her chest. She approached the dais, never once tearing her eyes from the ancient being lounging on the throne. His dark eyes glittered as he tracked her movements.

Thanar.

Shadows curled around him, both a warning and an invitation, as he lifted his chin to regard her with thinly veiled amusement. His long black hair hung loose and straight, a disapproving crease settling between his dark brows. He was handsome, there was no denying that, but he possessed a severity that made his features too hardened to appreciate.

"Here you are once again, Larkin." His baritone voice carved a pit of dread in her stomach.

Lark stilled, hands clenching into fists. She would not cower before him. Real or imagined, he had no power over her. Not anymore. This was a farce, an echoed imitation of what he once was. Now he was at the mercy of the witch queen of the Netherworld, contracted to do her bidding. The image of him, broken and lost, by Nereida's side, sprung to her mind—when he'd claimed Lark's debt and sacrificed himself to set her free of her contract. A slick emotion closely resembling guilt settled alongside her discomfort. "We both know I'm not really here."

He leaned forward in his seat, raven hair falling into his face. "As you well know, that is a matter of debate. Tell me, where do we go when we dream?" His obsidian eyes regarded her with careful consternation.

Reapers didn't dream.

Lark had guarded her secret, afraid of what it might mean that she —a Reaper—could fall into the world of dreams and nightmares. The place only mortals were permitted to go.

But she was mortal now, and she had nothing to hide.

"This is my dream. I decide what happens," she said. "I don't need to play your games."

His grin only widened, large hands curling to grip the armrests of his throne. "Since when have you mastered the art of controlling your dreams?" He arched a dark brow. "You waste your bluster here, Larkin. For in the recesses of your own mind, you cannot hide."

Lark's jaw clenched, heat rising up her neck. "I'm not hiding from anyone, least of all from you, Thanar."

He chuckled darkly, the low sound of it slithering over her and leaving a trail of ice in its wake. "You foolish girl." He stood so suddenly, Lark flinched. "Did you really think you could outplay fate?" He sauntered down the steps, a slow crawling storm.

Lark resisted the instinct to step back, to put space between them. Before she could respond, a wisp of gold fluttered out of the corner of her eye, and the scent of lupines and grass filled her senses. She turned —only to find nothing but that skies-forsaken throne room.

"Did you really think you'd get to keep your mortal pet? That the balance wouldn't demand a terrible reckoning?"

He towered over her, and she had to lift her chin to meet his eyes. "Fate may have determined my destiny, but it's mine to claim," she said.

His eyes softened, regarding her with what appeared to be pity, brows drawn together in an expression of vulnerability. "He will slip through your fingers, as you did mine."

Lark edged back, shaking her head. "I was never yours for the taking." But he'd tried to claim her. To own her.

His face fell at her words before he quickly composed his expression into a mask of indifference. "No, Larkin, you were never mine. Just as that mortal will never be yours. Don't say I didn't warn you. The pain of a shattered soul isn't one you walk away from. It consumes you until you recognize nothing of yourself anymore."

This wasn't Thanar. This was her fear given voice, reverberating against the walls of her mind. A less tangible enemy she hadn't the faintest notion of how to conquer.

She turned on her heel and stormed toward the doors. Without so much as a backward glance, she abandoned her fear in that empty throne room.

Awareness pulled at Lark, and she opened her eyes. Gavriel still slept beside her, his chest slowly rising and falling with every breath. She reached out to run her knuckles against his jaw, stopping just short of making contact. It felt like an intrusion. Their easy touches suddenly seemed weightier. Like she was taking advantage of a soul bond between two humans that were long dead.

"He will slip through your fingers, as you did mine."

Shaking the last vestiges of her dream, memories of that fateful day in Nereida's throne room took hold of her thoughts. Of what they'd learned, deep in the bowels of the Netherworld. The truth of why she and Gavriel were inexplicably drawn to each other.

Beyond reason and logic, her soul had screamed for his. Their joining was the result of magic from lifetimes ago. It wasn't Gavriel's choice to be near her. His body vibrated with the same incessant need and drive as hers. Now each touch felt stolen, rather than granted. The thought drained the warmth from her blood.

Lark sat up and crept over his bedroll, soundlessly opening the flaps of their tent. The crisp air of a morning chasing Autumn's call blasted her in the face. By midday, the sun would beat down on her back, driving away the chill. But for now, the cold air awakened her senses and sharpened her nerves.

She set about starting a fire, caring little for the tremor in her numb hands.

The same thoughts that haunted her, both waking and sleeping, unfurled in her mind. Nereida had Thanar and all his power at her beck and call. Images of him from before, great and terrible, to the crushing reality of what he was now. The pet to the Queen of the Netherworld. For as long as Lark could remember, she feared facing that same fate by his hand. But witnessing his downfall, the betrayal of his inner circle, and the trap Nereida had set long ago finally snapping shut, didn't offer Lark any satisfaction. Instead, potent dread curled in her chest. A deep sense of foreboding before the storm.

Nereida had all she needed to tear down the veil—the only barrier to keep the demons and Undesirables from seeping into the mortal world and scorching the earth. Each night, Lark prayed to the skies to be granted one more day before the world fell. Too afraid to ask for more. One more day to get that much closer to Inerys, to find answers.

If anyone knew how to restore the veil, it was her.

Lark had long since given up on contacting Solana, the Goddess she'd freed and then promptly been abandoned by. If there was one thing she'd learned to trust, it was that the gods cared little for the plights of mortals.

So she'd find Inerys, the witch of the woods, and with luck, she'd form a plan. An inkling of a plan, even. Anything to not feel so powerless.

Strong hands ran up her arms, startling her. Gavriel had a penchant for sneaking up on her, his movements silent from a life of training in the art of subterfuge.

"You're up early," he said, his voice a deep rumble, thick from sleep, "again."

She shrugged away from his touch, refusing to turn around to see if hurt flashed across his face. Even as the loss of his warmth ached in her chest. "It seems my body has a bit of an internal schedule. Must be the cold."

He took a step toward her. "If you're cold, there are ways to remedy that." His mouth curved in a suggestive smirk, tugging the scar bisecting his lip. It still lit a warmth low in her belly, but this time, the accompanying guilt smothered the feeling as quickly as it came.

"I've already remedied it," she said, turning away to sit by the fire.

"So you have." He walked around the circle of their campsite, dropping to sit across from her, and facing her through the flames. "Shall I cook us some apples?"

Langford was the first one to introduce her to that particular delicacy. They'd all parted ways weeks ago, Langford and Alistair staying behind to study the ancient archives of the Great Library in Koval. She missed him fiercely. His easy presence, the way he calmed her whenever he was near. She supposed she missed Alistair, too. And the way he always made her laugh. She even longed to hear his daily argument with Daciana.

Lark's heart clenched. Daciana had gone on her own journey, with no real indication of what she sought.

Soon enough, they'd reunite.

Well. Not all of them.

Losing Hugo was something Lark hadn't recovered from. But that wound was one she'd face down another day.

She swallowed the thick swell of despair that crept up her throat. "I'll just have mine raw, thank you."

Gavriel's face revealed nothing, though he busied himself with packing up camp.

If only she could find the right words.

Instead, they hung heavy in the air between them, unspoken.

DEEP IN THE EMERALD FOREST, they crossed that familiar lake. The only disruption to its glassy surface were the ripples from each dip of the oar. Lark and Gavriel approached the shore where Inerys' cottage stood.

Nothing about the façade had changed; the walls were made of stones forced to align and jutting out at odd angles. Vines wrapped around the cottage—as though the magic Inerys practiced within its walls called, and the forest had no choice but to answer. Trees loomed over the small hut. Guarding. Hawthorns glimmered like rubies against the dense thicket along her home.

The simple relief of finding the place right where they'd left it eased the tightness in Lark's chest. She wouldn't put it past the witch to have found a way to pick up her entire home and hide it deeper in the forest where she'd never be found. Especially after what happened the last time they were here.

Images of Balan, black horns curling out of a shock of white hair, crept from the darkest corners of her mind. The memory of how easily he'd sent Gavriel flying with a wave of his hand. How his body had careened through the air like a rag doll. A shiver crept down Lark's spine. She glanced at the boulder he'd hit his head against. The dark stain of his blood had washed from the stone since they were last here.

This was the life their soul bond had wrought. An existence rife with danger, a blade forever poised at their throats.

Gavriel's hand found hers as if sensing her thoughts. The scrape of his calloused palm against her own lit her nerves aflame. She almost melted into his warmth. The desire to turn into him and press her face against his chest overwhelmed her.

But she couldn't be sure of where that impulse came from. Not anymore. She gently tugged her fingers free, heart fracturing at the look of hurt that crossed his face for the briefest instant.

The door was firm against Lark's chapped knuckles, and its red paint was peeling off in long strips and cracks against the woodgrain. Inerys would know how to help. The witch was far more cunning than she let on. It was only a matter of willingness.

The groan of the door snapped Lark's attention to the dark eyes peering out from behind it. Inerys' gaze narrowed into sharp slits.

"Reaper. I thought I made it clear you were never to set foot here again."

Technically, she said never again would be too soon, but this was important.

"I need your aid."

Inerys opened the door wide to regard her with an impressive glower. Wisps of her dark hair curled away from her forehead, and her scarlet gown complimented her bronze skin. She was lovely in all her displeasure of their visit. "What have you done this time?"

"You might want to invite us in, it's a long story."

CHAPTER THREE

LANGFORD

The dry pages of the dusty tome crinkled their familiar comfort. Langford ran a hand through his dark hair, untidy from the hours he spent tugging on it, and clenched his eyes shut. He needed to regain focus on the blurry words before him.

He'd been so excited to return to the Great Library of Koval. It had been ages since he'd visited—since he attended the university, in fact. Setting foot in the massive building rife with knowledge filled him to the brim with a baffling mixture of melancholy and bitter nostalgia. Bitter, because he couldn't recall personal aspects of that time in his life fondly, but oh, the way the world had once seemed so vast. As if he had all the time in the world, and regret was a far-off notion reserved for the old.

He spent the first day on the upper balconies, peering down at the massive landscape of books. Stained cherry wood bookcases and tables, caught in an array of golds and reds, served as the burning beacon of knowledge begging to be devoured. Ornate paintings by the great Aureus Madizza spanned the ceilings—the artist, long gone but not yet lost to time. His work was magnificent, if a touch macabre for Langford's taste. Violent, bloody battles of the war that divided the continents, somehow made beautiful by the stroke of Madizza's brush.

It was humbling, that first day, surrounded by all the world had to offer. The promise of everything that could be—right at his fingertips.

But now the reality of Langford's task, along with the constant headaches from squinting at ancient texts and soreness from hunching over for days, waned his excitement.

If only slightly.

He massaged his neck, glancing over at Alistair. He'd rested the side of his face atop a stack of irreplaceable tomes, quietly snoring. The short beard dusting his jaw was more prominent than usual, and his black hair hung in his face. Langford studied Alistair's unguarded expression, smoothed of all the tension he wore as of late.

It wasn't without cause. Especially if Alistair felt half as torn up about what transpired as Langford did.

Nothing had been the same since the Forbidden Shrine. The shame and humiliation still set the skin beneath Langford's collar ablaze—his deepest desire made real, and the implications of what it meant. The life he secretly longed for. The love of a man who couldn't see him as anything other than a friend. He still carried those memories of an entire year, of a life that never existed. Yearned for a time that never came to pass.

Langford had always relied on logic and reasoning to keep him grounded while the rest of the world fell to baser instincts. But he couldn't even trust logic anymore. If he let himself dwell on thoughts of Alistair and the life they never shared, he'd unravel. The delicate balance, each tangible sense that insisted he was here, this was happening, would be thrown off kilter.

It was safer to stay focused on the task at hand.

He turned his attention back to the tome he'd been dutifully studying. He'd pored over countless volumes already, yet the answer he sought always eluded him.

After the news Lark brought from the Netherworld, of the imminent fall of the veil protecting the mortal realm, there was only one chance for survival.

They needed to kill Nereida, the Queen of the Netherworld. Even though she had Thanar, the master of death, at her beck and call. All while facing whatever monsters roamed freely once the invisible bulwark fell.

No pressure.

With luck, Lark and Gavriel would prevent this from ever coming to pass. But Langford couldn't be sure if fate or chance had a hand in this.

And he wasn't much of a gambling man.

Any advantage couldn't be overlooked. If he could but discover a way to slay the unkillable, his insurmountable task would feel possible.

Nearly possible.

Langford's gaze drifted from the page to once again regard Alistair and his rumpled clothes from days and nights spent in the library. The dirt and blood caked in the lines on his hands—hands far too elegant for his roguish skill set. Alistair stirred, as if sensing Langford's blatant examination.

Langford averted his attention back to the ancient text, eyes snagging on the word *Messorum*. He hunched forward, bringing his face close enough his breath ghosted against the page.

Messorum Ferrum.

Langford sat back in his chair, pinching the bridge of his nose. Trying to clear his vision of the tears his aching eyes conjured.

Reaper Blade.

It might be something, it might be nothing, but one thing was certain:

He was going to need more tea to analyze this finding.

CHAPTER FOUR

DACIANA

It was odd how memory filled in the gaps. How easily one fell into old habits and behaviors. Traveling alongside Kenna—blazes, fighting alongside her—felt as natural as breathing.

A fact that crept along Daciana's skin, unsettling her with the painful reminder of how easy it was to lose oneself.

Once they'd slain the Leśnik and pocketed the bounty, Kenna and Daciana made their way south. Back to the cluster of villages where Kenna might find couriers to send her letters to other hunters in warning.

Daciana slipped her hand into the fraying pocket of her favorite trousers, thumbing the stone from Hugo's grave marker. Once Kenna contacted the other hunters, she'd go search for Lark and wait for the others. Kenna would leave, and her conscience would be clear.

Daciana worried her thumb over the smooth surface of the stone, not at all feeling better.

"Full moon." Kenna ruptured the silence, glancing over her shoulder. "We should stay out here until it passes. I'd hate for you to maul any potential clients."

"I'm in full control of my urges." Daciana whipped her hand out of her pocket to grip the handle of her dagger. *Patience.* She exhaled a slow breath, searching for her center. It was always difficult to keep a steady hold on her reactions this close to her change. Being near Kenna wasn't helping.

"That's a shame." Kenna offered her signature grin—the one that dimpled her cheeks.

Daciana turned away, ignoring the flood of heat to her cheeks, and leaned against a nearby tree. She hadn't planned on staying with her this long, and the unspoken pull of her presence was already worrying. "You can go into town without me. I've told you everything I had to say. The rest is up to you."

"Is it now?" Kenna crossed her arms, canting her head to the side. Her red hood had fallen away from her face, black wisps of hair hanging in her eyes. "I'm not writing a damn word to anyone if you take off running now."

Daciana pushed off the tree fast enough, Kenna tensed. "What exactly am I running from?"

Lifting her chin, Kenna narrowed her eyes. "I don't even think you know anymore."

Every instinct in Daciana's body screamed to assert she was the predator, that she had the advantage, but she remained utterly still.

Kenna continued. "You'll go with me and help me complete a few jobs, then I'll chase your cause. I'm not abandoning people who need my help to clean up a mess your new friend made."

Daciana grasped Kenna by the throat, shoving her against the tree. She scarcely had time to register the action, but her own shock did nothing to dim the heat of anger in her blood. Beneath her anger, a thrum of need formed a heady undercurrent. It took every shred of Daciana's control not to press her face against the flutter of Kenna's pulse point when her breath hitched. "You think to command me. When has that ever worked?"

Even with a hand gripping her pale throat, Kenna rolled her eyes. "It's called a deal. Take it or leave it. You want the hunters' aid? You're going to help me first."

Daciana relaxed her hold. "It's your life's calling to shield the world from these monsters. What right have you to hesitate?"

Kenna placed her hand over Daciana's, tightening her grip on her narrow throat as if in challenge. "There are monsters everywhere. So long as I never stop fighting, I maintain my honor." Her hand fell away. "Can you say the same?"

Daciana released her, stepping back. The distance was an instant reprieve. "And there's honor in making coin off the misfortune of others?"

"I won't apologize for being compensated each time I put my life on the line, but I get to choose where and when I do that." Kenna wet her lips. "And I'm not dying for whatever war you're starting. Not without a show of good faith."

Daciana's heart hammered in her chest, blood simmering beneath her veins. The call of the moon beckoned. "What exactly do you need faith in?"

Kenna grinned—those damned dimples creasing her smooth cheeks. "That when you save the world, there are humans left to enjoy it."

To the blazing nethers with this girl. She wouldn't really refuse to alert the other hunters, would she? Daciana had no interest in calling her bluff. Perhaps it was weakness or selfishness. She had weeks to spare before Alistair and Langford would dock at the port. Lark was supposed to leave her a message at the Walden Inn and anywhere else she stayed to make it easier to track her down, but Daciana had time. Part of her wanted to send Kenna away, content she'd done her part and the rest was out of her hands. But a shameful part of her wasn't ready to be alone once more.

"Deal."

DACIANA FOUND a secluded spot to shift. After some convincing, Kenna swore not to come looking for her. Kenna was a lot of things, but she'd always kept her word.

In the nearby underbrush, a fox peered out. Daciana met its gaze, acknowledging another night bound hunter. The fox skittered away.

Animals knew to steer clear of her. Their senses recognized her as the predator she was.

She rolled her shoulders, preparing for the immeasurable pain that was soon to be lancing through her veins. The price of her power. The curse of her blood—of her bloodline she sullied with one act of vengeance.

Her nerves fired, oversensitive and seeking the change. The hairs on her arms and the back of her neck rose, awaiting the moon's command.

It was a terrifying and wondrous thing. Both a cage and unyielding freedom. To be so much and yet so bound. By time. By the skies.

She fell forward, gripping the earth between her fingers. Throwing her head back, she let a snarl slip free.

Here, she needn't be human. Alone in the woods, under a sky that knew exactly what lurked beneath her skin. She needn't be anything other than the monster she was.

THE NOTICE BOARD in Whitebridge was littered with tacked pages. Some were listings for unwanted furniture in need of a new home, day laborers advertising their services, and far too many missing persons. Those notices were faded and yellowed with age.

Kenna scanned the listings, eyes roving and never landing. She had a way of absorbing information in constant motion. Her hand snatched a parchment half concealed, the drawing of a girl with dark skin and bright eyes. The artist captured the delicate curve of her mouth, as if she had a secret poised on the tip of her tongue. Beneath her portrait read one word: MISSING.

Daciana peered over Kenna's shoulder, studying the image.

She was a beauty, a fact that meant little, but Daciana had learned never to ignore even the least significant of information.

Kenna hummed to herself.

"What is it?"

Kenna shook her head. "I don't know. This one's strange. All the other notices detailed their clothing and where they were last seen. This one has nothing. No leads. Just a picture of a pretty girl." She angled her head questioningly. "It's curious, isn't it?"

Daciana studied the image. The girl was young, eyes smiling even in the drawn portrait. "Whoever sketched this took great care to bring her to life."

Something knocked into her back. She turned to find a young boy sprawled on the ground, panting with a sheepish grin. Daciana helped him to his feet.

"Thanks, missus," he said breathlessly. His large, round eyes caught sight of the parchment in Kenna's hands. "Oh, that's Amara." He craned his neck, squinting to study their faces against the sunlight. "You going to kill the beast?"

"What beast?" Kenna stepped toward him.

"The one that stole her away," he said as if it was the most obvious thing in the world. "Everyone knows about it."

"Clarence!"

"Shit! That's my mum, I gotta run, good luck!" He sprinted away, leaving a trail of dust in his wake.

"Well, that was strange." Daciana stared after him, his figure receding in the distance.

"That is what I call a job opportunity." Kenna grinned, yanking her hood up over her head. "Let's ask around for any living relatives."

It DIDN'T TAKE LONG to discover Amara's only relative in the village was her father. But whenever they asked about the Beast, they were met with harsh glares and dismissive comments. "Mad Felix weaved the tale of the Beast rather than admit his daughter ran away," they'd say.

Rumor had it Felix was an artist who drove himself mad by seeking to craft the perfect masterpiece. He'd experimented with his creations, heating and bending metals to create ghastly sculptures that would send a shiver down even the bravest of spines. But one day he sliced his hand on the sharp edge of a metal form, blood weeping from the wound. He began smearing it against his creation, weaving bits of himself in his own art.

That was the day he learned that a true masterpiece takes sacrifice.

He sliced off his own fingers and skewered them onto his sculpture.

His daughter, Amara, was also the subject of ridicule and gossip.

Everyone thought her a great beauty, but it was widely accepted she'd bargained with a demon to grant her limitless beauty and knowledge. In every trade within the village, she seemed to have a keen understanding of their mechanics. Every subject broached, she was teeming with expertise. Whenever anyone would ask where she learned such things, a small smile would cross her face, and she'd simply answer, "I read it in a book."

The mad artist and his demon-dealing daughter weren't the village's most favored.

"We're actually going with the notion that a woman can only be beautiful and knowledgeable if she did, in fact, make a deal with a demon." Kenna stomped up the dirt path toward the dilapidated cottage where Felix lived. "That's what you're going with?"

"Of course not," Daciana hissed, urging her to quiet her voice, lest they scare him off. "I merely said we can't overlook any detail they've shared with us."

"What they've shared is a load of horseshit."

It was a load of horseshit, she wasn't wrong. But perception was evidence of its own.

Daciana knocked on the wooden door. Painted flower blooms and vines ran up the wood grains in vibrant yellows and greens. They looked so real; she was tempted to run her fingers over them just to be sure.

Footsteps shuffled from within before the door groaned open. A man with dark umber skin and wild hair peered out at them, his eyes alight with alarm. "Can I help you?"

"We wish to talk to you about your daughter," Daciana said. She'd been tempted to begin with pleasantries, but it seemed a waste of time.

He yanked the door wide, blinking at them owlishly. "Thank Avalon! I thought no one would ever help me get her back from him."

"From who?" Kenna stepped forward, eying him cautiously. "Who do you think has your daughter?"

He lifted a trembling hand to run along his unshaven jaw. "A Beast. A horrible, monstrous Beast."

CHAPTER FIVE

LARK

Inerys rubbed her temples. Her eyes slipped closed, dark hair falling over her face. Mud and soot blackened the hem of her scarlet gown. Lark gazed at it as she sat on the bench beside Gavriel, patiently awaiting the witch's response.

"So can you help us?"

Patience never was Lark's strength.

Inerys lifted her head to regard her with a pained expression. "Extend me the courtesy of a moment to process. It's not every day I'm informed of the impending arrival of the apocalypse."

They'd waited for more than a moment. After Lark had spewed the entire story, down to the last detail, Inerys sat in stunned silence. The longer they waited, the deeper Lark's worry carved into the pit of her stomach.

"I understand," Gavriel said, leaning forward, "but time is a luxury we don't exactly possess."

"Very well, I'll make this brief." Inerys leapt to her feet, and the floor groaned beneath her steps, muddy skirts swishing about her legs. "I can't prevent the fall of the veil, nor can I restore it. But in theory, there's a way to remake it."

Lark released the breath that had been clenching in her chest. "Thank the skies. What must be done?"

"This is all theoretical. It would be a new veil to prevent the dead from walking among the living. It would take considerable power. Power I don't possess. To answer your question, yes, there's a way to replace the veil once it falls. But it won't be by my hand."

"Whose then?" Lark rose, careful to avoid knocking her shoulder into the shelf overflowing with glass vials and greenery. It didn't matter if she left with more questions than answers, so long as she had a direction to travel in. "Who has that power?"

Inerys hummed, eyes darting between Lark and Gavriel as if she was mulling over her response. "No one within your reach, I'm afraid. But perhaps there's another reason you came to see me."

Gavriel glanced at Lark, studying her carefully.

Her heart sped up in her chest. "I don't know what you're talking about."

"Don't you?" Inerys smiled, revealing a row of straight white teeth. "I can't believe I didn't sense it before. Perhaps it was dormant. But now it's almost ear-splitting how loud the bond between your souls screams. A true soul bond that transcended death. Remarkable." She placed a finger over her lips. "Do you wish to retrieve those memories, long forgotten? The ones glimmering on the edge of your mind, just out of reach? Of a life once lived and lost?"

Lark fought to temper her impatience. "No, Inerys. I wish to halt the fall of the world." To save countless lives. To restore order and balance to a world threatened by chaos. That her heart fractured each time she looked at Gavriel was of little consequence. She would spend each breath fighting. Fighting for a way to right the wrong set in motion long ago. Ceto once asked what Lark was willing to sacrifice to make things right.

Everything.

"Who has the power to create the veil? I don't care if they're out of reach. Give me a name. Give me something, Inerys."

Inerys studied her with her impossibly dark eyes. Her irises were nearly black, depthless. Lifetimes passed behind those eyes, and here she remained. Hidden from the world, in the heart of the forest. "I don't have a name," Inerys said finally, "but I can tell you the source of power it requires."

Lark nodded, urging her to continue.

Gavriel remained seated, far too silent and still for Lark's liking. As if he was on his own mission to absorb everything around him. Even words unspoken. His sharp jaw was clenched, a muscle feathering his cheek. His forest green eyes found Lark's, and the unmistakable sensation of being analyzed swept over her.

There would be time to deal with that later.

"How familiar are you with Vitas Conjuring?" Inerys arched her brow.

"Life Magic?" Lark scoffed. "Familiar enough to know it's fallen into archaic myth." The practice died out long before her time. Such essence wielders drew magic beyond mortal limits. There was an essence in the blood they could call upon from the surrounding life—a guided sacrifice to uphold balance. She recalled Leysa once telling her of the wielders of old standing against the paragons, but it sounded more like a motivational speech than a true testament of history. "You can't actually mean to say there's a wielder of any significance."

A small smile crept along Inerys' mouth. "Allow me to rectify your ignorance."

Lark bit the inside of her cheek, stilling her tongue from any sharp response. Warranted or not.

"Vitas Conjuring, Life Magic, predates even the creation of the Netherworld. The creation of the Otherworld, where your kind is made. The practice was once revered for its impressive strength and wealth of power. To not be contained by one's own earthly limitations, but to derive power from the essence of life." She shook her head. "It was formidable even against the great warriors of Avalon, against the paragons you mortals seem so keen to worship." At this, she offered Gavriel a pointed glance.

"How do you know so much about an ancient practice long dead?" Lark asked, trying to slow the rising irritation of her own ignorance.

"Because it serves as a cautionary tale. When I was green and untested, I longed to dive into the forbidden arts. To experiment with how much power my mortal body could handle. My mother made me study this forgotten history, this well-kept secret, to keep me from harm" —she glared at Lark— "and unlike you, I heed the warnings of my elders."

Lark ignored the witch's misguided attempt to chastise her. There wasn't a mortal walking this earth who could claim to be her elder.

"Apart from *somniavi*," Inerys continued, "life wielders were the greatest threat among mortals."

"So what changed?" Lark asked.

"Do you think the paragons of Avalon appreciated mortals grasping for power? Of leveling the proverbial hierarchy? Of ascending to their level and offering resistance?" Inerys laughed humorlessly. "The most prominent life wielders were rounded up and slain, entire bloodlines destroyed to protect the fragile egos of the paragons. After the warriors completed the Great Purge, the paragons took it even further. They created the Netherworld. The pit for human souls to languish after their lives were spent, withholding the gift of Avalon from any who hadn't earned the right to ascend, as a reminder not to neglect offering their fealty. That was also when the first Reaper created the Otherworld."

Lark desperately tried to make the information fit with what she'd already known as a Reaper. Why had no one told her of the history of the Otherworld? "The first Reaper," she said. "It was Thanar."

Inerys nodded. "Thanar was once a guardian of Avalon, a warrior in his own right. His disdain for the way mortals were treated resulted in his banishment. The King of Avalon—"

"Sargon!" Lark blurted, unable to keep quiet.

Inerys cleared her throat. "Yes, Sargon crafted Thanar's punishment with great care. His love for the mortals would be rewarded with watching them die over and over and forever leading them to the pits of the Netherworld."

Lark's head spun, her mind barely clutching each piece of the puzzle, hastily fitting together to grant the whole messy picture. "We were told it was unknown where souls went. Fate kept their destination a secret."

Inerys shook her head, a sad smile on her face. "Probably a lie forged for comfort."

Lark glanced down at Gavriel, at his clenched fist at his thigh. She had the sudden urge to grab it, to yank him to his feet and forget about all of this. The end of the world. The lies crafted to keep them forever in darkness. Forget everything and try to find some small semblance of light. If only for a moment.

"Fate does play a hand in all of this… but the threads of fate aren't unpredictable. There is a source. Someone has to pull the strings."

Lark pushed the dread back down her throat, focusing on Inerys, her anchor point. It was too much, all of it. She needed to stay focused on the task at hand or else be swept away by the casual unraveling of everything she'd ever known.

"But there are some who reject fate. Solana crafted Arcadia, the peaceful afterlife in the Netherworld."

Inerys nodded. "She did, and she was punished."

Sargon banished her to the Forbidden Shrine and relegated her to live as an ancient relic that granted wishes. Her only hope for freedom was to destroy the small piece of paradise she'd crafted for the mortals.

Lark swept her hands over her breeches, agitated.

Gavriel eased to his feet, the movement smooth and measured. His motions were always saturated with lethal grace. "The paragons did more than slay the Vitas Conjurors. They punished countless others out of greed for reverence." He shook his head, pinching the bridge of his nose. "I can't say I was ever religious, but one would at least expect gods and goddesses to behave better than ill-tempered children."

Inerys shot him a catlike grin. "Careful, hero. You're sounding decidedly blasphemous. When Sargon crafted the Netherworld, and Thanar created the Otherworld, order had to be maintained. Avalon was so far, one had to cross planes of existence to access it. The Netherworld was so close, the twisted souls sent to live in agony were a constant threat to the living. So Thanar did what he had to. He employed a great and powerful witch, the last of the true wielders known to time, to use Life Magic to conjure a barrier between realms. Safeguards. And yes, she was unspeakably punished." She plopped down in the chair, crossing her legs. "With the veil in place, Life Magic became far more dangerous, and the last of the Life Wielders was no more."

"Why was it more dangerous?" Lark asked breathlessly.

"Because the call to life has far-reaching consequences when used blindly. The veil favors balance above all, however it must be sought. Without the powerful lineage feeding the power of a life wielder… at best, this form of magic is unattainable, and at worst? Chaos. Destruction. But it matters not, for they're all dead. Not even I could reawaken this power with a great magical anomaly. Not unless there's an ancestor I've never heard of who managed to hide their power long enough to pass on the bloodline." At Lark's brightened expression, she quickly added, "I've studied my ancestral tree for the better part of a decade. There is no such ancestor."

Lark worried her lip between her teeth. The layer of skin frayed from the wind. "No one still practices this form?"

Inerys shook her head.

"And Life Magic is the only way to forge a new veil?"

"Afraid so."

Lark glanced over at Gavriel, at the worry creasing his brow.

"Well, shit."

Lark hung back while Gavriel readied the boat, tension along his broad shoulders making his movements abrupt.

Inerys appeared at Lark's side. "You're disappointed."

Lark tugged her grey cloak tighter. "I'm disappointed when I order apple pie at the tavern, only to discover they've run out." She turned to face her. "I'm feeling a bit more than disappointed at the moment."

Inerys' mouth twitched. "I regret I have nothing comforting to offer." She turned to watch Gavriel, appreciating the view. "What of your man over there? Last time you darkened my doorstep, despite the grim circumstances, the two of you seemed desperate for each other. Now I'm feeling quite a draft coming from you."

Lark sighed, searching for the words. "Things are... complicated." Inerys waited with an expectant expression. "I'm having a hard time adjusting to the new information that's come to light."

Inerys' dark brows lifted. "You speak of the soul bond? I'd think you'd be pleased."

"I fought my very existence to escape fate. Can't you see why this feels like another cage?" All she wanted was the freedom of choice. To know her mind was her own, without influence and fate intervening. The soul bond threatened to unravel every decision she'd ever made. How much of herself was real, and how much existed to meet destiny?

"You confuse a soul bond with inevitability. You can always choose to walk away."

"Can I?" Lark turned to face her. "I can't be certain of what I feel, and what's bound by a thread of fate tethering our souls lifetimes ago. What about Gavriel?" Tears stung her eyes. She would not let them fall. "How much of what he feels is true?"

"You're afraid your heart isn't your own." Inerys shook her head. "Allow me to put that particular worry at ease—"

"Can you sever the bond?"

Lark couldn't halt the words from leaping from her lips, and even as her stomach churned at their release, she couldn't bring herself to regret the request.

Inerys' mouth thinned to a firm line. "You know what you're asking for?"

"Yes."

She shook her head, beckoning Lark with a wave of her hand, and disappearing into her cottage.

Lark glanced back at Gavriel, who watched her curiously from the shore. She held up one finger before following Inerys into her home. She chased the sounds of glass clinking and the metallic clang of hastily shuffled pans as Inerys rummaged through cupboards.

The hour had grown late, and the shadows along Inerys' walls from stacks of books and jars of herbs had grown taller.

"Here." Inerys stormed out from her untidy little kitchen, a brown glass bottle in hand. "I mixed the tonic in with some cheap cooking wine I won't miss."

Lark reached for it, only for Inerys to angle it away from her grasp, looking her over thoughtfully.

"I would be remiss if I didn't tell you I think this is a terrible idea."

Lark closed her fingers around the neck of the bottle, gently lifting it from Inerys' grasp. "Yes, well, as you indicated earlier, I'm not one to heed warnings."

CHAPTER SIX

LANGFORD

The door to the tavern offered little resistance against Langford's hand. A fact he momentarily mourned as the pungent scent of sweat and spirits blasted him in the face. The night air was heavy with humidity, but inside the tavern was even worse.

Moonlight slipped through arched windows, mingling with the warm light of the braziers against the stone columns. The marble floors were sticky from spilled drinks and gods knew what else. Langford tried not to cringe when the heel of his boot tugged against their surface. The thick floral scent of hyacinths set in numerous gold vases filled the air and irritated his sinuses. Raucous patrons and an abundance of body heat immediately made his collar tight as boisterous laughter boomed from the opposite end of the room.

Alistair strolled right past him, strutting up to the bar and leaning an elbow against its unwashed surface. How the man appeared completely at home in any environment would forever baffle him.

Taking shallow breaths, Langford paced up to his side, keeping a firm hand on his satchel. The ancient tome weighed heavily in the bottom of his bag. He couldn't translate the entire text in time for the rendezvous at the port to sail home. The importance of his task weighed on him, and his stomach churned with each step, the stolen book knocking against his thigh.

If he'd had his way, they'd have stayed in that library for far longer. Perhaps forever.

Someone slammed a tankard on the wooden bar top beside him, droplets of ale showering his arm. Langford gritted his teeth, silently reciting the mantra from the healer's oath he swore as a bright progeny to steady himself. *First, do no harm.* Not that he'd cause much harm, armed with an old book and a companion who was making eyes at the busty barmaid.

Langford wiped his sleeve, casually glancing around the tavern.

Most of the esteemed customers were three sheets to the wind, the volume of dozens of different conversations reaching a decibel suited for outdoors. Langford rubbed his temples, willing his headache to cease.

"You all right?"

He glanced up to find Alistair's brows drawn, mouth tight. His black hair hung in his bottle-green eyes as he scanned him over, assessing. It was awfully unsettling.

"I'm fine," Langford bit back, too irritated to soften his tone.

"That was convincing." Alistair crossed his arms, leaning his hip against the bar. His cutlass hung loosely from his side. His black tunic, which he'd been too lazy to tie up all the way, exposed the upper planes of his chest.

"It's just a headache. It'll pass."

Alistair's smile fell, a shadow passing over his face. He stepped up to Langford, reaching a hand to his forehead.

Langford held his breath as Alistair's thumb soothed over his brow, gently applying pressure to his temple. His hands were cool, a balm against the sweltering heat. Despite the blessed relief of his careful touch, Langford flinched, pulling away.

Hurt flashed across Alistair's face, before it vanished. "You should rest. You look like you need it. Personally, I feel invigorated. You missed the opportunity for a great nap. There's something to be said about the cushion of a centuries old book beneath your head."

"Your excessive sleep salivation smudged the handwritten text of a priceless tome."

"They need better security."

The tension in Langford's neck and shoulders was steadily mounting, and the thick, musky air of pipe tobacco wasn't helping. He pinched the bridge of his nose, squeezing his eyes shut. Some nights he could handle the noise, the overstimulation, even revel in it. He'd find a decent wine to drown in and a warm body to lie beside. But he was spent. He needed a quiet, dark room away from people.

A nearby patron drummed her fingers against the table, and the sound curved its way into his ears, pounding alongside his headache.

Alistair was still regarding him with maddening concern.

"Langford, go lie down."

"Would you silence your incessant prattling?" He pushed away from the bar, unwilling to witness if Alistair cared, and waded through the crowd. The stench of ale and fresh vomit burned his nostrils.

"Langford." Alistair's hand grasped his wrist, and the contact shot through him. He gently placed the brass key into Langford's hand.

Langford refused to meet his eye. Refused to see the pity they'd reflect. He couldn't stomach it. Not from him.

He tore away, not looking at the man he left in place.

LANGFORD AWOKE A FEW HOURS LATER. The skull-splitting ache in his head had all but abated, and his throat was as dry as the pages of his stolen tome. He groaned as he lifted his heavy body to stand, leaning uncertainly on legs that weren't fully awake yet. Rubbing his eyes, he glanced around the darkened room.

The space was small with two narrow beds on opposite walls. It only took three steps from his bed to bump into Alistair's. Which was still perfectly made. Coverlet untouched.

Langford stretched, joints popping.

Running a hand down his face, he avoided the small dingy mirror in the corner, not needing it to know his hair would be an absolute disaster. He crept to the door, careful to make as little noise as possible.

Alistair had likely passed out downstairs or was still up drinking and carousing with the best of them. But he'd need his rest for their trek to the port. Langford was accustomed to this mantle of responsibility—to being the one who reminded Alistair to take care of himself. Urging him to pause and rest when he'd sooner drink himself to death. It unsettled him that Alistair had taken that role from him earlier, sending him to bed as if he was a child. Langford couldn't dismiss the wisdom in it. He felt almost himself again, but now it was his turn to make sure the fool didn't get himself into too much mischief. At least until they were back in Ardenas, where the threat of being sent to the mines wasn't imminent.

Once they were aboard Ingemar's ship, Langford could study and translate the text. With luck, he'd have it all sorted by the time they docked and give Lark good news for a change. The girl could use it.

He descended the creaking steps, the wood groaning beneath his feet—only to find the dining area all but empty. A few stragglers still played a game of chance, testing their coin against the fate of the cards.

Perhaps the drunk fool had made his way outside to relieve himself and passed out in the stable.

Langford dashed up the stairs to grab his cloak, muttering the entire way, when he heard a groan from the room across the hall. He knew that voice. He'd heard that groan on far too many occasions, usually while Langford stitched the man up.

Alistair.

Dread pooled in the pit of Langford's stomach. But it became secondary to the irrefutable need to look. To know. His legs, suddenly heavy, protested every step to that door.

The door was silent when it swung open by his touch. The rhythmic creaking of the old bed frame and the unmistakable sound of flesh meeting flesh filled the room. A woman's moan rang out, rising to a note of near-distress. Her hair was a thick mane of blonde, hiding her face from view. The man's hands gripped her hips, bringing her toward him with each violent thrust.

They were thankfully facing away from him, both turned to the opposite wall. But the aching familiarity of the man's back shot through Langford's chest, hollowing him.

He'd seen Alistair bathe more times than he could count. He'd stitched him up thirty-seven times. Washed him clean from sickness on eleven separate occasions. There wasn't any part of the man he couldn't identify by sight.

Not for reasons that mattered.

Langford's shaky hand covered his mouth to ensure no sound slipped free as he slowly backed away. He didn't bother with closing the door as he crept down the hall to his room, shutting and locking himself in.

Leaning against the solid weight of his door, vision blurring, Langford allowed his first ragged breath to break free.

CHAPTER SEVEN

DACIANA

"What sort of beast?" Daciana was familiar with many beasts, but none that would hold a woman hostage.

Surprise dawned on his weathered face. "You don't think I'm crazy?"

"Well...?" Kenna shrugged noncommittally.

"We think you want your daughter back," Daciana said, giving Kenna a hard look. Kenna responded with an impish grin.

Felix eyed them both, shifting his focus between the two with a nervous energy. "Very well, come inside then." He stepped back to allow them entrance.

Daciana crossed the threshold, and the warm scent of aged wood enveloped her. Hundreds of metal and glass sculptures decorated every flat surface. Some were even suspended from the rafters, glimmering in the streams of afternoon sunlight spilling through the window. Butterflies and birds, forged of metal and colored glass, filled the air above them. From a distance, the soft tinkle of chimes wafted in on the breeze.

Daciana tore her eyes away, catching sight of Kenna's wondrous smile lighting up her face as she, too, was enraptured.

It was breathtaking.

Felix cleared his throat. "You must forgive the state of my home. I haven't had occasion to entertain guests in quite some time." He ran his hand over his head, peering around. He seemed almost embarrassed. Nothing about him rang of danger. Of the unhinged artist who wove blood and pain into his creations. The stories from the village were just that, stories.

"Blazes," Kenna murmured. "Did you make these?"

He wiped his hands on his soot covered apron. "I did, yes. It keeps the hands busy when the mind starts to fray."

Daciana tracked his movement. The ring finger of his right hand was missing the fingertip down to the first knuckle.

"What happened to your finger?" Kenna's voice cut through the air.

"Oh, this?" he held up his hand. "I used to forge blades, had a bit of an accident with the sharp end." He chuckled deprecatingly.

"Oh, I see," Kenna said with a grin. "That's an utterly boring story. You should make up something more exciting."

He shook his head, a soft smile on his face. "No, I think the village concocts enough excitement on my behalf." He pulled three clay mugs from the cupboard, setting them down on the table. Gesturing for them to sit, he busied himself with filling the cast iron teapot with leaves and water, before bringing it to rest on the fireplace crane.

He dropped himself to sit facing them, clasping his hands on the table in front of him. "Where do I begin?"

"How long has she been gone?"

Daciana wanted to question him about his daughter's comings and goings. What she liked to spend her time doing. Where she frequented. Get a sense of what her days normally looked like, so they might assess what was different about the day she went missing. But this was Kenna's area of expertise, so she'd defer to her judgment.

"Three weeks."

Kenna sucked in a breath through her teeth, her audible wince filling the air.

"Three weeks is a long time, Felix. But you already knew that." Kenna leaned toward him. "Why do you think she's still alive?"

"Kenna—"

"You're wondering the same thing, Daciana," Kenna cut her off before returning her attention to Felix. "Start there. Why do you think she's alive?"

"Because I know who has her." He lifted his hands to cover his face. "And it's my fault he took her."

"I think the time to speak in riddles is over," Daciana said as gently as she could. "We want to find your daughter. Tell us what you know." While they bantered in half truths and heavy-handed words, Amara was out there. Had been out there for weeks.

"Two months ago, I set out for the Midsummer festival in Brookhill. My plan was to sell some of my pieces," he smiled with watery eyes. "Amara was always a big fan of my work. Said the right eyes needed to see it. To appreciate it.

"The journey was harsher than I predicted. My wagon ended up with a broken wheel in the middle of the forest. They should have fixed that road years ago. I would have been fine, but the nights around here had been unseasonably cold—they still are, but this night brought heavy rain and bracing winds. I lost my way." He ran his hand over his unshaven face, the sound of calloused skin meeting thick bristles temporarily filling the space.

"Cold and drenched to the bone, I led my horse through the dark, desperate to find a shelter from the storm. It wasn't more than a few hours before I came upon a grand manor. I couldn't believe my luck. I'd traveled this forest enough times to know there was no such place, and yet, I couldn't deny my sight. It was huge! I don't know how I missed it before. A stone wall surrounded the estate, but the gate was left open. Abandoned or not, this place was the only thing standing between me and pneumonia, or worse. So I tied Pippa in the stable and pounded on the door. Freezing, shivering enough to rattle my teeth, I pushed open the door, not truly expecting to find it unlocked."

"Uh-oh," Kenna said with a smirk.

Daciana flashed her a warning glance. Now was not the time for glib remarks. Thankfully, Felix was undeterred.

"It was too dark to see. I stood there in this massive foyer, dripping all over the grand carpet. I probably would have curled up right there by the front door if he hadn't found me."

"I love it when they talk in pronouns. It only adds to the suspense," Kenna said, leaning as if to whisper to Daciana.

Daciana sighed, equal parts exasperated and amused with Kenna's commentary. "She's right. It would be in Amara's best interest if we dispel with the theatrics and get to the heart of it. Whose home were you in?"

Felix appeared dazed as he shook his head, a tear slipping over his cheek from the action. "Forgive me, he never gave me his name. He appeared as a shadowy figure at the top of the stairs. He was polite, accommodating even. He invited me in, let me sit by the fire for warmth and even ordered his servants to bring me a hot meal." He wiped the tear from his cheek. "But the strange thing was, he wouldn't step into the light. Not even his servants. They all remained cloaked in darkness during my stay. I assumed it was to offer me the courtesy of remaining ignorant of how underdressed I was."

"What happened next?" Daciana reached a hand across the table, lightly squeezing his. Encouraging.

"He asked me questions. What I was doing in the forest. If I had any family. I thought he was just making polite conversation. I did not know his intent, and I told him everything. About my art, about my village, about Amara—" He choked on her name. "I told him of her quick mind and love of reading. Even as a child, she would read and recall facts far beyond her years. Learning is the love of my daughter's soul. Always has been. He was very interested in her, and kept asking me what she was fond of, what she looked like, what her favorite flower was." He buried his face in his hands, sobbing.

Daciana and Kenna exchanged a quick glance. They needed to get him to focus so he might have a chance of remembering where that manor was.

"What a strange fellow," Kenna said with a laugh. "He should have at least asked you what your favorite flower was first. That's just good manners."

He lifted his head to regard her with confusion. "What?"

"Nothing," Daciana said quickly, relieved Kenna had at least torn him from his lament without slapping him across the face. Something she wouldn't put past her. "And then you left?"

"Not exactly." Felix sniffed, wiping his nose on his sleeve. "He told me I owed him a debt for his hospitality. Said if my daughter came to work for him, we'd be even. I told him it was up to her what she did with her life and I had no business trading her as if she belonged to me. I raised my daughter to have her own mind, as her mother did. Gods rest her soul."

"I take it he didn't much like that?" Kenna wrinkled her nose.

"He… *growled* at me and insisted I owed him this debt. That he'd be sure I paid. Well, I'd heard enough of that, so I fled. But I was so frightened, my foot caught on the corner of the rug and I fell. He advanced on me so quickly…" Felix shuddered. "That was when I saw him up close. That was when I looked into the face of the Beast."

The sharp whistle of the kettle caused him to jump in alarm. He paced over to the hearth, grabbing a towel to handle it and pour boiling hot tea into their cups.

Daciana murmured her thanks, gently resting her hand around the mug, but never taking a sip. If her change hadn't just passed, if she was close to the next moon, she could rely on her senses. But in the early days of waning gibbous, she couldn't trust anything someone else prepared. She doubted Felix would drug someone's tea with anything dangerous, but one could never be too careful.

He sat down, blowing on his steaming tea. "Whatever he was, it wasn't human. He had a long snout and terrible jaws, with sharp fangs. I ran like the coward I am. I ran to my horse and rode all the way home. Told Amara they canceled the festival. She didn't ask about the wagon—probably assumed I got cold feet and burned the thing. And I didn't tell her about the beast, a fact that will haunt me for the rest of my days. I could have warned her. I could have made her understand."

Kenna let out a low whistle, bringing the tea to her nose for a whiff. "So that's the monster that took your daughter three weeks ago? And you think he's got her holed up in his castle?" She shook her head and took a sip. "Sounds like an awful big job this short of notice."

Understanding dawned on his face. "Of course I'll pay! Do you require it in full upfront?"

Before Daciana could answer, Kenna waved her hand. "We get paid when the job's done. That's the deal. But we need to come to an accord." She leaned forward, raising her dark eyebrows. "If your daughter is gone, I'm still killing the beast."

He nodded fervently. "If you bring me the beast's head, you'll get your coin. No matter what."

She held her small hand out, clasping his in a firm grasp.

Daciana glanced between the two of them, the air heavy with a shared lust for blood. Hopefully, death wasn't the only thing his coin would buy.

CHAPTER EIGHT

LARK

Dusk approached, painting the sky in lush violet and deep indigo. The last light of the day bled from the horizon, as clouds rolled in bringing their promise of a dark night. Lark and Gavriel made their way through the rapidly darkening forest in silence. Gone were the evenings when the crickets and cicadas would hum. The only sounds were twigs snapping and the cracking of undergrowth beneath their steps as the breeze shook the leaves overhead. Tree trunks creaked in response.

The moon was hidden from view, offering no path of light. Overhanging tree limbs decorated the night sky in their desperate reach for the heavens.

Blindly they trekked. Neither speaking nor touching.

Once or twice, Lark swore he turned to look at her. As if about to say something. But the shadows concealing his face made it impossible to tell.

There was a time she felt right at home in shadows. Like she was darkness incarnate. When the power she possessed coursed through her veins. But then the reality of her cage would make itself known. She'd come crashing back down to remember she was a slave to fate.

But as a human, the shadows had grown taller. The dark held far more dangers for a mortal.

The breeze carried the scent of damp earth and rotting leaves. Tugging her cloak tighter, she shivered.

"Lark," Gavriel's voice lanced through the night air.

She wanted to demand he say it again. To hear her name from his lips and carry the music it made until the end of her days. But the words died in her throat.

"I've tried to give you space," he said. "I thought it would make things better, but perhaps that was a failing on my part." He leveled her with the intensity of his dark green eyes. Though she could barely see them in the shadows on his face, they froze her to the spot. "You've been distant since we departed the Netherworld. If something has changed, if your feelings are no longer—"

"Nothing's changed," she said before she could stop herself. Nothing had changed. Everything had changed.

Gavriel ran a hand over his face. "Help me understand. Why is it you feel far away?" His brows knitted together, his expression suddenly guarded. "Is it Thanar?"

Confusion temporarily stunned the ache from her chest. "What?"

"If I am not—if you feel something for him, I wouldn't hold that against you."

Was he actually suggesting this?

"The only feelings I harbor for Thanar are hatred and disdain," Lark said, shaking her head, "and maybe pity."

"For skies' sake, Lark, what is it then?" His jaw clenched, eyes burning through her as he begged to understand.

He should understand. He'd been bound by the Guild his whole life. What little he'd shared with her certainly didn't paint a happy picture. He'd been caged as well.

Inerys' tonic would likely be a comfort to him. He could leave with no form of guilt. It wasn't his fault things got so far so fast.

And yet... she couldn't bring herself to tell him about it. About severing the bond. The only way it would work is if he didn't know.

Damn his stubbornness, he'd convince himself of feelings that weren't there just to prove her wrong.

But she couldn't hide her feelings from him any longer.

The wind carved around the trees, whispering against her skin. She shivered as the ends of her hair tickled her cheek. She was flesh and blood and bone. Real and tangible. Reminding herself of this seemed to steady her nerves.

She sucked in a breath, marveling at how difficult these silly mortal words were to say. She gently pulled the bow and quiver Hugo had made her, setting them against a tree. "Gavriel, does the soul bond worry you?" Understanding dawned on his face, all but banishing the shadows. "How can you possibly trust that your feelings are real?"

"Lark," he said softly, "no spell or ancient soul bond determined what we have. What we found in each other."

"I've been bound to fate. Answering to a call far beyond sight. I fought my way to earn the right to choose. Only to discover something preordained my choice long before the thought even entered my mind. I thought I chose to save you, but it was just my soul calling to yours." Her chest heaved, aching with each breath. "Is this another cage?"

"Your soul may have called, but you didn't have to answer." He shook his head. "Just as now, you can choose whatever you wish."

How wondrous it would be to accept it as truth. She could let go of this, couldn't she? Accept this answer and claim her happiness. If it was truly that easy… why shouldn't she?

Such funny things. Mortals. The ability to simplify the most complex of ideals into bite-sized pieces. Anything to make it feasible and within grasp.

The strangest part was the truth in his words. The raw honesty in such a simple notion.

This was a choice.

Just as saving him was a choice.

There may have been larger things at play, greater powers at work, but when it came down to the moment; she decided. And maybe this was another moment, a crossroads, where she could yet again decide.

Decide what she wanted for herself, without allowing fear or fate to guide her hand.

She wanted this. She wanted to choose him.

The impulse to throw herself at this ridiculous man and slam her lips against his overcame her in a violent rush. She stood in place, clenching and unclenching her fists. Nerves screaming their outrage at her paralysis.

She could walk away.

The choice was hers.

Her soul would never be confined to a cage again.

In slow, measured steps, she approached. Drawing near until she had to tip her head to meet his stare. She cataloged his features, allowing herself a moment to bask in them. The sharp cut of his jaw, the scar bisecting his lip, and the one slashing across his cheek. The green of his eyes, like a dark forest. His achingly familiar scent of warm hearth and leather washed over her.

She'd made her choice.

In the barest of touches, she ghosted her lips against his. A soft noise escaped his chest. When she pulled back, his eyes were scorching, bearing down on her and setting her blood ablaze.

"Maddening woman." His hand fisted in her hair, and he claimed her mouth in a searing kiss. His unshaven jaw grazed her skin, leaving fire in its wake.

She gripped his black tunic, yanking him tight against her. The warmth from his body filled and sealed the cracks in her heart as it thundered against her chest.

This wasn't a cage.

This was life.

Unfiltered, scorching life, thrumming in her veins.

He lifted her easily into his arms. She clung to him, a breathless laugh escaping her lips as her chest swelled. She wanted to cry. To leap. To expel some of the joy that threatened to burst open her ribs.

She settled for taking his mouth with hers. He kissed her back, and his smile curved against her lips. "I don't know, Demon," he said as he pressed her against a tree, the bark scraping her back through her clothes. "Perhaps I should make you beg. You certainly made me wait long enough." His dark cloak offered the smallest semblance of privacy, shrouding them from view.

But it would have to go.

And the trousers, too.

"Careful, mortal." She leaned forward and caught his ear between her teeth, reveling in the sound it yanked from his throat. "I warned you against making promises you can't keep."

The wicked smile that stretched his scarred mouth sent a shiver through her. He raised his eyebrow in challenge—

—when the unmistakable scrape of rusty metal against the earth carried on the wind. Along with a shuffling stagger, disturbing the underbrush in long drags.

They weren't alone.

CHAPTER NINE

LANGFORD

Langford was familiar with heartache and disappointment. He was only ten when he lost his mother, and he'd spent the next six years in his family estate before he escaped to the University of Koval. Even in school, his father's influence was never far behind. When he was called home after graduation, the estate was far too small to house the both of them.

Langford sought diversions, and Ryker proved to be the next injury to his heart. Lord Windsor's arrogant son, brash and bold in all the ways Langford never could be, stole his attention. His handsome face, bright and open, a half-promise of devotion, and Langford had lost himself to it. He'd been charmed by ladies before, enjoyed their softness and how pliable they seemed beneath his hands. But his feelings for Ryker delved beyond physical exploration. Ryker had a way of stitching places Langford hadn't known were torn. When all the pressures of his family name, the expectations of lordship, and the role he would play, threatened to rip him to shreds, Ryker held him together. He never judged him for choosing books over hunting, or medicine over finance. Ryker enjoyed him, his company, his body, without the expectations of the masks of court.

But the affection they shared lacked the strength to go beyond hushed whispers and shaky hands clumsily unfastening buttons before the stableboy found them in the stalls. When he could no longer ignore the duty his father had passed down to him, Langford ran. He'd never do the Brenner name justice. He'd slowly disappear as court sucked the life and soul from his body. It didn't matter what he spent his time doing—his father made that perfectly clear. He could have whomever he wanted. So long as he produced an heir to the Brenner fortune. But he couldn't live that way, behind false smiles and empty titles.

The great legacy was to live divided. Split between his own ideals and the expectations he was born into.

The day he ran, he broke both his and Ryker's hearts.

Langford was sure he was done with the notion. That staying alive, staying sane, was to guard one's heart. To let no one penetrate the carefully cultivated wall he built around it.

Then he met Alistair.

He had more ego than any man had a right to. The sort of man to spill practiced lies from his lips—the absolute last choice for anyone who valued their heart to remain intact.

He'd be lying if he said he thought much of Alistair at first glance. He was obviously handsome, in a roguish way, but he was too aware of it. That made it harder to appreciate.

No, it took months for Langford to realize he had seeped beneath his skin and claimed his affection. It wasn't until one night—a night marked by its sudden drop in temperature—that he realized the depth of his feelings. Shivering beneath a thick wool blanket, Langford's breath escaped in wisps of steam against the dark night. He felt a hand at his shoulder. How Alistair sneaked into his tent without alerting him was still a mystery, though he always suspected the violent shivers wracking his body made him unaware. Alistair had placed his blanket over him, sacrificing his own warmth, and offering a soft smile that Langford could still see despite the dark.

Langford was foolishly besotted after that night, so he came up with ways to protect himself from the full onslaught. It started with a drinking game. Every time Alistair made eyes at someone across the room, Langford drank. Every time he made a comment about someone's physique, Langford drank. If he disappeared with one of his 'companions,' Langford emptied his cup down his throat.

It worked for a while. Until it didn't.

But after years of traveling with the man, Langford had mostly mastered his reactions. Mind over matter. They never were, they'd never be, so why care?

But then the Forbidden Shrine had to give him a taste of what he'd always yearned for, always wanted but never dared to hope for, and gone was his carefully constructed wall.

LANGFORD LIFTED HIS HEAD, the unforgiving sun leaking streams of ungodly light across the filthy floor, and illuminating spots and stains he had no desire to identify. Dust particles floated in the golden rays, swirling incessantly and hinting at how much the room needed a good dusting. He pressed his palms against his burning eyes.

Alistair hadn't returned. The perfectly made bed in the corner mocked him with its untouched covers. Langford stood on shaky feet, stomping over to where Alistair hadn't laid his head. No, his head was surely lying between the breasts he'd paid for. Whether in coin or charms.

Langford smoothed the wrinkles from his white tunic and rubbed against the ache making a permanent home in his chest. It ached the way it had when he was a child recovering from a nasty cough, though he doubted breathing steam and boiling herbs would help in this case. He carefully tucked the ends of his shirt back into his trousers before running a hand into his mess of dark hair. He should call for tea and run his tired eyes over the ancient text he should have spent last night working on. But the prospect of staying trapped in this room for even a moment longer set his teeth on edge. He allowed himself three full breaths. Forcing his lungs to expand and accept the air his chest desperately repelled. In and out. Until his nerves quieted to a gentle hum.

The dining area of the tavern was thankfully empty. Langford seated himself, offering a quick word of thanks to the barmaid who brought his steaming cup of tea. She smiled at him apologetically before she skirted away, wiping tables as she went. He must have appeared in quite a state to deserve a stranger's pity so early in the day. Either that, or she saw Alistair retire with his bedfellow, and drew her own conclusions.

It wasn't Alistair's fault. The tale of the scorpion and the toad came to mind. How the scorpion promised he wouldn't sting the toad if he would only carry him across the pond. The toad agreed, knowing it would condemn them both if the scorpion betrayed him. But sure enough, about halfway across, the toad felt the prick of the scorpion's sting. They both succumbed to the consequences of the scorpion's nature.

He brought the scalding cup of tea to his lips, gently blowing against the steam. It trembled in his pale hand. The image of Alistair and whatever anonymous partner he'd found for the evening still burned in the back of Langford's mind. He set the cup down, unable to stomach the sound of the teaspoon chattering against porcelain.

Perhaps something in him was broken and still convinced he was undeserving of any form of happiness. That must be why he longed for someone he could never have.

A firm hand clapped him on the back. "There you are!" Alistair's low voice grated against his ears, sending his thoughts spiraling into a tangled mess. "I thought you abandoned me when I caught sight of our empty room." He plopped down opposite him, crossing his boots at the ankle atop the table. Lacing his hands behind his head, he offered him a crooked smirk.

Langford dragged his eyes away, the mere sight of the man twisted his stomach into knots. "Our room, was it? I don't remember you sleeping there." He brought his tea to his lips, refusing to meet Alistair's stare. The hot swill was bitter on his already scalded tongue. He hadn't bothered to ask for honey.

"You seemed like you needed the rest more than I did," Alistair said, far too casually. "You always complain about my snoring. I thought I'd do you a favor and make myself scarce."

Apparently, in Alistair's world, to make oneself scarce is to plunge balls deep into the nearest warm body.

"How fortunate I am that you're always thinking of me," Langford said, taking great care to set his cup down gently. He chanced a glance at Alistair, to see his dark brows drawn in curious calculation. Impossibly green eyes scanning his face. As if searching for an answer Langford would never willingly give.

Alistair ran a hand down his face, scratching his unshaven jaw. He stretched his arms over his head, letting out a groan. "All right, well, I'll grab us some food for the road. But we better move on before anyone catches wind of my being here." He rose, snagging Langford's tea from the table and taking a quick sip. He grimaced. "Ah, Langford, that's terrible. There's no whiskey in it." He set the cup down and sauntered away.

Langford watched him go, rubbing the spot that ached in his chest.

CHAPTER TEN

DACIANA

Felix's directions were barely coherent, and that was once they calmed him down enough so he could explain. But Daciana had a keen sense of direction, of always knowing where she was headed. And there wasn't a forest in all of Ardenas Kenna hadn't traipsed through.

The tree branches stretched overhead as if trying to warn them to turn back. Leafless limbs scraped together in the breeze. Kenna and Daciana rode through the forest, having bought temporary mounts for the journey. They'd ridden hard for as long as they could. Now that her change wasn't so imminent, Daciana could actually ride without spooking the poor creature. It was another unfortunate side effect of her nature. She couldn't hold onto the same animal for long. They always sensed her predatory nature. She hadn't the heart to tell poor Lark that was why Alistair wouldn't let her keep her horse, but of course, it didn't matter. That girl got what she wanted, no matter the insurmountable odds.

Daciana's heart lurched at the thought of her friends. Soon enough, she'd reunite with them. She cast a sideways glance at Kenna, who sat effortlessly tall on her mount. She rode with elegant grace and casual finesse. Not that it was surprising. Everything came easily to her.

"Should be getting close." Kenna's voice cut through Daciana's thoughts.

"Do we have a plan?" She should have known better than to ask that question.

Kenna whipped her head to regard her with shock. "I'm offended you'd even ask. You know I don't believe in plans."

Daciana clenched her jaw. "Kenna..."

"Yes, yes, I know." She waved her hand dismissively. "Honestly, I don't have a 'sneaky cloak and dagger' type of plan. My plan is to get that girl out alive if possible—and slay the beast. In no particular order."

A harsh squall blew through the trees, rushing through Daciana's ears. The force of the breeze was deafening, carrying a note of despair. Somewhere, deep in the forgotten part of the forest, in a hidden castle, a girl was being held captive by a beast. It was like something out of a child's fairytale.

But those tales were a farce, a cleverly woven lie to keep children timid and compliant. That only goodness, whatever the definition meant to the person telling the story, always won out over wickedness.

Life was not so stark in its clarity.

Daciana had spilled enough blood to last ten lifetimes. She always hoped for a fight avoided. For the stay of her blade. But she would not mourn the loss of a life she chose to take. Only the ones she hadn't intended.

A whisper of a shiver swept through her. A soft hint of wrongness crept along her skin, raising goose pebbles on her arms. An imprint of magic thickened the air. A charged current that rode on the wind.

They were drawing near. She was certain of it.

There had been countless times her instinctive nature picked up on things. Things not meant to be detected by humans. The influence of repelling magic should have planted a need to turn around. To redirect. As if it wasn't magic, but human instinct warning this was the wrong way.

But she was no mere human.

And she could practically taste the magic someone doused the place with.

It wasn't as bad as the Forbidden Shrine. The place of memories stolen from the furthest expanses of her heart. From places, she never wished to revisit. She'd never felt repelling magic as strong as the enchantment that sang from deep in the bowels of the earth. When her nerves screamed of its wrongness, and every instinct cried for her to flee. No, this was faint magic, lacking in potency. And darkness. It reminded her of Inerys' magic, earthy and wild, like the gnarled roots springing from the ground in their desperate attempt at finding the light.

Keeping a firm grasp on the reins, Daciana ran a hand into her hair. She'd left it unbound for once, and now she regretted that decision and longed for the reliable weight of her thick plait. She caught Kenna staring, her face unreadable, but she twisted away.

The trees began to thin, the forest growing both lighter and darker without the heavy branches shrouding the sky from view. But the sky was darker than the one they left behind, despite the midmorning hour. As they continued, they came upon frost-cloaked ground and a freshly frozen path lined with icy branches tinkling with every pass of the wind.

"A bit early in the season for frost." Kenna angled an eyebrow. "And my pendant is going berserk."

That wasn't surprising. A hunter needed a talisman to warn when monsters and magic were near. It's how Kenna knew to be on guard the first time Daciana happened upon the young hunter, alone in the woods.

If only Kenna had heeded her pendant's warning.

"Should we tie the horses back here?" Kenna's brown eyes bore into her expectantly. "In case we need to escape quickly?"

Memories of the time when she, Lark, and Gavriel had done just that pulled an unwilling grimace from Daciana's mouth. Except Lark refused to tie hers, fearful the creature wouldn't be able to escape a grim fate. A fate both hers and Gavriel's horses succumbed to.

"No, we'll bring them in. I won't risk them wandering and getting lost." She turned her ear to the wind, listening. "Nor will I leave them to face any wolves on the prowl."

A mischievous grin slowly stretched across Kenna's face, dimpling her cheek and lighting her eyes with amusement. "Interesting turn of phrase."

Daciana dismounted, ignoring her comment. Her boots met the hard ground, disturbing the too-perfect dusting of white powder and ice. She gently led her horse forward, taking careful steps as she crept along the wintery landscape. Her breath appeared in misty clouds spilling into the air. The grey sky promised a great winter storm.

Only it wasn't winter.

Daciana tugged her cloak tighter, wishing she'd donned riding gloves. She glanced over at Kenna, who wrinkled her nose in discomfort.

Daciana huffed warm breath against her fist, spilling heat into her palm. They dressed for autumn—not for weather this cold—a fact her numbing fingers seemed all too keen to remind her of.

Kenna's teeth chattered, narrow shoulders beginning to tremble. Without thinking, Daciana wrapped her arm around her, pulling her close to walk alongside her. Kenna sucked in a breath that sounded suspiciously close to a gasp, body leaning heavily into her. Daciana immediately regretted the action—regretted the way her body responded to Kenna's touch, even at an awkward angle as they trudged through the spontaneous winter.

But she couldn't bring herself to let go.

The forest calmed, wrapped in a blanket of quiet. The crunching of their footsteps cut through the stillness of the air.

"You know," Kenna said evenly, "if we don't find the castle, we'll have to make shelter and warmth somehow. It's the first lesson of survival training, that in the event of life-threatening cold—"

"Do not finish that sentence."

Kenna rolled her eyes. "You don't know what I was going to say."

Daciana pursed her lips. "Body heat."

"Ha! Shows what you know." Kenna's breath ghosted against the side of Daciana's throat. "I was actually going to say body heat, unencumbered by clothing. Way more effective."

Before she could think of a good retort, the curve in the bend revealed a wrought-iron gate. Instead of rods, the iron was twisted like gnarled vines, wrapping their way up to the sky. Adorning the gate were bright red roses that hadn't wilted despite the chill. Beyond it stood a tall dark castle. The façade looked as if it had been crafted in the very depths of the Netherworld. Carved into the framework were gruesome faces, expressions of pain cast into stone, as if the repellant magic weren't enough to deter visitors.

Daciana and Kenna exchanged a glance before leading their horses to wait by the outer wall as they sidled up for a closer inspection.

Between the balusters, Daciana could see a frozen courtyard. Perhaps it had been grand once, but the enchanted winter had reclaimed it, burying and cracking statues until all that remained was a desolate field of broken pieces.

There was no padlock, a stroke of luck since it was too tall to climb and Daciana's hands were numb. It swung open against her featherlight touch, hinges groaning their protest.

"Well, this doesn't seem ominous," Kenna said. The words floated into the frozen air as mist suspended before they dissipated in a cool hush. The sight of her cheeks and nose, rosy from the bite of the wind, gave Daciana a pang in her chest. She stepped away, mourning the loss of Kenna's body so near to hers, and yanked her longsword from its sheathe.

"Let's get this done," Daciana said.

Kenna's broad, unrestrained smile left her breathless. "So commanding. I see some things never change."

Daciana crept through the snow, out of habit more than necessity. There was only one assured way of getting into the castle that warded away visitors while simultaneously offering no resistance to their intrusion. They'd be marching through the front door.

If Amara hadn't been missing for three weeks already, perhaps they would have crafted a plan. Studied the perimeter. Mapped out entrances, exits, and safeguards. But they were out of time. Daciana hated to admit it, but the likelihood of finding the girl unharmed was slim, and each moment they waited, the chances grew slimmer. At this point, it was a question of damage control. Any creature that kept a girl against her will had nefarious motives.

Daciana refused to track that path of thought. A moment of doubt could paralyze just as surely as a physical blow. She glanced over at Kenna, to find her mouth thinned in a firm line. Likely suffering the same thoughts as she.

Boots crunching in the snow, their tracks filled almost as quickly as they made them. As if within the confines of this courtyard, the storm was picking up speed. With each step, the wind blew harsher, stinging Daciana's cheeks. The hand gripping her sword trembled in the frigid cold, hundreds of pinpricks searing against her fingers and knuckles.

By the time they reached the door, shivers wracked their bodies. Daciana forced it open, spilling the brutal cold into the foyer. They staggered in, kicking the door shut with a loud thud.

The silence was heavy without the storm battering Daciana's ears. Cobwebs swayed in the residual breeze they'd allowed through the door. A lone candelabra, sitting on a small wooden end table, illuminated the dark entryway. As if someone had been expecting them and left it out as a small courtesy. Three little flames flickered in the dark. Daciana left it where it sat, unwilling to touch anything that might be laced with magic.

She swung her sword in a small circular motion, loosening her tight wrist and clenched muscles. Slowly, feeling seeped into her fingers. She glanced over at Kenna, who gave her a quick nod.

It was now or never.

They crept along the faded crimson carpet. Daciana took careful steps, lest her foot found a groan in the wood beneath.

From a distance, the sound of metal scraping pricked Daciana's ears and raised the hairs on the back of her neck. A slow drag of a knife, and she could practically hear each individual edge of serration.

She and Kenna exchanged a knowing look before they surged forward—

A large room greeted them, a long dining table in its center overflowing with pastries, fruits, and cheeses. Dozens of portraits adorned the walls, each grimly staring from their ornate frames. The massive hearth was aflame with a roaring fire, casting warm light across the room and over the banquet-sized feast.

But the strangest sight was the two individuals seated at either end, frozen in shock at the sudden intrusion.

A beautiful girl, with rich dark skin and cascades of black hair waving down her back and spilling over her shoulders, sat there, watching them. She wore a deep indigo gown of velvet that clung to her generous curves. Her large brown eyes widened in alarm, and her full lips were slightly parted as if she'd been about to take a bite of the glazed croissant she held suspended in midair.

Amara.

At the head of the table sat another.

Felix wasn't mad. Nor did he embellish.

For there sat an enormous beast. His fur-covered body had been stuffed into a too-tight gentleman's coat. His black horns caught the light of the flame that roared in the fireplace. His brilliant blue eyes were far too intelligent on the face of a beast.

A low growl rumbled from his chest, and his lips pulled back in a snarl, revealing sharp fangs.

CHAPTER ELEVEN

LARK

Undesirables came in many shapes and forms. A soul twisted from its original state could manifest in terrifying ways. Monsters made flesh by the journey.

Gavriel cursed as he dropped Lark to her feet. The metallic resonance of his longsword rang out as he tugged it free from the scabbard. Lark scrambled to retrieve her bow and arrows, and she slung the quiver over her shoulder. She nocked an arrow, loosely pointing it toward the ground as she regarded Gavriel. His dagger had found its way to his other hand, both of his blades poised and ready for a fight. They ducked behind separate trees, keeping each other within their sights.

And for a heartbeat, they waited.

Another scrape of rusted metal against the ground sang through the trees. The rhythmic drag, slow and steady. And growing ever closer.

Lark found Gavriel's face, wishing she could see his eyes. Dusk had settled over the forest, wrapping them in darkness. The all too familiar feeling of dread, from a night not long ago, coiled in the pit of her stomach. She pushed the images away—images of Gavriel on the ground, desperately fighting against the two Manananggal, seconds away from being ripped open.

If it hadn't been for Daciana…

Lark swallowed the lump in her throat, pushing down the terror that clawed at her chest.

Between the shadowed trees, a hooded figure emerged, its grey cloak tattered. The cloth was faded, as if it had sat out baking in the sun for decades. A great axe hung limply at its side, the blade dragging against the earth in long sweeps.

Lark's heart stuttered to a rapid thrumming in her chest. A rush of cold swept through her legs. Every nerve in her body screamed the danger of what stalked them.

An Undesirable.

It lifted its hooded head, face obscured by night and shadows. It dragged a large sack in its other hand. The dark stains across the canvas surface confirmed Lark's suspicions.

Fidelis Mortem. The loyal death. Commonly referred to as Collectors. Collectors were the purest of loyalists in life—to a fault. Blind loyalty to the wrong king rewarded no one in death. Their punishment for turning a blind eye to the crimes of their masters was to have their tongues torn from their mouths, lips sewn shut so they could never swear an oath of loyalty again. But their eyes would remain, ever seeing, ever watchful. A heightened sight to ensure they'd never fail to see their wrongdoings.

Fidelis Mortem that fought their way to the land of the living became Collectors. Lost souls who wandered the earth, unbound to a ruler and forever plagued to seek righteous justice by beheading—their swiftest form of cleansing.

Lark glanced at the bag. It bulged with bloody contents, and she swallowed the bile that rose in her throat.

"Is this… what I think it is?" Gavriel murmured low enough for her ears only.

The Collector stilled, eyes impossible to see beneath its dark shroud.

"We'll need to behead it." Lark's voice was distant to her own ears. "And bury the body separately." She could have swiftly dealt with this as a Reaper, but she couldn't help but send a silent thank you to the skies. It could be far worse.

"Is that it then?" Gavriel mused aloud. "I could have sworn there was something else we're forgetting."

"Don't lose your head?"

He frowned at her. "No, that's not it…"

The Collector shambled forward, dropping the blood-soaked sack and raising its giant rusty axe. The blade didn't gleam, too caked in gore and viscera for any glint of steel to remain.

Lark pulled her bowstring tight, aiming for the throat, and loosed an arrow into the night air. It sank with a thud; thick black ichor oozed from the entry wound. The Collector didn't even flinch, staggering forward without even yanking the arrow out.

Gavriel swung his sword, sinking it into the Undesirable's shoulder—where it remained, shallowly in place. With a growl, he pulled down tighter, using both hands, but his blade wouldn't budge.

Panic slammed into Lark's chest as she nocked another arrow, loosing it before she put much power behind it. It sailed through the air, narrowly missing her target. The wind it created in its wake blew the hood back from its face.

Beady, impossibly human eyes stared back at her. Seeing and not seeing. Like all the light had fled and given way to cool darkness. Its mouth—sewn shut with gaping sutures—cracked and bled black down its chin. It turned and regarded Gavriel with indifference, looking right through him before it knocked him back to land flat on the earth. The impact reverberated through Lark as she watched, stunned.

Gavriel shook off the force quickly, leaping to his feet with adept agility.

But the Collector had already turned its back on him, advancing on Lark in a slow, unyielding pace.

Bending down, Lark yanked Hugo's knife from her boot. She'd have to stay out of reach of the axe, but she was quicker with the smaller weapon. Her veins sang the familiar song she knew so well: the promise of violence.

Gavriel yanked the sword free from its shoulder, not even earning a backward glance as it continued its quiet trek to where Lark stood. "My blade can't pierce deeply," he said, terror lacing his voice.

"When's the last time you sharpened it?" She bent her knees, falling into a loose stance. "Didn't they teach you proper sword maintenance at that fancy Guild of yours?"

"That isn't it," he ground out. "There's no armor. It's as if the bone is made of solid iron."

Ah. Shit.

Lark's heart plummeted into her stomach, a free fall followed by a sickening landing. Her knife seemed downright silly in her hand as the Collector raised its giant axe. But wielding a weapon so large was cumbersome.

She feinted left, dropping to a swift roll out of reach. She slashed at its calves, only to be met with scalding blood, black and carrying the scent of rot and decay. The creature showed no signs of pain, merely swinging around to drop the head of the axe upon her. She scrambled away, dirt and leaves clinging to her sticky hands.

Gavriel charged the creature, brandishing his sword with lethal grace and speed—only to be met with a wall of indifference. He cut and slashed, swiping the edge of his sword against its chest, throat, gut. Strike, pivot, retreat, strike again. Gavriel was mesmerizing in his movements, and yet... the Collector would not fall. More black rot spilled from the wounds, as it never ceased its shambling toward Lark. No matter how many cuts Gavriel made, those dead eyes remained fixed on where Lark kneeled in the dirt. She aimed another arrow, and another, firing without pausing. Pull, anchor point, release.

Her arrows sunk their marks until they started going wide in her terror.

The Collector tilted its axe, knocking Gavriel back with the shaft. He hit the unforgiving earth with a loud thud.

Lark flinched, dragging her eyes up to the creature that now stood over her. Scrambling back, she tried to put as much distance between them as possible. The Collector flickered, one moment several paces back, and the next right on top of her. In a flash of movement, it gripped her throat in its large, clammy hand. Decaying skin pressed against her neck, its fingers squeezing a gagging breath from her lips.

It stared back, dull eyes lifeless and unyielding. Stitched mouth forever frozen in a frown. It released her throat and dragged its fingers through her hair, gripping tight enough Lark's eyes pricked with tears. She clawed and twisted, scraping her dagger across its dead wrist to release its hold on her hair. There was no excuse to fall now. She had so much left to do. She would not be felled by this silent creature, too cowardly in its human life to avoid this fate. Lark sank her dagger into its flesh over and over, screaming until her throat was sore and her voice was hoarse. The pestilential scent of death washed over her, the pungent ichor filling her nose and making her dizzy.

The Collector yanked her head back, exposing her neck as it slowly lifted its heavy blade. A cry ripped from Lark's lips as she tugged herself free and red strands of her hair tore from her scalp.

Gavriel leapt onto the creature's back, angling his sword to block its blow from aiming at Lark again. "We need the axe! Get the axe!"

With blood-blackened hands, Lark grabbed the shaft of the axe, tugging hard. The Collector held firm, turning to regard her with that dead stare. No anger. No fight. Its gaze chilled her to the very depths of her soul, freezing in her veins as she cried out and yanked harder. Tears streamed down her face, the skin of her palms biting against the effort.

"Get it free," Gavriel groaned as he slashed at its arm, holding fast to a monster showing no signs of fatigue.

"I'm trying!" Lark cried, biting her lips hard enough to taste blood. Finally, the axe shifted, gradually freeing from the impossible grip of its owner.

It loosed from its grasp, sending Lark careening into the dirt, the heavy axe landing on top of her. The impact rushed the air from her lungs. She coughed, searching for her breath, but Gavriel was already yelling for her.

"Quickly, do it now!"

On shaky feet, she stood. Blood, dirt, and grime coated her hair and skin. She shuffled forward, dragging the rust and blood-covered great axe in the dirt. Bracing with both hands, she heaved it up to her shoulder, groaning at the weight.

Gavriel stabbed his blades through its cloak, pinning it to the ground.

The Collector didn't fight, nor did it tug against its prison. It calmly waited, staring with unblinking eyes as Lark lifted the great axe high above her head—

And brought it down through its neck.

She released the axe, the weight of it stuck firmly in the ground, cleaving the creature's head from its body, whilst the blade kept the body joined. Lark staggered back, the dark forest spinning. She crashed to her knees in the dirt, the fight having fled her body.

Gavriel sank to his knees before her, his warm hands finding her face and lifting her chin to meet his eye. "You're all right. We're all right." His breathless words whispered against her mouth. A stream of blood trickled from his forehead down his face, a narrow river carving a path down his temple, down his cheek. Lark lifted shaky hands to wipe it away, smearing black blood against his skin.

"We should wash," she said, surprised by how even her voice was.

His dark green eyes studied her intently. As if afraid she might disappear at any moment.

It wouldn't be the first time.

Lark rested her forehead against his, not caring about the blood and dirt and grime that coated their skin. She gently pressed her lips to his, a soft ghost of a kiss.

And a promise.

She was here. She wasn't going anywhere. Not this time.

LARK SHIVERED despite the roaring fire Gavriel had built. The flames danced along the velvet shadows of the forest. She tugged her spare cloak tighter, their soiled clothing still drying on a tree branch nearby. Gavriel passed her a cup of steaming tea, a fragrant blend of cardamom and chamomile from the parcels Langford had sent with them. Her morning blend was whatever he brewed to prevent conception, and it tasted awful. But this was a gentle, mellow flavor, and instantly calmed her.

Gavriel settled beside her and wrapped his arm around her shoulders. She leaned into the contact, reveling in it once more. She'd allowed too much time to slip past already. Damned if she was going to waste another moment of her time on this plane pushing away the things that made her happy.

Firelight danced across his face, lighting up his sharp jaw and filling the scar that cut across his cheek. Her eyes dipped to the scar bisecting his lip, warmth fluttering in her belly when he smirked in response, as if sensing her thoughts. She wet her lips. "Gavriel, I need to tell you something." She needed to tell him what she asked of Inerys. What she nearly did.

He tucked a loose tendril of hair behind her ear, his fingers lingering at her throat. "What's on your mind?"

The way his touch tingled against her skin was the deciding factor. She needed something else first.

Lark pressed her lips against his, swallowing the small sound of surprise he made. He pulled her into his lap without hesitation, and she immediately wrapped her legs around his waist. She dropped her tea to the ground, hands sliding over the back of his neck, into his hair, touching and feeling everything she denied herself. He broke their kiss momentarily. "Is this what you needed to tell me?"

She clutched the neck of his tunic, twisting the fabric in her fists. "In part."

"Works for me," he said before claiming her mouth again in a searing kiss. His hand was gentle in her hair as he angled her head back. She gasped against his mouth, and he pulled her tighter against him.

Fire erupted across her skin, every nerve flaring to life. She felt his teeth along her jaw, the sensitive skin of her neck, as she tipped her head back, staring up at the night sky. Embers floated above, dancing among the trees in the darkness.

"Gavriel." His name left her lips in a desperate breath. He rose to his feet, lifting her effortlessly as he carried her to their tent. His movements slowed as he parted the flaps, placing her with heartbreaking gentleness upon the bedroll. She tugged at him impatiently, trying to pull him on top of her, but he braced himself on his hands, caging her body while searching her face.

"Lark," he whispered, "tell me you want this."

"I want this," she said, reaching for him. He caught her hands, lacing their fingers.

"If the soul bond… or whatever it is… if it's an issue—"

"It's not," she said quickly, sitting up so their breath mingled. "I swear Gavriel, it's not. I want you. Not just now." She swallowed the fear creeping up the back of her throat. "Always."

His eyes searched her face, their intensity almost searing. "I'm yours," he said, before sealing his mouth to hers.

She cupped his jaw, pulling him down with her. He slotted his thigh between her legs, never allowing his full weight to press on her. She yanked impatiently at his black tunic, trying to tug it over his head. His deep chuckle rumbled through her, ghosting a chill against her already sensitive skin.

"Patience, Demon," he said with a sly smirk before sitting up and tugging his tunic over his head. She ran her gaze greedily over the hard planes of his chest, the angry scars and lacerations across his skin. Every violent inch of him was perfection. She leaned up, pressing soft kisses to each one, as she had done the first time they'd lain together.

He pulled her to him, interrupting her exploration of his battle-worn form. "Am I to be the only one on display tonight?" he asked with a pointed look.

She grinned, untying her cloak and tossing it to the side. She grabbed her tunic and tugged it over her head, mussing her thick hair. Gavriel's eyes darkened, a ravenous expression crossing his face. Clad in only her breastband and leggings, Lark resisted the urge to cross her arms in front of her, instead firmly placing her hands against the ground and arching her back.

Gavriel's hunger lit up his face. His deft hands went to work unlacing her leggings, before peeling them down her legs and shucking them to the side of the tent. He pulled himself up to claim her mouth once more as he gently tugged the knot on her breastband free, her skin instantly goose-pebbling. He dipped his head, mouth worshiping her breasts until she was shaking with need. His hand ghosted down the plane of her stomach, stopping at the edge of her smallclothes. Lark's heart pounded in her chest, blood burning in her veins. He pulled back long enough to fix her with the intensity of his stare, eyes greedily devouring the sight of her beneath him, before his fingers slipped beneath the thin material.

Lark gasped, head thrown back against the bedroll. Gavriel leaned over her and devoured the sounds she made as his skillful fingers worked her higher.

She bit her lip, trying to keep the fire he was so masterfully stoking contained. He gazed down at her, as if admiring her form.

"I could spend hours like this," he murmured.

"You better not," she ground out between gritted teeth.

The rich timbre of his laugh crawled along her skin, kissing her already frayed nerves as he curled his fingers just so, blackness spotting her vision and a fluttering ache igniting within.

Breathing ragged, Lark glanced over at Gavriel to find him leaning on his elbow, a smug smirk on his face. She pushed him, so he flopped onto his back, a soft noise escaping his chest. She tugged his laces free, yanking his trousers and smallclothes off in one swift motion, tossing them behind her.

He laughed, and the sound filled every corner of her heart. Meeting his gaze, she waited for him to offer some remark before lowering her mouth over him, stealing the breath from his lungs in a swift hiss. She took him fully, addicted to the noises she coaxed from him. He carded his fingers through her hair. Firm, but gentle. She tipped her eyes up to watch. He was beautiful this way. Head thrown back, brow furrowed as if in pain.

Suddenly, his eyes snapped open, and he yanked her up to him, pressing her flat against his chest. Nothing between them. He searched her face, dragging his gaze over her in greedy pursuit. "I don't think I'll ever get used to you."

Lark ran her fingers along the scar on his lip. He leaned into the touch, gently shifting so she lay beneath him. He kissed her once. Twice. Each kiss melding into the next until she was writhing with need for him.

He lined himself up with her entrance, waiting to find her eyes on his. "Lark," he murmured, "my heart is yours." He sank into her, the slight burn as he stretched her, only increasing the fire in her blood. She gasped, arching her back. Every nerve in her body was alight with the rightness of their joining. He set a languid pace, unrushed, as he moved within her. She gripped his shoulders, nails biting into his skin.

"Gavriel," she gasped. Wishing she could form the words. To say she belonged to him. That her soul was his. That as long as time existed, she would be his. Instead, she ran shaky hands down his muscled back, heart pounding against his chest, as they moved together.

He groaned, pulling back to grab her hips and angle her so he could set a punishing pace. She shattered with every thrust, heart smashing and reforming between heartbeats.

Her body raced ahead of her, sprinting toward a culmination that pricked her eyes with unshed tears. Gavriel tightened his hold, murmuring whispers of praise as he brought his hand to where they joined, that final push crashing her over the edge. Plummeting off the cliff. He chased his own end, slamming into her with a brutal force until he stilled, a choked sound leaving his throat as his hand tightened on her hip.

Breath escaped her chest in heavy drags, and a lazy smile stretched across her face. Gavriel dropped atop her, still joined, burying his face in her neck. "You broke me," he murmured against her sweaty skin.

She laughed, the sound weak and stuttered. "I think you broke you. Must be out of practice."

Gavriel lifted his head to glare at her. "And whose fault might that be?"

Lark traced her finger in light swirls across his skin, delighting in the shiver she pulled from him. "We'll just have to make up for lost time."

He huffed a laugh against her cheek. "That is possibly the best idea you've ever had." He kissed her, before heaving himself off her with a groan. Lark laid back, resting her head on her hand as she watched him stretch, the impressive muscles in his broad shoulders rippling. Gavriel leaned over and grabbed a nearby bottle of wine, taking a long pull. Lark smiled, chest overfilled with unbridled joy. She wrapped the covers around herself, shivering in delight at the way they captured his familiar scent. Could it always feel like this?

He turned and pressed the bottle in her hand, pressing a quick kiss to her temple before standing to tug his trousers back on.

"Where are you going?" The words left her mouth against the lip of the wine bottle as she tipped it to spill over her tongue. She grimaced at the bitter flavor erupting in her mouth, and glanced down to study the bottle, searching for any signs of spoil—

Icy fear lanced through her heart. She squeezed the brown bottle in her hand, tight enough the glass shuddered.

"Did you hear me?"

Blood roared in her ears as she glanced up at Gavriel, who was smiling down at her.

"I said I was going to cook you some apples. I figured you'd need to bolster your strength." He gave her a wicked smirk. "I plan to spend the rest of the night buried in you."

She couldn't breathe. Her lungs had constricted in her chest and wouldn't expand. "Where... where did you get this?"

His brows furrowed in confusion. "I found it in your bag. It kind of reminded me of the time Alistair hid wine among your things." He smiled fondly at her. "Which reminds me of the first time I ever played the fiddle for you. I thought maybe you'd like to hear some music tonight while you feast on the labors of my cooking."

Lark shook her head, desperately trying to calm the racing of her heart before it leapt from her chest. "Don't go."

Shock splashed across his features. "I'm not going anywhere."

"Don't... don't leave. Don't leave the tent." She needed to figure out a way to reverse the effects. How would it work? Would he suddenly look at her and feel nothing? Would it happen the moment she was no longer in his sight, and the next time he saw her, he'd feel nothing of the bond? She had been quick to accept that the bond was nothing of importance to their affections. But when faced with the abrupt reality of severing it… Her stomach roiled, fear entwining in her gut.

"Lark" —he sat down and ran a soothing hand down her arm— "what's going on?"

She wet her dry lips, mind splintering. If their love was true, it wouldn't make a difference. Soul bond or not, he would love her.

And yet, the notion of leaving his side speared panic through her heart.

"Just," she said shakily, "stay."

"I will," he murmured, pressing a kiss to her hair. "I'll stay right here."

She glanced at him, terror still running through her veins, before she pushed him down onto the bedroll and rose over him again. His answering smile, though befuddled, never dimmed in its joy. She claimed his mouth, hoping to taste the carefree euphoria on his lips. She wouldn't tell him. They would have this, and then face the dawn together.

LARK AWOKE to a soft light of an early sunrise seeping through the stitching of their tent. Groggy, and with a head full of cotton, she blinked a few times, trying to push the heavy shroud of sleep from her mind. The canvas flaps fluttered in the breeze. She shivered against the brisk morning air, reaching for Gavriel's warm body.

All she found was the cold space beside her.

She sat up, throwing off the covers, and immediately regretted the action as a chill wracked her body. She wrapped the blankets around her shoulders and yanked the untied flaps back hard enough to tear the canvas.

Stepping out into the quiet morning, breath fogging the air before her face, Lark darted her gaze around the camp.

The fire had long been spent, not even a trace of smoke rising from the ashes.

The aching void suffocated as it surrounded her, mercilessly taunting her.

Gavriel was gone.

CHAPTER TWELVE

LANGFORD

*L*angford ran his hand over the dry page, the familiar sensation of paper beneath his fingers having a calming effect. Narrowing his eyes, he willed the words to make sense. He'd planned on waiting to study the tome more intently aboard Ingemar's ship, the ocean rolling beneath him as they traveled home. But here he sat, at another sticky table, in another crowded tavern. The sweet scent of wine and desperation permeated the already heavy air. The tavern's atrium granted a splendid view of the sky and of the boughs of a cypress tree nearby, but it offered little relief from the heat. Autumn nights in Koval were mild and balmy but trapped in this tavern, it was downright oppressive. Sweat trickled down his sides and dotted his upper lip. Absently, he unlaced the top of his white tunic. It did little to ease the sensation of being cooked alive. Wiping his hands against the rough fabric of his trousers, he focused on the book spread before him. This distraction was a welcome one, even if it didn't hold his attention long enough to form a coherent thought.

Alistair was across the tavern, holding court at a table filled with enraptured faces. Langford had to give him credit where it was due. The man knew how to entertain a drunk audience. Presently, he was regaling the tale of when he snuck into Cliffmount Prison and rescued a poor damsel wrongly imprisoned by a rival family.

"And of course, she was grateful." Alistair smirked, arching a dark eyebrow. "Very grateful indeed."

Langford rolled his eyes. Alistair left out the part where he downed a bottle of questionable rum and curled up by the fire after everyone retired to their tents, sobbing into the earth. Despairing over things he'd seen. Of what he left in that prison. Of what he couldn't do. Who he couldn't save. Langford had sat beside him, rubbing soothing circles against Alistair's back as he fell apart. In the morning, Alistair didn't remember a thing. Blaming the rum.

But Langford would never forget.

Another round of boisterous laughter boomed from the nearby table. Langford pinched the bridge of his nose, reaching to grab his tea. He wanted something stronger. The sweet call to oblivion was tempting, but he needed to focus. He glared at the page, taking a slow sip.

Messorum Ferrum. That damned Reaper Blade. A promise of advantage, only to be barred by his own incompetence. The translations still eluded him. Nonsense phrases that held no real meaning. *Forged by blood. Bound by fate.* He snorted. It meant nothing. It meant he stared at the pages of an ancient text for hours by dwindling candlelight and the very words he studied mocked him for it. Perhaps it would make sense in the morning, with fresh air filling his lungs.

He glanced at Alistair. The brunette with the ample bosom whispered in his ear, her hand trailing down his arm. Alistair's mouth curved in a devilish grin, emerald eyes darting to find Langford.

Heat swept up his already sweaty neck as he lowered his gaze back down to the tome he was studying. They hadn't spoken of what transpired the other night. What would likely occur again if the ravenous looks Alistair received from both the woman wearing too much rouge and the red-haired fellow at her side were any indication. Both kept finding excuses to touch Alistair—a caress against his arm, a touch to his chest, running their hands along his body as if he was theirs for the taking.

Langford tossed the rest of his tea down the back of his throat, ignoring the sharp bite of heat that seared his tongue. He wiped his mouth with the back of his hand, eyes drawn to Alistair like a magnet. Alistair watched him with an unreadable expression, eyes darkening across the crowded room.

Sweat erupted over Langford's palms, heart pounding in his chest as he quickly darted his gaze to the woodgrains of the table and the dark etchings against warm reds and browns. He would avoid his gaze for the rest of the night and distract himself from imagining Alistair with his temporary companions. Langford had more than enough work to keep himself busy.

The unmistakable sound of familiar boots thudded across the floor. There would be no distracting himself now.

"You seem awfully interested in my conversation." Alistair's voice was low and intimate as if he was sharing a sordid secret rather than mocking him. Langford lifted his eyes to find him leaning close. His warm breath fanned against his face, somehow still sweet as it mingled with the ale he'd drunk. He smirked, dark brow angling in silent question. "Put this away for the night, and come join us."

"I have a decent view from here," Langford said stiffly, ignoring the flush of heat in his cheeks. "I don't need to witness the spectacle up close."

"Spectacle?" Alistair leaned back, rolling his eyes. "Whatever could he mean, I wonder."

Langford snorted, ignoring the small smile playing on Alistair's mouth. "Are you so desperate for companionship?" Alistair's smile slowly faded, and Langford continued on, unable to halt the words. "You set your sights so low, you'll never go to bed alone. Even if you have to resort to spending coin on fleeting company."

Alistair touched a finger to his lips, as if in thought. "You're mad because I lack the integrity of a hunter? Seeking a greater thrill, a bigger kill? Is that it, then?"

"I'm not mad. I don't care what you do." Langford's nails bit into his palm as he clenched his fist. Alistair was a grown man. He could do whatever he damn well pleased with his time. It would be nice not to bear witness though.

"Vexed, then."

"I'm not vexed."

"Your reaction is a touch confusing."

Langford ignored him, silently fuming.

"I bet Niran over there would fancy your company." Alistair's voice held a mocking edge, and he jerked his chin toward his table of admirers. To the man Langford had already witnessed salivating over Alistair not moments ago. His red hair stuck out in jagged edges, and a wild smile played on his mouth.

"I have no need for any of your new *friends*. In fact, I have far more important matters to attend to than your inevitable infection I'll be treating on the morrow."

Alistair sucked on his teeth, the noise shooting straight to Langford's gut. "Fine, enjoy your books." He turned and sauntered away.

Langford kept his eyes dutifully trained on the words dancing across the page, even as they blurred out of focus.

MORNING CAME IN A GREY LIGHT, spilling through the thin gossamer curtains. Langford lay on his bed, surveying the ceiling. The wooden beams that stretched overhead were hardy and thick. Built to last. A shame. It would have been easier if the ceiling caved in and crushed him to death in his sleep.

That was too morbid a thought so early in the morning.

He swung his legs over the side, pulling himself to stand. Another night. Another day. Breathe in. Breathe out.

Langford shuffled to the door, rubbing his eyes. He hadn't ventured out of his room this night. He'd learned his lesson after the last time.

The first rays of dawn spilled through the atrium, pink and orange lighting the smooth floor. Stools sat atop their tables, and the floor held the sheen of mop water. From the back, the clatter of pots and pans rang out. Whoever had just washed the floor was prepping for another day of patrons, but the quiet morning was enjoyable while it lasted. Tankards hung from their hooks, chalices had been carefully stacked, and without the thickened air of too many bodies, the soft floral scent from the rose bushes outside crept through the glassless windows. The dining area was peaceful, empty, save for one drunkard leaning over the bar top to snag a bottle of rum. His dark hair was wild, his crimson jerkin askew on his broad shoulders, and beneath his leather gambeson, he'd loosened the top laces of his tunic. Langford recognized that drunkard.

"Alistair," he hissed. "What are you doing?"

Alistair froze, laying across the narrow wooden tabletop, one boot on his seat, the other suspended in midair. "Why 'f it isn't muh best mate," he slurred, falling back and nearly missing the seat as he stumbled to find a proper footing. "Drink?"

"Alistair, it's after dawn."

Alistair closed one eye, frowning. "Don' see the probl'm." He raised his glass, spilling its contents down the front of his leather gambeson. "Son offa bitch."

"That's quite enough," Langford said as he stepped forward, gently pulling Alistair to stand. Alistair grinned, swaying enough to knock into him. The firm planes of his chest rested heavily against Langford. He ignored the way his face heated at the contact. "Alistair, you're too heavy. I can't support all of your weight."

Alistair raised his heavy neck to regard him with a slight pout. "Tha's no 'vry nice, issit?"

Together, they shambled up the stairs, and Alistair's boots caught a few times. He tipped his head back and laughed, a deep rumble in his chest. Langford gritted his teeth, half-dragging him to the room he'd spent the night alone in. They fell into the door, knocking it open with a heavy thud. Langford kicked it closed behind him, bracing Alistair's arm over his shoulders as he pulled him to the small bed in the corner.

Attempting to flop him down, Langford angled him to fall as gracefully as possible. But Alistair held tight, dragging him down with him. Langford landed on top of him, heart beating erratically in his chest as he stared down at those impossibly green eyes, the black hair that was smoothed away from his bronze face. The small scar just above his right eyebrow.

Langford's breath hissed through his teeth as he pushed himself up.

Alistair's hands gripped him in place, an unreadable expression in his hazy eyes. "Langfor'," he breathed.

Langford's throat constricted. "Sleep it off, Alistair."

Alistair's eyes scanned his face, eagerly caressing every feature. "Your eyes… they're a calm sea a' dawn. I'see 'em when I close m'eyes. All I'see is'you," he said softly, breath ghosting against his face. "I'sleep… alls isee is'your face." He lifted his hand, running two fingers down Langford's cheek.

Langford held utterly still, frozen in place. Keenly aware of the trail of fire Alistair's touch left searing its wake.

A small smile played on Alistair's mouth, before he dropped his hand, head lolling to the side as his eyes slipped closed.

Langford sat transfixed, uncertainty burning in his gut. He pulled back and trudged to the door on numb legs and heavy feet, nearly tripping over himself as he swiftly darted past the threshold, yanking the heavy wooden door shut behind him—before finally exhaling a weighty breath.

CHAPTER THIRTEEN

DACIANA

"Ohat are you doing in my home?" the Beast growled, his voice a low rumble.

Daciana remained perfectly still, sword at the ready. Poised to strike, but avoiding antagonizing his predatory instinct with swift movements or sudden words.

Kenna had no such concerns.

She waved her sword around, not seeming to care when his eyes followed the movement. "If you didn't want people barging in, you might try locking it." Kenna shot a glance at Daciana as if to confirm the absurdity of the situation.

The Beast growled again.

Daciana stiffened, every nerve in her body, both mortal and primordial, preparing for an attack.

"Don't mind him." The girl's smooth voice cut in from across the table. Amara took a bite of her croissant, chewing thoughtfully. "He's a bit unnerved by the storm. It comes and goes," she said, waving her pastry around, flakes dusting her plate.

Daciana met Kenna's gaze with a silent question. *What in the blazing nethers was happening?*

"But on the bright side," Amara continued, lifting her chin to regard the beast, "you were right about that noise. He knew he heard intruders." She laughed, shaking her head. "And I insisted it was merely the storm. I suppose it'll be my turn to read aloud tonight, yes?"

Something that perhaps was meant to be a smile spread across the Beast's mouth, lips curling back to show his white fangs.

Amara returned his smile with a broad grin that lit up her already striking features. She busied herself with her assorted pastries, addressing Daciana and Kenna without looking at them. "Do you seek shelter?"

Daciana stepped closer to the girl. "Amara, we're here to collect you."

Amara froze, cherry danish balanced between her elegant fingers as she'd moved on from the croissant. "There's been some mistake," she said, white teeth flashing as she bit her lip. "I'm not leaving."

Daciana studied her. The glow of her healthy skin, her bright eyes, the supple curves of her well-dressed body, the amiable smiles that crossed her mouth as she chewed. She didn't appear to be in distress.

"This is awfully strange," Kenna said. "I don't think this has ever happened to me on a job before." She crossed the room, brushing past Daciana to lean over Amara and look her in the eyes.

The Beast leapt to his feet, the chair crashing behind him.

"It's all right." Amara held up a hand, meeting Kenna's stare. "What is it you're searching for?"

Kenna narrowed her eyes. "Signs of compulsion. Brainwashing perhaps. Why don't you want to leave?"

Amara scoffed. "Because my work here isn't done."

Daciana watched, her sword still ready to cut the Beast down should he get too close to Kenna. But for the moment, he seemed content to glower in place. "Amara," Daciana said finally, "your father is the one who sent us."

Amara's face fell, her finger tapping against the handle of her fork. "Yes, well, that is regrettable."

Kenna's expression screwed up in concentration as if she was puzzling away and couldn't make sense of what they'd stumbled upon.

"Perhaps we could take a walk," Daciana said, sheathing her

sword. "Kenna can stay here with… the master of this castle, and I can catch you up on how your father is faring in your absence." Daciana loathed the idea of leaving Kenna alone with him. In fact, it seemed a right shit idea, probably fated to result in blood and dismemberment. But judging from the glares Kenna was receiving from the beast, it was unlikely he'd let her anywhere near Amara without his presence.

"Out of the question," he growled, taking a step toward her.

"It's fine, Aidan," Amara said. "Stay, eat. We won't be long."

The Beast called Aidan gave her a look of pure adoration as he slowly righted his chair and smoothed down his gentleman's coat before sitting.

"Great, I'm babysitting?" Kenna hissed in Daciana's ear. Daciana resisted the shiver that ran through her. "Don't be long, or I'll take his head out of sheer impatience."

"Your tact is astounding as ever," Daciana hissed back, pushing past her to follow Amara out of the dining room and into the hall.

Amara's deep indigo skirts swirled around her feet as she elegantly paced down the hall, never breaking stride. Her black curls waving down her back shone like moonlight atop a dark river, and her full hips swayed with each step. She truly was a great beauty. Daciana could see why frightened villagers might concoct a story of demonic bargains to explain the otherworldly grace she seemed to possess.

There were no mirrors anywhere in the grand estate. Not even a silver tray one might accidentally catch their reflection in. Nothing but candles and dusty furniture lined the halls.

Amara slowed her pace, moving to allow Daciana to stride alongside her.

"You mentioned my father."

"Yes, he posted a missing person in town. We happened upon it, and he told us everything."

"Everything?" Amara arched an elegant brow.

Daciana stopped her with a gentle hand. "Apparently not. I suggest you fill me in on what he left out," she lowered her voice to a whisper, recalling the fond tenderness the girl seemed to reserve for the creature. "Especially since, in addition to rescuing you, our task is to slay the Beast."

Amara sighed, bracing her hands on her hips. "My father asked you that?"

Daciana nodded. Technically, he asked for her safe return and the head of the beast. Barring that, the head of the beast was enough.

"Fine. Where do I start?" Amara paced over to the great double doors at the end of the hallway, flinging them open.

A great room, with impossibly tall cathedral ceilings, stretched before them. Hundreds, no thousands, of books lined the walls from the floor to the rafters. Ladders even Daciana would be nervous to climb at every wall, granting access as high as the books stretched. Behind giant glass windows, the storm had softened to a quiet hush, blowing powdery snow drifts across the back garden.

Amara turned, hands placed on her generous hips. "What have you heard about me from the village?"

Daciana weighed her words. "I heard a great deal of misunderstanding."

Amara laughed, the sound high and bright. "That's a tactful way of putting it. Fine, let me ask you this, do you think I'd be happy in a place that never felt like home? A place where I'm scrutinized and vilified? A place where my father can't earn an honest living because the locals are too frightened of what they don't understand?"

"No," Daciana said evenly, "I don't think you're happy in the village."

Amara nodded. "My father is brilliant, you know. He once was one of the greatest blacksmiths in Koval, before he and my mother came to Ardenas, but his true calling is his art. He has no confidence in his abilities." She paced back and forth, worrying her track into the plum-colored carpet. "I think, if we lived somewhere else, things could be different." She paused her trek to level Daciana with a weighty stare. "Have you ever wished you could go somewhere where no one knows your name, or what you've done, or what you didn't do, and just start over?"

The question seeped beneath Daciana's skin, filling her with a keen sense of understanding. She cleared her throat. "Haven't we all?"

Amara stared at the floor, resuming her pacing. "My father was supposed to sell his pieces at the festival. I know people would have loved them. All we needed was enough coin to move somewhere new. When he came back empty-handed, I knew he'd abandoned the cart along with our chance of leaving Whitebridge. I set out after he fell asleep, tracking his journey," she paused, "and where he diverted from the path."

"Tracking you say?" Daciana ran a hand over her jaw. "That's an impressive skill to have. How did you learn?"

"I read it in a book," she said with a wave of her hand. "So I retraced his steps and came upon this castle."

"And that was when you met the beast?"

Amara nodded. "Aidan expected me to be frightened, and I was, but I couldn't help but feel utterly heartbroken that this poor soul was trapped in the body of a beast, cursed for all of eternity."

Daciana exhaled a long breath. "So it's a curse, then?"

"I believe so. He doesn't necessarily agree."

"Wouldn't he know if someone had cursed him?"

Amara held up one finger, a triumphant smile on her face. "That's just it, isn't it? I've read a great deal of theory on curses, and the aim is always to keep the curse from being broken. What better way to ensure a curse sticks than to deprive the victim of recollection of it?"

"Hm." It wouldn't be the first time a pretty girl made the mistake of loving a beast. It was all too easy to justify decisions by ignoring any signs of warning. His observable intellect made him something new and unfamiliar by Daciana's experience, but the fact that this girl wanted so desperately to find a curable explanation…

"Just listen, please. I told Aidan I'd help him break his curse if he promised to pay me enough so my father and I could start fresh in a new town. We struck a deal that was more than fair. When I went home to tell my father, he pitched a fit. Said he'd get a hunting party and kill Aidan himself rather than allow me to broker a deal. So I reminded him of his promise to never take my choice away. It was a promise he made to my mother before she died, and I wasn't going to let him break it.

"It took some convincing, but finally he came around to the idea so long as I lived at home and traveled to the castle each day." She held her hands out to her sides. "A library this big must have something in it I can use. Any answer you seek can be found in the right book.

"But the next morning, it was the strangest thing. It was as if he'd completely forgotten the entire conversation we'd had. As if it never happened. I had to fight the same argument with him. He acquiesced, reluctantly, and I set to work. Every evening, I'd come home, tell him of my day and my progress, go to bed, and wake up the next morning to his complete and utter ignorance of the agreement and of my task. Don't you see?" Amara waved her hands wildly. "It's the curse! It prevents anyone from remembering anything that might aid in its breaking. It was easier to just disappear until my task was complete. I hoped to have something more solid to go off of by now, but I have made little headway."

Probably because she was too fond of the creature to spend her time researching.

"Your father remembered stumbling upon... Aidan. He remembered where the castle was."

"Because that memory fuels the curse. You two coming here to take me away would prevent me from trying to break it."

This girl desperately wanted this theory to work, no matter how many holes it bore. "So it's a sentient curse?"

Amara's shoulders fell. "You think I'm crazy."

"No, I think you're chasing a happily ever after," Daciana said softly, "and I don't think that's how this story ends." Idealism was rarely rewarded with tidy endings of joy and life filled with love. These romantic notions often made those blind to the darkness of their path.

They fell silent. The only sound was the gusting of the wind as it rattled the glass.

What harm was there in having hope? Why did she feel she had to stamp it out?

"Let's say I believe you," Daciana began uncertainly. "Why is it you don't forget? Wouldn't the curse erase your memory?"

Amara's eyes lit up, excitement shining on her youthful face. "Because I never forget anything. Every word ever spoken to me, every word I've ever read—I never forget."

"That must be handy." Langford sprung to mind. He'd want to meet such a person. "And now my task lies before me. Whatever shall I tell your father?"

Amara rubbed her shoulder, chagrin washing over her features. "I do regret wasting your time."

"Don't be sorry you aren't in need of rescuing. I'd never despair over someone not being in mortal danger." Daciana grinned, the sensation oddly soothing. "Besides, you're not the one wasting my time." She wouldn't even be here were it not for a certain hunter determined to see how far she could push.

"Whatever do you mean?" Amara's brows furrowed in confusion, a small smile playing on her mouth.

Daciana sighed. They had to trek back through blistering cold, only to tell Felix his daughter was fine and wouldn't be returning home. The thought of purging some of her burdens was too enticing to ignore. "There is something of great importance I must deal with. But I won't receive the aid I require until I earn it." Or something like that.

Amara frowned. "What is your task?"

"Do you know anything about the veil between realms? About the planes of existence after death?" Daciana expected Amara's confusion, maybe even her disbelief. She wouldn't be the first person to deny the existence of the Netherworld. Depending on what she believed, this very conversation could be a slight against the Paragons of virtue.

"I have read little on that subject," Amara said thoughtfully, "but I'll look into it. Anything specific you want to know?"

"You want to help?"

Amara laughed. "Of course I do! I'll gather everything I can find on the subject, though if there's something in particular you'd like to know, it would give me a focus."

"Start with tears in the veil," Daciana said, blood burning with excitement. "Then look into the Queen of the Netherworld."

CHAPTER FOURTEEN

LARK

Lark hugged her knees to her chest, sitting beside a fire that no longer burned. Her tears had long since ceased flowing down her cheeks, a deep ache hollowing her chest. A pain so visceral she could have sworn it came from physical injury instead of the consuming despair that surged through her gut.

Gavriel was gone.

The soul bond was severed.

And yet, here she remained. Alone and heartbroken over the loss of a mortal that was never really hers.

It was funny really, the way a human soul carves out space for new aches. For wounds to fester. She was sure the pain couldn't be contained in her body; it was too large to carry. And yet, it stretched the space behind her ribs, pushing past the threshold she'd deemed possible. The tattered edges of her heart still clung to this idea, this hope for light. The light of a mortal life chosen, a vast horizon of possibility.

And it burned.

This was her recompense for seeking human emotion. For longing to *feel.*

She stood on shaky legs, tripping over to the tent. Images of hungry kisses, stolen touches, whispered confessions, all slammed into her, knocking the wind from her lungs. No, she couldn't go back in there. It would be too easy to pretend he wasn't gone. That he'd just stepped away. She could fall asleep and forget that he'd cracked her chest wide open and ripped out her heart, only to relive it all when she awakened.

She turned, surveying the silent camp with burning eyes.

It was as if he had never left. He didn't even bother packing his things, too eager to put distance between them as quickly as possible. Was it awful for him, when he awoke with no compulsion to be near her? Did it sicken him to remember every moment they spent lying in each other's arms? A wave of nausea rolled over her at the thought. Nothing had changed for her. Fate was punishing her yet again, for she still longed for his touch, his kiss. Nothing had slaked her need to be near him. It felt like her soul still called out to him, so why was it so damn easy for him to leave?

She cried out her frustration, picking up a rock the size of her fist and launching it toward the tree line. A panicked rustling in the underbrush was her only response. She grabbed a nearby log that never made it into the fire, throwing it hard enough her shoulder twinged. A dam inside her ruptured, giving way to exquisite fury. It wasn't fair. She was plagued with the remnants of a broken tether while he carried on living his life. Forget their connection. He abandoned her in the middle of the forest, leaving her to sort out the inevitable fall of the veil. She screamed, blood thrumming in her veins as she tore the camp apart. Grabbing the canvas tent, she yanked it to collapse against the ground. She kicked the pot he'd left out, the promise of cooked apples he never made good on, before she picked it up and tossed it into the nearby thicket.

Her pulse pounded in her ears as she panted. The last vestiges of anger waned, and a slow creeping cold spread through her veins. She staggered to the undergrowth, searching for the pot. She could feel sorry for herself, but she needed something to cook with. Her hand closed around something softer than metal—leather. Tugging it from the shroud of deadened leaves and fallen branches, Lark gasped.

Gavriel's boot.

She'd watched him lace up his boots enough times to recognize it instantly. Yanked them off him herself dozens of times, once going so far as to throw them out of the tent to teach him a lesson. It felt like lifetimes ago.

She sat back on her haunches, a new dread coiling in the pit of her stomach. Mind struggling to make sense of it. Meanwhile her blood ran cold.

Something had happened to him. Something unplanned.

A BRANCH SLAPPED Lark in the face. She hissed a curse, bringing her hand to the minor cut across her cheekbone. She'd been searching the forest for hours for any sign. After closer examination, she'd found a few sets of tracks. And drag marks in the earth that eventually disappeared. By the looks of it, a small group of people walked, dragging Gavriel along until they grew tired of that and lifted him.

But why didn't she awaken? If there was a scuffle, surely her human hearing wasn't that terrible. She would have known, would have heard something to alert her.

She searched the ground and the trees for broken branches, cataloging the night's events, searching for what she'd missed.

Their bodies had rejoined once more, before the pull of exhaustion beckoned like an impatient visitor. She'd fought to stay awake, eyelids growing heavier. Eventually, the drag of sleep was so strong, so overpowering, she'd succumbed to it, tumbling headfirst into unconsciousness, head pressed against Gavriel's chest as it rose and fell with each breath. She'd never felt so tired. If they'd been sleeping, why was she left unharmed? It would have been all too easy to kill her. Why risk her following?

She stilled, staring down at the tracks before her. They diverged. One set traveled east; the rest continued south. It would make sense to follow numerous sets of tracks. If he'd escaped, he would have found her. She was almost sure of it.

A crow cawed overhead, the sound cutting through her. She needed to decide. Damned if she chose wrong.

She continued on, heading south, and sending a silent prayer to the skies she was on the right path.

NIGHT BROUGHT A SHROUD OF DARKNESS, a black sky devoid of any stars. Lark's foot caught a gnarled root, shooting her straight to the ground. Her chin slammed against the solid earth, earning her a sore jaw and a mouth full of dirt. She turned her head to spit, cringing against the grit between her teeth.

This was hopeless. She wasn't a tracker, and her mortal eyes couldn't see a blasted thing in the dark. She should have halted sooner and set up a camp when she still had the faint light of dusk on her side. Pressing her hands into the cold ground, she pushed herself up. Gavriel could be anywhere by now. She hadn't the faintest idea how she could find him. They already had a head start and the knowledge of their destination. She had a mouthful of dirt and a severed soul bond.

She wiped her lips. She needed to rest until the sun returned, and then she'd set off at first light. There was no other option.

Pulling her arms free of her pack, she groaned at the stiffness in her muscles. There was no point in starting a fire now. She yanked the few ropes from her pack, walking along the nearest trees to set up a perimeter of large snares, tying her nooses and slipknots with numb fingers. It wasn't much, but it was better than nothing. Hugo had shown her one night how to add security to the camp, not that they'd ever needed it. Hugo never slept while the others slept, even if someone else was on watch. He always waited for the impending dawn to bleed across the sky before he finally retired to his tent.

She'd give anything to have him watching her back, whittling a new knife handle or fletching arrows by the fire. He would have known how to track Gavriel.

She didn't care enough to erect her tent, opting to lay her bedroll directly upon the earth. Not bothering to kick off her boots, she settled under the coverings, yanking them tight over her head. A shiver wracked her body as she burrowed deeper into her blankets. Gavriel's familiar scent washed over her, and her heart clenched in her chest. She rued the day his scent would fade. When all she'd have left were memories stolen from a heart, she had no claim over. But for this night, she squeezed her eyes shut and breathed him in. Allowing herself to sink into a dreamless sleep.

A RUSTLING in the underbrush tore her from sleep. Lark jolted awake. Without lowering the coverings, she crept a hand down to her boot, heart hammering in her throat. Closing her fingers around Hugo's knife, she gently tugged it free, gripping it tight enough the handle bit into her palm.

Whatever had made the sound, she wasn't alone.

A twig snapped, sharpening Lark's hearing over the sound of her own pulse.

Something heavy hit the earth with a surprised grunt. "Shit," a high voice said.

Lark tossed back the coverings, blade at the ready. On the ground near her feet was a figure—shrouded by the black night. Lark leapt up, grabbing the figure by the cloak. She pressed the knife between them, angling it against a slim throat. Yanking the dark hood back, a familiar face stared back at her with a frown of disapproval she could recognize even in the darkness. Icy blue eyes narrowed in disdain, tendrils of inky black hair spilling over bronze skin.

"Hazel?" Lark stared at her, dumbfounded. "What are you doing here?" She hadn't seen her since Connor and the assassins from the Guild caught up with Gavriel.

Hazel yanked herself free, and smoothed her cloak and tunic, leaves clinging to her clothes. "I could ask you the same thing." She crossed her arms, disapproval written on every hard edge of her body. "I didn't think you traveled alone. Where's Gavriel?"

The question speared through Lark's chest, reigniting the aching chasm. "He's gone."

"Gone?" Hazel's dark eyebrows furrowed. "Gone how?"

"He was there, and then he disappeared." Lark's cheeks burned with shame. The shame of knowing she failed to keep him safe. The shame of wondering if he even still wanted her. "He's missing."

Hazel exhaled a long breath through her teeth.

Lark still held Hugo's dagger out defensively. She felt silly doing so, but couldn't bring herself to put it away. She let her arm fall to her side. "There were… signs that he didn't leave of his own accord."

Hazel nodded. "Any blood?"

"None that I could find."

"Well, that's a relief. Had it been a member of the Guild, chances are you'd have found his corpse absent of his head. Tell me exactly what happened."

As Lark accounted the details of how she awoke in their tent alone, she left out the part about how they spent the night prior to falling asleep. Instead, she focused on the fact he took nothing with him, including one of his boots. When she finished, Hazel nodded and lowered her pack to the ground.

"The good news is, he's likely still alive," Hazel said.

Despair filled Lark's belly like a sinking ship taking on water. "All right, what's the bad news?"

"The bad news is it was probably bounty hunters who took him. And I'd bet every coin to my name they're bringing him back to the Guild." She shook her head. "How could you let this happen?"

"Me? How is this my fault?"

"You swore you wouldn't let anything happen to him. You said, should he fall, you're already lost to the void to stop it."

"Well, he's not dead yet, is he?" Lark's hands clenched into fists, blood roaring in her veins. If any harm came to him, she'd burn the Guild to the ground.

Hazel studied her intently. "I'll help you find him."

Lark couldn't trust her, even if she did aid her when Connor and the others caught them. "I never asked for your help."

Hazel called over her shoulder, already building a fire. "And yet, here I am."

Lark cataloged everything she knew of Hazel so far. She was an assassin from the Guild. She'd hired Alistair to kill Talbot. Lark suspected something had happened between her and Gavriel from an undercurrent of familiarity that set her teeth on edge when she witnessed them interact. Hazel didn't want Gavriel caught, or else she'd be forced back to the Guild alongside her brother Gregoir—

"Where's your brother?" Lark demanded, raising her dagger again. If this was all a trick. If they'd had a hand in Gavriel's disappearance… she turned her head to search the trees for the silent archer.

Hazel struck the flint to produce a spark of a flame. "He isn't here."

Lark eyed her, wishing she knew her well enough to determine if she was lying. "He goes everywhere with you."

A shadow passed over Hazel's face, eyes darkening. "Not this time."

Lark let that remark slide. Hazel leaned forward and blew on the embers, slowly breathing life into the fire.

Hazel settled into the sleeping roll she'd somehow produced from her pack without Lark's notice. She laced her fingers behind her head, closing her eyes. "You can take the first watch," she said lazily. "You already got some rest before I stumbled upon you."

Lark glared at the lounging assassin. "What's stopping me from leaving you the minute you're asleep?"

Hazel cracked an eye. "Because I'm your best chance at finding Gavriel. Alive."

Lark swallowed a curse. Should Hazel prove useless, she'd cut ties the first chance she got. But for the time being, she settled to sit beside the warm fire, bringing her hands to hover above the flames.

By the skies, please be all right, Gavriel.

CHAPTER FIFTEEN

LANGFORD

The last of daylight hovered on the horizon as the gloaming claimed the sky. Langford sat on his bed, elbows braced on his knees, mouth pressed against his laced fingers, and watched Alistair gently stir. He'd slept through the day, awakening once or twice to call out, "I need a bucket." Only to collapse against the coverlet—fast asleep—before Langford could get him anything to retch into.

Sleep eased Alistair's face of the insincere smiles he wore all too often. Langford had to halt himself from brushing his dark hair back. It seemed too intimate. What did he know, though? Every line between them had blurred beyond recognition.

Alistair's drink-fueled words echoed in Langford's thoughts. He couldn't possibly mean them, not in that way. They were close, sure, and likely Alistair felt a sense of responsibility for him. Memories of the Forbidden Shrine, of Alistair's nightmare, danced along the edges of Langford's mind. Of his greatest fear made flesh. Images of bloody knuckles and broken glass, of that hateful glint in Alistair's eyes—

Alistair couldn't bear the idea of anything happening to a member of his crew. He sent them out on missions, and the very thought of one of them falling as the result of his oversight led him to nearly kill Lark in a fit of rage and self-loathing. That's all it was. And that's all that bound them in this twisted dance. Alistair felt responsible for him, and the weight of that must have been such a burden.

Langford ran his hand over his mouth. They shouldn't have stayed an extra day. They should have left at first light as they planned.

Alistair groaned, rolling over. Sweat matted his black hair to his forehead. Langford stood and wet a cloth in the wash-basin. Gently, he placed it over Alistair's forehead, smoothing it to lie flat. He told himself it was his duty as a healer. But the warmth in his chest as he watched Alistair sleep echoed back, calling him a liar.

Yes, the lines between them were blurry indeed.

And yet Langford reveled in the quiet moments where he felt almost needed.

Almost.

Alistair groaned again, stretching his arms over his head, knocking the cool cloth from his forehead. He squinted blearily at Langford, confusion written on his face. "Where am I?" Alistair's words squeezed out through a yawn.

"We're still at the Dew Drop. You were in no condition to travel." Langford swallowed, pushing down his heart determined to climb up his throat.

"How late is the hour?" Alistair regarded him with bloodshot eyes, making the green of his irises burn brighter than Langford thought possible.

"Late. The day is at its end."

"Shit." Alistair tugged on the covers, and Langford leapt off, allowing Alistair to swing his legs over the side and rise to his feet with surprising agility, considering the hangover he'd just slept through. "Water," his voice rumbled as he brought a hand to his face, massaging his forehead.

Wordlessly Langford passed him the pitcher. He went to reach for a cup, only to find Alistair had already brought the lip to his mouth and was spilling water down the front of his tunic and jerkin as he guzzled. Tossing his head back, he gurgled the water in the back of his throat. With a sigh, Alistair lowered the pitcher heavily to land on the table, wiping his mouth with the back of his hand. "Now, rum."

Langford shook his head. "Absolutely not. We've tarried long enough as it is. We need to keep our heads on straight."

"I never think more clearly than with a belly full of rum." Alistair arched his back, hands on his hips as if limbering up. "Then we'll need to move along quickly."

Langford bit the inside of his cheek. Weighing his words carefully. "Are you nervous your bedfellow from last night will catch wind you're still here and demand another session?"

Alistair paused his stretching, glancing over with a dark brow raised in suspicion. "I'm fairly certain my only bedfellow, as you so aptly put it, was you." He grinned. "So unless you want to have another go…"

Heat crept up Langford's face. "Nothing happened," he said through gritted teeth, cursing himself for even bringing Alistair back up to their room to rest. He should have let him pass out on the bar.

"Aye, but there was some aggressive cuddling, wasn't there?"

Langford quietly fumed, ignoring the predatory grin aimed his way. The man was mocking him once again. Langford swept past, stuffing his books, pages, and quills into his bag with more force than necessary. Soon they'd be aboard Ingemar's ship and he could lock himself away to focus on what mattered. Though he prayed to the gods they stopped by a stream or a more reputable inn before then. There was only so much a washbasin could do in the name of cleanliness.

"There's the little bugger," Alistair called out triumphantly, as he held up a half-empty bottle Langford hadn't noticed him sneak in. He tipped it back, swallowing hard. Langford tried not to watch Alistair's throat, turning to glare out the window. They'd be traveling in complete darkness. On foot. It was a wonder Alistair was still alive. Sometimes the man was simply more trouble than he was worth.

"Ah, much better," Alistair said, replacing the cork and tucking the nearly empty bottle into his pack. "Are we ready, then?"

Langford didn't even offer a sideways glance as he pushed past him out into the hallway. Bounding over to the narrow rickety stairs, he barreled down, shoving his way to the bar and slamming the key down on the wet bar top. The grey-haired fellow paused his task of wiping down a glass to raise a bushy eyebrow.

"Did you enjoy your stay?"

Langford exhaled a heavy breath, trying to keep his focus. "No, as a matter of fact, I didn't."

"That's nice." The man returned to wiping down glasses and over-serving sloppy drunkards.

Langford huffed, spinning around to see Alistair—

The brunette woman from the night before was draped over him, arms wrapped around his neck as she pressed her sizable charms against him. She angled her head in a coy manner, dark ringlets hanging down her back.

It was too much. The throbbing headache returned as the old wound ripped open again in his chest, raw and tattered about the edges. Vision spotting, Langford stalked out of the tavern, not caring if Alistair realized he'd left. He thought he heard his name being called, but he didn't glance over his shoulder, instead forging a path through the crowd. The throng parted only when he shoved hard enough.

Finally reaching the door, Langford swung it open, to be met with a blast of warm air. It whipped through his hair, tugging gently at his scalp. He took a deep breath, inhaling the fresh scent of roses.

Soon they'd rejoin their friends. His heart ached at the thought of seeing Daciana and Lark again. Gods, he missed them. He missed every gentle touch and prod from Daciana, the fierce warrior who missed nothing and sensed everything. He missed the easy affection he always received from Lark. Her head would fall to his shoulder so naturally, a steadying and grounding touch that offered trust and security. He even missed the good-natured ribbing he received from Lark's favorite assassin. He missed Hugo's—

He swallowed a lump that formed in his throat.

How had everything gotten this mixed up?

Normally it wasn't this difficult with Alistair, but everything was so complicated now. Every touch, every word, every smile, every night he spent losing himself in someone else—landed heavier blows.

Langford just needed some distance. Once they regrouped, he

could demand Alistair assign him far, far away from him. He could even stay at the Walden Inn, taking up near-permanent residence while they traveled about, leaving him in solitude.

He'd finally have peace.

Langford shivered despite the warm breeze. The scent of rain carried on the wind as a few cool droplets fell, hinting at more to come. He wiped his cheek, cursing the fates that deemed him worthy of the pain of never ceasing longing.

The door to the tavern slammed against the side of the building. Alistair stormed out, a murderous expression on his face. "What in the fucking abyss is wrong with you?"

Langford screwed his face up in what he hoped appeared to be confusion. "What do you mean?"

"What do I mean?" Alistair mimicked as he stomped his way to stand dangerously close to Langford, his breath fanning his face and sending a shiver down his neck. "You've been acting erratic, much more than typical Langford neurosis, and I can't keep up," he growled. "Everything I say and do is wrong. I'm at my wit's end here."

Langford swallowed, his tongue thick. "I don't know what you're talking about."

"Stop lying." Alistair grabbed him by the shoulders, grip bruising. "You've barely looked me in the eye since the Forbidden Shrine." He let his hands fall away. "What did I do?"

Langford exhaled a shaky breath, heart pounding in his chest. "Nothing. You didn't do—"

"I said stop lying!" Alistair's voice echoed against the night sky, filling the space they shared. His handsome face contorted in rage and anguish. It was the look of a man in desperate need of willow bark or one of his poultices.

Langford pushed his hands into his pockets, desperate to hide the way they trembled. "Last night," he began, "you said, when you close your eyes… all you see is me."

Alistair's eyes widened. "I said that, did I?"

"Yes," Langford said hesitantly. "And I understand if it was just the drink talking, or if you thought I was someone else, or if you were saying something else but just—" He ripped his hands from his pockets and ran them through his hair impatiently. Alistair's eyes followed the motion. "You can't just say whatever pops into your head. We aren't children, and it's time you stop acting like one. If you want to plow all the willing partners you come across, be my guest, but you can't turn around and say shit like that to me. It's not fair Alistair. It's not bloody fair." Langford's chest heaved with each breath as the anger subsided.

A few more cold drops of rain splattered against his nose.

Alistair's face was frozen in an expression of shock.

Langford shook his head and rubbed at the spot in his chest aching from their conversation. "It's fine. I shouldn't have said anything. We have much ground to cover, and we've wasted enough time on things that don't matter."

That snapped Alistair out of it. He reached out and gripped him by the tunic, yanking him close. Their breath mingled, and the sweet scent of his mouth made Langford's head spin. "You remember what you saw in the Shrine, yes? When you and Lark brought me back?"

Langford nodded, not trusting his ability to speak.

"You realize that means my greatest fear is losing you." Alistair's impossibly green eyes shone with such intensity. With promises Langford didn't dare hope for.

"You fear causing my death. The guilt—"

"Hush," Alistair said, shaking him. His dark brows knitted together, worry lines creasing his forehead. "Listen carefully, my greatest fear is *losing you.*"

Langford swallowed, the action near impossible with how tight his throat was.

Alistair laughed, a pained sound. "I'm… not very good at this. I can't seem to say the right thing."

Langford placed his hands gently over Alistair's. He immediately stilled under his touch. "I'm not very good with actions." Langford exhaled as he softly pulled Alistair's hands away from his tunic. A brief flash of pain crossed his face, but he let his hands fall. "Words I can do." Langford bit his lip, ignoring the pounding of his heart. A few more drops of rain, more insistent this time, landed against his forehead. "I can't stop thinking about you. Not for one second. In the years since I've met you, I've known you as selfish, arrogant, conceited—"

"This is you being good with words?"

"I'm not finished. But you're brave, compassionate…" Langford met his stare, forcing himself to focus on those eyes he'd fantasized about for so long. Willing himself to lay it all bare. He could be courageous with his heart if he only dared. "You're loyal and strong. You pretend not to give a damn when, deep down, you and I both know how much you carry. You're bad with money, and have a weakness for strays, and… I would very much like to know, even just once, what it's like to kiss you."

Alistair froze in place, his expression utterly blank. "You know me, Langford… and still… you want me?"

Langford released a ragged laugh. "Yes, you bloody fool."

Alistair's face lit up in a dizzying smile of joy and wonder. He grabbed Langford's face with both hands and crushed his lips to his. Langford gasped, heat flaring from his mouth to his entire body. He fisted his hands in Alistair's jerkin, gripping and pulling and desperately trying to stay upright despite the loss of sensation in his legs. Alistair smiled against his mouth, demanding more with each pass of his lips, his teeth, his tongue. He didn't kiss; he conquered. Claiming Langford's mouth in bruising kiss after bruising kiss as he soothed his thumbs along his jaw. The taste of him was sweet, like vanilla, spices, and rum.

Raindrops pelted them, the sky opening up in earnest.

Langford couldn't feel the ground. He couldn't hear a thing beyond the roaring in his ears. Everything else melted away until all that remained was this man and every scrape of his unshaven jaw against his own. Tears filled his eyes and rolled down his cheeks.

Alistair pulled away to press his forehead against Langford's, breathing hard. "I've wanted to do that since the first moment I saw you." He kissed him again, softer this time. Gentle and sweet.

Langford huffed a tight laugh. Alistair's fingers ran along his jaw, and he could have sworn they trembled. He lifted his eyes to meet his, unable to form the words.

Somewhere behind him, a twig snapped. Probably a deer.

Alistair tasted better than Langford had ever dreamt, and now he was determined to have more. Have everything he offered and damn the consequences.

A sharp pain at the back of his head knocked the thought from his mind—and it all went dark.

CHAPTER SIXTEEN

DACIANA

"You're doing all the talking, right?"

Daciana slid her gaze to where Kenna waited expectantly for her reply. Her features tightened, betraying the casual way she kicked a few loose stones.

"Because you kind of sank the job. I was more than happy to kill the Beast. Just to be safe."

Daciana felt an unwilling smile tug at her mouth. "No you weren't. I daresay you even *bonded* with the creature." It was one of those things about Kenna she'd always marveled at. Her ability to see past what was right in front of her. As a hunter, trained in the art of slaying beasts—a practice steeped in tradition—Kenna was a breed of her own.

Kenna batted her dark fringe from her face. "It was still terribly awkward waiting for you and Amara to return. He didn't answer any of my questions."

"Such as?"

Kenna bit her lip, fighting a smile. "I may have asked him if he and Amara took part in any interspecies carnality…"

A sharp laugh burst from Daciana's chest before she could halt it. It didn't even surprise her. Kenna's favorite pastime used to be attempting to shock Daciana with deeply personal and inappropriate questions. She would probe and prod, uttering scandalous thoughts and questions, all punctuated by her laughter. The simple solution was to shove her down and silence that mouth with her own. Daciana quickly shoved that thought away, clearing her throat. "Why would you even wish to know?"

Kenna shrugged, her smile spreading across her lovely face. "I like to think the best questions have uncomfortable answers. Plus, I was bored."

Turning away from the amusement on Kenna's face, Daciana rapped on the door in three hard successions.

The door hinted open. Felix appeared, even worse for wear, eyes wild with anticipation.

Daciana heaved a deep breath, already regretting the conversation she was about to have. "Felix," she began, as gently as she could, "we need to talk."

KENNA GRIPPED HER STOMACH, shaking with laughter.

"It's not funny," Daciana growled.

"Do you jest?" Kenna wiped her eyes, where moisture from her mirth had gathered. "That was amazing."

Daciana gritted her teeth. Felix had lost it, unable to handle the reality that not only had his daughter willingly left, but refused to return until the curse was broken. A curse she had no proof of and no basis for apart from theory.

"Amazing," Daciana said, shaking her head. "That's not how I would describe it."

"He makes the strangest faces when he cries. I can't even handle it."

Daciana spun around to face her. "Are you so callous?" How could she find amusement in that? Pain was pain. And watching that man fall apart in despair, to lose himself to hopelessness? There was nothing amusing about that.

"His pain?" Kenna arched an eyebrow, laughing. "Remember when he told us his daughter was of her own mind? That he'd raised her as such? That he'd never presume to decide on her behalf? I guess that understanding only extends so far."

"That doesn't mean he can't mourn her choice. Nor fear for her safety." Daciana crossed her arms, desperately trying to slow the rapid beating of her heart. "It's unbearably difficult to watch someone you love trust the wrong person."

Kenna scowled. "He doesn't have to trust the Beast, he has to trust Amara."

"That's easily said, not so much done."

"Believe me, I know that."

Their conversation was edging dangerously close to a topic Daciana had no wish to broach. Images of blood and carnage swept through her mind. The reeking stench of burning flesh and hair. Of pain and betrayal, and how easily the skin split beneath her claws. She swallowed the bile that rose in her throat. She couldn't face those horrors.

Not willingly.

Her nightmares, though. That was another story. She hadn't had a decent night's sleep since that damned Forbidden Shrine. It had torn down the barricades she'd meticulously built in her mind. Memories better left consumed by the darkness.

She took a deep breath.

She was more than her pain.

Daciana thumbed the hilts of her daggers as she remembered what mattered. "I held up my end. Now you hold up yours."

Kenna kicked a rock with the toe of her boot, tugging her red cloak tighter. "Very well. My word is my bond."

Daciana offered a curt nod. Once Kenna sent her missives warning the other hunters, the balance of debt between them would be that much closer. They could part ways, and she'd never have to see her again.

The sooner she was rid of Kenna, the better.

"MY HAND IS CRAMPING," Kenna whined. "Can't you pen a few of these for me?"

Daciana glanced up from her array of blades she'd been tending to, whetstone still in hand. With nothing better to do than sit and wait for Kenna to write her letters, Daciana found she needed to keep busy lest she go mad. The poorly stitched patchwork of the homespun quilt on the bed glared up at her. Images of sunflowers, crooked hearts, and leaves that were meant to feel homey came across as stifling.

What was she even doing here? She should follow Lark's trail. Lark had promised to leave her messages at each place they stayed, but she needed to journey in the opposite direction to have any hope of retrieving them.

"Wouldn't a letter by a strange hand be suspicious?"

Kenna's freckled nose scrunched up as she groaned. "I suppose so, but I could always just sign my name down here." She pointed at the bottom of the page. An impish grin dimpled her pale cheek. "Or you could just massage my hand and wrist. And shoulders. And my neck has been aching something fierce—"

"Why am I even here?"

Kenna blinked at her, face uncharacteristically devoid of any emotion.

Daciana huffed in frustration before running the whetstone down her longsword with a satisfying resonance. "I've done as you asked. Why must I sit on my ass while you drag your feet to complete a task that should weigh of importance? That I needed to exchange a favor for you to do so leaves me worried for the safety of the people you claim to care about."

Kenna stared at her, dwindling candlelight dancing across her smooth skin. The warm scent of burning tallow hovered in the air between them.

"Where else would you sit, but on your ass?"

"Kenna—"

"I'm sorry I got distracted. But really, think about it. Can you even sit without your ass?" She shook her head. "One for the philosophers, I guess."

"I suppose taking things seriously fell out of fashion some time ago. Had I known this, I might have had the good sense to stay away."

Kenna's brow furrowed. Slowly, she set her quill atop the stack of letters. They gently crinkled as she stood. Kenna adopted slow, careful steps as she approached.

Daciana tracked every movement, her pulse quickening. Want and dread battled for dominance.

Kenna sat on the corner of the bed, the only spot that wasn't littered with the sharp edges of steel and silver.

"Dac," she whispered. A shadow passed over Kenna's face, before her mouth lifted in a smirk that failed to reach her eyes. "Is my company so terrible?"

It would be so easy to push her flat on the bed. To climb over her and tear away the layers of clothing hiding her smooth skin. Daciana would run her mouth over familiar curves, finding all her dips and valleys with a ravenous hunger. She'd finally taste her sweet mouth again and lose herself in Kenna's intoxicating scent.

But that was a dangerous road, especially with Kenna. Daciana couldn't afford to make the same mistake again.

Daciana released a sharp exhale as the spell broke. "No, your company is not terrible. But I have grave matters to attend to."

Kenna rolled her eyes, though the action seemed forced. "Yes, we know. You're very important." She canted her head to the side as if pondering something. Her next move, most likely. She slapped her hands against her thighs, the sharp crack of it cutting through the room. "All right, fine. Let me finish these and we'll be on our way."

Head spinning, Daciana watched her leap to her feet and dance back over to the desk. "I'm sorry. We?"

"You didn't think I'd let you have all the glory, did you?" She reclaimed her seat at the writing desk, snatching up the abandoned quill and began scribbling away. Blatantly ignoring the dumbfounded expression Daciana was sure she wore.

"Kenna, I don't understand."

Kenna glanced up, giving her a cheery smile. "I'm coming with you, of course."

CHAPTER SEVENTEEN

LARK

Lark was alone in the Twisted Woods. No sounds of life met her ears, not even a breeze ghosted against her skin. She stared up at that ancient yew, in all its unyielding glory. Gnarled roots, thick and wet, curved through the soil. Empty branches clawed at the grey sky as if hungry for sunlight. Something ached in her chest at the sight. At the notion that this once was a living forest, and this tree was the home of the bond she and Gavriel unknowingly forged lifetimes ago.

Had she not bound herself to him, tethering their love to the very roots of this ancient tree, what would have happened when Thanar dragged her across to the Otherworld? Would the damage to the veil have been a negligible thing? Or would it have made no difference, the destruction predestined in impact?

That scent... lupines and spring grass, of fresh earth in the sunshine, it wafted over her before dissipating. It was a fleeting sensation, the flash of a memory before it was once again forgotten. The light of the sun dipped behind the cloud, and in its sudden absence, Lark's senses heightened, searching.

A chill scuttled down her spine, a warning that someone was watching.

"Have your memories returned?" The familiar voice, the one that made her skin crawl, shattered the silence of the Twisted Woods.

Lark turned to find Thanar watching, his obsidian eyes unreadable. He looked different. Where his immaculate leathers and formal robes normally carved an edge of danger and authority to his presence, his simple black tunic, rumpled and worn, was a jarring sight. His hair lacked its sleek luster, now hanging limply over his shoulders.

Lark's muscles tensed at his intrusion. "What must I do to rid myself of you? You are a plague I want nothing more than to eradicate."

Pain flashed across his face before he smoothed his expression of any emotion. "You accuse me of haunting you, when it is you that's been the blight of my existence."

Lark clenched her teeth. "You chose your fate, as I did mine. I never asked for your help—"

"And you never needed to." He advanced swiftly, invading her space. "You've never acknowledged all I've done to keep you safe, to keep you from harm. You're nothing more than a howling echo of my failures."

Lark stepped back, carefully avoiding the giant roots. "You wished for my gratitude? All I knew was I awakened in a life I did not recognize, and I felt nothing. I remembered nothing."

Brows knitting together, his voice lowered to barely a whisper. "I was not aware of how your soul would respond to the connection to the Otherworld."

He might not have known, but he didn't make it any easier. "Thanar, you... punished me. For asking questions. For thinking and searching for my own way. You stifled me without mercy." Emotion she hadn't been prepared to explore thickened her throat. "And when I finally found something that called to me... you hurt me. You tortured me." That day in the throne room, he'd shattered her mind over and over, forcing his will through hers, weaving himself through her thoughts. It had been an agony she never could have fathomed. Reapers didn't feel—at least she didn't—and she felt every slice of his influence through her mind.

All for the want of a mortal.

His face crumpled, anguish stealing his features. "I didn't seek to hurt you. You must know, I've never wanted that. I acted in anger and meant to force your memories so you might understand what would happen if you betrayed fate, if your affection for a mortal were to govern your actions and disrupt the balance. I searched and searched, but I couldn't find the tether to your humanity, and I couldn't bring your memories back." He swallowed, his gaze searing. "I only wanted to show you my mistake, and how much the world has suffered from it."

"You tried to make me into someone else. You sought to control me."

He shook his head, lowering his gaze to the forest floor.

Thanar never lowered his stare. Not for anyone.

"I sought to replace that which I'd lost. That which I destroyed." His voice lowered, falling with the force of a whisper. "I only wished to find you once more, before my time came to an end. To ensure the balance would be restored before you took my place."

That... couldn't be. It couldn't. He hurt her; tormented her; punished her, and he showed no remorse. Lark recalled whispers of his plans to train her as his heir, but hearing him confirm them—

It was too much.

"You were a monster—the very heart of what I feared most. You threatened to take away my thoughts, my free will, all to command loyalty."

"I know what I said. I couldn't risk losing more support than I already had. Authority is a precarious thing. One thinks strength and power determine who rules, but it's the belief in those things that fuel loyalty. And you've seen how much I've lost in the absence of loyalty."

Ceto and Nyx. The Commander and Spymaster. His left and right hands. Both now pledged to Nereida. Was it Lark's doing that they were able to break their oaths to Thanar or had he assumed their loyalty and failed to see their growing discontent? Nereida had said Lark took a piece of Thanar, a piece of his power when he dragged her to the Otherworld. That piece she'd given to Nereida when she made her mortal. Had Ceto and Nyx been waiting for the opportunity to betray him or had Nereida poisoned their minds with Lark's help?

It mattered nothing. It was done, and Lark couldn't bring herself to regret escaping Thanar and his oaths. "And what of Ferryn? You banished him to Lacuna when he didn't even aid in my escape. What excuse have you to justify that?"

"It was the only way to punish him without breaking him. As I said, power is a precarious thing, and had I shown leniency, I would have lost the trust of those who follow me."

Laden silence filled the air, almost smothering in its blanket of quiet. None of this changed anything. He had more than enough time to spin his lies, to make himself seem the victim when he terrorized her for lifetimes. She could never forgive him for his crimes... but an edge of pity softened her anger, a flutter of guilt forming in her belly. It was far easier to hate him, and she couldn't readily give up that comfort, but if what he said was true, and now he was well and truly alone in his regrets...

"What would you have done? If I hadn't escaped, and I'd refused to kill Gavriel, would you have forced the oath?"

Thanar's eyes slipped closed, as if the question itself was a fatal blow. "I hoped it wouldn't come to that. I had already grown accustomed to your indifference, then your fear, and I was ready to face your hatred." His voice fell quiet once more, almost too soft to hear. "I am grateful you escaped."

He hoped her fear would have been enough to force her hand to do his bidding, which meant if it hadn't been...

Thanar's jaw clenched, and he stalked toward her. "Ask me if I would do it again. If I would prevent your death, halt the pain that was sure to echo for centuries. Ask me if I would rip open the veil, pull you through, and face the fall of my throne, as I have done. If I would weather your disgust and disdain, knowing countless lives would be lost all for the love of a mortal who despises me."

Lark shook her head, anger coursing through her like a living flame. She did not want to hear this; she did not—

"I would do it. I would relive the path to this fate until the end of

days to keep you from harm." He gripped her arms, pinning her in place. "Because you are right about one thing, Larkin. I am a monster. This is why Reapers do not love. This is why your mortal shall fall and the pain will consume you." His fingers dug into her skin, and she wrenched herself free from his grasp—

Lark lurched awake, fear and panic tightening her throat. Her erratic breath was harsh and labored, and tears pricked her eyes. It wasn't real. It was only a dream. But the feel of him clutching her arms, trying desperately to make her believe, clung to her skin.

What if it was real?

His words echoed in her mind, twisting and tangling everything she believed. He swore she would lose Gavriel. After everything he shared, everything he revealed, he still set out to influence her decisions. Whether it was real, Thanar's soul seeking her in the expanse of dreams, in the plane meant for humans, or the lingering ghost of her fears, it changed nothing.

She would find Gavriel.

The cold ground offered little in the way of comfort. She rolled over, groaning at the sensation, to find a small fire burning. Hazel sat beside it, watching her curiously with her pale blue eyes.

"You remind me of a dog when you sleep," Hazel said with a vicious smile. "Your arms and legs go all crazy like you're imagining you're running through a field."

Lark ignored her remark, sitting up and scooting closer to the flames, and holding her hands out to warm them. The last vestiges of her dream faded and burned away as the heat licked her palms.

"You said you were my best chance at finding Gavriel." Lark darted a glance at where Hazel absently picked her teeth. "Where do we start?"

Hazel sighed, dropping her hand to her lap. "Once the sun is high enough for me to track properly, we figure out which town they dragged him to. With any luck, they holed up for the night. I'd much prefer catching up to them on the road than setting foot anywhere near the Guild."

Lark stared into the flames, willing the gut-churning fear to abate. "And if they beat us to the Guild?"

Hazel's face darkened. "Then I'm sure you'll remember him fondly."

Panic speared through her blood, numbing her limbs and sinking into her stomach. "Don't say that."

"It's not something I take lightly," Hazel said, shaking her head. "It's in my best interest that he stays alive. They've only tolerated my absence this long because of the mark on his head. Once Gavriel is returned, I risk being labeled a renegade."

Lark bit the inside of her cheek, eternally grateful for Hazel's motivations of self-preservation. It seemed like the only driving force she could trust.

THE FAINT LIGHT of the autumn morning peeked through the trees, casting shards of pale sunlight across the forest floor. Dead leaves littered the ground and crackled under every step they took. Each sign they uncovered—marking the path they'd chosen—was a hollow victory. Proof they'd taken the right course, and confirmation of what had befallen him.

Gavriel would never leave these blatant signs behind. The eerie silence in his movements was a carefully adopted practice from years of remaining undetected. It transcended into his skill at leaving no evidence behind.

Either the ones who took him were very foolish, or he was leaving her a trail of breadcrumbs to follow. The thought swelled her heart in her chest though she squashed it quickly. It was his self-preservation, nothing else, that fueled him to seek her aid. That he hadn't escaped on his own, was troubling. Who were these men? And how had they gotten the jump on him so easily?

"We're getting closer to Bridgebarrow. To The Little Philosopher pleasure house."

Did Alistair know of this place? He must have, even if he'd never mentioned it by name. Perhaps he'd already been blacklisted. The thought almost brought a smile to Lark's face. It reminded her of the night Alistair, Langford, and Hugo were thrown out of the Horse and Feathers Tavern. The way the three of them sprinted from the tavern, followed by the sounds of angry shouts and accusations of cheating—

Lark's throat tightened. Grief was a funny thing, with the ability to cast a pall on unrelated memories. It wasn't a particularly good night, especially with Gavriel still bent on killing her, but it was a time when Hugo was still alive and they were all together.

"I'm guessing they rested there for the night. That's where I'd go," Hazel continued with a sideways grin.

"So we'll go in, ask a few professionals if they've seen anything suspicious, and then what?" Lark spun to face her. "Isn't stopping there a waste of time? We should proceed to the Guild."

Hazel shook her head. "You poor, simple creature. Do you truly know nothing of the hearts of men?"

The hearts of men? As a Reaper, the motivations of mortals were strange. She would inherit the mark, learn their death, and wait. What they revealed on their final walk to the crossroads, and the manner of their death were the only insights she was truly offered. Death had a way of unearthing truth that life could never afford. But that was another time, another life. And she had learned the capricious nature of humanity. One never knew the deepest motivations until the very end.

"Coin speaks, dearest Lark, and bounty hunters answer to one thing." Hazel hitched her bag higher on her shoulder. "The heaviest purse. So if there's a chance they stopped in there, we need to know who they spoke to, what they did, how much of their own coin they spent. Because believe me, if they can cut a deal that lines their pockets and keeps them clear from the Guild, they will."

"Why?" Lark didn't understand. If the Guild placed the bounty they sought, why in the world would they seek a different benefactor?

Hazel raised a dark brow in question. "Do you really think anyone wants to be noticed by the Guild? The task is meant to be completed by a Guild member. They'd be setting themselves up as competition." A bitter laugh broke free. "No one wants to challenge the Guild of Crows. We don't suffer unworthy rivals."

She seemed angry about that fact. Gavriel's mother had sold him when he was only a child. It seemed most of the Guild's members were either forced to join or without any other options. So how did Hazel come to be a Crow?

"Would the Guild kill them?"

Hazel shrugged. "Most likely, if not under orders, then by whatever member let it slip there was a call for Gavriel's blood."

Dread gnawed at Lark's gut, and a deep unease crept along her bones. "One of your members specifically hired them to find Gavriel?" But why? Why not do it themselves?

"All I'm doing is taking shots in the dark. I'm privy to nothing more than my suspicions."

"Fine, I'm opting to trust you." Lark ignored the stone in her stomach at the prospect of trusting the assassin. It was a funny thing, human emotions. How a feeling in her gut could war with the logic of her mind. How it could sow seeds of doubt. It was a dangerous thing, to put so much in another's hands, and hope not to be rewarded with a knife in the back. "What do we do?"

Hazel's mouth curved, pale blue eyes lighting up against her bronze skin. A promise of mischief. "First I'm going to need you to trust me even further."

"Is this really necessary?" Lark asked breathlessly. The air was thick with warring perfumes, the conflicting scents burning her nose and watering her eyes. The back room of the brothel, off limits to patrons, was a bustle of activity. Women laughed and dressed in finer clothes and in cuts of fabric more revealing than Lark had seen. Nudity didn't make her uncomfortable. But the lack of light in the eyes of some women as they rouged their cheeks and painted their noses left her feeling a rush of cold through her veins.

Hazel tugged the laces of her dress tighter, ignoring Lark's sharp inhale. "Yes, well, if someone hadn't failed spectacularly at remaining discreet when Talbot was handled," she hissed in her ear, "we wouldn't have to be this cautious."

Security had indeed been tighter than Lark expected. They'd planned to waltz right in, ask a few questions, then leave, but they hadn't even made it through the front door.

Damn Gavriel for crashing her last assassination plan. She would have had Talbot handled easily and quietly were it not for his barging in. Probably.

"Couldn't we disguise ourselves as patrons seeking companionship?" It would have been far easier and far more comfortable.

"You know we're nothing more than tits and ass to these fellows. Best to keep it that way."

Lark supposed she was right. This way, they could meander about the establishment and strike up a conversation with anyone.

It was safer this way.

"Turn around," Hazel said impatiently.

Lark turned to find Hazel's face twisted in concentration. She'd painted her bronze skin with a dark rouge, giving her a fresh sun-kissed glow. Her pale blue eyes were a stark contrast to the red pigment on her eyelids, and the black kohl rimming her lashes. She looked the part of a high-end companion. Hazel eyed her with a speculative gaze, a slight frown forming on her lips.

"How do I look?"

Hazel made a noncommittal noise. "A bit frantic." She crossed the room, snatching a bottle of wine that had been left out for the girls getting ready. "Drink this. You'll need that glassy look to keep your eyes from giving us away."

"Drinking on a job hardly seems professional," Lark muttered as she took a swig, grateful for the soft burn that deadened some of her fears to a gentle buzz. When she realized what she'd said, she froze.

Hazel gently took the wine from her. "That's it, Lark, it's just a job. There's nothing beyond that for the moment." She took a generous pull from the bottle, sighing in satisfaction. "There's no shame in playing one move at a time. Whatever it takes to keep paralysis from kicking in."

Lark nodded, stomach tying itself in knots. Damn her human reactions. If she let herself, she'd spiral out in terror of what might have befallen Gavriel. She swallowed, pushing it down where it might quietly fester.

Hazel pushed the bottle back into her hands, picking up yet another color palette. Lark narrowed her eyes, regarding it with suspicion.

"What's that for?"

"Hush, my little strumpet. We need to put your mask on."

FACE heavy with paints and pigments, Lark strode out from behind the gossamer curtain.

A steady drumming undercut each plucked string of a harp as the music created a rich atmosphere of warmth. Plush velvet-lined seats of crimson and deep lacquered cherry wood furnishings filled the establishment. Each post, each chair leg, every damn table had been carved by the finest craftworker. Detailed etchings of bears, wolves, and graphic depictions of the female form were whittled into the backs of the chairs. Heavy chandeliers sparkled without candles, adorned by deep rubies casting red light about the room.

Lark held her head high and allowed a sultry smile to curve against her mouth. She kept her eyes half-lidded, but ever watchful as she sauntered about the room, seeking lips loose enough to give her what she wanted.

She spied a raven-haired woman, undulating her hips by a nearby post, eyes closed as if she was lost to the music. The beat of the drum thrummed through Lark's blood as she approached. The woman must have sensed her arrival, for she opened her eyes and regarded her with a lazy smile. "You new?"

Lark let a smile, coy yet confident, spread across her face. "Is it that obvious?"

She shrugged a bare shoulder, the small bells on her blue skirt tinkling. "I don't pass judgment, but I'd remember you."

Lark peered up at her from beneath her lashes. Hoping it conveyed the right balance of shyness and daring. "You flatter me."

She tossed her head back, raven hair falling in dark waves down her back like a tumbling sky full of stars. "You forget where you are. Now move along before you scare off any potential customers."

"Wait." Lark edged closer, earning a raised brow. She saw Hazel from across the room, perched on the lap of a red-faced man, running her hands through his sparse hair. "Yes, I'm new and I don't want to step on any toes," she whispered. "Point me toward a regular I should approach. I'll leave the new customers to my more experienced colleagues."

The woman's green eyes flashed dangerously before they resumed their heavy-lidded stare of seduction. "Come, let's freshen up and I'll help you choose your client for the night." She gripped Lark tightly by the wrist, steering her toward the backroom.

She threw Lark behind the curtain, brandishing a small dagger from beneath her skirt. "Who are you, and why are you here?" She angled the small blade with a shaky hand, the steel trembling in the firelight.

Lark held up her hands in supplication. She could disarm her, but the last thing she needed was to alert the guards. Not before she discovered if Gavriel had been here. "It's not what you think. I'm looking for someone."

"Who?" Though her hand shook, her voice never wavered.

Lark bit her lip, debating telling her the truth. Trusting her was dangerous, especially if she had any ties to the men who took Gavriel. But the chance she might yield valuable insight was too tempting to ignore. That and Lark couldn't spin a convincing lie now that she'd already gained suspicion. Perhaps it was a mortal failing, but she would avoid bloodshed if possible, and she desperately needed to know where Gavriel was.

Lark held her stare. "Someone very dear to me was taken. I suspect they might have come through here, and I need to know if they did, who they are, if he's… still alive." The last words were the hardest to force out.

The woman furrowed her dark brows, staring at her with mistrust before she finally lowered her arm. "We don't want any trouble here. If someone came through with your man, it wasn't any of our regulars. They're good folk. Well, as good as can be these days." She slipped her dagger back beneath her skirts.

Lark ran a hand into her hair, gripping it at the roots. "I just need to know if there was a group of men here last night. They would be unfamiliar, possibly rowdy, and likely one of them stayed outside the entire time." To watch Gavriel and ensure he didn't escape from wherever they'd stashed him. Lark's belly churned at the thought.

She nodded. "Aye. There were men here last night. Strange and wild. A bit too manic to be sheer excitement. One of them took Layla to bed for the night. She came back on the morn covered in bites and bruises, but didn't tell us a thing. The odd love-bite is to be expected, but he left imprints of his teeth, even drew blood. Some men are like that, ya know? Mixing pain with their pleasure. The pain of others, that is."

Lark pushed down the revulsion at the thought. "Where is she?"

"She took the night off. The rest will do her good."

"Would anyone else know anything?"

The woman nodded, scanning her with a critical eye. "I know who to talk to." She grabbed Lark by the hand and tugged her to the slit in the curtain, gesturing to the bar. "See him?"

Lark followed her gaze to find a young man seated on a stool. His blond hair was swept back from his face in a way that made her heart clench for its passing resemblance to Langford's preferred style. He wore a simple tunic beneath a black jerkin, and no visible weapons. "Yes, I see the man."

"He was here last night, and even dined at their table for a spell. He hasn't taken with anyone since his arrival. Maybe he's picky or just waiting for someone." She turned the full force of her emerald eyes on her, and Lark could see how many would fall under her spell. "If you want my advice, don't come on too strongly. He seems easy enough to spook. Men like him are much more at ease when they feel they have the upper hand."

"I know what to do," Lark said with a nod.

"Now go, shoo. I can't keep the masses waiting all night," the woman said with a wink, before slipping out and swaying her generous hips as she took up her post and resumed dancing. As if she cared little if she were approached or not.

Lark eyed the man at the bar. He lifted his tankard and brought it to his lips, casting a bored expression around the room. Lark adjusted her hair to make sure everything was in place.

With a deep breath, she strode out into the fray. The warmth of a room full of opulence, lust, and desperation enveloped her.

CHAPTER EIGHTEEN

LANGFORD

Langford awoke with the coppery taste of blood and dirt between his teeth. Skull pounding, he lifted his head with a groan. Black spots danced along his hazy vision, dim lighting making it difficult for his eyes to adjust. His muscles ached as if he'd slept in an awkward position all night. He twisted to stretch—

Only to find his arms wouldn't budge. They were tightly bound behind his back, trapping him in a hard wooden seat. He wrestled against his bindings, panic mounting in his chest.

"Are you all right?"

The single most beautiful voice Langford had ever heard in his life called out from the darkness.

"Alistair? Where are we?"

"Well, there are two possibilities. One is we're in some sort of hideout, likely awaiting hours of torture before we succumb to a most gruesome death."

Langford held his breath. "And what's the second option?"

"Someone has some very ambitious ideas about what qualifies as role-play seduction."

His heart sank. The last time he was captured, he'd found himself in Adler's dungeon the night of his masquerade. Adler might have been an abhorrent person, but he followed his own twisted code, which ruled out ritualistic dismemberment and torture. The gods had a stroke for irony for making him long for that bastard's nefarious schemes.

Langford took a steadying breath. "What's the plan?"

Alistair sighed, and shifted against his bindings. The soft *creak* of rope tightening whispered through the darkness. "Well, they took all my weapons."

"Naturally."

"But lucky for us, my sharpest weapon is my cutting wit."

Langford blinked into the darkness, trying and failing to come up with a proper response to that. He didn't have his pack either. Even if they escaped, he couldn't venture far without that tome.

He wriggled his hands, shoulders aching, and tried to stretch his ropes enough to yank himself loose. They held firm. Not even the sweat on his palms could help him slip free.

How had they gotten here? They had committed no crime he was aware of.

"Langford," Alistair called out, "you didn't answer me. Are you all right? Did they hurt you?"

Langford's heart clenched in his chest. "I'm fine." He had a nasty headache, but that was nothing new. "Did you see who attacked us?"

Alistair's voice hardened. "As a matter of fact, I did."

Gods above. He didn't like the sound of that.

The door slammed open. Three figures strolled in. The first was a large man with dark curls and a big bushy beard. His face was illuminated by the lantern he carried, revealing the dozens of small gold hoops along the shells of his ears.

The second man had white hair and a leaner build. An angry scar cut down one side of his face, right through his eye. His long fingers were wrapped around a torch. He cut across the room, heading directly for the tables along the back wall.

The third had dark skin and black hair cropped short. His wiry frame swept across the room until he came to a shadowed wall at the far end. He leaned against it to fiddle with one of his knives.

The scarred man began lighting each candle waiting in the dark.

The tables gleamed, rows of glittering metal caught the light. Langford's stomach turned at the thought of what those must be.

"Alistair," a thick voice drawled, the one belonging to the bearded man with gold in his ears, "you are one tough son of a bitch to track down."

"Apologies," Alistair said, cheek creasing against his usual smirk. The candlelight lit up the side of his face, granting Langford the sight of his bloodied eyebrow, dried and matted from an hours old injury, and a faint bruising along his eye. "Had I known how warm a welcome awaited me, I'd have sought you out myself."

Langford shot him a look of terror, hoping he'd curb his words before he landed them into even more trouble.

The man chuckled, a deep scrape from the chest that sounded more like a growl. "Ah, I've missed your quick tongue, Alistair." He leaned over and grabbed a knife from the table. The blade flashed beneath candlelight. "Mind if I keep it?"

"Martell, after everything we've been through, you'd deny me my right to a farewell monologue? It's the least you can offer me after the Rosemoor haul."

"What about Rosemoor?" the scarred man asked. "What do you suppose you've earned after you double crossed us, betrayed Zephyr, and stabbed us in the back?"

"Shut up, Quintan," Alistair snarled. "You weren't even on that job."

"Nay, but Zephyr was, and he said you left him for dead. You even sought refuge at his family home. Dined at their table and broke bread with them, knowing what you'd done." Quintan spat at him.

"Zephyr is a liar. I left him in a safe place." Alistair nodded his head to regard Zephyr, the thin man leaning against the wall. "And I patched your leg, I might add. Getting cut off from the rendezvous point was merely rotten luck. *You* were the one who suggested we hide out for a night or two with your contacts should things go badly."

Langford resisted the urge to roll his eyes. Of course Alistair's previous penchant for selfishness would come back to bite him. The key was to keep them talking long enough he could figure a way out of here. As long as Alistair said nothing stupid to set them off.

"I certainly didn't plan to bed your sister, if that's what you're implying." Alistair's voice cut through Langford's train of thought.

Bleeding nethers.

He barely had time to register the blow, but he heard Martell's fist collide with Alistair's face. The dull thud of thinly cushioned bone on bone—a sickening hollow sound that made Langford's insides twist. Alistair spat blood on the floor, a wry chuckle leaving his lips.

"You think you're invincible. Untouchable." Martell dragged a chair over, the legs scraping against the floor. "You've been flying too close to the sun for ages. You were always going to get burned."

Alistair canted his head to the side, his cheekbone already darkening. A thin layer of blood coated his lips, probably from biting down on his tongue. He raised a dark brow, a wicked glint in his eye. "I always liked you, though your threats are too rehearsed for my taste." He spat again, a splatter of blood landing on the wooden floor. "What story did you spin for Zephyr and Quintan after Rosemoor?"

A dangerous grin stretched across Martell's mouth. "You're slippery, Alistair, I'll give you that. But why don't we discuss the matter at hand?" He sat backwards on the chair, leaning over the backrest. He jerked his head in Langford's direction. "Who's this?"

The blood in Langford's veins froze to ice. He stilled, hands he was trying to wriggle free, suddenly gone numb. He darted his eyes to Alistair, silently begging for him to have a plan.

Alistair's expression froze, and for the first time, fear shone in his eyes before he let his face smooth into his carefree, amused expression. He ripped his gaze from Langford's. "He's nothing, someone I picked up on the road for a good time." Alistair shrugged dismissively, though the action was strained with his hands bound behind his back. "Nothing special, but he got the job done."

Langford bit the inside of his cheek. His heart thudded painfully in his chest, hard enough he was sure they could all hear it. Alistair still refused to meet his eyes.

"Hmm…" Martel rubbed his jaw. "That's not what it seemed like to us."

Quintan and Zephyr laughed, dark chuckles that sounded less like humor and more like threats.

Langford's face heated in shame of their private, intimate moment being so intrusively observed.

"In fact," Martell continued, "I'd wager this little wisp matters a great deal to you."

Langford held his breath.

Alistair scoffed. "You always made the worst bets, Martell." Finally, his eyes met Langford's, desperate and pleading.

"We'll see about that." Martell waved his hand, and Quintan stepped forward, grabbing Langford roughly by the hair and yanking his head back. Pain rippled along his scalp, and he cried out. Langford darted a glance to where Alistair sat dangerously still.

Quintan loosened his grip and slid his hand down the base of Langford's throat. Langford trembled, muscles quaking against tight bindings. Images of that night—the night he waited for Alistair to make the trade and save his life—flashed through his mind. The terror of facing the fact that he might not come. The burning pain of humiliation at each hour that passed. It felt the same as Quintan continued his exploration, trailing a hand down his arm.

"You can stop this at any point. Just say the word." Martell's voice was a distant thing.

"I told you, he's nothing. Cut him loose and let's get on with it." Alistair adjusted in his seat. "I grow bored of this."

"Well, if he's nothing but someone to warm a bed, perhaps we can each take a turn with the lad before we cut him loose."

Tears pricked Langford's eyes. A sob threatening to form. *Not like this. Gods, if anyone up there is listening, please not in front of him.*

Stunned silence followed the remark before a low growl rumbled from Alistair's chest. "If you harm a fucking hair on his head—"

"Why, Alistair, that almost sounded like a threat. Did you hear him, boys?" Martell angled his head over his shoulder, grinning.

Quintan sneered down at Langford.

"Alistair McCall, have you gone and found yourself a weakness?" Zephyr grinned from where he leaned against the wall, turning his knife in both hands. "Awfully foolish of you."

"Indeed." Martell eyed Langford with a speculative expression. "Quintan, take a small piece. Something he won't miss."

"With pleasure."

Langford didn't have time to catch up with the words. To grasp their meaning. To turn them over in his mind and ponder them. All he felt was the immediate flash of pain. Searing pain and cutting through skin, nerves, and bone. He cried out—the agony too large to keep contained to his chest. It was like fire in his hand; the nerves ignited against the scrape of Quintan's blade. His fingers were now slick with blood, each pulse sent more streaming from the angry wound made raw by the air around it. Tears rolled down his cheeks as he lifted his head to meet Alistair's unwavering stare.

Alistair fought against his bindings, brows furrowed in concentration as his eyes bore into him.

Quintan tossed something to Martell.

Dizzy and disoriented, Langford squinted through the haze of tears to see what he now held.

Martell held it up to the light, the ghastly sight of it violently punching Langford in the gut and dragging a deep heave from his belly.

Martell held Langford's finger—cut from his hand—up to Alistair.

It was fortunate they hadn't eaten yet. Langford was sure he'd have deposited his stomach's contents onto the floor.

Alistair went still, jaw clenched and eyes alight with such fury, a chilling calm spread over him.

Langford blinked, his vision going dimmer. He was losing too much blood—it was getting harder to focus. He needed some sort of tourniquet, something to staunch the bleeding before he passed out.

"He'll survive without this," Martell said, holding the finger close to Alistair's face. "I can't promise that for the next cut."

Alistair said nothing, remaining perfectly frozen like time had halted to a standstill.

"Are you ready to confess your sins against us, brother?" Martell's voice had gone soft. Like he was beseeching a child to tell the truth about swiping sweets before dinner. "Are you ready to own what you've done? Or is the boy to pay the price?"

Langford's stump, where the middle finger of his right hand had been, was pulsing its reminder slower now. It was getting increasingly difficult to keep his eyes open. Langford recognized his symptoms—he was going into shock.

Another tear tracked down his cheek.

"My sins?" The rich timbre of Alistair's voice, now dangerously low, swept a shiver through Langford as he fought to remain awake. "I took my share and left the rest at the spot you designated should the city guard get the drop on us. You swindled the others and blamed me because you're a gutless coward. So my greatest sin was trusting you." He glared at him. "My next sin, I don't feel too shite about."

Alistair leapt from his seat, hands unbound, and drove his fist into Martell's nose with a sickening crack. Spinning on his heel, he grabbed two knives from the table, turning to face his three opponents.

"Slit the boy's throat and then end this." Martell coughed as blood streamed over his mouth and chin, slowly rising to his feet.

Quintan glanced down at Langford, uncertainty on his scarred face.

Whether he was going to follow the order, Langford would never know. A faint *squish* filled his ears, and, protruding from Quintan's belly, was one of Alistair's knives. Quintan's face twisted, before he lumbered back to the wall, slowly sliding to the floor.

Langford slipped his blood-soaked hand free of the bindings, his gaze following Alistair's every move.

Zephyr darted toward him, dagger glinting in the candlelight. He feinted and slashed, quick and lethal in every movement. But Alistair was both precision and rage—a deadly combination. He caught the edge of Zephyr's knife against his forearm, bellowing in anger or pain.

A spike of fear shot down Langford's spine as he watched, cradling his injured hand and kicking Quintan's weapon away from his unconscious body.

Alistair advanced, pushing Zephyr closer and closer to the opposite wall, meeting him strike for strike, blocking and slashing any blows that would be fatal. He absorbed and caught every other swing of his blade, showering them both in blood. Finally, Zephyr's back hit the wall—

And Alistair's knife met him there, his blade jutting out from Zephyr's throat.

Zephyr opened his mouth as if to say something, only for blood to come burbling out and dripping down his chin.

Langford closed his good hand around Quintan's knife, standing on shaky feet. The fog of having his own finger crudely sliced from his hand was slowly lifting as his body's response to danger took over.

Martell was the shadow they'd nearly forgotten. He leapt from the dark, plunging his knife into Alistair's side.

Alistair tossed his head back, a cry of rage leaping from his lips.

Langford staggered without thought. He drove his dagger home into Martell's back before yanking it free. Hot droplets of blood hit his cheek.

Martell spun around—shock written on his face.

Langford didn't wait. He couldn't wait. Alistair was hurt, and he'd lost too much blood. His strength was waning.

Langford dropped to the ground and plunged his blade into the front of Martell's thigh.

He'd never been more grateful for his healer's training. For knowing the places on the human body that bleed the fastest.

Langford fell back, landing on the filthy floor. If Martell was strong enough, he could kill him before he bled out. So many things he hadn't done. So many words he still hadn't said. He would never taste Alistair's kiss again. Never see Lark or Daciana. He'd never get that tome to Ardenas. Never halt the fall of the veil. So many things he hadn't learned.

At least he'd die having known Alistair's kiss. He had said 'just once.' The gods weren't generous enough for more than that.

Martell raised his blade, face contorted in rage, when a bloody hand caught his arm.

Alistair shoved him to the floor, carefully climbing over him. "I'm not letting you fade into the void without a clear sense of justice." He bared his teeth, and the sight was enough to make Langford's stomach flip.

"I'm a dead man anyway," Martel said, laughing. "There's nothing you can do to me now."

"Care to test that theory?" Alistair grabbed Martell's hand that had already slackened, and dug his blade into the knuckles, hacking and sawing until he broke through bone. Martell screamed, the sound of true human anguish, as his fingers dropped to the floor.

"Quintan's the one who hurt your man there," he panted as Alistair raised his other hand. "Why do you torture a man bound for the Netherworld, anyway?"

"Weak men follow bad orders all the time. Quintan will get his, but now it's your turn," Alistair growled, "and the Netherworld isn't punishment enough for you." He grinned, bloodied teeth clenched and eyes wild as he brought his blade down to hack away the other fingers before digging his knife into Martell's stomach.

Martell's cries diminished to inhuman sounds of pain.

Again and again, Alistair sank his knife into every spot of flesh until Martell's eyes faded, and he was stabbing into a bloody mess of a corpse.

Langford couldn't watch any longer. Tears blurring his vision, he sat up and looked around the room. Quintan lay bleeding out on the floor. It could be hours before he succumbed to his injury. There was no chance he'd survive it, not without the help of a healer.

Langford once swore an oath to render aid to any who should need it, regardless of who they were or what they'd done.

A squirming sensation twisted in his gut as he turned from the man.

Some oaths didn't account for such colorful circumstances.

Langford's wound throbbed. He yanked his own sleeve down, ripping it free and wrapping it around his hand. Using his teeth to pull it tight, he winced. Blood bloomed across the white fabric.

The sounds of Alistair's knife piercing flesh ceased, and the following silence was smothering.

Langford hesitantly turned to find Alistair watching, his eyes greedy in their survey.

"Langford," Alistair rasped, his voice thick.

"We need to find the tome."

Alistair wiped his knife on Martell's trousers. He tried to push his dark hair back from his face, but his hands were coated in blood. His blood. Theirs. He stood, faltering and wincing. His hand flew to his side, where Martell's blade drove home.

Langford leapt to his feet, black spots dancing across his vision. He staggered to Alistair, using his good hand to peel back the opening in his shirt from the knife wound.

"We need to disinfect this and suture it closed," Langford said, shaking his head. "I can't imagine their weapons were clean." He lifted his gaze to find Alistair staring intently at him. His intensity was enough to steal the breath from his lungs.

Alistair raised a shaky hand, gently cupping Langford's face and running his thumb along his jaw. "I'm so sorry."

Langford almost missed the words he whispered, too caught up in the heat of his touch. He didn't know what to say. Words came easily, but at this moment they abandoned him, leaving his filth and blood-crusted body to fend for itself.

He did the only thing he could think of.

Bending his head forward, he caught Alistair's mouth in a kiss, fisting his uninjured hand in his shirt. Alistair wrapped his arm around him, steadying, while the other hand held firm to his jaw. He tasted of Alistair, like vanilla spiced rum, but with the sharp tang of blood. Their kiss grew more frenzied, messy and violent as they searched within each other for comfort and forgiveness.

Langford broke away first, fighting for breath. They needed to get out of this room of corpses. They needed to find the tome and get somewhere he could tend to their wounds before any sort of infection set it.

The thought was enough to wipe any notions of romance from his mind.

Alistair grinned at him, eyes glassy. "I wasn't finished."

Langford laughed, the sound of it slightly hysterical. "Well, it's a relief to see they did not injure your libido in the scuffle."

Alistair shook his head, still grinning. "No, but I'll need my favorite healer to make sure everything's working right."

Covered in blood, lips still burning from Alistair's kiss, and missing a finger—Langford still felt the heat sweep up his face at his words. "How you're able to stand there flirting whilst probably bleeding out is beyond me."

"It's just a scratch. I've had worse."

Langford rolled his eyes, regretting how dizzy it made him. "Come on then, off we go."

CHAPTER NINETEEN

DACIANA

The first time Daciana saw Kenna, she was sure she was under a spell—a trick of the senses crafted to ensnare. The sight of Kenna's flawless, pale skin, black hair as dark as a night under a new moon, and deep brown eyes that crinkled when she smiled, held Daciana captive.

Coming together was as natural as breathing. The world shaped around Kenna, like she was the center of everything, and Daciana was merely pulled into her reality. Nothing about them made sense, and yet it was as if everything fell into place when she found her. Her entire life had been comprised of jagged edges that didn't fit anywhere, until Kenna filled all the cracks and sharpened points, smoothing out the parts that threatened to cut.

It was a free fall of her need for this girl. As if she was always meant to be in her arms, pressed heart-to-heart, as the rest of the world fell away. In those moments, there was no duty. No pack she was sworn to. No heavy looming mantle destined to be her burden.

Kenna was fire—a wild force that burned and smoldered and destroyed. The only light in this gods-forsaken world. And Daciana would burn for her.

But some things were never meant to be.

Daciana would endure. As she had each day before the last.

WHEN THEY ARRIVED at the town of Stormfair, Daciana hurried to the Crooked Bottle Inn, just in case Lark had left her a message.

But there had been nothing.

Lark should have already spoken with Inerys and been on her way by now. She must have bypassed Stormfair in favor of Oakbury, a town Alistair regarded as home. They all considered it a place of refuge with Mrs. O'Connell's warm hearth and welcoming smiles at the Walden Inn and Tavern.

Alistair and Langford would be back from Koval in a matter of weeks. Docking at the same port they'd all traveled to not so long ago.

"No word from our favorite Reaper?" Kenna offered a silly grin that dimpled her impossibly smooth cheek. A girl that ran headlong into danger as often as her should have worn the evidence in scars. Though she couldn't speak for the skin beneath Kenna's clothes. Daciana frowned, and Kenna's expression flickered. "Should we go see Inerys?"

"I'm not sure yet," Daciana said, finally glancing around the town of Stormfair. In the center square, a silent fountain stood unfilled. Stone steps led to the central feature—a bear's head, but no water spurted from its mouth. Everyone that passed kept their heads down. Villagers mulled about at a cautious pace, as if afraid of catching one another's eye. The scent of fear and hopelessness permeated the air.

Kenna's dark brows furrowed, and she canted her head to the side. "Awfully slow-moving village."

"Do you notice anything in particular?" Daciana rolled the town name, *Stormfair,* around in her head, over and over. Realization struck her hard and hot as it slipped between her ribs. "Where are all the children?"

Kenna's eyes widened. "I didn't even realize I haven't seen a single little shitter this whole time."

Daciana bit down on her tongue. *Stormfair.* The center of trade, owned by Adler Bennett. Lark had found evidence of nefarious activity involving the children of this town. Something was systematically hunting them. The mayor begged Adler to do something before people fled to live somewhere they wouldn't have to worry about their children coming to harm. Adler offered his former business partner's son up as a lamb to slaughter.

Lark had searched Adler's estate for blackmail material while Hugo and Gavriel had broken him free from prison. The last real job Hugo went on.

Daciana worried her thumb over the stone in her pocket, pushing the thought of him away. Instead, she searched for that anger, the injustice at letting the actual monster go free to keep Adler's pockets lined.

Exhaling through her nose, Daciana reached for the calm she'd need to handle this efficiently. "That's because the children here are in danger."

Kenna eyed her, calculating. "What sort of danger?"

"The kind that requires our aid," Daciana said. She had not forgotten those crimes. The ones Lark whispered to her when they were alone. The ones they mourned never having rectified. This seemed a good day for justice.

Whatever held Lark up from contacting her, she could hold her own. And knowing Gavriel guarded her back, Daciana could stand to delay a day or so until this matter was sorted. If they were to hunt a beast, they'd follow it to the ends of the earth and then some.

"What do you say we go have a chat with the mayor?"

BRONN, the mayor of Stormfair, wasn't a charismatic fellow. His face was weathered and creased with permanent frown lines. He wore his long, greying hair tied at the nape of his neck. His frown only deepened when Daciana and Kenna sat across from him, his large oak desk the only barrier between them in a mostly empty lodge. Letters and parchments spilled across the surface of his desk. A narrow mattress and simple end table sat tucked into the corner. An odd home to be owned by the mayor of a wealthy town.

"Apologies," he scraped out. "We don't take too kindly to strangers these days."

"Isn't this a major trade center?" Kenna scoffed. "That's not a viable marketing ploy."

"I don't give two shits about the trade in this town. We're far beyond that," he growled.

Daciana studied him carefully, searching his face for signs of duplicity. "Tell me what's happening here." This wasn't a time to mince words. There was no room for concealing agendas. If there was a monster to be hunted, they needed to lay their cards on the table.

Before they lost another child.

Bronn sighed, the heavy gust of a weighted conscience. He tapped a gloved hand on the massive stack of correspondence atop his desk. The papers crinkled with every dull thud. "What have you heard?"

Lark had told Daciana everything. The slayings. The poorly patched blame they placed on Davin's son—the boy Hugo and Gavriel had freed.

"I know someone is killing your children," she said evenly, "and I know you went through a great deal to hide it. When that didn't work, you assigned blame without cause."

"And you know the little shit escaped?" Bronn said, ignoring the accusations leveled against him. He brought his elbows to rest on his desk, caging himself as he hunched over the stack of missives laid out before him.

Daciana cast a sideways glance at Kenna, who restlessly shifted in her seat as she stared back at her. Her dark eyes were wide and bright with excitement. The promise of a hunt. Daciana turned her attention back to the mayor. "Who do you think helped him escape?"

Bronn's face paled. "You had a hand in that? How could you release him?"

"How could you condemn an innocent to death? Out of fear of losing a few coins?"

"You keep calling him innocent. Do you know what he did to those children?" Bronn shuddered, yanking open the bottom drawer of his desk, and pulling out a bottle. The gentle sloshing of liquid against sides of the bottle murmured between them as he tipped his head back, taking a deep pull. "Egregious, really."

Daciana reached out, beckoning for him to pass it to her. "Tell me what happened, Bronn." She brought the lip to her mouth, hand clenched around the slender neck. She reveled in the pleasant burn that passed between her teeth, rolling over her tongue and sending vapors down her throat. The easiest way to reach a place of trust and under-standing was to share a drink with the man. That, and Daciana could identify a decent whiskey when she saw one.

Crestfallen, he lowered his chin to stare down at his hands. A few wisps of grey hair hung in his eyes. "First the Delmarro boy went miss-ing. He was prone to runnin' off, so we weren't too worried when a day or so went by." He clenched his weathered hands into fists. "Another day passed, no sign of him. By the fourth day, we started to worry and sent out a search party." Bronn reached a shaky hand to Daciana. She passed him the bottle wordlessly, waiting for him to gather his strength. "When we found his remains, I couldn't comprehend what happened to him. He was…" He trailed off, eyes finding the ceiling.

Daciana took pity on him. If the words weren't ready for release, she wouldn't push, not yet anyway. "What was your initial suspicion?"

"Everyone wanted to believe it was an animal."

"But you didn't." Daciana took note of every action, down to the way he rapped his knuckles against the flat surface of his desk, in three hard successions as he steeled his nerve.

"No," he said finally. "No animal could have made those cuts on his body. They were careful. Precise." He shook his head, as if trying to clear away the memory. "Everyone was much more cautious after that, keeping a close eye on their young ones. It made no difference. Somehow that slimy bastard lured them out one-by-one."

"And you never thought to hire a hunter?" Kenna crossed her arms over her chest and tossed an annoyed expression Daciana's way. "This is what happens when townsfolk try to do my job."

"Perhaps we should have hired a professional. But we thought we could handle it. We thought if everyone locked their doors, and we instated a strict curfew, nothing would get by." He ran a shaking hand over his mouth. "The next child to go missing was a month later—Torrin's daughter. Skies, I've never seen anguish like the day he found her. Then there was the Fillon boy, found buried alive. When we examined the body, his mouth and lungs were full of soil. What kind of monster subjects a child to that torture?"

Daciana ran a hand over the hilt of her dagger, exhaling hard. "How does Declan fit into all of this?"

Bronn's neck bloomed bright red, the blood traveling to tinge his cheeks. "I sent a letter to Adler, telling him of what this village was facing. He came swiftly, along with some of his best guards, to hunt the bastard down." He took another swill of his whiskey, groaning at the taste. "His partner, Davin, was already here. He oversaw the guard and collected taxes to be delivered to Adler quarterly. We never had an issue with payment, *I* always did my job, but Adler wanted one of his own close by. Davin had been stationed in Stormfair for the past year, along with his son, Declan. Strange that these attacks never occurred *before* they moved to our town."

Bronn poured himself another, sloshing dark amber liquid over the side and onto his paperwork. His hand trembled, drink shaking as he raised it to his lips.

Daciana allowed the stilted silence, giving Bronn a chance to collect himself.

Finally, he cleared his throat to continue. "Another child went missing the day before Adler arrived. We mounted a full scale search of the woods and nearby river, searching for the Rainier boy."

"Did you find him?" Kenna leaned forward in her seat.

"We found him alright; it was too late, but we found him." His lip curled back in disgust. "Declan stood over the boy's mangled body, obviously trying to hide his crime when we intercepted them. We knew we'd found our monster." A humorless laugh escaped his lips. "Not that Davin would see reason, but we knew."

"Was he arrested immediately?" There'd been enough time for Davin to contact Alistair, for Hugo and Gavriel to free Declan, and for

Lark and Langford to attend Adler's masquerade. All the while, Daciana's task was to wait in the wings and watch for any urgent messages, tipping Adler off.

"We held him for a month, that was the pattern. If another child went missing, it would confirm his innocence. If not, then we knew we had our killer." Bronn leaned back in his seat, the chair groaning beneath him. "A month came and went. And no child went missing. We had him. He was locked up and due to hang. It would have given those poor families some closure." He glared at Daciana, eyes bloodshot. "And you're here telling me you fucked it all up?"

Daciana's jaw clenched. Pushing down the anger that swelled in her chest. "We were hired to save a man's innocent son from an execution he didn't deserve." At least, that was their understanding. She was starting to wonder.

"Yes, well," he said, tone dismissive, "tell that to the families who buried their children."

"We were only trying to stop another parent from burying their child."

Bronn met her stare, expression softening. "Perhaps, but now we'll never know. I thank the skies for each day that passes without the loss of another child. But you've seen our town. We're broken. The wounds have festered, and the rot set in. Without closure, without a certainty that the beast responsible has paid for his crimes, Stormfair will become a thing of the past."

"People endure," Kenna said, "even in the face of unimaginable grief. We'd all be wiped out were that not the case."

"Maybe you're right," he said, running a hand absently over the rim of his cup. "But I don't see how we can keep going like this. This town is an echo of what it once was."

Daciana didn't doubt it. She'd seen firsthand how pain can linger, crumbling walls and weakening strongholds. The citizens of Stormfair seemed like ghosts themselves.

Perhaps if she and Kenna could find the killer, some life would return to this village.

CHAPTER TWENTY

LARK

Lark's stare never wavered from the blond man studying his ale with a vague expression of distaste. As she strode across the room, she remembered what the dark-haired woman had suggested. She quickly let her step falter, swaying her hips in an exaggerated motion that was sure to look forced. As if he could sense her gaze, he lifted his head, locking his stare on her.

She stumbled, just to be safe.

He grinned, dimpling his cheeks. Amusement danced across his features as he ran a hand through his hair, tracking her every step.

She pushed her fears down. Fear of failing. Fear of whatever fate Gavriel might be facing. She forced them into the pit of her stomach, and plastered a smile on her face, audibly clearing her throat. "It's a pleasant night, isn't it?" The woman had instructed her to allow him to believe he had the upper hand.

It was good advice. The human failing of trusting that which seemed weaker was a lesson she'd learned long ago.

His smile only widened, crinkling the corners of his brown eyes. His bronze skin glimmered in the soft candlelight. A sharp dimple cut through his chin. He might have been handsome, but to Lark he was a means to an end. "It is now," he said.

Lark hid a demure laugh behind her hand, casting her eyes down as if embarrassed. If her performance was convincing, then he was a fool to think he could make a professional blush. She didn't care to know his name, but she knew she had to ask. "What's your name?"

"Maddox. But I'm more interested in your name."

"Oh, Lana," she said with a deprecating smile, as if she were ashamed she hadn't come up with something more exotic sounding to titillate him with.

"Sit, Lana," he said, kicking a stool out.

She lowered in the seat, pushing it closer to him. Even these stools were carved to perfection, the wood as smooth as silk. She quickly angled her body to face her new companion, schooling her face into animated interest. "Don't tell anyone, this is my first night."

Maddox leaned toward her. "Your secret is safe with me," he whispered conspiratorially. "But I confess, I gathered as much. I would have remembered you."

"You come here often, then?" she asked innocently.

He took a long sip of his ale, eyes narrowing. "Does that matter?"

"No, of course not!" Perhaps the dark-haired companion who aided her earlier led her astray on purpose. Everything about Lark's act seemed to put this guy on edge. If the woman thought her a threat, the easiest way to dispose of her would be to throw her to a dangerous client. There was a sharp glint in his eye, something she hadn't noticed from afar.

But she was dangerous, too.

Lark felt the unmistakable sensation of someone's gaze. Turning, she found Hazel watching from across the room. Her expression was one of alarm. But why should she worry? If she had to take a man to a private room, she would, but for answers and a quick incapacitation.

Maddox ran a warm hand over her knee. "Let's go somewhere more private?"

Lark's mouth went dry. "You haven't finished your drink yet," she said with a tight smile.

His smile came easier. As if it was always meant to grace his features in a wolfish way. "I'm in the mood for something else."

The dagger from Hugo pressed against her inner thigh, beckoning. Whatever it took, she'd get answers. But if Maddox thought it was going to be pleasant, he was sorely mistaken.

Lark glanced at Hazel again. Hazel's eyes flashed dangerously before she shoved the man away who'd been running his fingertips up and down her side, and strode over to them.

Lark's stomach dropped. This wasn't part of the plan. Did she unknowingly give Hazel a signal for help? Did Hazel really think her incapable of completing her task without help?

Hazel was the dark sky in a storm, a tempest of icy cool rage. "Lark, get away from him." Her words left her lips in a growl.

"I thought your name was Lana," Maddox said with a lazy smile. "You expended little effort coming up with that, didn't you?"

Lark's head spun. Stomach churning in tandem. Ignoring him, she addressed Hazel. "You know him?"

Hazel bared her teeth in a snarl. "No. I recognize his brand, though. The Lions are little better than cattle."

Peeking out from beneath the sleeve of Maddox's tunic was the sharp curl of a tail inked into his skin. *Shit.* If Hazel meant the rival guild, the Den of Lions—Lark had reaped enough souls that had fallen prey to their assassins to recognize danger. The Guild of Crows operated on discretion. Nameless and faceless in their pursuits. The Den of Lions was a different story. Known for taking political sides, openly and unabashedly. If the Lions were sniffing around Gavriel—

Lark would not give Maddox the satisfaction of seeing her fear. She used to make mortals like him cower in their own pungent terror.

Maddox frowned, pushing his sleeve up to reveal a lion coiling around his forearm. "What of you, little crow?" Maddox watched Hazel with the eyes of a predator. "At least they let me out of my cage once in a while. What will happen to you once we deliver the goods?"

Rage burned through Lark's veins. "Where have you taken him?"

They ignored her question, sizing each other up. Hazel spoke first. "What do you want? Coin? A favor? Name your price, you little shit."

Maddox chuckled, the sound slithering over Lark's skin. Her hands itched for steel.

"There is literally nothing you have that I want." He eyed Lark with distaste. "You either. I was told to stay put until someone came looking for the handsome beast." He rolled his eyes, crossing his arms. "You women are so predictable. So which of you is the lover?"

Hazel's murderous expression never faltered. Lark clenched her hands, waiting for some sort of signal. They hadn't considered this. It was a foolish oversight. Of course, Gavriel hadn't been taken by common bounty hunters. Though it begged the question of why they left her alive.

"Or have both of you warmed his bed?"

The urge to punch that smile off his face was nearly impossible to ignore.

"Everyone wants something," Hazel said with a dangerous glint in her eyes.

Maddox hummed thoughtfully. "Sure, I want a bevy of well-built men and an endless supply of ale and debauchery," he said with a flippant wave. "But I'll settle for my cut of the reward when we serve your man's head up on a platter. Proving once and for all that the Den of Lions are rivaled by no guild."

Lark slammed her elbow against the middle of his chest, pinning him against the bar. Her dagger had made its way into her hand without thought, now angled against his throat. The roaring in her ears drowned out the sound of the brothel and its patrons.

"I think you've talked long enough," she hissed. "I don't give a shit how many bear witness. You will answer me or I will cut the answers free from your flesh." Maddox's hands hung by his side, but Lark wasn't foolish enough to think they'd remain there. At least she had Hazel watching her back. "Where did they take him?"

"You haven't thought this through—"

"It would be wise to think before speaking," Hazel warned.

Lark's hand shook, rage thrumming through her. It was madness, the call to violence. As if spilling his blood would somehow keep Gavriel safe. If she thought there to be any truth to that, she'd leave a bloody trail in her wake. She chanced a glance over her shoulder, expecting to find the brothel guard storming over. But the dark-haired woman held him completely in her thrall, undulating her hips invitingly. When she caught Lark's gaze, she offered a wink.

Maddox swallowed, eying Lark with disapproval. "He's on his way to Aelcliff. We're going to let his master come for him." A muscle feathered in his cheek as he fought a smile. "Or he'll fight in the gauntlet. Earn back some of the coin he's tallied before he falls."

Slowly, Lark relented her grip. Stumbling back, her chest deflated with a sharp exhale. They planned to keep Gavriel alive long enough to fight through a tournament and return him to his master on their terms. She couldn't be certain this was a blessing or a curse, but it was a direction. That's all she needed. Aelcliff was the largest town in the Western Desolates. The harsh and inhospitable climate made it difficult for many villages to thrive. Lark had never reaped souls from some death tournament that supposedly existed in Aelcliff, but she had reaped more than enough souls who'd fallen victim to the blistering sun and unforgiving sand of the Western Desolates. But that was when she could appear anywhere the tether dictated. The world was much bigger now.

"Do you know where Aelcliff is?"

Hazel nodded. "It's a two-day ride to the Desolates. After that," she shrugged, "depends on the winds and the reliability of our mounts."

Lark bit the inside of her cheek. They would need horses, at least until they reached the Desolates boundaries, then they'd trade for *hiekka hevonens*, or sand horses. Ardenian chargers wouldn't survive that heat. They couldn't delay. It would be a hard and fast ride to have any hope of catching up with them. Hopefully, Gavriel's captors stopped to rest.

"What do we do about him?" Lark inclined her head toward Maddox, who'd taken up sipping his ale. Unconcerned.

Hazel sighed. "We should kill him to ensure he doesn't tip them off."

Maddox shook his head, narrowing his eyes. "I've answered all your questions and without kicking up much of a fuss. The least you could do is let me live. It isn't as if I'm in any great rush to leave, and what do I have on you? Hm?"

It was true. Even if he slipped away and somehow beat them to Aelcliff, what could he report they didn't already know? That two instead of one came looking? Besides, then he'd have to explain how they wrestled the information out of him.

"How much trouble would he face, if news of his loose tongue traveled to the Lions?"

Hazel grinned. "Oh, his punishment would be great indeed."

Maddox held his hands up in surrender. "I wish for no part of this. I've enjoyed my time waiting for you to show." He winked at a man nearby, who offered him a shy smile in response. "I could stand to wait a little longer. Now that I don't have to watch for you lot, I can be my charming self."

Hazel and Lark exchanged a look. Was it really worth it to let him live? It seemed like an uncalculated risk. Though based on what he had to lose, he shouldn't prove to be a problem.

Yet.

Lark pushed the feeling of unease down. She hated leaving things to chance like this. But they needed to move on.

Once she knew Gavriel was safe, she could lament all her mistakes.

CHAPTER TWENTY-ONE

LANGFORD

It was fortunate Martell and his men had kept their belongings close. Langford almost wept for joy at finding his pack with the tome, and all his necessary provisions accounted for. What was left of his finger still throbbed its painful reminder, wrapped as it was in the sleeve of his shirt, but he found himself utterly grateful just to be alive.

Perspective and whatnot.

They'd taken the Silent Mountain pass since it let out at the discrete port where Ingemar would be waiting. The Bereft Coast had many bluffs and cliffsides, making it less popular for ships to dock. But Ingemar refused to make berth anywhere near the capital. Langford wasn't complaining. He had no desire to traipse through the most densely populated city of Koval. Additionally, the Silent Mountain pass supplied freshwater springs to clean their wounds.

Langford rolled the remaining sleeve of his tunic up to his elbow, washing his hands in the impossibly cold stream, like ice slipping through his fingers. He winced at the sharp pain of his ragged edge where his finger used to be. It was vanity to mourn its loss—he was left-handed anyway. Even so, each time he looked at the stump, he felt a painful lurch in his chest. Casting a sideways glance at Alistair, he hoped he didn't notice his reaction. Alistair stripped off his tunic—he appeared about ready to keel over.

They'd fled that dingy warehouse and immediately headed for the coast, avoiding trade routes in case more of Martell's connections were nearby. It was a calculated risk, journeying instead of finding somewhere to hole up and tend to their injuries. But they couldn't be sure if any more of Alistair's old friends had caught wind of their arrival.

"I need to assess your injury," Langford said, reaching out to Alistair.

"Your wound needs tending, too." Though his voice left no room for argument, Alistair turned, offering him his side.

"True, but if one of us passes out and the other has to carry them to safety, I'd rather you bear that responsibility." Langford gently wiped Alistair's knife wound, careful not to agitate the torn flesh.

Alistair laughed, his body shaking. Goosebumps broke out along his deep bronze skin beneath Langford's hands.

"Pass me the rum." Langford held his hand out.

"You read my mind," Alistair said as he tugged it free of his pack. He brought it to his lips with a quiet sigh. Langford reached over and yanked the bottle from his grasp, ignoring Alistair's cry of outrage.

"It isn't for drinking." Langford studied Alistair's wound intently. Wine would have been better. Or some sort of alcohol base he could be certain was clean, but they didn't have the luxury of pickiness. He needed to act fast before any infection took root. Placing a rag over the top, he flipped the bottle upside down, coating the cloth. "Hold still."

Alistair winced as Langford gently pressed the rag flat against his wound. Really, he should douse the area, but he was kind enough to spare a few mouthfuls for Alistair when it came time to sew him up.

Langford chanced a glance up to find Alistair's gaze smoldering as he regarded him with a heated stare. "You shouldn't look at me like that," Langford said, ignoring the way his face burned under Alistair's scrutiny. "Especially when I'm about to stick you with a needle."

"We should take care of you first." Alistair's expression hardened.

Langford huffed his disapproval. "There's a very good chance I may go into shock immediately following the procedure I need." He stretched his spine, limbering up as he pulled catgut thread from his pack—carefully threading it through the eye of his needle. He'd need to resupply soon. Perhaps they could avoid any great injuries until they docked in Ardenas and hit the market. He flexed his remaining fingers, preparing himself to stitch Alistair's wound. Langford was more than familiar with stitching up wounds, but performing it absent a finger would be new. He held his hand up, daring it to tremble.

Steady as a rock.

"Langford," Alistair said, placing a heavy hand on Langford's thigh, leaning in close, "I'm sorry." There was no pity in his gaze, but a deep shame. The squirming sort of guilt that dug beneath one's skin.

"I know," Langford said, eyes drifting to where Alistair's hand burned through his trousers. "Now turn, and hold still."

Alistair took a greedy pull from the bottle, saving a few mouthfuls at the bottom.

It was calming, really, the familiarity of weaving skin back together. For his hands to occupy the task they were made for. The middle finger of his right hand, just beneath the second knuckle, was achingly raw. It throbbed in time with his heartbeat. But for just a moment or two, everything else faded as he focused on suturing Alistair's side closed. It had always been this way, almost meditative, to discipline his mind. He might freeze when it came to cutting down a man—but stitching him back together? That was easy. Just parts in need of fixing.

Alistair exhaled a shaky breath as Langford tugged the thread tight, skin joining once again. He snipped the thread, finally finished.

Alistair's hand found his. "Thank you." The breath from his whisper ghosted against Langford's mouth, chasing a shiver through him.

It wasn't the time for that. They had a far more unpleasant task to deal with first.

"I'll clean the area, but you need to build a fire." Langford forced his hand back into the icy depths of the stream, biting back a hiss.

"A fire? You wish to cauterize it?" Alistair's disbelief made his tone sharp. "Langford, you can't be serious."

"What would you have me do?" Langford said through clenched teeth. The pain really was becoming troublesome. Hopefully, it wasn't the first stirrings of infection.

Alistair gathered nearby sticks for kindling, his movements abrupt. "I don't know. Can't you sew it back on?"

A sharp laugh leapt from Langford's chest. "Why ever would I do that? It wouldn't restore sensation or mobility. I can't rejoin the bone, Alistair." What a mad idea. Though now he said it, he supposed if he had the right sort of witch or conjuror near, perhaps there was a restoration spell that theoretically could have aided in bone growth and reattachment. But magic wielders were rare, and apart from the green witch Lark had ventured to find, Langford couldn't think of a single known location. Besides, his finger would never survive the journey to locate such a person. Not that he'd grabbed it when they left. It seemed too morbid an idea to carry a small piece of himself in his pocket in hopes they'd miraculously find a way.

Langford snapped his head up, whipping around to face Alistair. "Do you have it?"

A sheepish expression crossed Alistair's face as he reached into his pocket. He had, in fact, brought Langford's finger with them.

"You carried it in your pocket?" Langford's stomach twisted at the thought. He wasn't a squeamish man, his chosen profession dictated as such, but the thought of his own finger in Alistair's pocket made his skin crawl.

Alistair shrugged, chagrin washing over his face. "I didn't realize you couldn't reattach it. I thought I was being helpful."

Langford pulled his hands from the water, shaking them dry and ignoring the sting. "Gods above, get rid of it."

"How was I supposed to know? I thought you'd be pleased. I even wrapped it so it wouldn't get dirty."

"Get rid of it!"

Grumbling under his breath, Alistair stomped away, disappearing for a moment. When he came back, he dropped to his knees and used the flint to light a spark, the first embers hinting at fire.

Langford pushed down his nausea at the idea that Alistair had been carrying his finger around in his pocket. Once they cauterized the wound and sealed the nerves and vessels, he could wallow.

"Is there a knife you care about least?"

Alistair regarded him with a puzzled expression, before understanding dawned his face. "Ah, of course." He pulled an impressively adorned dagger from his pack. The hilt sparkled in the moonlight, small stones catching and refracting the light.

It must have cost a small fortune.

"Alistair… where did you get that?"

The boyish expression on Alistair's roguishly-handsome face disarmed him, sending his heart pounding.

"What do you think I'm doing while drinking in every tavern? The pocket of a fellow drunkard is easy to steal from, especially if I'm staggering about." Alistair studied the dagger, turning it over in his hands. "I was going to free the rubies and emeralds for some spare coin. We could get more honey for your tea."

Something about that last part made Langford's chest swell.

Alistair leaned close to the smoldering embers. Slowly, he blew, his breath fanning the flame. The glowing coals brightened in response.

The fire was catching now, yawning and stretching as small flames licked at the sticks and branches Alistair had arranged. He needed to temper his impatience. If he didn't heat the steel to the correct temperature, which was guesswork, he could severely damage himself and botch the whole procedure.

Patience was something Langford was good at. When pain wasn't stealing his focus.

He needed a distraction.

As if sensing this, Alistair quickly scooted over to sit by him. "What do you think the others are doing right now?"

That was something Langford wondered over time and time again. "Hmm… let's see," he said, as if giving it considerable thought. "Daciana is doing something very mysterious and important. Perhaps she's completing a rescue mission of a kidnapped baroness."

Alistair laughed. "I'd bet the baroness would end the evening right lusting for her."

Langford rolled his eyes. Of course Alistair's mind went there. "Not everything is about sex."

"Yes it is." Alistair tossed a pebble into the stream. The ripples fanned out beneath the light of the moon. "The drive of every living creature is sex. It's the nature of life, Langford." His tone implied how obvious it was. "In fact, I'd wager our little Lark is currently mounting a certain assassin, even as we speak."

Langford snorted, ignoring the smile that stretched across Alistair's face at the sound. "Just because you can name two individuals with a proclivity for copulating with one another doesn't mean you've proven your point."

"But I, too, can admit to thinking of little else other than ripping your clothes off and ravishing you." Alistair raised a dark brow. "The evidence stacks in my favor."

Alistair was teasing. He thoroughly enjoyed both making others uncomfortable and winning arguments. This was an opportunity to accomplish both at the same time. Still, a pleasurable flush erupted over Langford's skin.

Damn him.

Langford wet his lips, Alistair's eyes tracking the movement. "I think the fire is hot enough to heat the blade."

And just like that, the spell was broken. Alistair's face darkened, his brows pulling together. He held the blade over the fire and word-lessly handed the rum to Langford.

Langford tipped it back, swallowing hard against the vaporous liquid burning the back of his throat.

This was going to hurt.

There was a featherlight touch against his hand. Alistair tugged him closer, soothing his thumb over his knuckles. "Ready?"

Langford nodded, not trusting himself to speak. His eyes slipped closed, clenching tight as he braced against the pain.

He heard the sizzle before he felt it. The scorching pain of searing flesh. He cried out, eyes fluttering open.

"Look at me." Alistair's voice was hoarse. He'd removed the blade, granting Langford a moment's respite.

"Again," Langford panted. "Once more to seal it."

Alistair nodded, his mouth a grim line, before he pressed burning steel against Langford's flesh.

Langford bit down on his lip, hard enough he was sure to bleed.

Four throbs of his pulse later, Alistair dropped the dagger to the ground. Collecting Langford up in his arms, he pulled him against his chest.

Langford's vision blurred. But he wasn't ready to give way to unconsciousness. "Alistair."

"What do you need?" Alistair's voice rumbled in his chest. The chest Langford was pressed against.

"Need you to wrap it." Langford's tongue had thickened—or the words were too big for his mouth. He felt a sharp pain through his hand as Alistair wrapped it as delicately as possible. "Thanks."

"Sleep, Langford." Alistair still held him tightly, soothing his hand up and down his arm. "I've got you."

Langford mumbled unintelligibly. He liked to think it was along the lines of 'just a short rest.' Eyelids heavy, they finally fluttered closed.

"You'll always have me."

It sounded like that's what Alistair said, but before Langford could be sure, he tumbled headlong into a dreamless sleep.

CHAPTER TWENTY-TWO

DACIANA

*R*ather than question the mourning families regarding their losses, reopening old wounds that had never healed right, Daciana pored over the coroner's reports, scanning each document chronicling the crimes committed against these poor children. Leaving no stone unturned. It was atrocious, really, the details she never wished to know. Even more unsettling was confronting that part of herself she never wanted to face.

How not even the grisly truth of these acts could turn her stomach.

Daciana scanned critical eyes over words like *dismembered, asphyxiated,* and *exsanguinated.* The parchment never wavered in her ever-steady hands. She was focused, and her anger remained sharp and cool, like the surface of the Permafrosts region.

It was disturbing how much she'd come to accept as fact in this blighted world.

Her only comfort was Kenna, who leaned over her shoulder, scanning the reports with as much stern calculation as she possessed. If there was one person to understand the way the world can harden a heart, it was Kenna.

"Any theories?" Daciana passed the report to her. She'd already read it three times.

"None that stick," Kenna said thoughtfully, her usual glib demeanor absent. "There's no pattern, apart from the severity of the crimes, and all committed against children." She sighed, stepping around the desk and plopping herself into Bronn's chair—it groaned in protest, even under her slight frame. "I hate to say it, but I have no idea what we're dealing with."

Daciana had already suspected as much. But some small part of her hoped it might be something they understood; something they could study and lure to its demise. "What's our next move?"

"I hate to say it, but since the kills aren't fresh, I have little to go on." Kenna didn't soften her words; she, too, was accustomed to the uglier face of the world. "I don't want to call it a dead end; more like a gap in the trail. We'll pick it up again. The minute the bastard hears whatever calling drives him to torture innocent children. Or we won't. If he doesn't kill again, I have no way of finding him." She dropped the report onto Bronn's desk.

Daciana snatched it up again, examining it with razor-sharp focus. There had to be something—anything that would give them a hint. "Harick Ranier... this was the boy they found with Declan." *Bite wounds... claw marks on his arms... defensive cuts...* Her eyes widened. "It says here they found a strip of cloth in his fist—but it doesn't say if it matched what Declan was wearing."

Kenna crept closer to peer over her shoulder. "What are the odds they kept the evidence?" Her breath blew against Daciana's neck, and Daciana tried to ignore Kenna's familiar scent of fresh rain and berries. Sweet and wild.

Daciana slid away from Kenna's warmth. "I'll ask Bronn. What are the odds your witch will perform a locator spell?"

Kenna's brows pinched, a frown forming on her lovely face. "She isn't my witch... but she'll do the spell. Of that much I'm certain."

WAS it fate or chance that guided Bronn's decision to keep the only evidence from a series of terrible crimes when he was convinced they'd found the killer? He gave Daciana a tattered piece of cloth, a faded greenish grey. He didn't ask why they needed it, and seemed all too willing to part with it. Daciana had promised him answers, a promise she wasn't certain she should have made.

The fraying cloth sat bunched in her pocket, beside the stone she'd taken from Hugo's burial.

They departed while their shadows were still long, leaving Stormfair behind and traveling to a far more welcoming destination.

Oakbury was the closest thing to home for Daciana. If home was a place, sturdy and standing, no matter how many times one left it behind. But Daciana liked to believe home was wherever she and her companions made camp for the night. The ache in her chest, the longing she felt to be reunited with the others, hurt something fierce as of late.

The Walden Inn and Tavern held a familiar warmth. The giant stone hearth still blazed in the corner. Round wooden tables they'd all dined and drank at still filled the large space. Mrs. O'Connell, covered in flour from a day spent baking pies, came bustling over to yank Daciana into an air-restricting embrace.

"Where's Alistair?" Mrs. O'Connell demanded, peering over Daciana's shoulder as if she expected him to come waltzing through the door.

"He had some business to finish, but he sends his love." Daciana offered her a warm smile. It was rare for Alistair to be anyone's favorite, apart from the ladies who knew he lined his pockets with the intent of their company for the evening. Was he still up to his old tricks? Things between him and Langford had been tense the last time she saw them. Like they were on the verge of hurdling off a cliff. Perhaps they'd finally admitted their feelings. But Daciana had witnessed them dance around each other for years without ever taking that next step.

"You look so familiar. Have you stayed here before?" Mrs. O'Connell eyed Kenna with calculating scrutiny.

Kenna grinned, the effect dizzying. "I was through here maybe a year ago."

"Oh, that's nice. Before I forget!" Mrs. O'Connell bustled over to the bar and darted behind the heavy wooden table-top, dipping out of view for a moment or two before she popped back up with a sealed envelope. Daciana's name appeared hastily scrawled across the front. "Lark left this for you nearly a fortnight ago."

Daciana nearly leapt over to Mrs. O'Connell, her eager fingers snatching up the letter and gripping it tight enough the parchment crinkled its rebuttal. Lark kept her word.

This overwhelming sense of connection came over her. She was holding a message penned by Lark's hand. The vast expanse of the world—all the time that had passed between the two friends—folded in on itself, bringing Lark within Daciana's reach. She wanted to rip it open and devour its contents. She wanted to find a quiet spot alone to read.

"Do you have any rooms available?"

"For you?" Mrs. O'Connell gave a hearty laugh. "Always. Even if I was full-up, I'd kick their arses out and make room. Now go on up, the room at the end of the hall has been freshly cleaned. Go get the smell of the road off of you and be down here for supper."

Lark's message burned in Daciana's hand, demanding her attention. "Thank you, Mrs. O'Connell. You're too good to me."

"Nonsense." Mrs. O'Connell wiped her hands on her apron. "Now go, I'll see you in a few hours."

It took every shred of Daciana's control not to sprint up the stairs in her impatience. She allowed a brisk step in her walk until she made it into their room, Kenna hot on her trail. Midday sun streamed through the window, basking the solitary bed in a warm, hazy glow. Daciana bit the inside of her cheek, silently regarding their sleeping arrangements.

Kenna let out a low whistle. "Now this looks mighty cozy." She dropped her pack and sauntered over to the bed, jumping to land on her back, elbows bent as she laced her hands behind her head. "I hope you don't mind if I snag this side of the bed."

Daciana ignored her. She yanked the door to the bathroom open, thanking the skies their bathing tub wasn't in the middle of the sleeping quarters, but behind the privacy of a door she could slide the latch across to lock. There'd be time enough later to worry about how she was supposed to get a wink of sleep with Kenna's warm body in the same bed as she.

Daciana perched on the edge of the large, round wooden basin. She broke the acorn wax seal, ripped open the envelope and yanked the letter free. The air constricted in her chest as Lark's familiar scrawl stared up at her.

Dac,

Gavriel and I will be off to see Inerys soon. Mrs. O'Connell lent Apple to a local farmer, so we'll travel on foot, which will slow our journey considerably, but it's all right. We're keeping to the forests anyway, just in case Adler is looking for me, and we didn't dare set foot in Stormfair in case anyone recognized Gavriel. Once I know more, I'll leave another message.

I pray to the skies she has answers. If not, then I really don't know what the next step is. Hopefully, Langford has found something useful. And that he and Alistair have finally given in and ripped each other's clothes off. All right, fine, if I only have one wish, it'll be that we find answers. And that Alistair and Langford come home safely. And that you find whatever it is you're looking for and come back to us. Yes, I know, that was more than one wish.

I miss you. Be safe.

-Lark

Daciana reread Lark's words over and over. Memorizing every single splotch of ink, every place where Lark pressed too hard.

Blazes, she missed her. And the others.

Daciana knew Lark would go see Inerys, but she'd hoped Lark's message would explain what she learned. That she hadn't stopped by afterward to update her findings left Daciana feeling a bit rattled. She glanced around the modest washroom. The privy in the corner had a wooden door that closed over the top, creating a bench seat. There were fresh, white towels hung off the back of the door, and the washbasin she perched on was large enough to accommodate two people. Daciana's face heated at the unbidden image of Kenna, unclothed and half concealed by water sloshing over the sides of the tub, giving her that mischievous grin that lit up her face and creased her cheeks.

Daciana stood abruptly. Perhaps she'd sleep in here tonight rather than sharing the bed with her. It was likely the only way she'd get any rest.

Making her way out of the washroom, Daciana found Kenna softly snoring. Careful not to disturb the bed with her weight, she shifted onto her side of the bed, making sure to leave enough distance they didn't touch. Kenna's unguarded expression softened her face, and Daciana took the opportunity to appraise her. The splatter of freckles across her nose. Her full lips. The slick, straight, black fringe hanging over her closed eyes. With a whisper of a touch, Daciana brushed the hair from Kenna's face. Her long, dark lashes rested against the swell of her cheek. Kenna didn't stir. Daciana held her breath, eyes greedily drinking in the sight of the most bewitching woman she'd ever seen.

THE JOURNEY through the Emerald Woods was decidedly tense. As they drew nearer, Kenna's posture seemed to grow stiffer like she was bracing herself for an unseen threat. Either that, or she was still vexed from when Daciana shoved her away upon waking and discovering their bodies had intertwined.

It had been fortunate Mrs. O'Connell kept Lark's horse, Apple. The local wheat farmer had been more than happy to return the animal since his yield had recently been harvested and transported to town. The horse showed no signs of fear, allowing Daciana to ride her through the forest. A damp chill had settled in the air, and the sky was a thick swirl of grey mist. The Emerald Woods no longer held the warm green life of both spring and summer. A dank fog shrouded the foliage-laden forest floor. The spindly branches of bare trees loomed above, twisting toward the dark sky.

Daciana dipped her head, narrowly avoiding a low-hanging branch. High above, a crow cawed its lament.

Daciana tugged her cloak tighter. It wasn't far now. The mist was gradually thickening, a sure sign they were close to the water. By the time they reached the boat that leaned heavily on the shore, Kenna's mouth had firmed in a tight line, her shoulders tense.

A thick haze hovered over the lake, casting the water in an unearthly warning. Inerys' cottage stood, smoke billowing in thick clouds from the brick-stack chimney. The greenery that hugged her outer walls had shed its leaves, dark barren vines wrapped around her hut in a threatening embrace.

Daciana shook of her head, tasting the faint hint of warding magic in the air as they paddled across the lake. Witches with their spells. This witch had better be willing to use her magic to locate the dark shadow hounding Stormfair's children.

And if the spell led her to Declan, to the boy they'd freed, she'd kill him herself.

Daciana leapt out of the schooner, landing in the shin-deep water that immediately filled her boots. The hem of her cloak danced atop the lake's surface. Kenna joined her, leaping in with a splash to push the boat ashore.

The chill in the air showed no signs of abating, despite it being midday and likely the warmest it would get. The wind whipped through Daciana's hair, sending thick black tendrils into her face. Her wet clothes instantly chilled against her skin, and she fought a shiver.

The steps to Inerys' cottage were slow and weighted with the lake water still sloshing around Daciana's boots. She leaned against the door, tugging her boots off one by one to dump them out. Without the spring moss that once covered Inerys' home, the grey stone walls were visible, peeking out from behind dark vines and roots.

"Daciana," Kenna said, finally breaking her silence. "I have to tell you something."

Daciana paused her scrutiny of the dwelling, slowly yanking her boot back into place. "All right."

"The last time I was here… when I used to visit Inerys—" Kenna's words halted as she ran a hand to grip the handle of her sword.

Painful understanding slid through her like a knife between the ribs. "You don't need to explain anything to me."

"No, I know. But I didn't want you to be caught unawares in case it came up…"

Daciana crossed her arms, hoping it conveyed a casual ease she didn't feel. She'd suspected something had gone on between Inerys and Kenna. The familiarity in Inerys' tone last time Daciana was here had hinted at it. But Kenna's visible discomfort during the entire trek here from Oakbury and her awkward posturing now were the more blatant clues. "You needn't explain anything to me," she repeated.

Hurt flashed across Kenna's face, but was quickly smoothed into casual amusement. "Quite right. No need to share the sordid details, I'm sure."

Daciana sucked on her teeth, reining in the anger and regret flaring in her chest. "Let's just get this over with."

"Fine by me."

Pounding on the door with more force than necessary, Daciana counted backward from ten, slowing the pounding against her ribs. Kenna was free to do as she pleased. Daciana had no claim on her. In fact, should Kenna find herself desperate for a quick fuck, Daciana could simply slip out and make her way back on her own. Kenna could swim the lake for all she cared.

The door disappeared from beneath Daciana's fist. An unimpressed looking Inerys stood there, dark eyes narrowed as she regarded them with suspicion. Her deep chestnut hair hung down in soft waves, offsetting the warm tone of her golden skin.

Of course, Kenna had lain with her.

"What do you want?" Inerys spat. "I already told Lark everything."

"I need to know everything you spoke of." Daciana still didn't know where Lark went after meeting with the witch. She couldn't guess Lark's path without Inerys' help.

Inerys slid her gaze past her to regard Kenna. A wolfish smile spread across her face. "Well, if it isn't my favorite hunter."

Daciana felt Kenna move closer. "And my favorite, incredibly *helpful* witch."

Inerys rolled her eyes, pulling the door open wide for them to enter.

"Yes, yes. Keep reminding me why I stay in the forest where I wish to be left alone."

"You don't mean that," Kenna said in her cheery tone. "I recognized a few protective laurels on the doors of the villagers' homes when we came in through town." Kenna flashed Inerys a brilliant smile. The one that never failed to leave Daciana feeling a bit dazed. This time, it only made it difficult to breathe.

Inerys closed the door behind them, a smirk playing on her lips. "I was merely taking advantage of the superstition that runs rampant on this side of the country."

"Liar," Kenna said affectionately.

Inerys dusted her hands on her deep auburn gown. The garment accentuated her slim waist, ivory buttons running all the way up her neck. The homespun cloth conveyed a simple elegance. Daciana shifted uncomfortably in her filthy ram-leather leggings and deep brown cuirass. The green tunic she wore beneath her leather protective layer was torn and stained, her cloak dripping mud and lake water on Inerys' wood floor. The steady drips rang in Daciana's ears.

"Lark left a message saying she spoke to you." Daciana trailed the respectable distance between Kenna and Inerys. Yet it still felt far too close. "I've heard nothing since. I need to know what you told her." And hopefully, a locator spell to track the beast stalking Stormfair, but one matter at a time.

The corner of Inerys' mouth lifted, only slightly. "Very well, but it's a long story, so allow me to prepare us some tea." She turned to leave, pausing to regard Daciana with a hard look. "And you both need to change. I can't have you dripping all over my furnishings. Kenna will show you to the bedroom."

Daciana's jaw clenched. At both Inerys' haughty tone, and the notion that Kenna was familiar enough here to offer a tour.

"Come," Kenna said, placing a gentle hand on her arm. The contact seared even through layers of wet cloth.

Daciana trudged behind Kenna, ignoring the audible squish of her boots. Kenna cut straight through the sitting room, the one Daciana remembered from the last time she was here. Glass vases still adorned the table top and mantle, though without the summer sun glaring through the windows, they no longer cast a glimmering light. Thick books still covered every surface, some left open as if Inerys paused her reading and forgot to return. Living greenery crawled up the walls, life begging to be close to the witch. Despite autumn's hold on the land, inside Inerys' home, it was still decidedly spring. Verdant, living, breathing, spring.

With a firm hand, Kenna swung the door to Inerys' bedroom open, stepping in without waiting to see if Daciana followed.

The room echoed the voice of nature. Flowering vines climbed the walls, creating an indoor forest. The chair and table were hewn from branches, still wet and living. The large bed, dressed in glimmering white covers, was half hidden by a pale gossamer curtain. A thick tree had grown right through the floor, leaves hanging heavy in the corner.

Claustrophobia crawled up Daciana's throat. Like these living walls were threatening to become her cage. The forest was meant to feel free, not confining. It sang in her veins—her very blood called for the forest beneath a bright moon.

Suddenly Kenna's hands were on Daciana's shoulders. Heat flared through her, scorching through her nerves.

"Dac," Kenna said, soothing her hands down Daciana's arms. "What is it? What's wrong?"

Daciana forced her eyes to Kenna's face. Her deep-set brown eyes stared back—tightened with worry. Her delicate pale skin, dusted along her nose with soft freckles, was far too perfect for the number of times Daciana had seen it painted in blood. Kenna's black brows were drawn tight as she continued to search Daciana's face with unwavering concern. Her scent filled Daciana's senses. Intoxicating her. Daciana made the mistake of lowering her gaze to Kenna's mouth. Memories of tasting Kenna's lips flooded her, making her head spin.

It was too much. It wasn't enough. She needed to shove her away. To feel her beneath her hands. To search every curve and plane of Kenna's perfect body that she already knew by heart.

Daciana's heart was split between two fierce longings. Deep aching loneliness, and unwavering need to remain alone.

At her hesitation, Kenna's face fell before she turned from her, blessedly making the decision for her.

It was better this way.

Daciana took a shuddering breath, repeating the mantra in her head, even as her chest ached. She could never allow herself to make the same mistake again.

"Here."

Daciana caught a bundle of clothing, a simple pair of softened, tanned leather breeches, and an oversized white linen tunic. Kenna yanked a similar handful of clothing from the top drawer of Inerys' moss-covered dressing table, slamming it shut with enough force, the leaves trembled. Before Daciana could say a word, Kenna stomped out of the room.

It was better this way.

CHAPTER TWENTY-THREE

LARK

This is not the same as riding Apple.

Lark shifted in the wool saddle atop her *hiekka hevonen*. Her sand horse. She sat nestled between two of the hard arches of its back, the exaggerated position sending shooting pains through her hips and thighs.

Hazel showed no signs of discomfort, riding beside Lark as fast as she could. Which wasn't very fast at all.

Once they'd taken the shortcut through the mountain pass, the air gradually thickened, and the vegetation slowly thinned. The ground gave way to a dry soft reddish clay, long before they reached the Desolates.

The hazy sun beat down on the reddish-orange sand, shimmering along each grain like a living flame. The horizon danced in her vision, and the blazing heat sent beads of sweat rolling down her back. Hazel had acquired them appropriate attire to trek into the Desolates when she'd traded for their sand horses. Instead of her usual fighting leathers and breeches, Lark sported light tan linen leggings; a matching tunic hung loosely down her body, and a hood draped over her head.

Sand shifted beneath their mounts, and an occasional wind, that offered no cool reprieve, whipped against Lark's face. Her stomach dipped as they trekked down a steep dune, her sand horse lowing with the tug of its reins. They'd only been traveling across the Desolates for a day and a half, but Lark's cheeks and nose were already raw and tender to the touch.

This region was impervious to autumn's charms.

A small fennec fox darted out from behind a tall boulder of sandstone, its large, white ears twitching.

Lark swallowed, her dry throat scraping with the action. "How far is it now?"

"You realize you asked me that not two hours ago?"

"Yes, I know."

"And I believe I made it quite clear we'd be there by sundown." Hazel straightened in her saddle. "Oh, and look! The sun is still high in the sky. So either the heat has cooked your memory or your impatience needs governing."

Lark bit her dry, cracked lip. With each passing moment, the panic in her chest twisted, coiling deep. She needed to see Gavriel's face. She needed to know he was all right. The terror and absurdity of her mission nearly tore a laugh from her lips. Here she was, with the fate of the world in the balance, and all she could think about was the life of a man her heart still called for now that she'd unbound their souls.

History seemed determined to repeat itself.

But fate be damned—there was no question. Soul bond or not, she wouldn't rest until she knew he was safe, and his heart still beat in his chest.

Memories of his warm smile tugging his scarred lip, of fevered kisses and softer ones, of calloused hands running over her—into her hair, across her skin—smothered the air in her lungs. The gnawing ache of it all was deep and ravenous.

What felt like lifetimes ago, Nereida had warned Lark that she didn't know pain anymore.

Her humanity was all too quick to acquaint her with various forms of pain, and now she knew another. This ache… it carved her from the inside, and for every fleeting moment when she felt it retreat, it returned with a vengeance.

Lark tugged the waterskin free from her saddlebag, tipping it between her lips. Water spilled onto her tongue, filling her mouth. Her throat immediately felt less dusty, and her head cleared.

She commanded her own fate—that had included Gavriel's once.

She would not lose him. Not this day.

THE CITY of Aelcliff sprawled before them, beckoning between tall canyon walls made of sandstone. The sun had not yet dipped below the horizon—a fact Lark was more than happy to point out to Hazel.

"What can I say? We made good time. Must be because you stopped swooning in your saddle every time you heard Gavriel's name carried on the wind."

"I did not swoon."

Hazel chuckled, turning her gaze to the city that lay before them.

Layers of wooden scaffolding connected the canyon walls, offering passage across rickety bridges. Beneath the shadow along the gorge, small homes resided within the dug up ground. The walls and roofs were of some sort of animal skins, drawn tight like a drum. Lark and Hazel passed through. Under that shadow, the air was significantly cooler.

"We're getting close now," Hazel said with a note of warning, as if realizing this was a mistake, one they should quickly reverse.

"Where would they have taken him?" Maddox had mentioned the gauntlet in a fighting arena. But this was a community, a village, and it didn't appear anyone was in these homes. A laundry basket of freshly folded clothes sat beside a clothing line, with a single garment still billowing in the breeze. It was empty, abandoned. Like everyone was in the middle of living their lives and suddenly vanished.

"He'd be in the center of town," Hazel said darkly. "This is just the outskirts."

"But where is everyone?"

There was a low rumble in the distance, steadily building. Like a wave cresting. Lark felt it, a raw edge of panic that she couldn't explain. She glanced at Hazel, who grinned back, though it failed to meet her eyes.

"You hear that, Lark? That's where we'll find him."

The sound only grew until, instead of a rumble, it was a collective shout. And then each singular voice broke away until it was a shapeless mass of dissonance. Calls for more, for blood. Jeers and cries of triumph alike. Just around the canyon wall, the city center came into view. Tall buildings carved from sandstone towered from above, children in light clothing ran around the market. Carts overflowed with brightly colored fruit Lark had never seen. Canvas overpasses were erected with numerous merchants peddling their wares.

Lark leapt down from her sand horse, hips and back screaming their protest. The exaggerated seat of her mount and the hours spent riding without respite were a reckoning. She tugged the creature over to the trough and tied it to the hitching rail. Yanking her pack from the saddle, she followed the sound of the vicious crowd.

Lark and Hazel elbowed their way through throngs of people, forcing a path. Lark tugged her hood tighter, unsure of why the cover of a shroud suddenly felt like a safety measure.

The sun was just hovering above the horizon as dusk approached with its soft embrace.

But there was nothing gentle about this night.

Before them stood a large wooden circle of walls towering overhead. Upper decks were built into the surrounding scaffolding, accessible by a series of ladders and bridges. Lark and Hazel exchanged a look before Lark marched up and began climbing. The voices were louder now, deafening.

Lark stood on her tiptoes, glancing around the crowd, but she was stuck behind a pair of tall men. She pushed past them, desperate to see what everyone was so up in arms over. Her heart in her throat, she trailed down the ramps, knocking into people to keep on her path. She couldn't halt. She couldn't wait.

On the lower level, the crowd was thin enough for her to lean over the rail and take a breath that wasn't laden with the reek of perspiration and warm bodies.

And then she saw him.

The harsh roar of the crowd evaporated as the blood pounded in her ears.

Gavriel.

Sweat and blood matted his dark hair, and his mouth drew into a cruel sneer as he faced off with two opponents in the center of the ring. A formidable broadsword in one hand, and a lean gladius in the other. He raised them high with a mighty battle cry that shook Lark to her very core. As he slashed and carved a path of rage and fury, he was a force of nature. Of power and vengeance. Gavriel's body was a map of wounds, rivers of cuts and slices that bled angrily and stained his torn clothing.

Lark's heart fractured.

Gavriel's head snapped up, his eyes finding hers. Shock flashed across his face before settling on something else.

Fear.

Lark couldn't breathe.

The momentary distraction cost him as the warrior in ruddy armor sliced his blade across Gavriel's thigh. Gavriel staggered, and swept his swords against the man's throat with a swift, merciless pull.

The man's head remained perched on his shoulders for a heartbeat or two before it toppled to the ground.

Lark gripped the rough wooden rail tight enough that splinters dug into her palms. She leaned back, preparing to launch herself over the edge—when a hand gripped her shoulder. Hard.

"What in the fucking abyss do you think you're doing?" Hazel hissed. Her impossibly blue eyes blazed with fury as her expression twisted in equal parts disgust and disbelief. "Were you seriously about to go down there?"

"It's Gavriel." Lark tore her gaze from Hazel, searching for him. He advanced on his remaining opponent. A man with olive skin and long black hair twisted into a knot at the nape of his neck. A thick bushy beard hid most of his face, but his arms were bare and covered in a smattering of tattoos similar to Hugo's. Vallemerian. What was a Vallemerian warrior doing fighting in the Den of Lions' gauntlet?

He lunged, missing Gavriel by a hair's breadth. Gavriel swiftly leapt back, faltering under his wounded thigh. He stumbled, righting himself quickly. The sun was just starting to disappear beneath the horizon. It painted the bloody sand in a violent orange and reddish hue.

"I know, Lark. But you can't just leap into the arena like that. You'd be forfeiting your life. Maybe his. There are rules, and you don't get to change them without facing consequences." Hazel jerked her chin at Gavriel. His handsome face was contorted in anger and pain and something Lark couldn't quite name. He narrowly blocked a cutting blow. The sound of steel on steel struck like an angry chord, setting Lark's teeth on edge.

"I can't just sit by and do nothing. He needs help. I—" What was she hoping? That she'd leap over the side and run into his bloody arms? Kiss him senseless, and the crowd would go wild? That there was even the smallest chance they might release him? Or that perhaps between the two of them, they could fight their way to freedom?

How utterly foolish was she?

"Lark, no," Hazel said, as if sensing her thoughts. "Whatever you think will happen, it won't."

The edge of a sword snaked across Gavriel's stomach. Gavriel threw himself back in time to keep the cut from hitting deep. The graze, though shallow, wept blood down his stomach.

Lark tightened her grip on the rail.

Gavriel swung wide, forcing the man to leap back. Gavriel spun his broadsword—casting a ripple of wind in its wake—catching the curved blade of the man's falchion and holding, before Gavriel swept his gladius across his throat, splitting the intricate tattoos that encircled his neck.

Gavriel didn't wait for the body to hit the ground before he turned away, stalking back to the middle of the arena. His darkened gaze found Lark once more. The sight of his handsome face, painted in blood as his chest heaved with every violent breath, constricted the air in her lungs. His eyes never left hers, his expression still holding all the fury of his fight. Even as the guards swarmed him and placed him in shackles, he didn't tear his gaze from her.

A hot tear slipped down Lark's cheek as her chest hollowed.

When they dragged him away, the sun finally gave way to night, and shadows crept along the blood-soaked sand.

"IF YOU DON'T STOP FIDGETING, I'm going to tie your arms down," Hazel said with a scowl.

Lark hadn't stopped moving since the guards led Gavriel away. She couldn't halt her nervous pacing—her frantic energy and fear pulsing with every heartbeat. Hazel had promised that during guard rotation, they'd venture to the dungeons where Gavriel was being held.

Hazel and Lark had tracked the journey the guards took to the farthest building. There was no mistaking where Gavriel was being held. Death Drop Prison. Aptly named because the fortress sat at the edge of a steep cliff. Lark had never reaped souls from this particular prison, but she'd heard enough to know how busy it kept her fellow Reapers.

Hewn from clay, sand, and silt from the Lost Spring in Death Drop Valley, the fortress stood just beyond the arena. Pillars beneath the terrace lined the lower entrance where the guards remained ever watchful. The structure reached three stories high, its arched windows dark, as if they hadn't bothered to light any torches. Swathed by night, and a bright sky full of thousands of stars, the prison seemed almost serene.

Lark and Hazel waited in the shadows of the canyon, watching two guards casually converse. Something about the meal he'd cooked for his wife. He promised to give the fellow guard on duty the recipe.

Lark shot Hazel a desperate look. If they incapacitated the watchers too soon, they risked the next shift discovering their colleagues were missing.

Even knowing this, impatience dug at Lark's chest. Each moment that passed, Gavriel was alone in that cell, possibly succumbing to his wounds. She couldn't imagine they'd offer a healer to look after him. "How deep was the cut to his thigh?"

"If any of his wounds had been fatal, you would have seen his corpse for yourself." Hazel thumbed her dagger absently, turning the handle over in her palm.

It was a comforting thought.

Lark still wasn't sure what would await her in that dungeon. She couldn't shake the image of his face, twisted in monstrous fury. The look he gave her when he saw her in the stands offered no insight. Would he be angry, now that the soul bond was no longer forcing his feelings to draw them together? Might he feel she'd somehow duped him? Would he be relieved to see her? At least grateful she was here to set him free? She didn't dare hope for anything beyond that.

The memory of his impossibly handsome and open face that day so long ago—when she'd held his head in her hands and changed their fate—flooded her mind. With blood in his teeth and a smile on his lips, he'd gazed up at her with trust and wonder. When she'd forced the draught down his throat, effectively healing and inheriting his mortal ailment so he might live—and then when he'd looked upon her with disgust. With hatred.

Yes, they'd come a long way from that fateful day, but how would he look upon her now that the soul bond was severed? She couldn't bear the thought of his indifference.

Lark tugged her familiar grey cloak tighter. The Western Desolates were perilous under a blistering sun, but under the cover of night, the harsh winds blew. Lark and Hazel had changed back into their own clothes, into darker colors, far more practical for remaining hidden in the shadows. Lark yanked Hugo's dagger from her boot. She clenched her fist around the handle, sending a silent prayer to the skies for strength. It was funny, really. Habits and rituals. Even when they'd lost their purpose and one can't be sure they hold any meaning anymore, comfort can still be found.

Hazel turned back, offering Lark a grin. "It's show time."

INCAPACITATING THE GUARDS WAS SIMPLE. Namely because Hazel had a specific weapon.

Hazel whipped out a thin wooden tube from her pack about the length of her forearm. She raised a dark brow, her blue eyes glinting with mischief, as she loaded a small needle edged dart into the end. In the time it took for the first guard to lift a hand to his neck to extract the dart, she'd already reloaded and shot the second. Both crumpled in a heap beneath the terrace.

Lark couldn't help but grin as excitement bloomed in her chest. This was it. They were going to free Gavriel. There was still the veil to worry about and the matter of finding an archaic wielder Inerys insisted no longer existed…

Lark yanked her focus back on the task at hand. Hazel once told her to think of it as a mere job to keep the fear from creeping in.

It's only a job. A job that will determine if Gavriel survives.

They crept up to the unconscious guards and dragged them to sit with their backs against the pillars. It was too laborious to pull them much further.

There was no door, only an open archway. A stroke of luck—they wouldn't have to waste time picking the lock. Well, this lock anyway.

Lark's footsteps echoed through the dark stone hallway. Like a rabbit warren, corridors twisted and turned, hidden rooms popping out. But Hazel seemed determined in her stride, never wavering as they twisted deeper into the fortress. Her movements were silent, a skill she, too, must have mastered alongside Gavriel at the Guild. Lark remembered the way he kept light on his feet, trying her best to do the same.

When the corridor ended in a steep set of spiraling stairs, there was nowhere to go but down. A deep pit of pitch blackness awaited them, darkness threatening to devour them whole. It had been some time since Lark had seen true darkness. There was always a ribbon of moonlight or a hint of stars.

But this was a void.

Exhaling a shaky breath, Lark descended the stone steps. Hazel trailed behind, her hand soft against Lark's back. It must have been to keep aware of her.

When they reached the base layer of the fortress, Hazel grunted in displeasure. "For fuck's sake. This is ridiculous."

There was a rustling of fabric, the unmistakable strike of a flint, and a spark that illuminated Hazel's face as the torch caught with the hint of a flame. Her expression was drawn, as if annoyed she had to resort to something as silly as a light source. Wordlessly, she handed it to Lark, somehow sensing she needed it more than she did.

Lark held the torch out, turning to face each cell she passed. Terrified of what she'd find.

Unable to stop herself, Lark called out to him. "Gavriel?"

"Lark?" Gavriel's low voice rang out from the end of the room. On numb legs, Lark hurried toward the sound, heart climbing up her throat.

A set of hands braced the bars. Hands she'd recognize anywhere. Hands she'd seen commit violence and beauty. In the furthest cell of that filthy stone dungeon, Gavriel leaned as far as he could to catch a glimpse of her.

"Gavriel!" she cried, nearly dropping the torch. Her hand immediately found its way into his.

His large callused hand gripped her tightly. "I thought I imagined it today. But you came." His voice was hoarse.

"Of course I did. I couldn't—" Lark froze, unsure of what to say. Instead, she let her eyes drag over his face, searching every feature. His dark green eyes, flecked with gold. His impossibly sharp jaw. The scar that trailed down his cheek. Her favorite scar that bisected his lip. He was here, he was whole. Filthy, covered in blood and skies knew what else, but he was alive. "Even if things have changed, I had to find you."

Gavriel's expression turned bewildered. "What are you talking about?"

The path leading to this moment was one fraught with worry and fear. Worry over his safety. Fear she would be too late. But now, a yawning chasm of possibility stretched before them. It mattered not to her that they'd severed the soul bond, but what of him?

A few heartbeats passed in silence, save for the sound of metal clicking and scraping as Hazel deftly worked to pick the lock to his cell.

Gavriel's face seemed frozen in confusion.

"Fancy meeting you here, huh Pearson?" Hazel said.

Gavriel startled, as if he hadn't noticed Hazel kneeling beside Lark. "Hazel? How did you…" He trailed off, gaze darting back to Lark's face. His brow wrinkled.

With a click of the tumblers and a satisfied sigh, Hazel tugged the door open. The hinges groaned their protest at Gavriel's freedom. "I was in town anyway, hoping to win a few coins on the fights." She snatched the torch from Lark. "Seeing you is merely a fringe benefit."

If Gavriel had a retort, he kept it to himself, choosing instead to gather Lark into his arms. She went willingly, pressing her head against his chest. A sense of resonance rang through her body.

Lark tilted her head, desperate to see his face. Gavriel stared down at her, a small smile playing on his mouth. Skies, but the way he looked at her.

"Now, what were you saying had changed?"

"Gavriel, I…" The words died in Lark's throat. But what could she say? She drugged them by accident with a tonic that effectively severed their soul bond? What if the tonic temporarily weakened them while the magic took hold, causing his ease of capture? If the severed bond wasn't enough to hinder his feelings, that detail surely would.

"Is now really the best time for this?" Hazel cut in, impatience lacing her tone. "Perhaps you might defer this moment to when we're under an open sky instead of layers of stone."

Gavriel narrowed his eyes at Hazel before tilting Lark's chin and sealing his mouth over hers.

Fire instantly erupted in Lark's belly, igniting a yearning she'd been terrified they'd lost without the bond. His mouth was hot and demanding in its pursuit. With eager fingers, she clutched his filthy clothes, tugging him closer. His grip on her chin tightened before he released it to cup the back of her neck. Pressed against him, heartbeat to heartbeat, Lark realized what a fool she was.

Fate be damned. This man belonged to her, and she to him.

Lark pulled away from his dizzying kiss, still wrapped tightly in his arms. "We should go," she said with a shaky breath.

Gavriel frowned, but released her with a nod. "You're right. If they catch you here, I don't know what they'll do."

"I do!" Hazel said cheerfully as she marched ahead toward the stairs. "They'll string her up by her toes and peel her skin off." She grinned. "After they've each had a turn plundering her depths."

"Fucking abyss, Hazel." Gavriel ran a hand down his face.

Lark hooked Gavriel's arm around her shoulders. He staggered along beside her, only allowing a fraction of his weight to rest on her. Lark tightened her grip on his wrist, her other arm she wrapped around his waist. She darted a glance down to his thigh, where they had indeed treated and bandaged it. Crudely, but it would hold.

Gavriel followed her line of sight, smirking when he glanced down at his wound. "I didn't have someone as skilled as Langford sew me up. He'd at least have made the stitches uniform."

Lark shook her head. "We could all use Langford and Daciana right about now."

"Alistair?"

"Eh."

Gavriel laughed, wincing. Hazel waited at the bottom of the steps, one hand on her hip, the other held the torch out to the side. "No, by all means. Take your time and have a friendly chat. There's no rush."

Lark glared at her. "You could help me. That might move things along."

"I'm the lookout, besides if we get caught, I need a clean getaway."

Lark rolled her eyes, tugging Gavriel back as he attempted to pull away and limp on his own.

"I'm slowing you down," Gavriel said, bracing a hand on the stone as he tried again to take the first step on his own.

"You're the reason we're here," Lark said with a hiss, anchoring her arm around his waist. "Stop making this harder than it needs to be."

Hazel doused the torch in a nearby bucket, which, judging by the smell, was filled with human waste. Plunging them into darkness. No more glib retorts passed their lips. Under the cover of the deepest shadows, they became silent as wraiths.

Lark and Gavriel crept up the stairs, keeping close to Hazel, or at least Lark hoped she was close. It was like she was blindfolded. The darkness pressed on her, weighty and smothering.

When they reached the summit, thin shards of moonlight cut across the sandstone floor, illuminating their path. Hazel strode forward, determined in her gait yet silent while Lark and Gavriel ambled along. They needed to hurry. How many moments had passed since Hazel incapacitated the guards?

The sound of voices carried down the hallway. Hazel froze, shooting a look at Lark that she couldn't quite make out in the dark.

One heartbeat.

Two heartbeats.

Hazel darted to the window, yanking her lithe body through. Lark watched in horror, bracing Gavriel against her.

This wasn't happening. Hazel couldn't leave them like this.

"Hazel," Lark hissed.

But all that greeted her was silent darkness. The coward had actually abandoned them at the first sign of trouble.

Gavriel shrugged out of her hold, beginning to shove her toward the window. "Lark," he hissed, "get out of here."

"Gavriel, stop," Lark said, elbowing out of his hold.

Before she could wrestle him toward the window ahead of her, a deep voice curled out of the shadows.

"Yes, Gavriel. I believe the time for games is at its end."

Three figures stepped into view, faceless in the dim corridor. Three on two, in a narrow hall, was a risk. Especially since Gavriel was unarmed and injured.

"Let her go. She has nothing to do with this," Gavriel said, voice firm and commanding. As if they weren't completely at the mercy of his jailors.

"In due time, boy." The shadowed voice was patient, amused even. "Come, we have much to discuss."

Lark threw a desperate glance at Gavriel. A pained look flashed across his face before it smoothed into stone. He grabbed her hand, his rough calluses pressed against her palm.

Whatever they faced, at least it was together.

CHAPTER TWENTY-FOUR

LANGFORD

Captain Ingemar's stunning face, deep brown from both her dark olive complexion and hours in direct sun on deck, remained impassive as Langford and Alistair walked across the dock. Their footfalls thudded against the weathered wood. Captain Ingemar's narrow brown eyes—so dark they almost appeared black—regarded them with little interest.

"Ingemar, you dazzling creature," Alistair began with a half bow that ended in a hiss of pain through his teeth. Langford peered at Alistair's side to check if he pulled his stitches.

"Captain," Ingemar bit out as she lifted her narrow chin. Her thick, black curls hung heavy over her shoulders, teased by the wind, and blowing across her cheek. The brim of her high cocked hat slowly drew back the shadows on her lovely face, revealing her brows drawn in disapproval. "Last time you were aboard The Jewel, something of mine went missing."

Langford exhaled a tight breath, glaring at Alistair. Was it possible for the man to go anywhere without forging enemies out of old allies?

Alistair glanced over his shoulder at Ingemar's ship, *The Savage Jewel*. At the snarling Lion figurehead. "Curious. It almost sounded like you said it belonged to you." He turned back to regard Ingemar with one of his devilish smirks. "And we both know that isn't true."

"I won it. The rules of fair play state that you forfeited ownership." Ingemar gripped the golden handle of her cutlass that gleamed in the sunlight.

"It held far more sentimental value than its weight in coin."

"A man willing to part with his belonging in a game of cards can't claim sentimental value." She wrinkled her long, elegant nose in amusement.

Alistair's jaw ticked. His hand flexed by his side before he jammed it into his pocket and whipped out the familiar compass.

Langford's cheeks burned at the sight. He'd seen it resting atop Ingemar's maps in her quarters when he'd gone to speak to her about her pirating routes. *Trade routes,* he mentally corrected. Langford knew it was the very gift he'd given Alistair that one year he'd discovered Alistair's precise nameday. Seeing it so freely given away had turned his stomach to lead. And now Langford knew he had gambled it away.

Alistair's pale hand clenched around the worn and filthy brass compass. "What do you want for it?"

Ingemar's full lips parted to reveal straight, white teeth. "An apology. And you'd better make it a good one."

Alistair took a deep breath. "*Captain* Ingemar, illustrious goddess of the sea, dusky rose among thorns—"

"Ugh, I can't stomach this," Ingemar said, taking a step back. Either she was preparing to flee or brandish her blade. Knowing her, it would be the edge of her cutlass.

"I am truly, truly, sorry." Alistair bowed his head, dark hair hanging in his eyes. "I never should have been arrogant enough to place something this important in the hands of fate."

The heat from Langford's cheeks crept down his neck as his stomach flipped.

Alistair continued, "It matters more than any earthly possession that's ever passed through my hands."

Langford swallowed thickly, palms pricking with sweat. The air between them felt suddenly charged. Tension snapped into place, pulling taut with warning. He found himself unable to look away. Needing to do something with his hands, he adjusted the strap of his leather satchel to sit higher on his shoulder.

"I said make it good, not dramatic," Ingemar's voice cleaved through the static-charged air, releasing Langford from the hold of Alistair's stare. Langford exhaled a shaky breath, unsure of why his legs suddenly felt ready to give out. Ingemar grinned, eyes twinkling with delight. "All right boys, off you go. Make yourselves comfortable."

Langford shuffled forward. His shoulder grazed Alistair's, and it was impossible not to notice the jolt of energy he felt at the contact. Langford clenched his fist, wincing at the pain in his hand. He cursed his foolishness at forgetting his harrowing injury.

Alistair only seemed to notice his tight expression. He placed a hand on Langford's shoulder, oblivious to what his innocent touches did to him. "Are you in pain?"

"I'll manage," Langford said stiffly. Alistair didn't appear convinced, but he relented, letting his hand fall away from his shoulder.

Langford mourned the distance immediately.

"Alistair, I almost forgot," Ingemar called to them.

They both turned to regard the stunning captain.

"Paw through my things again, and I'll relieve your cock from betwixt your legs."

Langford glanced over to find Alistair unconsciously shielding the body part in question, his eyes wide with terror.

"Enjoy your stay!" Ingemar called cheerfully, before marching past them and straight up the wooden ramp to her ship.

Alistair seemed frozen in place.

"This can't be the first time someone threatened you with phallic dismemberment." Come to think of it, not receiving some sort of threat of bodily harm was highly uncommon where Alistair was concerned.

"No," Alistair admitted, face ashen. "But she's the first who'd actually do it."

LANGFORD RAN a hand through his increasingly untidy hair, scanning tired eyes yet again over the same page. His candle, once tall, now dwindled from the hours it spent illuminating the ancient tome for his research. His room was private, as Alistair had found his own accommodations. It should have helped him concentrate, but it was too quiet. The gentle rocking of the ship, even in his cramped cabin, was irritatingly peaceful. He needed alertness, not rhythmic lulling.

Alistair had kept his word and left him to work without distraction. Who knew the next time he'd have this much time, uninterrupted by kidnapping, threats of rape and dismemberment, actual dismemberment, and brushes with death? Langford glanced down at his right hand resting loosely beside the weathered pages. At the padded and wrapped shape of the rest of his finger.

With a sigh, Langford straightened in the hard, unforgiving seat. He arched his lower back, trying to stretch out the twinge aching above his tailbone as he glanced about his temporary quarters. He'd been fortunate enough to receive a room with a writing desk, a simple enough piece of maple furniture that adequately held his stack of books and papers, a narrow bed tucked into the opposite corner, and a small round window he discovered actually opened. A sliver of pale light asserted its place across the floor. The heavy scent of brine and night air swept through the room and occasionally ruffled his pages. Langford didn't mind. Each gust of cold air livened his senses, waking his mind when all he wanted to do was sleep.

Perhaps some time on deck would serve him well. The idea of getting out of his room and stretching his legs was too tempting to ignore.

The floorboards creaked underfoot as Langford made his way down the hall and up the wide staircase. It was quiet on the main deck, save for the whipping wind that skirted off the churning waters and the gentle groan of the ship. The vastness of both sky and sea settled something tight in his chest.

Langford stepped up to the rail, leaning his elbows against the cool wood. Amidst the dark night, the clouds had parted to allow the moon its rightful place looking over the ocean, casting silvery ripples over impossibly black depths. Each time the wind blew, the reflection scattered, sending fragments of the moon across the dark sea.

"There you are."

Langford turned to find Alistair, stripped of his usual attention seeking wardrobe in favor of a white linen tunic and dark breeches exposing his muscular calves and bare feet.

"Where are your boots?"

Alistair draped over the rail at Langford's side, releasing a gusty sigh. "I'm convinced Ingemar cheats at cards."

"You didn't learn your lesson the last time?"

"Come, now. I never make the same mistake twice. I'm far more creative than that." Alistair reached into his pocket and pulled out the compass Langford had scoured the markets to find. Beneath the cracked glass of its face, the needle dipped and circled in search of north. Langford had saved every spare coin he could to afford the bronze piece as a surprise gift, and Alistair's face had lit up with joy when he gave it to him. Langford carried the memory of that smile in the months that followed, keeping him warm on the nights Alistair sought company for his bed. He may have given them his time and his nights, but Langford claimed that smile.

"How goes the diligent researching?" Alistair's voice pulled Langford from his thoughts. His vivid green eyes burned against the shadows, undimmed even by darkness.

"I can't focus." It was true. Langford couldn't keep his mind occupied on the task for over ten minutes without wandering. Exhaustion had eroded his mental fortitude until all he had left was a fleeting awareness.

"I could help, you know," Alistair said, his voice barely carrying over an abrupt gale. He was picking at the raw skin just beneath his cuticle, a habit Langford recognized as nerves. But what did Alistair have to be nervous about?

"I'd never condemn you to such a punishment."

The corner of Alistair's mouth lifted. The sight was enough to make Langford hyper aware of his own skin. Alistair was close enough to touch. All Langford needed to do was reach out…

"I'm fucking freezing." Alistair shivered as he ran a hand through his thick, black hair. Langford followed the action, noting the wide neck of his tunic and how it exposed the top of his chest.

Langford nodded, mouth dry. "You should head inside."

Alistair turned the force of his gaze on Langford, and the effect was dizzying. "I want you to join me."

Langford gripped the rail, not trusting his legs to keep him upright. They'd shared a tent before. Even a room in an inn to save on coin. But they had separate quarters aboard Ingemar's ship, and this felt decidedly different.

"Or rather, I'd like to join you. I think the illustrious captain hasn't quite forgiven me." Alistair arched a dark brow. "She's relegated me to the bulkhead with a rickety hammock."

Oh. So that's what it was. He wanted a more comfortable space to relax in. All the tension fled Langford's body. He almost sagged in relief, even as his chest ached.

"You can go let yourself in. Would you rather I take your room?" It didn't matter where Langford went, he wouldn't find sleep tonight.

Alistair regarded Langford with a puzzled expression. "I want to join you in your quarters." He bounced on the balls of his bare feet, rubbing his arm for warmth. "Do I have to beg?" A dark grin slashed across his face. "Because I'm more than happy to oblige."

Heat bloomed on Langford's cheeks, dipping down his throat and setting his chest on fire. His tongue felt too big for his mouth. He should say something. Anything. Words were always easy for him. He could spin them any way he wanted. He could dazzle Alistair with his eloquence if he could only open his mouth and spit them out.

"Very well, then."

Ill-equipped with words, Langford hoped his swell of courage was enough. He turned, all too aware of Alistair's close footsteps trailing behind him. The wind and the sea roared in his ears as Langford led the way back down the stairs.

The door opened beneath his shaky touch. Langford swallowed

against his thick throat. He'd lain above and beneath enough bodies to know his way around pleasure.

He knew why his hands trembled, and his stomach fluttered with anticipation, fear, and excitement.

This was Alistair.

The sound of the door closing was loud and resolute. Langford turned to find Alistair watching him as he leaned against the door, dark hair hanging in his eyes. His familiar brand of upkeep shadowed his jaw, and Langford had the sudden urge to run his hand along it.

Instead, Langford smoothed his hand down the front of his tunic, worried he appeared rumpled and unremarkable. That Alistair would take a closer look at him and laugh, realizing what a silly notion it was to find Langford anything more than a source of amusement. That Alistair would evaporate and reveal this moment to be fraudulent, a vision cooked up by his own selfish desire and lack of sleep.

Alistair's stare could very well set Langford on fire for the heat in his eyes. He lifted his hand, crooking his finger in an unmistakable gesture. "Come here."

All those little thoughts scattered until all that remained was Langford's incessant need. As natural as breathing, he stepped toward Alistair. Like he'd been walking toward this moment since the day Alistair found him on the road, trudging away from a title he didn't want, a home he'd never belonged in, his weary pace leading him toward something he couldn't identify.

Langford drew close enough he could smell the sweet hint of vanilla and spices that permeated the air around him. That and something sharp and distinctly Alistair. Langford ran his gaze over his face. Alistair's emerald green eyes, the jawline he refused to shave clean, the small scar above his eyebrow.

Alistair drew a sharp breath. His warm, calloused hand found Langford's neck, thumb running gently against his jaw. His eyes searched Langford's face, desperate in their pursuit, as if he, too, was utterly starved for this.

This breath. A heated mingling upon the precipice. This moment of exquisite agony as Langford waited to taste Alistair's kiss. The beautiful torture of a heart filling and yearning in utter silence.

Langford pressed a featherlight kiss to his lips. The heat of Alistair's mouth sent a wave of dizziness through him. Before his mind had time to catch up, Langford sealed his lips over Alistair's, swallowing his guttural response. The sound shot straight through him, making his stomach flip. His hand fisted Alistair's loose tunic, clutching for dear life as the liquid heat of his mouth made standing a feat of great difficulty.

Alistair's hand still gripped Langford's neck, a firm pressure that kept him from pulling away.

As if he'd ever want to.

Alistair's arm found the small of Langford's back, tugging him to press against him fully. Evidence of Alistair's arousal was hot and hard against his thigh. Langford pressed into him, instinct taking over. Alistair growled, the slide of his mouth turning near violent, as he spun them to press Langford against the door. The scrape of his jaw stung, and yet Langford was desperate for more, as if he couldn't get close enough. Alistair pulled back to regard him with a ferocious expression, stealing the breath from Langford's lungs.

"What did I do to deserve you?"

Before Langford had a chance to formulate a response, Alistair invaded his mouth once more. He tasted sweet and sharp, and Langford was utterly addicted to the liquid slide of his scorching kiss.

Alistair gently pulled Langford away from the door, steering him toward the tiny bed. Slowly, he lowered him onto the mattress, climbing over him and refusing to release his mouth from his punishing kiss.

Langford tugged at the laces of Alistair's breeches, cursing his injured hand.

Alistair finally broke away to laugh, low and deep. "Langford," Alistair whispered, pressing soft, quick kisses to his mouth and jaw. Langford squirmed beneath him, seeking some sort of friction. "Let me make you feel good."

Langford stilled, a slow creeping shame threatening to spread over him. Did Alistair think he owed this to him? That enough years spent pining for someone somehow earned them some form of release?

Alistair pulled back to regard him with a curious expression. "I can always tell when I've somehow said the wrong thing," he said thoughtfully. "You make the face you're making now, it's all weighing my words before you react." Alistair rested on his elbow. "Perhaps I should just say what I mean. I want to make you tremble and cry my name." Alistair's sensual smirk graced his sinful mouth. "I like the sound of my name, and I have a feeling it'll sound like fucking music from you. So it's selfish, really."

Langford choked on the air that his already tight throat struggled with. But how did Alistair always render him impossibly speechless? Langford wet his lips, searching for an equally titillating response.

"That would be permissible."

Alistair laughed, the rich timbre coming from a place deep in his chest. He ran a hand to the laces at the top of Langford's tunic, tugging them loose. Langford helped Alistair pull it over his head. His skin blazed, and the freedom of shedding that layer almost made him shiver in delight.

Alistair's fingers crawled their way down the flat pane of Langford's stomach, slowly descending to the waistband of his breeches. His eyes sought Langford's, searching for permission.

It had been ages since Langford had been touched in any real way. He had indulged in the occasional copulation with fleeting company on their travels. But clothes were hardly shed, and it was the quick heat of a body. Nothing like this. Laying here, still wearing his breeches and small clothes, Langford hadn't felt this naked in a long time. He nodded encouragingly, afraid he might go up in flame if Alistair didn't get his hands on him.

Alistair's hand slipped beneath Langford's trousers, gripping him both firmly and gently. Possessive with a careful reverence. Langford groaned, unable to halt the sound. Alistair's eyes never left his face, watching with his lips parted, a glassy expression on his face as he worked Langford with his skillfully adept touch. Langford fisted the blanket with his uninjured hand.

Alistair leaned forward to catch Langford's mouth in a messy kiss, before he lowered himself to eye level with his breeches. Still steadily working him, he yanked his waistband down, exposing him.

Langford tossed his arm over his face, shielding himself from seeing whatever Alistair was about to do. A growl and a firm tug on his arm was the only warning Langford got that Alistair was displeased by the notion he wanted to hide.

"Don't you dare," Alistair said, voice dangerously low. "I want your eyes on me."

Langford's cheeks inflamed, and he nodded.

Holding Langford's gaze, Alistair lowered his mouth over him. The hot sensation of a tightly sealed mouth—Alistair's mouth—had Langford tossing his head back with a hiss. Remembering himself, he brought his increasingly hazy vision to watch Alistair. To watch his hands and mouth obliterate any sense he had left.

Every nerve in his body flared—a fire with no chance of abating without release. He threaded his fingers in Alistair's hair, and his answering groan shot straight through him.

"Alistair," he whimpered, surprised he found his voice. Alistair doubled down his efforts, pressing Langford even deeper as he consumed his diminishing sanity.

Langford tightened his hold on Alistair's hair, unable to stop from crying out. The base of his spine tingled, and spasms of heat fluttered through him as he trembled beneath Alistair's wicked mouth. Alistair held him there until the last wave subsided. Running his tongue in vicious thorough pursuit, before he finally relented.

Langford laid there, panting and slicked with a sheen of sweat, as Alistair slowly crept up his body. His mouth curved in an indulgent smile, a self-satisfied look of contentment as he gazed down at Langford.

"Why didn't we do this ages ago?"

Langford huffed a quiet laugh. "Because you were determined to plunge into every other warm body that permitted you entry." It appeared climaxing helped Langford find his words again.

Alistair laughed. "Right, that. Well, I hope you're not about to fall asleep on me." His expression turned serious. "Unless… if this was all you wished for, we can stop. We can always stop."

Langford cupped Alistair's jaw, searching his face and finding nothing but fond affection. "I want you to stay, and if you wish to continue—"

"I'm not nearly done," Alistair whispered, before lowering himself to press against Langford and claiming his mouth in a soft kiss. "I will never be done with you."

Langford sank into his warmth and tugged at Alistair's tunic. Removing his clothes was decidedly faster. There was no more hesitation, only an urgency to feel skin against skin.

Alistair smoothed Langford's hair out of his face. "I promise to be gentle with you."

"I just want you." In whatever way he could have him. Every dark corner, every jagged edge. Langford wanted Alistair, just as he was.

Alistair smiled; the sight banished the shadows from his obscenely handsome face. He rose over him, allowing Langford a chance to appreciate his full, naked form unabashedly. His golden-brown skin glinted in the warm candlelight, casting his form like a painting of a paragon. The sharp muscles of his perfectly crafted abdomen, his thick muscular thighs bracketing his hips. The man was sin incarnate.

And he was his.

Alistair angled a brow, regarding Langford with a knowing look. "Admiring the view?" He curled a firm bicep, striking an exaggerated pose.

Langford snorted, shaking his head and refusing to feel abashed for being caught ogling him. "You certainly think highly of yourself."

"As a matter of fact, right now I feel like a king. Want to know why?"

"Hmm… because that's how you regard yourself every day?" Langford kept his voice steady, even as he shivered beneath Alistair's finger running down his stomach.

"Because I finally have you." He punctuated his words by gripping Langford with exquisite pressure. Langford gasped, falling back to lie flat on the bed. "And now that I do," Alistair said, running lazy strokes up and down, "I'm never letting go."

Langford opened his mouth to respond, but only a whimper came out. Alistair's fingers wandered as he readied him gently, a featherlight touch so full of care and adoration, it made Langford's chest tight. And when Alistair aligned himself with his entrance and slowly sank in, Langford cried out in feverish pleasure. Alistair's name was a prayer of devotion falling from his lips.

Alistair growled, driving deeper as he ran trembling hands down Langford's body. As he pressed desperate kisses to his neck and raked his teeth over sensitive skin.

Langford found Alistair's hand and threaded their fingers, the last piece needing joining. Alistair's eyes blazed, a fire so fierce his gaze was searing, and he tightened his grip on Langford's hand, bringing it to press against his chest. His heart pounded beneath Langford's palm, and their movements slowed.

There was nothing else. No fear, or shame, or doubt. Only the achingly tender touch of Langford's greatest desire. When his body found new heights to plummet from, Alistair held him through every wave, whispering unthinkable promises against his skin.

For once, Langford dared to believe them.

CHAPTER TWENTY-FIVE

DACIANA

"So you turned Lark away with little more than a vague history lesson?" Daciana had maintained a polite tone—until Inerys revealed just how little help she'd been to Lark and Gavriel. A fact she could have quickly revealed without the long-winded tale.

Inerys huffed an impatient breath. "I told her the truth about the type of magic it takes to restore the barriers, the same magic used to create them."

"Vitas Conjuring," Kenna said with a frown. She kept her dark stare fixed on the mismatched wooden floorboards, refusing to meet Daciana's eye. Daciana wiped her hands on the tan leather breeches she'd borrowed. They didn't fit quite right, snug in the wrong places.

"Where do you suppose Lark would go upon hearing she needs a lost and forbidden power?" Inerys rested her chin on her delicate hand, lifting her chipped teacup that had long since stopped steaming to her lips.

Where wouldn't she go? Daciana drummed her fingers against her knee. Lark would go to unfathomable lengths in pursuit of what she wanted, especially if guilt played a factor. But she wouldn't be rash enough to travel to Koval in search of the Great Library. Not when

Langford was just returning from that very destination, research in hand. Perhaps he'd already found something of note. There was also Amara, dutifully searching for answers on their behalf. If only Lark had left another message, a hint regarding her next step. Lark knew Daciana would come looking for answers upon reading she'd gone to Inerys. So why would she leave without another word?

"What else?" Daciana lifted her chin. "What else did she ask you?"

Inerys lowered her cup with a soft clink of the porcelain. "She asked me about severing the soul bond between her and Gavriel."

Daciana merely blinked at her, unsure of what to think.

Kenna laughed. "In the middle of all this, she's worried about a soul bond?" She shook her head, lifting her own teacup and mismatched saucer. "I wish I had that focus."

"What do you mean, soul bond?" Daciana had never even heard of such a thing, and Lark certainly hadn't mentioned it.

Inerys sniffed. "It would seem our favorite Reaper is bound by more than affection to the man that follows her steps like a tethered and domesticated little beast."

Daciana scoffed. Though it was an accurate description. "And she wanted you to cut the ties that bind them?"

Inerys nodded.

Of course, Lark did. She'd been answering to fate long enough to reject anything that didn't stem from free will. She likely didn't even trust her affections to be her own, so long as that bond was intact.

"And did you?"

Inerys sighed, adjusting the skirt of her auburn dress. "I might have done something… unethical."

Kenna grinned, and the wooden bench she shared with Daciana groaned as she scooted closer. "Oh, do tell."

"Well, soul bonds aren't exactly common knowledge. I daresay you'd be hard-pressed to find many who believe in their existence— outside of romantic fiction, that is."

"Sure, sure," Kenna said, unaware that her thigh had ghosted against Daciana's.

Daciana clenched her teeth.

"It's tricky business, ancient magic. One might say it's impossible to sever a bond forged between two souls," Inerys said.

"Did you tell her as much?" Daciana had little patience left for the witch's particular brand of storytelling.

"Not exactly," Inerys said with a sheepish smile. "She looked utterly miserable, and you should have seen her man! He was like this lost little spirit haunting her. I knew she'd never be content with just accepting the bond as it was. She'd never believe me that forging the tether didn't determine their feelings so much as merely draw them to one another."

Daciana eyed her carefully. "So what did you do?"

Inerys shrugged. "I might have… given her my least favorite cooking wine laced with a sleeping draught."

Silence hovered between the three women for several breaths.

"Classic Inerys," Kenna said with a chuckle.

Daciana pressed her fingertips between her brows. "How strong was the sleeping draught?"

"Strong enough to grant them a deep sleep 'til morning. They probably woke up well-rested, and ready to seize the day. They should thank me, really."

Daciana exhaled a slow even breath, crossing her arms and leveling Inerys with the full weight of her scrutinizing stare. "Consuming a sleeping draught on the road is a terrible danger. Who knows what they might have slept through? Who or what might have stumbled upon them while they were unconscious?" Was this why Lark hadn't written to her following her visit to Inerys? If any harm came to her from the witch's meddling, she'd dismantle her cottage stone by stone until there was nothing left but a pile of rubble.

Inerys' cheeks tinged a lovely pink that somehow made her appear girlish rather than ashamed. "I assumed they would stay at the inn. It isn't far from here."

"They never made it back." Daciana was assuming, because if they had, Lark surely would have left her an updated message. They could have moved on without resting another night at the inn, but unless she had given them a genuine lead, they should have headed back toward the port to await the others. Walden Inn was an easy stop along the way —it made little sense.

"Oh." Inerys had the good sense to look regretful. "Well, how was I supposed to know? I thought I was being helpful."

"Yes, being lied to and drugged is such a big help," Kenna said, rolling her eyes, but a small smile played on her lips.

They could speculate about Lark and Gavriel's whereabouts all they wanted, but unless Daciana's change was imminent, she couldn't track them. Not after the rain they'd had a day ago. Any trail her human eyes could pick up would have washed away. Before she could deal with that worry, there was one more thing to ask of the witch.

Daciana pulled the faded cloth from her pocket, gripping it tightly in her fist. "Can you perform a locator spell?" She placed the material in Inerys' outstretched hand.

"I can…" Inerys began cautiously. "But it's hit or miss, and the ingredients for such a spell are scarce." She turned it over, examining it with detached interest. "I'm assuming this belongs to the individual in question. It's not Lark's, is it?"

"No." But perhaps they should perform the spell to find Lark instead. Only she had nothing that belonged to her except… Apple. Daciana wasn't familiar enough to know if any harm would come to the horse or if it was even possible to complete the spell with a living creature. And if the ingredients were as rare as Inerys claimed, should they allocate them to finding Lark instead? She could take care of herself… wherever they were, she would survive. And Gavriel would sooner die than let harm come to her.

"We think it belongs to a murderer," Kenna said, lip curling in disgust. "The children of Stormfair dwindle thanks to this bastard."

Inerys nodded, holding the cloth between careful fingers. "I'll do what I can. But it will take time to gather what I need. I already have a raven feather. It's the wolf mushroom that will be tricky to find. No matter. I'll track one down. Where can I contact you when I'm ready?"

"How long will it take?" Daciana still needed to meet Alistair and Langford at Emeraude Port when they docked. Lark had better be there, too.

"I do not work on a timetable. It will take however long it takes."

That wouldn't do. They couldn't risk missing Ingemar's ship. Daciana stood, and her borrowed leathers creaked with the action. "I can't wait an indeterminate amount of time. We'll return with the others, unless Kenna wishes to stay." There was nothing tying her to Daciana's side. She was free to do as she pleased.

Inerys stared up at her from where she still sat, her dark eyes narrowed in scrutiny. An unmistakable look of calculation on her face. Kenna's knee bounced as she glared at the floor.

Not waiting for a formal dismissal, Daciana stepped out of the room, seeking solace in Inerys' forest of a bedroom. She'd draped her dark ram leather leggings and deep brown cuirass over the thickest branch of the tree that sprouted along the corner of Inerys' room. Her cloak and tunic hung from a lower branch. She'd change quickly. Her clothes were probably dry enough from how long their conversation took.

Kenna made no move to deny her wish to stay.

Daciana pushed the thought away and stepped out of Inerys' pants, standing clad in only her breastband and smallclothes. She turned uncertainly to the looking glass that hung on the wall framed in ivy. She bore new scars. That was to be expected. Her dark skin was taut over firm muscles, and her thick hair hung in wild waves around her face and over her shoulders. Daciana met her own hazel eyes, refusing to look away.

Her mother used to sit her down to stare at her own reflection.

"You are never to lower your eyes first. You command every room you enter."

There was no vanity in this task. It was an exercise of control, of patience. Of precision and fortitude. To look upon one's own face without fear. Without shame. Shame was for those who begged for scraps instead of demanding their feast. For those who relied on another's opinion to make it in this blighted world. Daciana's mother always warned her shame was the most desirable accessory a woman could bear. So instead of desirable, Daciana became so much more. And even after her mother was long gone, she practiced looking upon her own face in the mirror. Of staring down her own weaknesses until they vanished from her eyes. Her pack didn't need to want her. She was next in line to be Alpha, and could take her pick of any man for breeding purposes when the time came. No, they needed to fear her. To fall under the weight of her dominance as easily as breathing. Her ascension to Alpha was imminent. Her father had prepared everything. Even Lyall had sworn his loyalty as her second. Every piece was falling into place.

And then she found Kenna.

Daciana turned from her reflection, yanking her still damp clothing from the thick branches. As she dressed, she carefully avoided the mirror.

When she emerged, Inerys' voice abruptly halted. Both she and Kenna seemed to stiffen in their postures. Daciana narrowed her eyes as she tugged her belt into place and stepped into the parlor. They'd obviously been talking about something that wasn't intended for her ears. Daciana hadn't heard even a murmur from Inerys' room—the witch must have certain privacy spells in place. The sort that not even Daciana's hearing could overcome.

"I'm heading back to the inn. Kenna, stay if you wish, but I need to find Lark."

Kenna's pale face pinched in confusion before smoothing into understanding. "No, I'm ready to go." She and Inerys stood facing each other with matching expressions of significance, like there was something weighty and important between them. Kenna pulled Inerys into a soft embrace. "Thank you, I'll keep in touch."

Inerys stepped away, laughing humorlessly. "That's more of a threat coming from you." Her hand found its way to Kenna's arm. "Be careful."

Kenna smirked. "You know better than to expect that from me."

Inerys planted a quick kiss on Kenna's cheek. "Off you go then." Her dark eyes found Daciana's. She offered a quick nod in acknowledgement.

Daciana returned the gesture, feeling hollow.

It mattered little whatever connection Kenna and Inerys still maintained. There were far more important things at stake. Like finding Lark, preventing the fall of the world, locating a Vitas Conjuror, and finding the monster responsible for slaying the children of Stormfair. One step at a time. First, Daciana had to walk out of this blazing cottage that seemed to grow smaller with each passing breath. Then she could figure out the rest.

One step at a time.

KENNA PACED the modest room they shared at the Walden Inn.

Daciana sat crossed legged on the narrow bed, sporting her most comfortable tunic and breeches. Her fingers itched to sharpen their blades, but she'd only recently done so and they maintained their edge. An impatient energy hummed in the air. With Lark's lead turning into a dead end, Daciana felt... listless.

Kenna's white gauzy tunic reached halfway down her bare, pale thighs. Her inky black hair spilled over her shoulders and down her back. Her bare feet tread the same path over and over as her hands remained perched on her hips. Nothing about her expression revealed if she knew how alluring her lack of coverage was, so Daciana made sure to only appreciate the view in her periphery.

"Dac, I—" Kenna stalled mid sentence, shaking her head. "No, never mind."

Daciana turned her attention to the wool blanket, running her fingers across the soft and somewhat oily surface. Her newly cleaned hands from a long soak in the bath were nearly unrecognizable. The dirt caked beneath her nails had almost seemed a permanent feature.

Kenna dropped to the bed, Daciana bounced from the weight. "We need to talk."

"That much is clear."

"It's about something Inerys mentioned."

"Ah." Daciana shifted her focus to the way Kenna's tunic had hitched up her thigh. For once, the expanse of pale skin seemed an easier distraction to bear. Thick, white scars slashed across her skin.

Those were new. The overwhelming urge to trace them washed over Daciana, before she cleared her throat, and forced the thought away. "What did the witch say?"

"It was about Life Magic."

Daciana flicked her gaze to Kenna's face. Kenna worried her bottom lip between her teeth. The sight might have caused a familiar flutter in Daciana's stomach were it not for her deep brown eyes, tight with worry.

"Is there a reason you're drawing out the suspense?" Daciana spoke as gently as she could, but her annoyance won out.

Kenna blew out a sharp breath, running her fingers through her long black hair. "The way she explained it…" Kenna swung her leg that dangled off the bed. That girl physically could not hold still. The wide neck of her tunic slipped over her shoulder, revealing more pale skin and silvery scars. "Like manifesting power through the essence of another's life."

Daciana froze, holding dangerously still as Kenna's words sank beneath her skin. "What of it?" She already knew what Kenna would say.

"Sounds an awful lot like your ascension." Kenna swirled her finger in the loose fabric of her tunic, tightening it like a coiled snake until the very tip of her index finger was bright pink. "Or what little was shared with me after the fact."

Daciana hummed, letting her gaze drift to the woodgrains of the floorboards. A far safer focus since the conversation was heading for a downturn. "I'm not a witch, Kenna."

"Daciana." Kenna's voice was achingly soft. "What happened that day…"

"I don't want to talk about that." Daciana pushed off the bed and prowled around the room, pacing the increasingly cramped quarters. Why hadn't they made camp in the Emerald Woods? The stone walls of this room were far too close.

"You think I enjoy remembering it? You think this is pleasant for me?" She rose, stepping right into Daciana's path. Kenna's overpowering scent of fresh rain and sharp berries washed over her. "But pretending doesn't alter the past, Dac."

Daciana growled, shoving away from Kenna and aiming for the door. She didn't miss the flash of hurt that shone in her eyes.

Daciana needed air that didn't carry Kenna's scent. She needed to think in a space she wasn't filling. To quiet the storm that raged. Kenna always pushed. She didn't have the tact to know when it was too much.

Daciana fled down the stairs and through the empty dining room until the night greeted her. When she finally met the cool air, she sucked in a greedy breath. Exhaling a wisp of vapor, she knelt in the shadows by the crumbling stone wall that lined the road. Rubbing her eyes, she desperately tried to dispel the images that danced on the edge of her mind. A memory she wished to forget.

The smell of freshly baked sweet rolls. The air was heavy with burnt sugar and cinnamon. It was a gift from one of the pack mothers, a show of respect for what was to come. Her ascension. The ritual that granted Daciana the role as alpha. To follow in her father's footsteps as his sole heir. Her lineage guaranteed her supremacy. The royal blood of the wolf king scorched through her veins. Daciana was eager to complete the hunt. The blood spilled would seal her rule and ascend her to her greatest potential. It was her sacred duty to follow the scent marked by fate, to the kill that would solidify her place and grant her mastery of her power.

In the old days, they would wait until the moon was high. Blindfolded, she would walk the path, relying on her sense of smell alone. But times had changed, things were far less formal. Her father had even given her permission to sense out the trail early in the day, to practice before the Great Hunt commenced.

But when the path led to Kenna, the hunter she'd met and loved in secret—the girl whose kisses Daciana still tasted on her lips from mere hours ago—it was clear fate demanded the ultimate sacrifice. She turned from her destiny, and knew she would never complete the ritual and ascend. She would never be the alpha her mother promised she would be.

Daciana begged Kenna to leave. To take her grandmother and flee, lest her pack learn of hunters in the area. Especially since the Great Hunt had claimed her scent as the prize.

But Kenna never knew what was good for her and demanded Daciana come with them. To leave her pack behind and forge a new path by her side.

It was a fantasy, nothing more. But Daciana was young and foolish and came to believe the girl who tasted of forbidden fire. They tumbled to the forest floor, smothering laughter with heated kisses, worshiping every inch of skin. As if the depth of their affections would halt time.

Hours later, Daciana snuck into her home, grateful her father was out readying the feast for after the ceremony. She packed the few items that held sentimental value, her mother's silver ring—etched with two rival wolves snarling, and the leather cord her father made her. Daciana tucked the braided leather into her pocket and quickly began scrawling on the spare parchment. The least she could do was leave him a letter, begging him to understand. To find it in his heart to forgive her. To even come to respect her for choosing love over duty.

But love is ultimately a selfish act.

Daciana wended her way through the dark forest, a smile blooming on her face. The entire world was wide open for her and Kenna. A whole life awaited them.

Nothing would keep them apart. This thought fueled her courageous and foolish heart, propelling her faster to claim her love.

It was the smell that hit her first. Like meat cooking. And that sharp pungent scent of burning hair.

Daciana sprinted. There were no thoughts, no plans. Just a heavy, sinking dread that her legs refused to acknowledge.

When the trees parted, the grisly scene that lay before her should have emptied her gut onto the forest floor. Perhaps it would have offered a modicum of relief.

The charred remains of something distinctly human shaped roasted over a roaring fire. Her pack, her brethren, crowded around a wooden stake. Whatever was tied to it, she couldn't see over the broad shoulders of her brothers and sisters of the moon. They all wore their finest livery, the ceremonial garbs of silk and satin that wrapped around muscled bodies honed for power.

On steady legs, Daciana approached. Her father, her proud, noble king, stepped into view. His dark, handsome face wore a fierce expression of anguish. The Wolf King bore no crown, save for the tattoos that shone across his dark forehead. Stars and the crescent moon that almost appeared to glow upon his skin. The tattoo she would have proudly received if fate hadn't led them down this path. Stains marred his emerald green robes.

Blood.

She pushed past him, needing to know. Afraid of knowing.

Her pack brothers and sisters parted. If they wore expressions of anger, Daciana didn't notice.

Kenna's body hung limply from the wooden stake, her face hidden by the black curtain of her hair. Blood dripped over her boots, pooling on the ground and staining the pyre. The steady dripping against the branches and bramble they'd assembled was deafening.

It was a nightmare. A warning. To end things before they got this far. She'd wake up in Kenna's arms and face the harsh truth of the morning. She'd return to her pack, to her father and take up the mantle of alpha, and years later could wonder what happened to the girl with kisses like fire. She'd—

"Oh, child." Daciana's father spoke gently. "Look what you've done."

He had followed her when she scented the trail early in the day. Learned of her betrayal, her intent to flee rather than uphold her duty. And like a wolf stalking its prey, he had waited for Daciana to disappear long enough to sink his claws into the girl she loved, ripping away the life she foolishly dreamt could be hers.

Rage. A fiery pit of rage roared in Daciana's ears. Kenna's limp body steadily trickled blood from the bite and claw marks that had shredded her perfect, pale skin to ribbons.

Daciana couldn't think. She couldn't see.

She could only feel.

Feel the ease with which flesh shredded beneath her nails, her claws, her teeth. Feel the scalding flow of fresh blood over her chin, filling her mouth. Snarls erupted in her ears but were quickly muffled by her own. She was nothing. She was everything.

She was chaos.

Daciana came to, covered in the blood of her people. Blood, flesh, and hair were caught in her teeth. Her body hummed a deep dissonance. She felt the change. Every nerve fired with its call. With its dark promise. An electric charge filled the air, and the wind sang of her betrayal, trees violently shaking in their grief.

Every bone snapped and reformed, every muscle was tearing and stitching back together. It was wrong. It was meant to be easier. As the full moon bathed her in silvery light, Daciana stared down at her twisting hands, her body mangling in the harsh light of her ascension.

She'd completed the ritual—with the blood of her own.

Daciana howled in agony.

"Oh, child, look what you've done." Her father's voice rang in her ears, echoing from cold grey lips as she broke and reformed. Into something unnatural. Something grotesque. An abomination and violation of her pack.

"I'm sorry," Daciana sobbed, her voice slipping into a growl. Until she was no longer human. No longer anything but a monster.

The ascension was meant to grant mastery of her legacy, of the change. But the way her body broke again and again, reforming only to splinter again, made it clear—this was to be her curse. This was the price of all the destruction she'd wrought.

She slipped in and out of consciousness, simultaneously blissful and punishing. Until she collapsed, body spent.

When she awoke, the shards of moonlight no longer splayed over her naked body. Her human form was restored. She stood, wild strength and power singing in her veins. Whispering dark secrets. She stepped over her father's corpse without a backward glance, to the girl still tied to a stake. Standing in the bloody pool at Kenna's feet, Daciana untied her and lifted her easily into her arms. Cradling her to her chest, she carried her away from her grandmother's burnt remains. Away from her own pack she'd slaughtered.

Gently, Daciana laid her on the mossy ground. The moon was kind in its glow now, no longer holding the violence of its judgment. Its light bathed Kenna in a soft, ethereal glow.

Daciana pushed Kenna's black tendrils of hair from her face. Her impossibly beautiful face, smoothed of the cruelty of her last moments. Were it not for the mangled state of her body, Kenna would have appeared almost peaceful in death. Beauty preserved like one of those fairytales she'd recited through giggles and lazy kisses.

Daciana would never hear Kenna laugh again.

The power of her ascension roiled in her blood. Daciana pressed a kiss to Kenna's lips, leaving behind a smear of blood.

Kenna didn't wake. Because this was not a fairytale.

Daciana reached deep within her soul. Deep in her blood. To that dark well of power that coiled inside her. To the place light would never reach. To the rot that already started to fester, a power borne of betrayal of the worst kind. She would bring Kenna back to this world. No matter the consequences. She would bring her back.

Daciana imagined Kenna's soul as bound by a thread. She tugged, ripping it from the Netherworld, from Avalon, from whatever blighted world thought it right to claim her. Daciana wasn't sure what the afterlife held, whether all that awaited each of them was a gaping abyss or paradise, but by the skies and whatever gods may or may not exist, she'd bring Kenna back.

She felt it, the power singing in her veins. She felt it search for a source. For an essence to fuel the demands she made. Demands to bring the girl she loved back to the land of the living.

Whatever the price, she'd pay. Daciana knew this as she dragged Kenna's soul back into her body. As the rush of heady power filled her near to bursting, Daciana had the fleeting thought of where it was coming from. Who it was coming from. Something fueled this unspeakable power, and she called to it. Gluttonous and all-consuming, she demanded it all until Kenna's wounds stitched back together. And when Kenna sucked in her first mouthful of air, Daciana forgot to mourn whatever she'd stolen to bring her back.

"Daciana." Kenna's voice ripped Daciana back to the present.

Daciana's palms stung from where'd drawn blood from clenching her fists too hard. Her nails had bitten crescent moons into her skin. "You want me to be the asshole? Fine, I'm the asshole, but you can't run away from this. You have the power Inerys spoke of. I felt it firsthand, so don't tell me you don't want to talk about it."

Daciana stood, unyielding in her decision. "How many lives were lost that night, Kenna?"

Kenna narrowed her dark eyes. "You're not the only one who suffered loss."

"Kenna, how many lives were lost?" Daciana's body vibrated. A need for a violent release. To breathe life into the truth she'd shielded Kenna from.

"That's a sorry excuse—"

"You don't get to lecture me on this. You do not know what it cost."

Kenna's mouth parted in shock. Her face froze in an almost youthful expression of surprise. Of innocence. Like she couldn't imagine that much death and suffering left behind their wake.

Daciana stormed off toward the forest, leaving Kenna alone in her judgment and ignorance.

It was unfair to throw that in her face. Kenna didn't know because she couldn't bear to tell her. But Daciana had counted each body. Each life she stole. She committed every face to memory. They paid the price for her selfish act.

That day, she'd made herself a vow.

She would never allow herself to love another as she loved Kenna.

And she'd never call upon that power again.

CHAPTER TWENTY-SIX

LARK

A bright slice of pale light spilled through the arched windows and onto the floor. The room appeared as if carved out of the sandstone building. Lark and Gavriel sat beside one another, and the man who'd yet to offer his name sat across from them. His hands were elegantly steepled, his elbows braced on the narrow table of petrified wood that served as his desk. It was more like stone than any material that had once been living. Lark lifted her hands to mirror his casual posture, and the *clink* of her shackles filled the silent room.

Gavriel hadn't taken his eyes off the man, as if expecting a sudden attack.

He appeared a few decades older than Gavriel, with rich dark skin and black hair shorn to the scalp along the sides and braided in a long thick plait down his back. The candlelight danced across his face, illuminating zig-zagging scars across the bridge of his strong nose. Despite the beard peppered with grey along his upper lip and chin, Lark could detect a strong jaw, tightened even further in disapproval.

"Well," he finally said. His deep voice had an edge of a growl to it. Like he'd swallowed something sharp long ago and scarred the back of his throat. "This is an interesting development." He leaned back in his chair, crossing his thickly muscled arms. His bronze plated armor ended at his shoulders, leaving them bare. He stared at Lark with his dark brown eyes, tilting his head to appraise her. Light shone off the small gold hoops lining the shell of his ear. Finally, he sighed. "It would seem the timing of your arrival is most… fortuitous."

"How's that?" Lark demanded, leaning forward.

"For starters, Gavriel here has been a spectacle. But it was only a matter of time until his motivation waned." He cast a disapproving eye at the table concealing Gavriel's leg wound, as if getting hurt in the arena was a show of disobedience. "Your presence is neither unwelcome nor unexpected."

"You knew I would follow?" Lark leaned forward in her seat, earning another *clank* of her shackles.

"Do you think you were left alive by accident?" The man chuckled, shaking his head. "You live because I plan for every outcome. Since you're here now, perhaps we can come to an arrangement beneficial to all."

"Yuri," Gavriel hissed, tugging at the chains that bound his wrists, "you gave me your word."

It was interesting to think Gavriel trusted the word of his jailor. But Lark wasn't knowledgeable on the inner workings of assassins' guilds. Perhaps there was a certain level of honor he'd come to expect.

Or perhaps Gavriel was foolish to expect honor in a place like this.

"I kept my word. None of my men laid a finger on her. She chose to come of her own free will. You're wounded and barely keeping it together." Yuri turned the force of his glare on Gavriel. "You're no good to me dead, boy."

There wasn't time to dissect his meaning, not while Gavriel's fate hung in the balance.

"I'll know what you propose, Yuri, is it?" Lark ignored the glower she received from Gavriel. "So I might decide for myself." Honor or no, she wouldn't sit out this negotiation.

"Lark, no."

Both Lark and Yuri ignored Gavriel.

"I need a fight tomorrow. We have a special guest arriving specifically to see Gavriel, and if he dies too quickly, it'll all be for naught."

Yuri waved his hand through the air. "I can't let him go, but I'm open to reaching an accord. Have you any fighting skills to boast of?"

"No, she doesn't fight. Hasn't lifted a weapon a day in her life," Gavriel quickly said.

"I can handle myself," Lark said. She'd faced Undesirables, slave traders, guards, and even some of the assassins from Gavriel's guild. His concern was unfounded.

Yuri pursed his lips, nodding. "Gavriel stays here, as do you. You may fight in his stead until my guest arrives. Should you fall, he'll take over."

"She wasn't part of the agreement." Gavriel braced his hands on the table, trying to stand.

"And what if I win?" Lark wasn't about to strike a deal without clarifying all the terms. She'd never make that mistake again. Lark stood, peering down at him with the type of stare Thanar would use to make it clear who was in charge. "I want both Gavriel and I to walk out of here, free."

Yuri stood, his thick, imposing frame was all edges and corded muscle. His considerable height towered over Lark. "The winner will go free; you have my word."

"Both of us will go free. Gavriel and myself." If he thought her stupid enough to trifle with technicalities, then he was sorely mistaken.

"If everything goes as I hope, you both will be free." Yuri grinned, flashing a row of straight white teeth. He held out a large, dark hand.

Gavriel rounded on her. "Lark, don't. Trust that I can do this."

Lark glanced down at the leg he was still trying not to put any pressure on. The memory of all that blood pouring from his wound before they dragged him away was still fresh in her mind.

She placed her hand in Yuri's, giving a firm shake.

LARK LEANED against the cool stone, letting her head fall back. Gavriel hadn't uttered another word the entire trek back to the dungeon. He was just on the other side of the solid slab of a cell, still ignoring her.

Her cell was little more than a stone room with a bench and bucket to piss in. Even so, she felt a relief she hadn't known in days. Gavriel breathed the same air as she, his heart still beat in his chest. Even if he was angry with her, at least he lived.

Lark ran her fingers across the iron bars. The guards had been kind enough to light a brazier and unlock her shackles once she was safely behind a locked door. Gavriel hadn't received the same courtesy. Probably because of how he reacted when one of the guards pushed her toward her cell.

"Why did you come here?" Gavriel asked with a groan.

Apparently, he was ready to speak to her.

"Truly? I came to rescue you." Though she didn't do a very good job.

"The only comfort I had was that you were nowhere near here. That you were safe and far away."

Lark huffed. Easy for him to say. He was the one carted off in the dead of night. "Gavriel, I woke up alone in our tent." Lark's eyes pricked at the memory. "Do you know the thoughts I entertained to explain your absence? I thought..." She thought he abandoned her once the soul bond had broken. Though now, perhaps it would have been better if he'd just wandered off, done with her without the tether. "I thought you left me, which was... bad enough. But then I realized someone took you. Do you have any idea how terrifying it was, not knowing if you still breathed?" A hot tear snuck to the top of her cheek.

"Lark," Gavriel's voice had gone soft, "why would you ever think I left you?"

Lark wiped her face. She had to tell him. There might not be another chance. "I asked Inerys to sever the soul bond." When only silence greeted her, Lark continued. "She gave me a tonic for us to drink. I didn't tell you because I wasn't sure I even wanted to go through with it. I feared you'd take it for me, and then pretend to feel the same out of some sense of honor or obligation. But really, I was just terrified." Lark sucked in a shaky breath. "I didn't want to lose you. I should have just told you."

"The wine I found in your bag," Gavriel said softly.

"Yes." Lark ran a hand through her filthy hair. Her chest was raw, yet somehow lighter. Like telling Gavriel the truth had carved out a piece of her but cleared away the rot as well. "That's why they took you so easily, I suspect. Inerys' tonic must have had some sort of sleeping agent while the spell took effect. I didn't wake until morning and you know what a light sleeper I am."

"Yes, I can't even get up to take a piss without receiving a swat for waking you. Which, incidentally, is what I was doing."

Leave it to him to focus on the wrong part of her explanation—

"You weren't asleep when they took you?" Lark scrambled to her knees, pressing herself to the corner where iron met stone, as close as she could get to Gavriel's voice.

"No. Whatever was in that tonic must have already worn off for me. You know how many poisons and toxins I've had to build base immunity to. I snuck out to take a leak—I was very impressed I hadn't woken you. I still maintain I don't make a sound when I rise first. You just have a tendency to wrap your entire body around me."

"You were outside the tent when they took you." Lark exhaled a sigh of relief. If nothing else, she hadn't directly caused his capture. "You must be losing your touch then."

"Attacking a man with his prick out seems the coward's way. As does keeping him sedated."

"Sedated?" Lark laughed, feeling worlds lighter. "Isn't that what assassins do? Strike where it'll inflict the most damage? Exploit every advantage?"

Gavriel made a noise of disapproval. "Perhaps, but there's an art to it. A finesse that the lions sorely lack. And drugging a man with Dreams of the Dead is the epitome of cowardice." A heavy silence settled over them before he continued. "How did you find me?" There was a grim note to his voice, a blatant disapproval that she had in fact found him.

Lark tucked her filthy hair behind her ear. "Maddox. He stayed at the pleasure house in case anyone was tracking you. I think he was supposed to kill me but instead he told me where to go." Perhaps she should have killed him. Skies, she hoped the decision not to wouldn't bite her in the ass.

A humorless laugh, more akin to a growl, came from Gavriel's cell. "He wasn't supposed to kill you. He was supposed to send you in the wrong direction. I should have known better than to expect a shred of honor from the lions."

Maddox was supposed to send her elsewhere? Then why would he risk his position? Unless… he did exactly as he was told. "Yuri said he feared your motivation was running out. He always intended for me to find you."

"Who fucking knows with this lot? They say one thing and do another. I was told since the mark was placed on my head, you would be left alone and deterred from following me to this place so long as I cooperated and gave them a good fight each day. I wasn't exactly in any position to argue during the trek because they maintained a steady dose of Dreams of the Dead to keep me compliant, but I believed him because the only thing he's been after is drawing the eye of the Crows." Gavriel exhaled a sharp breath. "Yuri is a snake, and I'm the fool who took him at his word."

Keeping her alive was a tactic to make Gavriel cooperate. They must have left all the obvious signs on the trail for her to find. Whatever their motives, she was grateful for their duplicity since it brought her to his side.

The sound of shuffling wafted over to Lark's cell. Goose pebbles rose on her arms, as if she could feel Gavriel's presence through the stone.

"Lark," he whispered. The soft sound of her name on his lips made her want to weep with joy. "You never answered my question. How could you ever think I'd leave you willingly?" From the corner where their cells met, Gavriel's hand snuck through the bars, splayed open and waiting. His chains scraped against the floor, granting him limited reach.

Lark gave him no answer, and he pressed no further. Neither of them spoke of what it might mean, severing the soul bond. She didn't ask after his feelings, nor he hers. She was a fool for ever doubting him, and couldn't bring herself to fill these moments with her mistakes. In the cold, filthy dungeon, the shadows swallowed any questions or answers they had left to offer.

With a sigh, Lark stretched to place her hand in his. He threaded their fingers. His rough calluses pressed against her, eliciting a shiver. Where their hands were joined, Lark felt a steady pulse. And though that was the only point of contact, warmth flooded her whole body just the same.

"RISE AND SHINE, LOITER-SACKS." A voice far too chipper for Lark's liking cut through the dank air. Morning must have come, though one would never know it in the dungeon that saw no light.

Lark groaned, releasing Gavriel's hand. Her shoulder ached from sleeping in such an awkward position. Not her brightest idea. Bracing against the thick iron bars, Lark pulled herself to stand, rolling her shoulder to loosen her stiff muscles.

A blazing torch appeared in front of her, held by a woman with intricate face tattoos and a wide, splitting smile. Beneath the black swirls and shapes, her tawny skin practically glowed in the firelight. Her dark eyes crinkled in amusement. "I hope you rested up, kitten. You're going to need it."

Lark rolled her eyes, too tired to bother with a retort, and hung her wrists through the bars. The man standing beside the tattooed woman clapped Lark's shackles in place, none too gently. His face was impossible to see beneath his dark cowl. The door to Lark's cell swung open, and the ancient squeal of metal lifted the hairs on the back of her neck. Lark stepped through, her eyes immediately finding Gavriel's shape waiting in the shadows.

"Not yet, kitten," the tattooed woman said, leading her up the stairs. "Once you're in the cage, we'll let him out to watch. Don't worry."

The cage? Lark's mind buzzed with a thousand questions, questions she desperately needed answered. Would she get to choose her weapon? Would they feed her before the fights began? Who was she facing first? But the stubborn part of her didn't want to give the woman the satisfaction of knowing how worried she was.

"The cage is where you await entrance into the arena." The man beneath the hood spoke for the first time. He had a smooth, melodic voice. Lark glanced over at him, seeing nothing but the square cut of his dark bronze jawline. A thick scar cut across his chin.

"Oh," was all Lark said.

They veered away from the front entrance, taking Lark out the side path. She tried not to let her fear show—to keep her head held high and still the tremors in her hands. This differed from the heat of survival in an ambush. She had time to think, to worry, to play out all the ways she might end up a skewered corpse.

Lark swallowed the panic that climbed up her throat.

Fear is not my master. I will never submit.

THE STALE BREAD they'd given Lark sat like a rock in her belly. Nerves still shook her to her core as the unmistakable clash of steel reverberated through the crosshatching of the cage. She had to lean close to press her eye between the zigzags of metal that made up the walls of her confinement. From the look of it, they made it from swords melded together to form the enclosure. Lark shook out her hands, swinging her arms in front of her to stay loose and prevent fear from locking her muscles tight.

They still hadn't given her a weapon.

Was she to scavenge the sand for weapons from fallen competitors? The idea of not knowing what she'd wield until the moment she was to defend her life made the meager meal in her gut threaten to reappear.

Lark tugged at the unfamiliar, hardened leather armor she wore. Her arms were bare, and they'd given her a deep tanned cuirass, light canvas pants, and leather boots—similar attire to the fighters she'd watched. Although the garb didn't fit quite right, at least they hadn't made her fight in her dark clothing and leathers. With the unforgiving sun baking her, she'd probably cook before she'd have a chance to be properly slain.

"You're up next."

Lark turned to find the hooded man, still hidden beneath his cowl, stalking toward her with a satchel in hand and… was that her bow and quiver slung over his shoulder?

He tossed the burlap sack at her feet. Lark knelt and carefully opened it. Inside was Hugo's knife, atop the stack of blades and daggers they'd confiscated.

"Here," he said, yanking the bow and quiver from his back and dropping them into her eager hands. "That's a well-crafted dagger, but you should really arm yourself with a short sword, at the very least. And I doubt you'll have the time to fire off too many arrows."

Lark ran her fingers over the familiar grooves of her Ash Wood bow. It was the last thing Hugo made for her—a stronger pull that could pierce armor. It lacked the decorative etchings he'd included in her first bow, probably because she complimented his craftsmanship enough to embarrass him, but it still felt so wholly him. She'd never want to rely on a bow Hugo hadn't crafted for her himself, and the truth of that thickened her throat. She slid his dagger into her boot and sighed with the rightness of the weight. "I don't have a sword."

With lightning reflexes, he whipped his cloak to the side and yanked a steel sword from the sheath at his hip. Flipping it in the air, he handed it to her, pommel first.

She stood, running her hand along the wooden grip. The design was simple enough, with an intricate knot at the base of the steel. She grasped it, bringing it closer for further inspection. It was light, but sturdy. The simple design wasn't to be confused with poor quality.

At her close examination, he said, "They don't make these around here. That's Kovalian steel. Surpassed by none, apart from fairy stories of magical blades."

A blade like this was a rare find in Ardenas, so why give it to her?

"Why do you hide your face?" Lark meant to say something else, something disarming so she might gauge his character, but the words slipped from her lips with damning ease. She blamed it on her nerves.

His dark mouth quirked before he dropped his hood, revealing a stunningly chiseled face. Faint scars adorned his dark skin, his black hair was shaved close to the scalp, and thick, dark lashes lined his golden-brown eyes.

"Oh, it's because you're pretty?"

His brow furrowed and disapproval tightened his mouth.

The deep vibration of the horn blowing sang through Lark's bones, through her teeth. The round was complete. Someone had fallen.

He frowned, whipping his head in the blasting horn's direction. "It's time," he said in that smooth voice.

Lark slung her quiver onto her back, sheathing her blades in place before gripping her bow tightly.

"Listen," he said, stepping away, "aim for the easy kill. This is no place for honor."

Why he felt compelled to offer any advice, Lark couldn't guess. But honor was something she hadn't bothered to maintain. From the moment she was remade as mortal, her hands were full of all the little ideals she tried so hard to carry. There was no room for honor. Not when survival was on the line.

Lark took her place at the mouth of the cage, counting down the seconds until they released her.

One heartbeat.

Two heartbeats.

Exhale.

The door lifted; blinding light flooded the space. Lark shielded her eyes. The roar of the crowd was already deafening. She strode onto the reddish sand; each step sank into the soft ground. The walls of the fighting ring were hewn from the same sandstone of the prison. Roughly carved and towering high enough, Lark would never be able to reach the top. Not that she'd ever run. Rows of rickety looking ramps overlooked the arena, floods of people crowded above, clambering to witness bloodshed.

Lark tightened her hold on the Kovalian short sword, circling the blade through the air.

Across the arena, a man the size of a mountain stood. He rested a great axe over his shoulder, watching Lark with a carefully concealed expression. Most of his bronze skin was exposed, and he wore only a pair of dark trousers and boots. The broad expanse of his chest was covered in intricate markings—the markings of a Vallemerian warrior.

Shit.

His dark shoulder-length hair and beard hid most of his face, but his eyes remained ever watchful as Lark trekked across the sand.

Lark swung the Kovalian sword again, marveling at how light it felt. It was about to be put to the test. She couldn't imagine crossing blades with a great axe that large without being sliced in two. Both she and the sword.

"I don't want to kill you," his thick brogue was low and sharp. "I won't enjoy this." He said it without an ounce of emotion. No taunting. Like he was merely stating a fact.

Lark couldn't find it in her to be offended. She did not know who this man was, or what brought to this arena. Vallemer was a long way from here—across the sea. What path had he taken for fate to bring him here? Lark wet her lips, weighing her words carefully. "Of that, we are of the same mind."

His blue eyes widened before he took a step back, readying his axe.

Lark turned and sprinted to the opposite side of the arena. Dropping her sword to the sand, she yanked her bow off her shoulder, reaching behind her to whip an arrow from her quiver.

There is no place for honor here.

Nor in me.

She nocked the arrow, aiming for his throat. His face twisted in rage as he charged, bellowing. She released, watching her arrow sail through the air and land in his chest. A little low from her mark, but the sight of blood weeping from the entry point was a welcome one.

Only he didn't stop.

Lark nocked another arrow, aiming for his gut. It sank with a thickening squelch; more blood painted the sand.

And still he didn't slow.

Lark yanked an arrow and fled, needing more distance to nock another arrow. If he caught up to her, one swing and it would all be over.

A sharp pain exploded in her calf. Lark dropped, sand and salt burning her wound. A small throwing blade jutted out from the back of her leg. Cursing, Lark flipped to her back, nocking an arrow just in time to find a massive shape blotting out the sun. With a cry, Lark loosed the arrow. It sunk into the shadow mass. The silhouette of his axe was still raised high. He stumbled back, lowering his weapon to the sand before he fell. The sun instantly blinded her. She squeezed her eyes shut as she scrambled over to his body, not trusting herself to stand just yet. Sure enough, there was her arrow sticking straight out of his left eye.

The crowd was screaming, but all Lark heard was the blood rushing through her ears.

Lark tore two strips of fabric from the trousers of the man she'd just killed, carefully avoiding eye contact with his remaining eye. She wrapped the thick, dark material around her calf as a tourniquet, wincing when she pulled it tight. Only then did she remove the small blade. Dizziness hit as she swiftly wrapped the wound with the second piece of cloth. It warmed with the slow, wet trickle of her blood, but it would hold. She stood, nearly buckling under the weight of her injured leg. She ignored the bloodthirsty crowd as she allowed herself one last look at the man she'd sent to the Netherworld. Who was here collecting his soul? Were Reapers even guiding anymore? The Otherworld had likely descended into chaos without Thanar's rigid rule. What would come of this man's soul now?

Lark couldn't bring herself to apologize. There was more than just her survival at stake. Somewhere Gavriel was watching, his life hanging in the balance. It was him, or them. Whomever they tossed at her.

An easy decision to make.

Lark bent down to retrieve her bow and quiver and slung them over her shoulder. She yanked the arrows from the man's chest and skull. Hugo once told her killing never got any easier. That he found a way to live with it, but it always stayed with him. Lark sank the blood-soaked arrows into her quiver.

Hugo was wrong.

The sand was scorching beneath Lark's feet. Even through her boots, she could feel it. She trekked across the arena to the spot where her sword awaited. The reddish sand was a graveyard of abandoned weapons and bloodstains. No bodies, though. The guards came and collected the corpses. As they were doing now, dragging that giant man off to the side. What did they do with all the bodies? Burn them? It seemed too hot to consider setting a pyre alight. Unless they waited until nightfall.

Lark wiped the sweat from her brow, certain she'd just smeared some of his blood across her face.

The commanding horn sounded.

Another fight.

Another death.

So long as it wasn't her own.

Trudging with uneven steps, Lark approached her discarded weapon. She pulled it from the sand and swung it in a circular motion, readying her stance.

I am death's master. I yield to none.

LARK SANK her sword into the man's thigh. He'd bleed out quickly. It was the only kindness she could offer. He stared up at her with panic in his wide brown eyes. His dark curls clung to his tan forehead, matted with sweat. He trembled. Whether he was cold from losing all that blood, or terrified to meet his own end, Lark wasn't sure. She should walk away or deal him another blow to speed this along. But something about his expression froze her to the spot.

He wasn't like the Vallemerian, who died before Lark could determine what emotion locked in his gaze.

But this boy—that's what he was, a mere boy—stared up at her in terror.

And for a moment, for one fleeting moment, Lark wished she was still a Reaper. That she could end his pain and grant him peace. To guide him so he wasn't alone as he faced the unknown. But the truth of what happened to souls after death wasn't as simple as she'd once been led to believe. The memory of Aislinn, the bright soul she'd led to the afterlife, struck Lark like a dissonant chord.

She couldn't lead this soul anywhere, but he wasn't alone.

Lark bent down beside him, yanking the sword from his feeble grasp and tossing it to the side. Clasping his hand in hers, she held tight. Was this a kindness, or torture? Lark would never know because the light fled his brown eyes before he could utter a word.

Lark's heart clenched, and she wished she could have offered him some words of comfort before he faded. Something to carry with him as he ventured to the unknown.

Lark stood, taking his blood and her sword with her. The memory of the first life she took as a human flooded her mind. The weight of it on her conscience had been a shock to her system.

Hugo was wrong.

She wasn't carrying these kills with her. She was leaving bits and pieces of herself with each corpse.

How much of her would remain?

The oppressive sun beat down on Lark's back. Its unforgiving rays already burned her arms and face. She tugged on the collar of her leather cuirass. Sweat, sand, and blood coated her skin, creating another smothering layer to cook her through. She lifted her sword, the effort far more difficult now. Her arms and shoulders ached, and her calf still throbbed. It was a wonder she hadn't suffered a worse wound, but it made no difference. If not injury, her flagging strength would end her. Hopefully, she'd finish before her body failed her. Eventually, this had to stop. It had to be enough.

She almost missed the commanding horn, its deep bellow reverberating through her bones.

Out of the cage strolled not one, but two fighters.

Skies above.

CHAPTER TWENTY-SEVEN

LANGFORD

old light from the midmorning sun streamed through Langford's small round window. Alistair had draped his arm over his side, holding and guarding. His heated body pressed against Langford's back, curved around him in an almost possessive way. Langford smiled, gently running his hand down Alistair's arm.

This was the first morning in a long time that Langford had woken without a mind-rending headache. Probably because it was the first decent night's sleep he'd gotten in a while. Even if Alistair kept him up most of the night.

Langford sighed, warmth spreading through his chest.

He'd grown accustomed to the notion that he wasn't meant for happiness. It was something that would always remain just out of reach. He found enjoyment in things. Studying, healing, belonging to Alistair's crew and the family he'd found. But Langford was so sure he was doomed to want. To pine. It was recompense for all the disappointment he caused in his life.

Again, he ran his hand down Alistair's arm, marveling at how soft his skin was between each scar. His body was a map of brutal memories and old injuries. The sharp edges of a life hard-fought between the soft valleys of a man who hid his heart.

A deep groan rumbled against Langford's back. Alistair's firm embrace tightened, pressing Langford flush against his considerable arousal.

"Good morning," Alistair said, voice thick from sleep.

Slowly, Langford turned to find Alistair's eyes still closed, his sinful mouth curved in a smug smile. "I can't stay in bed all day," Langford said, attempting to extricate himself from his hold. Alistair didn't budge.

"Yes, you can. You can do anything you set your mind to."

Langford snorted, trying to pull away again. "I have so much reading to finish now that I've actually slept."

With a sigh, Alistair released him, rolling onto his back. "I see how it is," he said, stretching. "You have your way with me and then kick me out for the sake of your precious *books*."

Langford laughed, yanking his trousers on. He immediately regretted the decision. He needed to wash, but there was no way he'd get anything done with Alistair in the room. "Perhaps you could find some way to amuse yourself until later."

Alistair arched a brow, eyeing Langford's trousers in a way that heated his cheeks. "What's happening later?"

Langford pulled his tunic over his head. "We have dinner with the captain this evening." She'd insisted on dining with them at least once during their journey back to Ardenas. She called it a matter of civil discourse, but Langford was fairly certain she'd end the night threatening Alistair's life and manhood. Again.

Alistair groaned. "Sargon's knickers, I forgot about that. Can't we just tell her we're busy?"

"Don't blaspheme," Langford said, but there was only amusement behind his chide. "We're on her ship. What matter of social engagement might we commit to?"

Alistair's mouth curved, his eyes glinting. "I can think of a thing or two."

Langford shook his head and turned away, eager to set his desk for work. He preferred arranging his research in a careful organization, so when it inevitably devolved into chaos, he'd at least begun with a plan.

Taking dinner in Ingemar's quarters would put a damper on his plans to research straight through mealtimes, but if it meant patching whatever had damaged her friendship with Alistair, it was worth it. From the first time they boarded her ship, back when they all sailed to Koval to reach the Forbidden Highlands, there was unnamed animosity between Inegmar and Alistair. It was Langford's understanding that they used to smuggle exports from Koval together, and Alistair always spoke highly of her. It could only mean one thing:

Alistair must have botched up somewhere along the line to earn her ire.

"You're the reason we're in this mess with Ingemar. If you apologized for whatever grudge she holds against you, then maybe she wouldn't regard us with distrust." Langford jumped when Alistair's hands snuck over his hips. Heat flared through him, making rational thought impossible.

"What if I promise to apologize tonight?" Alistair's fingers were already tugging at the laces of Langford's trousers. "In exchange for an hour of your morning." His hand slipped beneath Langford's waistband, gripping him firmly. He began a decadent rhythm that had Langford's eyes fluttering closed.

"Alistair." Langford couldn't bring himself to care that his voice pitched to a reedy whine. "I need to work."

Alistair pressed his lips to the juncture between Langford's neck and shoulder, humming softly. "Is one hour going to kill you?" he asked against Langford's overly sensitive skin, before he laved the spot with his tongue, languid and unhurried.

Langford braced his hands on the desk, legs shaking. Yes, it would undoubtedly kill him. This man would be the death of him.

Alistair gripped Langford's jaw, turning his head to thoroughly claim his lips. Alistair kissed like a man starved, and Langford could do nothing but endeavor to remain upright.

Alistair spun him and pressed him into the desk.

He could have every morning of the rest of his life. It was that thought that swelled Langford's chest near to bursting as Alistair freed him of his clothes and worshiped every inch of him.

Every morning of forever.

"MORE WINE?"

Reluctantly, Langford turned away from the large angular windows of Captain Ingemar's cabin. The wooden table was laden with the picked remains of their dinner. Kovalian fruit was a rare export. He'd made it a point not to ask Ingemar how she'd gotten her hands on pomegranate seeds and enough loquat to make preserves, which Alistair was shamelessly spreading in a thick layer over a cracker. When he caught Langford watching, his eyes darkened as he slowly licked the vibrant yellow jelly from his finger.

Langford's cheeks heated, and he cleared his throat. "No, thank you. I have more work to do later."

Alistair stretched, crossing his ankles above the worn boots he'd bartered for after losing his to Ingemar. He arched a dark brow at Langford, thoroughly enjoying the effect he had on him.

"What is so important you'd turn down my Anquan Red?" Ingemar studied the bottle in her dark slender hand. "A good year, too." She wore her hair loose in thick black curls. For once, her captain's hat hung off the hook on her door.

"Maybe a sip or two," Langford said reluctantly, as Ingemar grinned and filled his bronze chalice nearly to the brim.

He couldn't afford to muddle his mind tonight. As soon as Alistair left their room, which took two full hours instead of the one he promised, Langford dove into research. He was on the cusp of understanding. The text kept mentioning *Messorum Ferrum* or Reaper Blades. Blades that, if Langford understood correctly, were forged by some sort of transference magic. This method of conjuring was archaic and unconfirmed by scholars. Langford would have to conduct more research.

He caught a pained expression from Alistair, as if the man could sense his thoughts.

"Normally I mind my own business," Ingemar said as she swirled her wine in her chalice. "Live and let live, and all that. But since Alistair is involved—and your merry party has returned divided—my curiosity grows." Her dark, narrow eyes were piercing, as if by her gaze alone she could sink beneath the surface and uncover the answer. "There were six of you, yes? Once I drop you two off, I'm still short four. Are they going to crop up at an inconvenient time and demand passage? Or has Alistair's particular brand of loyalty lost him more allies?"

It was an obvious oversight to assume Ingemar wouldn't ask about their missing companions.

"Alistair did nothing untoward, and no one harbors any ill feelings. We parted ways. I'm sure you can understand when plans need to adapt. Three of our members found alternative passages home. As for our sixth member" —Langford carefully stepped around the thought of his name— "he didn't make it." He didn't owe her any more of an explanation than that—not yet, anyway. It was better to guide her into tipping her hand first. Langford took a sip from his cup. The taste of deep, musky plum and notes of berry slid on his tongue. He hadn't had wine of this quality since he fled his father's home.

Ingemar's mouth thinned into a firm line.

Alistair groaned. "I swear to the rutting skies, Langford, if I catch you sniffing and spitting and whatever else you're planning to do with that wine besides drink it…"

Langford rolled his eyes. "You'll what?"

Alistair's eyes darkened with wicked promise as his sinful mouth curved in a smirk. "You'll find out later."

Ingemar kicked her boots up on the table, crossing them at the ankles. "See, I think you're lying."

"Oh no, I really will punish him. He just might like it," Alistair said with a shrug.

Langford's cheeks burned as he took a bracing drink from his cup.

"Not that. There are two things I'm good at reading. Maps and people." She crossed her arms behind her head, thick black curls spilling over her dark, bare shoulders. Her thin, tight undershirt left little to the imagination, barely tied closed over her ample feminine charms. "You're hiding something."

Langford's grip tightened on his chalice, but he kept his voice steady. "Every word I've spoken is true. I can choose to share that which bears repeating and withhold unnecessary details at my discretion."

A lazy smile stretched across Ingemar's mouth, revealing her chipped, white teeth. "True enough. But I'd like to consider myself counted among your trusted allies." She cut a sharp glare Alistair's way. "Unlike some, you seem the type to honor such a partnership."

Curious. "Allies, you say?" Langford took another pull from his wine, a small mouthful, but he savored it. He'd witnessed the stall tactic employed by his father during many a conversation, an intentional power-play. Judging by the amused expression on Ingemar's face, she knew what he was doing. "What could you possibly stand to gain?"

"Trust is a powerful thing. You never know when you might need a favor. I like to collect my allies before I need them. Keeps me from making foolish decisions out of desperation."

That was the first lie. Langford might not have Alistair's skill with a sword, or Lark's with a bow, or Daciana's with—well, everything— but there was one thing Langford excelled at. He knew when he was being lied to.

Whatever Ingemar needed, she wasn't yet willing to share.

He chanced a glance at Alistair, who was uncharacteristically silent. His chin rested in his hand as he observed the exchange, frowning.

"There are things that are difficult to understand unless you're the faithful sort or you've seen them firsthand." Langford placed his wine down and leaned forward. "I can tell you everything, and you can choose not to believe me. But I need your word—this stays in this room."

All humor fled Ingemar's face. The candlelight glimmered in her dark eyes as she yanked the stiletto dagger from her boot and placed the blade in her palm. Without so much as a wince, she swept it across her hand, and blood ran between her fingers.

"Really, Ingemar? Of all the ridiculous—"

"You, too," Ingemar cut Alistair off, handing the dagger to Langford.

Langford took a deep breath and shook his head. What would his mother say if she could see him now? Swearing a blood oath to a pirate. He swept the blade across his palm and a shallow cut blossomed. He gripped Ingemar's hand, trying not to calculate the chances she disinfected her blade often.

"A blood oath is binding. Not even Alistair was willing to swear one."

"I stand by that. If we're swapping fluids, there's a better way of doing it," Alistair called over.

Langford ignored him. "I understand." As soon as they let go, Alistair was pressing a napkin into his hand, and Langford closed his fist. Blood crept along the white cloth, red traveling over the fine fabric. It was a barbaric practice, but one Langford was willing to partake in if it meant gaining trust from the captain. It couldn't hurt to have a ship and crew on their side should the veil fall and the true fight begin. "We need to start at the beginning. You remember Lark?"

Ingemar grinned, leaning back and coiling a bandage around her hand. "Oh, yes. I remember her fellow, too. What was his name? Gorber? Gundry?"

"Gavriel," Alistair said, laughing.

"That's it. Gavriel. You sent him to my quarters—very transparent of you, Alistair. I was disappointed with the effort. But he was pleasing to look at, and I hadn't had a good lay since the last port, so I figured we'd fuck and he'd leave empty-handed." She shook her head, snatching her wine up. "You'd have thought I asked him to drown a cat from how offended he was at the suggestion. How was I to know they were attached?"

Langford smirked into his chalice. He could imagine the look on Gavriel's face. Though the man was insistent he'd had plenty of opportunity for subterfuge in his days as an assassin, there didn't seem to be a duplicitous bone in his body.

Unlike a certain someone.

Langford glanced over to find Alistair looking decidedly uncomfortable. His posture remained relaxed, but there was a line of tension in his shoulders and a tick of his jaw that gave him away.

"I needed to reclaim my property, which ultimately failed. So no harm done."

Her eyes darkened, and Langford hoped Alistair didn't offend the captain enough for her to throw them overboard. Langford tossed him a withering stare, and Alistair sighed, sitting up in his seat and eying Ingemar with grim determination.

"There was something I wished to discuss with you," Alistair said in a strained voice. "Among other things." He laced his fingers in front of his chest. "About our old partnership... our last... *shipment.* Mistakes were made."

Langford's face landed in his palm. Oh, Alistair. That was bloody well the worst apology he'd ever heard.

Ingemar blinked. "That's all you have to say, 'Mistakes were made?' I should have gutted you when you betrayed me, you little shit."

"I had good reason to go back on my word," Alistair said. "I didn't take that decision lightly. I knew you could handle yourself."

"And what about the people who depended on me, Alistair? They counted on me to get them out of Koval, to get their children out. You ratted me out to the city guard, and I left them behind."

Langford's heart sank. If Ingemar was trying to ferry people out of Koval—that could only mean one thing.

"You came back. You made good on your word," Alistair said. "But we couldn't delay. It was the only way to get her out."

"Do you think they were all waiting for me? While I was lying low, some of those people—*people,* Alistair—were carted off and sold. I gave them my word. That means something to me. And I failed them."

A muscle feathered in Alistair's jaw.

The evening's meal and wine churned in Langford's gut. Alistair sold Ingemar out to the city guard for freeing people from the labor market. For some woman. A deep ache twisted in Langford's chest.

"I didn't know what to do, Ingemar." Alistair's voice broke. "I— I'm sorry. I can't change what I did. And in the end, it didn't matter, did it?"

Ingemar's hard stare slowly shifted as pain twisted her lovely face. "I guess not," she said.

"For what it's worth," Alistair said. "I'd do it differently. If I could go back, I would have begged you to take her and thrown myself into the fire. That's what I should have done."

A heavy silence filled the room. Langford stood and paced over to the tall windows that nearly spanned floor to ceiling. Through the glass, the silvery ripples of a black tide swelled and rolled beneath the moon. Langford's throat constricted. He knew Alistair. He'd seen the best and worst in that man. But this… he wasn't prepared for.

Ingemar cleared her throat. "You had something to tell me, Langford. Something I might have a hard time believing." Her voice was firm and clear, as if Alistair's confession hadn't just happened. "Let's have it, then."

How quiet it must be, in the depthless-black of the sea. Even in violent storms, the silence below the surf must be the truest form of peace.

Langford turned from the window, refusing to glance at Alistair. "Allow me to start at the beginning. Our friend, Lark, is more than what she seems…"

"You didn't have to slice your hand open, Langford. As my healer, your hands need to be ready and able at a moment's notice." Alistair raised an eyebrow suggestively. "Not just for healing, either."

Langford propped his elbows on the pile of pages flooding his writing desk. His head hung heavy in his hands. Despite ignoring Alistair the entire trek back to his quarters, he still behaved as though nothing was amiss. Langford had spent the rest of the evening catching

Ingemar up on everything they knew, everything they'd learned. The impossible, the nonsensical, all of it. She didn't say a word, merely resting her sharp chin on the top of her fist, eyes narrowed as she listened. When Langford concluded his account, she promptly kicked them out. She didn't seem angry, but contemplative. Probably trying to determine if he was delusional or a liar.

Langford couldn't blame her.

He wasn't sure where Ingemar hailed from, or what beliefs she held. He only knew that not too long ago, he considered Lark's tale a work of fiction, an echo of old ideologies and an active imagination. Though he carried the reverence of the gods and warriors of Avalon, it was a far-off notion. The truths that came to light, horrible and grotesque, were real and too close for comfort.

No, it wouldn't surprise him if Ingemar didn't believe him.

Langford lifted his head to regard Alistair. He was sitting on the bed, already yanking his boots off to stay for the night.

"I should get back to work."

Alistair froze, boot midair. "You're kicking me out?"

Langford sighed. "No, I'm suggesting you sleep in your quarters so I can get some work done without keeping you up."

A muscle feathered in Alistair's jaw. "I don't mind the candlelight. And I can't imagine reading and scribbling to be that disruptive an activity."

"Well, I'd focus better if I had the room to myself." Langford was offering the most blatant of excuses, but he couldn't let go of what he learned about Alistair's betrayal. He needed to know the circumstances, who the woman was, why he had to jeopardize the rescue mission, what happened to her after the fact. All questions bursting in his chest for answers. Answers he wasn't ready to hear.

Alistair's expression darkened. "That's some horseshit, Langford."

"No, it isn't. It's the truth." His mouth dried with the bitter lie on his tongue.

"No, you've been weird ever since I apologized to Ingemar."

"Apologized?" Langford gave a tight laugh. "You barely owned up to what you did." Heat crept up his neck. "You haven't even explained yourself to me." So much for waiting for answers.

Alistair's face softened. "Langford, I'll always tell you anything you wish to know. So long as you promise not to hide it when something upsets you." His throat bobbed. "I don't... I can't handle when you do that."

It was a fair enough request. Langford was so used to hiding his feelings, sometimes it was hard to switch off. "Fine. Tell me everything. Make me understand why you did what you did."

"All right," Alistair said. "But we need to clean your hand. Rutting skies only know where Ingemar's blade has been." He crossed the room, grabbing Langford's pack and dipping a cloth in the washbasin on the small dresser.

Langford heaved himself up, trudging the few steps it took to reach the bed. Alistair appeared at his side, gently lifting his hand and pressing the damp cloth into the shallow graze.

Alistair's eyes found his. "Ingemar was set to transport a large group of people to Ardenas. Too conspicuous for my taste, but there was no time for multiple trips. They'd either fallen on hard times, failed to pay their taxes, or had petty charges brought against them— either way, they were all set to enter their servitude."

"Slavery," Langford said. "Their slavery."

Alistair nodded, dark hair falling into his eyes. "I was the middleman. It was my job to collect them and bring them to her ship. In covered wagons, disguised as employees, as companions, whatever it took to get them out of the city and onto her ship without notice." He dipped his finger into the clay jar of honey from Langford's bag and spread it over his wound. "I drew some unwanted attention. A former partner of mine noticed my comings and goings—said he wanted in." A shadow passed over Alistair's face. "You need to understand, some of my colleagues were collected out of necessity, not preference. I couldn't let a man like that anywhere near these people."

Langford swallowed. "Did he threaten the woman, the one you had to choose over everyone else?"

Alistair wrapped a fresh bandage around Langford's hand. "Worse.

He handed her over to the city guards. Said she'd stolen from the market frequently, had seen it with his own eyes. Claimed it was his civic duty to turn her in."

"And had she?"

Alistair made a noncommittal noise. "Yes, but that's beside the point. They were going to hand her over to the auction. Theft isn't tolerated in Koval."

"That's when you gave Ingemar up and all those people?"

Alistair lifted his head to regard Langford with the intensity of his stare. "It wasn't like that. I traded the intel for her freedom, but I kept the details vague enough Ingemar wouldn't be specifically implicated. We'd already forged the details of her business under a false name at the port. All Ingemar had to do was lie low for a bit and come back. It would have been fine." He tied the bandage but his hands lingered on Langford's.

The heat of his touch nearly made him shiver. "What happened?"

"I told them of the time and place the ship would be arriving and departing. Then I went straight to Ingemar and told her we'd been found out and we had to go. But she refused. She wouldn't leave until everyone was accounted for." Alistair released Langford's hand. Immediately Langford mourned the loss. "We had to leave. There was no telling what they'd do to Ingemar if they caught her. So I knocked her unconscious and carried her onto the ship. Told her crew she got into a scuffle with the city guard. I'd been working with them long enough, none of them questioned me."

"Oh, Alistair." Langford groaned and ran a hand down his face. "Was the woman worth it? Worth all those lives and Ingemar's trust?"

"I need you to understand something—something I've been shit at making clear in the past." Alistair leveled him with a penetrating stare, ruthless in its intensity. "My people aren't expendable. I'd let the entire world fall to ruin if it meant saving the ones I'm responsible for. If that makes me a right bastard, then fine. I never claimed to be otherwise." He closed his eyes, sighing. "But to answer your question, yes, she was worth it. In a perfect world, they all would have made it out and I would have stayed behind to face the consequences. Sometimes I wonder if I should have just let the asshole in on the job."

That was Alistair. When it came to saving his own, no effort was spared. "What happened to her?"

Alistair gave Langford a grin that didn't quite meet his stormy eyes. "She escaped while the guards were busy hunting down the ship. She sent word once, said she settled down in a small village in Valle-mer, and not to come looking for her. Pity, it was ransacked by bandits. There weren't any survivors."

He said it so casually. As if the death of the woman he sacrificed so much for was the equivalent of a turn of bad weather. Langford cupped Alistair's unshaven jaw, gently turning him to meet his eye. "I'm sorry."

Alistair searched his face with a sort of desperation that made Langford's chest ache. Unable to stomach his anguished expression, Langford closed the distance, brushing his lips against Alistair's. A broken sound escaped his chest as he surged forward, bearing down on Langford and lowering him onto the bed.

Alistair had his demons. They all did. But maybe these small moments of light could one day banish them, once and for all.

CHAPTER TWENTY-EIGHT

DACIANA

*D*aciana awoke, sore and stiff from sleeping up in a tree. She couldn't stand being in the same room as Kenna, so she'd taken to the forest. Like a coward.

Pulling her cloak tighter, Daciana shivered. The faint orange glow of the early morning sun spilled through crimson leaves, setting the surrounding maples on fire. The warm scent of burning hickory seeping from puffing chimneys, and damp earth cut through the chilled fall air. With a groan, she stretched, savoring the way her muscles trembled. She untied the rope she'd fastened around her waist to keep from falling and climbed down.

Daciana made her way out of the woods toward the Walden Inn. She and Kenna needed to move on. Regardless of Lark's whereabouts, Daciana needed to make it to Emeraude Port to meet Alistair and Langford. She just hoped Lark would be there. If she didn't show—

Lark would show.

The low, crumbling stone wall came into view. The Walden Inn was just beyond the small field.

Kenna was already waiting for her outside, sipping from a steaming mug and leaning against the outer wall of the inn. If Kenna had questions, Daciana had no answers. But she didn't say a word. Not as she drank deeply from her tea, staring off into the distance with an unusually somber expression.

"We need to head out by midday if we want to make it to the port on time," Daciana said, because it was true, and because she couldn't stand her silence a moment longer.

"Why wait? Let's depart now," Kenna said, voice flat. She dumped her tea on the brown grass and stomped away, letting the door slam behind her.

IT WAS STRANGE, Kenna's silence. Like a sinking beneath a wave during a raucous storm.

They traveled without speaking. The hayfields had long been cut, baled, and transported to neighboring towns and villages to feed their animals over the winter. Acres of barren land sat under a muted sky.

Autumn in Ardenas was precarious. One moment filled with a violent splash of color—leaves of blood and sunlight—then the next it was as if all the pigment was drained from the world, like the sickly pallor of a corpse.

Daciana felt every change in the air. Felt it roil beneath her skin as the shift in the air sang in her bones.

A storm was coming.

Dark clouds, heavy with the threat of rain, rolled in.

Daciana's jaw clenched. At the first drop of rain, she'd halt their journey. She had wanted to make it past the cornfields abutting Oakbury before they even considered resting. Stormfair wasn't a far cry from the edge of the seemingly never-ending farmland, and then, just beyond, lay Emeraude Port. But she wanted to arrive with ample wait time. There was something calming about having time to spare instead of always chasing it.

A cold drop from the sky landed on Daciana's nose, slicking its way down to her lip.

"We should head for the cover of the trees before the storm picks up." Daciana didn't care she was the first to break the silence. Kenna could keep her pride.

"You're sure it isn't a passing cloud burst?"

"I'm sure if we don't find shelter, we'll be soaked through."

Kenna bit her lip; the graze of her teeth left a band of white where the blood disbursed. Her dark brows drew together as she surveyed the remaining distance. "It's too far and in the wrong direction. I'm not in the business of moving backward. If you feel a veritable storm coming, we should find something closer."

Of course she remembered Daciana's instincts.

Kenna didn't wait for an answer. Instead, she gave a resolute nod and marched forward.

Daciana trailed behind the girl with the red cloak, content to follow her into the storm.

DACIANA SHIVERED beneath her rain-soaked cloak.

The sky bellowed another rumble of thunder, pelting them with an unforgiving storm. Days like this were rare in the autumn season. It was a farewell from summer, come too late. The wind had a bite, and the clouds were just as violent in their release. Daciana wiped the thick drops from her eyes, pushing forward.

They'd made their way through most of the farmland, but the miles of open terrain weren't safe. It was fortunate they hadn't been struck by lightning already. In the distance, sat a thick forest, but it was beyond their reach with the way the thunder shook the air around them. Though it would seem their luck was finally restored, in the middle of the field was something even better than the cover of trees.

A dilapidated barn stood against the stormy sky.

"Paragon's nethers, is that what I think it is?" Kenna shielded her eyes.

Daciana's teeth chattered. "It's shelter."

They hurried across the field. Daciana's steps were heavy under the weight of soaked clothing. She trekked through muck and puddles that seemed to find every opening in her worn boots.

The makeshift shelter sagged under the weight of the storm. The wooden structure was littered with holes and openings, but at least it had a roof. Thatched with old hay, it would shield them from the brunt of the storm.

Kenna yanked on one of the double doors, fighting against the wind. Daciana reached over to help. The two slipped into the dark barn, and the door shut with a heavy thud. The air was dank and musty like the shed hadn't been opened in months. A large mound of forgotten grain sat waiting on the floor, filling the corner.

"It's a tithe barn," Daciana said through clenched teeth. If she continued chattering and shivering, Kenna was bound to suggest taking their wet clothes off for warmth. And as smart as that would be, the temptation to lick the rain from her skin—

"Ugh, fucking zealots," Kenna said with a huff.

She had every right to be annoyed. There were still a few circles of the faithful that so revered the Paragons of Virtue and the Warriors of Avalon, that they would gather tithes for the silent gods. Even if their children starved.

Daciana shivered, clutching her useless cloak tighter. It squelched against her soaked tunic.

"You know we need to take these off." Kenna was already tugging her wet clothing free, oblivious to the way Daciana turned away and tightened her grip on her wet wool fabric.

Daciana's mouth went dry. "I'll be fine."

"Don't be stupid. It won't do you any good if you catch your death."

Practical. That's all it was. A practical survival strategy. Daciana pushed away her lingering doubt and unfastened her cloak. It fell with a thwack against the stale, straw-covered floor, and a violent shiver wracked her body. Toeing off her boots, she tried not to think too much as she pulled her tunic over her head with shaking fingers. She left her breastband in place—there was no reason to remove the strip of fabric —and instead moved to her leather breeches. They clung to her legs, shrunken with rain. She shucked them off and immediately set to work, fixing the legs to hang-dry them.

Down to her smallclothes, Daciana turned to find a low hanging beam to set them on and froze.

Kenna stared at her, eyes wide, and pale pink mouth gaping.

Daciana stood a little taller, ignoring the shudder threatening to spread through her. Despite the flush of something forbidden close enough to touch, the cold had seeped into her marrow.

Kenna crept closer. Her pale expanse of skin pebbled with the cold. Her dark breastband concealed her modest chest, and she still wore her soaked breeches. Both her tunic and cloak were abandoned on the floor, and with each step, her expression grew more desperate and unsure. Her black hair clung to her neck and forehead.

Daciana opened her mouth to either say Kenna's name or tell her to stop, but no sound came out. Kenna's steps were too fast and too slow. Daciana wanted nothing more than to pull her flush against her body and taste every word she hadn't said.

"Dac." Kenna's voice was an aching whisper that landed like a heavy blow. She stood before Daciana like a ripe offering or a damning temptation. Who could be sure anymore?

With trembling fingers, Daciana pushed Kenna's black fringe, messy and uneven, away from her face. Kenna leaned into the touch, her eyes fluttering closed. Daciana ran her hungry gaze over Kenna's face. Her skin was brighter than the moon, and a dusting of freckles across her nose begged for her kiss. Finally, those eyes opened. Warm brown with shades of gold. They were elegantly arched, and for once not sparkling with mischief, but with a want so fierce it stole the breath from Daciana's chest.

Daciana traced the side of Kenna's face, cupping her chin and marveling at how such pale skin flushed pink. Her mind felt cleaved from her body, watching herself touch and stroke as if there were no consequences in this blighted world. She was dizzy, flushed with an aching desire she never let herself feel anymore. With a steadying breath, Daciana closed the space between them. Kenna's lips parted in a gasp, and Daciana took her chance to taste the sound. Kenna was sweet—she always had been. Sweet with a hint of sharpness, like a nearly ripened berry. Daciana explored her mouth, alternating between tasting and caressing her full, soft lips.

Kenna gripped Daciana's hip with an edge of desperation, her other hand running to grasp the back of her neck. Their bodies melded, and it was maddening how much she missed the feel of Kenna's skin against her own. Daciana tangled her fingers in Kenna's wet hair. Despite the chill, fire seared through her veins, nearly sending her to her knees.

Daciana was freezing. She was burning. Drowning. Falling.

Kenna pulled away, eyes hazy. Her mouth was reddened, raw with their kiss. "Daciana."

Daciana shivered and leaned in to catch her mouth again, tasting deeply, and wrenching a soft moan from Kenna's throat. This was everything, *every* sensation she'd been dreaming of. Kenna's kiss still tasted of fire, and the scorching slide of her touch was enough to banish every fear and doubt Daciana desperately clung to.

"Dac, you're burning up."

Her words made no sense. Of course she was burning up. She was on bloody fire and needed her to douse the flame. With her body, her hands, her mouth—

Kenna placed the back of her hand against Daciana's forehead. "Shit, you're feverish."

Daciana opened her mouth to respond when a wave of dizziness spun her vision. Kenna's arms came around her, keeping her upright.

"Come on." Kenna pulled her deeper into the barn. She tipped her bag, dumping out a grey linen blanket. "Now you can't berate me for lifting this from the inn."

A thin, scratchy blanket draped over Daciana's shoulders, and the barn spun. Rotted beams lurched to the side as the world tilted. She sank to the floor, shocked to find her head resting on something soft. Cool fingers found her forehead. A soothing touch that barely held the spins at bay.

"Rest."

CHAPTER TWENTY-NINE

LARK

The warrior, a thickly muscled woman, flashed Lark a dangerous grin. She wore a long, brown tunic under the mantle of a wolf pelt. Her light-red hair was twisted in a top knot, her impressive arms flexing as she tossed her bo staff—razor-sharp blade flashing at the top—from one hand to the other.

A lithe woman sauntered beside her. Her long snowy hair was shaved to the scalp on one side of her head. She wore simple, light leathers. On her back gleamed two thick hilts of her swords, and at her hip an ornate handle jutted out from a thin scabbard. A rapier by the look of it. How many swords did one person need? She could have been a duelist, or at least someone with enough vested interest to master multiple methods of swordplay. Duelists were hired blades but regarded with far more respect than mercenaries. Duels were an art form, a bridge between the old ways and the new. It was common for noble families in Koval to settle legal matters by dueling. Sometimes to the death, sometimes to first blood, and duelists were swordsmen hired to fight in the name of conflicting parties. It was a profession marked by study and training of many forms.

So what in the blazes was she doing here?

The possible duelist bore no discernible expression. Just a cold, quiet acceptance. Like killing Lark was a job, and nothing more.

Lark circled her sword again, wincing at the twinge of protest in her muscles.

The warrior and duelist split up, both advancing with lethal swiftness. Two directions to block. Two ways to die.

Lark's sword caught the edge of steel. The clash rang through her teeth. Barely enough time to spin. To block. To dodge. Lark leapt back, throat tight. They weren't like the others.

They advanced; the sword wielder was lithe on her feet. Lethal and graceful. The tower of a woman spun her bo staff, formidable and agile. A dark smile graced her face.

Lark shot out, striking and feinting. A push-pull. But it wasn't enough. She couldn't exhaust them. There was always a blade to block, a blow to parry. Lark's sword was heavy in hand as she fought for each breath. The duelist was faster, blocking and dodging, sure-footed with the beginning of a smile on her lips. She was always just out of reach, a heartbeat faster in anticipation than Lark could maneuver.

Fire lanced up the front of Lark's thigh. She cried as she jumped back, blood blooming across the front of her trousers. It wasn't deep, but the sting of it burned.

Beneath the shroud of snowy hair, the duelist lifted her blade for closer inspection. Her pale hand ran down her sword, collecting Lark's blood. She held her stare as she smeared a trail of red across the bridge of her nose.

Was that for her benefit, or for the amusement of the crowd?

Lark's distraction was rewarded with a blow to the back of her skull. The sand rushed up to meet her, scorching her cheek. At least, the fine, soft grains were deceptively gentle. With a shaky hand, she felt the back of her pounding head. Her touch burned, and her hair was wet with her blood.

Lark pushed up to all fours. A firm kick to her gut knocked her flat. The air rushed from her lungs in a violent surge. A deep cough pulled from her throat, ripping through her. She gripped her stomach, trying to inch away. A throaty laugh came from above, before a boot barreled into her face.

Lark dropped, rolling and clutching her jaw.

A sharp cut across her bare arm, and more of her blood fed the sand. The crowd was ravenous, begging for more.

Another cough wracked Lark's chest. Her mouth filled with blood. Choking her.

A heavy boot lowered over her hand. Lark cried out as the crushing weight stole the strength of her grip. Her sword was kicked out of her limp grasp, skittering along the sand.

The butt of the staff came down hard in a blow to her ribs. Lark curled on her side, a small sound escaping her throat. They could end it at any moment—they were toying with her. Perhaps Yuri even asked them to put on a good show. Perhaps he knew she'd never walk out of this arena. She pulled herself tighter, bracing against the kicks against her back, her legs, her head.

Beneath her fetal form, Lark's hand snuck into her boot, dragging Hugo's dagger out. She cracked an eye, waiting for the stomp she knew would be coming. As the shadow descended, Lark positioned the blade to strike. Hugo's knife sank through the bottom of the large warrior's foot. Her howls of pain echoed around them. Lark bolted upright, barely blocking the end of a sword. It was close—much too close. She needed to get her sword to have a chance.

Lark rolled away, trying to leap to her feet. She buckled, landing on her knees. The thrill of the fight had fled long ago. Every blow she'd received—every slice in her skin screamed.

The warrior hobbled back, favoring her injured foot. Splatters of her blood adorned the sand. Her bo staff whistled against the wind as she circled and spun the long, thick weapon. Too fast for Lark to halt the strike—the blade pierced her shoulder. A flare of heat erupted in her skin. Lark cried, grabbing the end of the staff. The warrior grinned, yanking it out with a slice through Lark's palm, showering the reddish sand with drops of her blood.

The duelist had unsheathed her rapier now, also brandishing one of her short swords. She must have tossed the other at some point.

Lark lifted her hazy stare at the women standing before her. A blade snaked out to her throat, and Lark's dagger caught it, shoulder aching with the movement. The sword still bit into the side of her neck. A sharp kiss of steel. Lark swayed on her knees. Another flash of steel, and her cheek wept blood with a stinging bite.

She'd failed. Failed Gavriel. Failed all of them. Daciana, Alistair, Langford, Hugo—

Would she see him in the afterlife? What was the afterlife now? Was it a great gaping void with no one leading souls on? Would she linger, forced to watch the destruction of the world as Nereida tore down the veil and unleashed her wrath upon the earth?

Lark's blood roared in her ears. What she wouldn't give to see Gavriel's face one more time before it all went dark.

The force of the bo staff slamming against her knuckles dropped Hugo's knife to the sand.

The warrior wore a smug expression, amusement in her eyes as she stared Lark down—before her face went slack. Without warning, her body tipped forward, landing in the sand. Lark blinked, shock washing over her, until she spotted the small dart in her thick neck.

A grin stretched across Lark's face. It was tight beneath the layers of blood, grime, and sand, but triumphant. She glanced up at the duelist as another one of Hazel's darts speared into her delicate neck. Her hand flew up to grab it, before she dropped to her knees, glaring at Lark. The duelist lifted her swaying sword, trying to slash at her before the sedative knocked her out. She collapsed in the sand, the rapier still in her grip.

Lark struggled to stand, needing her weapons before they unleashed the next threat. A firm hand gripped beneath her arm, yanking her up. Lark turned, finding icy blue eyes, bronze skin, and dark hair neatly plaited around her head in a crown. *Hazel.*

"You came back."

Hazel arched a brow, mouth quirking as she released Lark. "Maybe I just couldn't let you hog all the action."

Lark laughed, a hysterical edge of a sound. "By all means, I'm more than happy to share."

The commanding horn bellowed, calling for more carnage. Lark and Hazel exchanged a look.

"Get your weapons and get ready. I expect you to hold your own." Hazel's face was tight.

Evidently, playing the part of the rescuer did little to soften her demeanor.

Lark spat out the blood coating her tongue. "I watch your back, you watch mine."

"Deal. Now go get your sword. I'm not dying here today."

Lark bent down, cringing at the way her ribs popped. She yanked her sword from the sand, soft grains cascading to the ground. Her bow was still on the other side of the arena, discarded when she'd realized her opponent was a mere boy who looked as if he'd never held a sword before. Curse her foolishness.

The horn bellowed again, in two shorter successions. With luck, it meant the end of sanctioned bloodshed.

The crowd had turned their attention to the uppermost deck. Lark followed their line of sight. Yuri stepped out from the shadows of the light canvas tarp, shielding the upper seating from the retreating sun. He held up his hands, quieting the crowd. "Good people, you may have noticed our new fighter this day." His mouth slanted as he angled his head. The setting sun glinted off the gold hoops lining his ears. "I know many of you must be wondering after our Bastard Crow. But don't fret!" His grin turned savage, stretching the scars across his dark face. This was not the bargaining leader Lark made her deal with. This was the king of the arena, and his words riled the crowd like a compulsion born of magic. A call for blood.

Lark shifted, gripping her Kovalian sword like a lifeline. Dreading whatever came next.

"I couldn't possibly leave him out of the arena on a day such as today." Yuri swept a hand to the opposite side of the arena, where an older man stood, his grey hair tied back. He wore a deep frown. Lark recognized this man from Gavriel's nightmare in the shrine. *Hamlin.* Gavriel's former master, who only released him to place a bounty on his head.

Maddox was right, that bastard. He'd told them as much in the heavily perfumed brothel. Hamlin was Yuri's honored guest. Brought here to witness the fall of one of his assassins at the hands of the rival guild.

"Today, we welcome our most esteemed guest, and what sort of host would I be if I denied him the thrill of witnessing our newest up-and-comer?"

The crowd roared with a violence reserved for the battlefield. Lark and Hazel exchanged furtive glances.

The metal grate of the cage door lifted, and the screech of the mechanism was almost lost to the rumble of the spectators.

Lark's breath caught in her throat as her heart plummeted to the pit of her stomach. Yuri was a lying bastard.

Gavriel stood, every inch the proud warrior. His bare chest heaved with each breath, lean gladius in one hand and a formidable broadsword in the other. Gone was Gavriel's cool, collected demeanor —of sharp blades and careful control. He'd become the beast again.

Perhaps it made the arena easier to endure.

His leather armor comprised straps crossing his back and chest, layers of covering guarding his shoulders. His chest and torso were bare in the diminishing sun. Shadows crept along every scar, every muscle, and carved a path of dark lines across his expanse of skin.

His steps were heavy with purpose as he advanced onto the sand. Lark's gaze darted to his wounded leg, noting the slight limp he tried to hide. Gavriel's eyes found her face, and a glimmer of worry crossed his features before he schooled them into a vicious mask.

When Gavriel was only a few paces away, he let his gaze run over Lark, surveying her wounds. His face tightened as he marked the cuts to her face, her arms, her shoulder, before landing on the way she stood, off kilter to avoid putting too much pressure on her calf. A sound loosed from his chest that sounded suspiciously close to a growl.

"It would appear we'll be witnessing teams forming today!" Yuri's voice boomed from the stands. "A decision sprung from the moment when the lovely viper joined the fight uninvited." His voice hardened to a sharp edge on the last word. Yuri didn't appreciate

Hazel's last-minute help. Lark cast a desperate look Gavriel's way, but he was staring off into the crowd, at where Hamlin stood, watching.

"The team left standing will be proclaimed the winner." Yuri's white teeth flashed in what looked more like a snarl than a smile.

Oh, he was pissed.

The commanding horn thundered—a sound Lark was beginning to hate.

Three fighters strolled out onto the sand: A hooded figure, compact and small in stature. His steps were tight and quick, frantic even. A thick leather bandolier ran from his chest down to his opposite hip. A row of spherical glass vials glowed with an iridescent shimmer like he'd bottled moonlight. His tattered cloak billowed behind him as he paced toward them in his hole-riddled boots.

Beside him, a tall, broad man sauntered at a leisurely pace. His golden hair was tied at the nape of his neck and the buttons of his ill-fitting guardsman uniform glinted with every step. The Kovalian colors of red and gold were faded and smudged with dirt, but he held his chin high, a proud smirk on his tan face. He kept one hand on the longsword he wore at his waist, but his eyes zeroed in on Gavriel, and his smirk widened across his face.

The third figure was hidden beneath a dark cowl. He moved with a fluid grace as he approached. His lean but firm frame was familiar, as was the dark bronze and scarred jaw that tightened. He was the same man who brought Lark her weapons and told her to fight free of honor. Though his blades remained hidden, she'd bet he carried more than any of them. He dropped his cowl, revealing the sharp edges of his striking face.

Beside Lark, Hazel stiffened and yanked her daggers free. Lark swung the Kovalian sword, anything but ready for another fight. Aches wracked her body, reminding her of how close the last fight came to ending in her demise. Gavriel turned and met her gaze. A violent ache of longing glimmered for but a moment before his mask slipped back into place.

The golden-haired swordsman yanked his weapon free, and the

scrape of steel resonated in a sustained note. He pointed the tip of his blade in Gavriel's direction.

"Guess he picked his favorite," Hazel muttered. "I want the tall one."

"That leaves me with—" But before Lark could finish, the man beneath his ragged hood yanked a glass flask free from its hold and launched it straight for her. It exploded in the sand at her feet. Lark flew back from the blast, landing flat on her back. Stars exploded in her vision, ears ringing. Lark groaned, struggling to stand. She needed her bow; he'd never let her get close enough to strike him down. Lark pushed herself to stand, the earth spinning with the movement. Again, she cursed her foolishness for leaving the bow across the arena. The awful sound of another glass clinking free from its hold rang out.

Gavriel skidded in front of her and knocked the bomb away. It exploded somewhere off to the side, blasting red sand to rain down.

The golden guardsman brought down a heavy strike, taking Gavriel's distraction as an opportunity. Gavriel caught it and spun it away.

Lark needed to get as far from them as possible. Find her bow, take out the bastard, then assess who could use her help. Not Gavriel. He had a tendency to make foolish mistakes where she was concerned. Hazel then. Lark limped across the arena, to where she'd left her bow and quiver from the first fight—to where they still sat, waiting. Hazel seemed to hold her own against the pretty assassin. His hood had blown back to reveal his dark, chiseled face, calm and controlled, as he met her strike for strike. Almost like a choreographed dance.

A bomb exploded at Lark's feet, sending her face first to the ground. Sand filled her mouth and stung her eyes. She didn't stop to wipe them, just crawled as fast her body would allow, spitting out blood and sand. She'd seen her bow, just a few paces ahead, and needed to get to it before—

Another clink of glass. Lark waited a heartbeat, then covered her head with her arms and rolled. A blast spewed sand into the air beside her. This was her chance. Lark squinted against the sand stinging her eyes and scuttled toward the blurry shape of her weapons. When her fingers closed around the smooth wood of her bow, she nearly wept. She staggered to her feet and grabbed an arrow, yanking and holding at her anchor point. Her ribs and shoulder screamed in protest with sharp, jabbing pain. Her bloodied hand nearly slipped as the bow pressed against her stinging wound. She whipped her mark from side-to-side, searching for that damn tempest. Her vision was still blurred, but she didn't dare lower her bow.

Breathe. Hold.

The sound of glass clinking to her right brought a smile to her filthy face. She turned, his compact shape was poised to toss another bomb, or so she assumed. She loosed the arrow and rolled, praying to the skies she didn't miss and hit Gavriel or Hazel. When she landed on her back, she hissed. She wasn't doing her injuries any favors. The air left her lungs in a rush as the bomb hit its mark beside her, showering small rocks and sand over her face. Lark wanted to just lay here and wait for this horrible day to end. But a deep groan of pain sounded, followed by the whoosh of a body hitting the sand.

Heart hammering in her throat, she waited, listening. The clash of steel rang from the opposite side of the arena, and the roar of the crowd continued in angry jeers, but all was quiet where she lay in the sand. She bit back her cry as she stood, staggering back a few paces. Bow still in hand, she nocked another arrow. Her ribs creaked in objection. If she hadn't hit him, chances were she'd hear another of his glass containers. She staggered across the sand, blinking rapidly until her vision cleared enough to see two sets of fighters still going strong. She glanced at the body on the ground. The alchemist lay unmoving in the sand, her first arrow jutting from his chest. Lark released her next arrow, letting it sink into his side. Not even a flinch, but at least she was certain he was dead. Lark slung her bow onto her back and rubbed the heels of her hands against her eyes.

The fading sun had lit the arena ablaze in the last glow of the day. And another body fed the sand.

Gavriel bellowed, cutting and slashing.

Hazel leapt, kicking and jabbing.

Lark gripped her ribs—she suspected they were broken. With each breath, they rattled a sharp pain. As her energy ebbed, more aches shuddered through her body. She loosened her hold on her bow, granting the barest of relief for her bleeding palm. Her calf burned, soaking the back of her pants with fresh blood. Heat flared in her thigh at each shuffled step she took toward Gavriel. Her bloody shoulder burned and her entire back was slick with sweat.

Hazel was still engaged in a fluid dance, battling the assassin with grace and speed.

Lark was close enough now that Gavriel's fierce stare met her own over the shoulder of his golden-haired opponent. With a guttural sound, Gavriel slashed, driving his blade home. Blood rained across his obscenely handsome face, painting his snarling rage a violent crimson. He knocked the man down and stepped over him, ignoring the way he coughed and bled his final moment. Gavriel's intense focus zeroed in on Lark as he charged up to her. His limp had returned in full force, but it didn't slow him down.

Lark's chest seized as he closed the distance and pulled her into his arms. Sweat, grime and blood mingled on their skin, but Lark sagged against him. Relief and exhaustion nearly sent her to her knees. Was this to be their fate? A lifetime of death chasing after the mark she cheated?

"Let me look at you," Gavriel's voice rumbled. He gently lifted her chin with two fingers, turning her head to examine the cuts on her cheek. He made a noise in his throat. "I'm still furious you're here."

Lark laughed, then groaned, gripping her side. Gavriel's stare dropped to the movement.

"You're injured?" His broad hand swept over her ribs.

"Only everywhere." Lark offered a weak smile. "Should we go help Hazel?"

Gavriel eyed her with disapproval, before glancing over to where Hazel continued her dance of death. "No. She's been toying with him this whole time. When she's done playing, she'll finish it."

It would be better to finish it now. They still needed to put as much distance between them and Hamlin as humanly possible. They had the entirety of the Desolates to cross before she'd feel sure they would not be dragged back into this skies forsaken arena. Lark groaned. Gavriel smoothed his hands down her arms, searching her face for signs of pain, but she brushed him off.

"I'm all right. You saw who was in the stands?"

Gavriel stiffened, hands stilling. "Yes. I wish he didn't have to witness this."

"Didn't he train you to be an assassin?"

"Yes, but this is different. I never wanted to bring him shame." Gavriel's voice had gone quiet. He placed a whisper of a kiss on her forehead. "Let's tell Hazel to finish."

They traipsed across the sand, to where Hazel and her opponent had suddenly ceased their fight and were staring each other down. His dark, chiseled features were shrouded in a wary shadow.

"Leander…" Hazel murmured.

"I invoke the right to a stalemate," he said smoothly, sheathing his daggers with practiced ease. "I will not fight you."

"Don't be stupid." Hazel edged a step closer. "They'll punish you… it's not worth it. Fight me."

He grinned, and the beauty of that smile didn't belong in the harsh, bloody sands. He held his arms out to the side, gesturing all around. "What more can they do to me?" His golden-brown eyes bore into her like he didn't possess the ability to look away before he forced himself to turn and stride back to the cage.

Hazel stared after him, face falling. She thrust her daggers back into place, never tearing her eyes off his receding form.

"You know him?" Lark asked.

Hazel's face melted into cool indifference. She turned to Lark and made a noncommittal noise. "It doesn't matter." Surveying both Lark and Gavriel, she let out a whistle. "You look like shit."

The commanding horn blew, and for the first time the deep vibrations were music to Lark's ears. The crowd was a buzzing dissonance. She couldn't tell if they were angry or cheering. Did it matter? Blood had been spilt, their hunger should be sated. Her knees sagged in relief, and Gavriel caught an arm around her waist before she hit the sand.

"It's over," Lark breathed.

Yuri stepped out to face the crowd once more. He ran a large hand over his beard, a tentative smile dawned across his dark face. "We have a winner!" His voice boomed, cheers erupted in the stands.

Lark smiled up at Gavriel—his expression remained wary.

"But who amongst the winning team will be crowned champion?"

Lark felt the smile on her face freeze. That bastard couldn't be serious.

"That's right, good people! There can only be one crowned champion. Since the lady viper reached a stalemate with her opponent, she was disqualified."

Ice froze through Lark's veins. She cast a panicked glance at Hazel, who appeared just as shocked. If he was suggesting—

"The Bastard Crow and the Living Flame will have to decide who shall stand!" Yuri's eyes found Lark's. They were empty and dull as he delivered his parting words. "And who shall fall."

Gavriel's arm tightened around Lark. She gasped against the pressure in her ribs, but couldn't bring herself to loosen his hold. This couldn't be happening. She'd only just got him back. Her muscles locked up as Lark stared up at him, grabbing a hold of his pauldron to hold herself upright.

"Gavriel," she choked.

"Shh," he said. He pressed his mouth to hers in a shaky kiss. "It'll be all right."

All she'd ever done was try to save him. Perhaps this was what fate had been trying to show her all along. That he'd always slip through her fingers. Like this skies forsaken sand.

She would not fight him, and he would not fight her. But even they couldn't take on the whole of Yuri's guards.

Thanar's words echoed in her head.

This is why Reapers don't love. This is why your mortal shall fall and the pain will consume you.

Angry tears rolled down her filthy cheeks. It wasn't fair. It wasn't fucking fair. But when had she ever relied on fate for kindness? She wouldn't start now. "It doesn't end this way. I will not allow it. You will not die here."

He shook his head. "You never should have come here, Lark. I accept my fate. Why can't you?"

"I'll never accept it. I'll never stop fighting against your death, Gavriel. Don't you get it?" It went against every instinct in her body, both mortal and before. She'd never sit by and watch him fade from this world.

Gavriel ran a hand through his blood and sweat matted hair. "Can't you just kiss me and let me go?"

"Could you?"

His eyes tightened, face falling. He shook his head, exhaling a sharp breath. Two heartbeats passed before he crashed her against his chest, sealing his mouth over hers. Lark gasped in pain—her ribs were definitely broken, and fresh tears tracked down her face. Teeth clanged, and Lark bit down on his lip. Their kiss was angry and brutal. Angry at this world. At all that stood to keep them apart. At the way it would end.

"What's this?" Yuri's voice called out from his post. Someone must have designed the space to optimize the acoustics. "I believe we might make history, good people. I see a challenger, eager to step in for our fighter."

Lark and Gavriel turned to find none other than Hamlin, calmly walking across the sand. His arms were tucked behind his back as he regarded them with an indulgent expression.

Gavriel's hold on Lark loosened as he gaped at his former master.

Hamlin stopped a few short paces away, cocking his head. "Hello, Gavriel."

LARK'S HEAD SPUN. The man standing before her, with keen blue eyes and perfect posture, was the man who shaped Gavriel into the weapon he was.

Gavriel's throat bobbed. His eyes were glassy. "Master Hamlin."

Hazel kept a safe distance. As if just being near Hamlin might send her back to her cage.

"And a hello to you, too, Hazel." Hamlin peered around them with an affectionate smile. He turned his stare back to Gavriel. "Well, I'll admit this isn't how I hoped we'd meet again."

"What did you hope?" Lark couldn't halt the words from leaping off her tongue. "You placed a bounty on Gavriel's head, cursing him to be hunted for the rest of his life. I'm curious. What did you hope for a reunion?"

Gavriel had gone utterly still beside her.

Hamlin chuckled, a rich warm sound. "I hoped I'd never see him again, actually. So I guess a reunion in the afterlife. I thought he'd live his life in a quiet fashion—free from too much excitement." Hamlin regarded Gavriel with a disparaging look. "I can see your penchant for trouble hasn't faded."

"Master Hamlin, I—"

"Oh, I think we can do away with the formalities," Hamlin said, cutting a hand through the air. "After all, I'm no longer your master, am I?"

Gavriel tightened his lips and nodded.

Hamlin gave Lark a hard look. The lines on his face deepened, as if just looking at her aged him. "You keep him out of trouble. This" —he circled his finger in the air, indicating the arena— "can't happen again."

Lark swallowed her retort and nodded. If he was using his social capital to free Gavriel, she could stand to be civil. Maybe.

Hamlin stepped forward, clapping Gavriel on the shoulder. Lark watched his movement warily.

"Gavriel, I have failed you in so many ways." Hamlin's blue eyes softened. "I can't atone for everything you lost. But know this" —he rested his hand on the back of Gavriel's neck— "you never failed to make me proud."

Gavriel lifted his head, face tight.

Hamlin backed away a step, eyes wet with unshed tears. "Allow me to do one thing right." He turned to where Yuri stood and gave a curt nod.

Gavriel's face froze, uncertainty warring with lingering pain.

Hamlin whipped off his black cloak and tossed it. The dark shroud billowed before it landed in the sand. He pulled a short sword from the scabbard hanging from his belt. "Make it quick, make it clean."

Gavriel shook his head. "I'm not fighting you."

Hamlin's eyes flashed before he darted a glance at Lark. "You will, boy. You'll end this the right way." He lunged, aiming to strike where Lark stood.

Gavriel's sword was an extension of his arm. A knee-jerk reaction as he deflected and pulled Lark behind him. "I said no."

Hamlin spun. His blade glinted, shooting out to strike once more. Gavriel blocked. The clang of steel was sharp and unforgiving.

Hamlin disarmed him with a rapid spin of his sword. Gavriel's weapon sang through the air, landing in Hamlin's outstretched hand. He tossed it back to Gavriel with a growl. "Stop playing and fight me, boy." Again, he aimed around Gavriel as if posing to strike at her.

Gavriel halted his pass with a blinding flourish of steel.

It happened so fast, Lark couldn't be sure what she'd witnessed. Hamlin's expression was serene, a calm contentment. He appeared almost pleased—until red bloomed across his throat. It poured so viciously, even as he dropped and tipped forward. The sand beneath his corpse deepened in violent color.

All around them, the crowd erupted. The last sacrifice to the blood-thirsty arena.

Lark stood frozen, unable to breathe as Gavriel sank to his knees.

CHAPTER THIRTY

LANGFORD

Langford fiddled with his sleeve, tugging and pulling as if it would somehow ease his impatience.

Ingemar had called on him to meet in her quarters, without Alistair, but when Langford arrived, she was nowhere to be found. Her desk was a pile of chaos and parchments. Wax from over-burnt candles spilled over the side of the short brass prickets. Beyond the disorder of her desk, large windows cast a ghostly light across the space. Grey waters gently lapped against the ship beneath a fugue of thick mist.

The night before played in Langford's mind—how quickly she'd dismissed them after learning the truth about everything. About Lark, about the world. Truths even Langford scarcely believed. It was difficult, this balancing act between what he knew and what he felt. Like carrying his mother's beliefs through University. His education and traditions were always at war with each other. But his mother's faith was all Langford had left of her, so he kept it close. Even as the gods of Avalon remained silent.

Minutes slipped by. Ingemar's crew remained above, working away as they sailed closer to Emeraude Port. To Daciana and Lark. He had enough of the text translated to hold a discussion, at the very least. But part of him hoped he could give them more. An answer, whole and defined. He'd had more than enough time to prove himself. Why did he always seem to come up short?

The creak of the door made Langford jump in his seat. Ingemar swept in, kicking the door shut behind her. Her boots were heavy against the floorboard as she strutted to her desk. She collapsed in her seat with a huff, tossing her hat across the room and pinching the bridge of her elegant nose.

Langford wiped his sweaty palms on his dark trousers.

"I'm sure you're wondering why I called for you." Ingemar still hadn't looked up at him. She wore the same clothes from the night before, the wine stain from when she spilled down her chin was a stark red against her white tunic.

"Admittedly, I'm curious," Langford began. "I suppose whatever it was, you couldn't share it with Alistair."

Ingemar dropped her hand. "You're a smart boy, Langford. Do you really need me to tell you not to trust Alistair?"

Langford bit the side of his cheek, halting his response until his mind could catch up with his tongue. "I'm not ignorant of Alistair's way of doing things," he finally said. "Nor am I ignorant of the way truth gets muddled between two perspectives."

Ingemar's narrow eyes crinkled with mirth. "Spoken with careful diplomacy." She reached for a brown bottle on the corner of her desk, yanking the cork off with a *pop*. Tipping the bottle against her lips, she swallowed with a groan. "But I didn't bring you here to listen to your pretty words."

Langford scraped a hand through his hair. He wished Alistair were here to tell her to get on with it.

"I thought about what you said last night, and I'm inclined to believe you."

A rush of pleasant relief spread over him even as his curiosity piqued. What matters of impossible truths had Ingemar faced to believe his tale so readily? He wouldn't voice his question, not yet. For now, her trust was more than enough. So he said, "That's good because I'm not one for false stories."

"No," she said with a soft smile, running her finger over the lip of the bottle. "You're not, are you?"

A nagging twist of nerves formed his stomach. Langford was raised with words that were fashioned for hidden cuts and blows. A threat unspoken weighed heavier than one out loud. "You don't wish for my pretty words. Offer me the same courtesy, Ingemar." He leaned forward. "What do you want from me?"

She pinned him in place with a razor-sharp focus of her dark, narrow eyes. "You're Kovalian, are you not? And of noble birth?"

"Your point?" Langford fidgeted in his chair. If she hoped to capitalize on his family name, she'd be sorely disappointed.

"Have you noticed how much worse things have gotten?" Ingemar was gripping the neck of the bottle hard enough for bloodless knuckles. "King Zaire is losing it, and he's destroying what little progress his parents made."

Koval was always advanced, a wealthy country built on the backs of indentured servitude and heavy taxation. It took years for King Efrain and Queen Zibiah to turn the tide and lessen the burden on the people. Centuries-old traditions refused to vanish overnight, though Langford suspected they hadn't tried very hard. There were no safeguards in place when they died—nothing to stop their heir from wreaking havoc in the capital. His younger sister, Demetria, would not challenge him, not that she could achieve much as second in line for the throne under her tyrant brother.

Langford cleared his throat. "I wasn't exactly sight-seeing during my brief visit."

Ingemar let out a humorless chuckle. "Three years since Efrain and Zibiah's passing. Zaire has raised the taxes and filled the mines and indentures market tenfold." Ingemar drank deeply from the bottle. "I think the bastard is searching for something."

"Men in power always seek more power."

"No, there's something in those mines he's desperate to find."

Langford snorted. "That's presumptuous. You leap to conclusions based on what grounds? That he's a spoiled little boy posturing with a crowned head?"

"He's not a little boy anymore, and dismissals like that keep him in power."

Langford's cheeks burned. He'd spoken rashly, and having Ingemar, of all people, shame him, stung. He knew nothing of Zaire, who had always been pompous and arrogant when they ran in the same circles in his youth. He knew nothing of Demetria, the young princess he'd only seen at a handful of events when she was a child. He'd fled years ago, and when he was in Koval, the politics weren't his particular interest. But now, his judgment and dismissal were too quick for comfort.

Ingemar was right. If unchecked, Zaire wouldn't be satisfied with just Koval. If his gluttony truly knew no bounds, the peace between Ardenas and Koval was delicate.

"I acknowledge the threat he poses, but what do you expect me to do about it?"

Ingemar's face lit up in a dazzling smile. "I want your help."

Langford tugged at his hair, gripping tight enough for his scalp to burn. He trudged up the steps to the deck.

Alistair wasn't going to like this.

Langford had convinced Ingemar to let him tell Alistair before they docked. To give him time to process. Langford could scarcely believe what he'd agreed to. As if they didn't have enough on their plates. But to take on responsibility for—

Langford smacked into the low hanging ceiling. Sharp pain bloomed across his forehead. He gripped his head as he staggered up the last few steps to the upper deck. The wind was damp with mist, a welcome balm against the spot he was sure was going to bruise. The salty brine of bracing sea air filled his lungs. He glanced about until he found the very man he sought.

Up above, Alistair's bronze muscled back was to him, bare. He wore no shoes, only a tight-fitting pair of breeches he'd rolled to his calves. His dark hair was damp and clinging to his neck. Langford schooled his expression into one of curious fascination, hoping it wasn't obvious he'd been gawking at him. Alistair finished shortening the sails—they must have been worried about the masts in this wind—before he glanced over his shoulder and met Langford's gaze. An eager grin lit up his face as he hurried down.

Langford stood in place while Alistair bounded toward him. That maddeningly alluring smile never left his mouth.

Without so much as a greeting, Alistair gripped Langford's tunic and hauled him in for a lazy, open-mouthed kiss.

Langford choked, pushing him back. His cheeks were hot as he glanced around. A couple of whistles rang out at the display. "What is the matter with you?"

Alistair laughed. "You know better than to ask that." His sea glass-green eyes zeroed in on Langford's forehead.

He must have a mark.

Langford rubbed the spot furiously, as if he could erase it. "We need to talk."

"That sounds ominous."

In case Alistair took this badly, they needed a private space. Alistair harbored no great love of Koval, despite the two of them technically being compatriots. Convincing Alistair to aid in anything that didn't benefit him specifically was always a gamble.

But Alistair was turning Langford into a gambling man.

Langford tugged him by the hand, pulling him from the deck to their private quarters.

Once they were safely behind the door, Alistair gripped Langford by the chin, plundering his mouth with a possessive kiss.

Langford melded into it for a moment or two before pushing him back with a sigh. "This is important."

Alistair dropped onto the bed and laced his hands behind his head. He still hadn't put a shirt on. His golden skin glistened with salt water. "So serious. Out with it then."

Langford rubbed the spot on his chest that ached each time Alistair flashed him one of those unguarded smiles. "As you know, I met with Captain Ingemar."

Alistair nodded, crossing his feet.

"Well, she needs a favor."

"Of course she does," Alistair said with a laugh. "What's the little minx want this time?"

Langford dragged the chair over and sat, bracing his elbows on his knees. "Transport."

Alistair quirked a brow. "What are we transporting?" At Langford's hesitation, he sat up. "Langford…"

"A girl." Langford swallowed the lump in his throat. He hadn't even gotten to the hard part yet.

"For fuck's sake. What's this, penance for that transport I cocked up?"

"It isn't like that."

"Bleeding abyss, it's not," Alistair said. "I suppose we aren't getting paid for this?"

Langford winced. "Not by Ingemar."

Alistair rose to his feet. Warm fingers tilted Langford's chin. "We can't take a babysitting job and help Lark with her mess. The last time I took responsibility for a stranger, we ended up with an assassin, more unpaid work, and the task of saving the world. Also unpaid, I might add."

Langford pulled his face away from Alistair's touch. "None of that is Lark's fault."

Alistair's eyes softened. "I know. I meant we have enough going on. Tell Ingemar to find someone else." He took his hands, running his thumbs across Langford's knuckles. "It's not the end of the world if we can't be everything to everyone. Poor choice of words, but you know what I mean."

He wasn't wrong. Not in a general sense, that is. "I already told her we'd do it."

Alistair pursed his lips. "Of course you did." He paced to the corner, lifting a tunic out of his pack to tug over his head.

"Alistair," Langford began, standing. Alistair hurried past, straight for the door. "Would you just listen to me?"

Alistair glared at the wall. But at least he was waiting. "What?"

"I couldn't say no. I couldn't turn her down." Langford suspected Alistair wouldn't have been able to turn his back on this, either. Whatever it took, they'd keep her safe. "We have to protect her. The fate of Koval depends on it."

Alistair's brows knitted together as he turned his stare on Langford. "Who are we protecting?"

"Princess Demetria."

CHAPTER THIRTY-ONE

DACIANA

Daciana stumbled through the lonely woods. The unforgiving moon cast harsh light on the forest floor, but never illuminated her steps. She tripped over angry roots and fallen branches that were all too eager to grip her ankles. Her blood pounded a steady beat of power she didn't want, didn't deserve, as she fled Kenna's side. Fled her father's corpse. Her massacred pack.

Daciana's skin was tight with dried blood. The blood of her people. Kenna's blood.

She'd felt the call to her power, the pull in her veins. If she had ascended in honor after the Great Hunt, Daciana's power would have come from her people. Freely given and reciprocated. An enduring cycle of life. But her power came from death. Betrayal. It was tainted beyond measure, and when she felt the call, it was wrong.

Daciana chased the imprint of her power, following the thread.

She had to know.

She had to face what she'd done.

Her footsteps led her through the dark forest, beneath the loom of the shadows. Until the trees thinned, and a small village crept into view. In the distance, the wail of an infant carried on the wind.

Daciana swallowed the cramped space in her throat and moved forward.

A small lamppost swung from a low wooden gate, beckoning her to enter, and the rickety gate creaked under Daciana's touch. The village was silent, save for the lone cry of a babe. The piercing anguish of the sound was shrill and consuming. Suffocation swelled in Daciana's chest. Where was its mother? Why did no one answer its call?

The village comprised simple homes of wood and mud, thatched roofs, and doors left open. More than one hearth was lit that night, warmth spilling out of doors with an orange glow.

And still no answer to the babe's cries.

Daciana crept closer to the sound, pausing at the stone-laid well in the center of town. Bracing a hand against the cool edge, she listened. It was coming from inside the home. She pushed away from the well, marching straight toward the sound of the child. Her foot found something firm.

Daciana glanced down to find a man passed out on the ground, his merchant pack still on his back. She crouched down, placing a hand on his shoulder to shake him awake.

He didn't stir. The chill of death against her hand constricted her chest in panic. Daciana leapt back, finally seeing what her eyes should have glimpsed upon opening the gate.

Bodies. Some only hidden by the shadows of their homes. Others only visible at certain angles peeking in through doors left ajar. A limp hand here. An unnaturally angled leg there.

The screech of the infant pulled Daciana's feet into motion. She staggered into the home, pushing open the cracked door. In swaddling clothes, face scrunched up and red from screaming, the babe shook as if angry.

Daciana lifted the delicate thing into her arms, bringing it to lie on her shoulder. It wailed even harder.

"Shhh, shhh." She bounced gently. "Hush, now. I'm sorry. I'm—"

Daciana stilled. A pair of feet, scarcely larger than the child she now held, stuck out from the corner.

Unmoving.

Daciana bolted upright in a panic. She felt around for the baby, searching her side for the tiny person whose life she'd forever altered. A warm body was beside her, and she ghosted her touch along smooth skin, heart thudding in her chest. Her fingers snagged on a linen cover as her eyes adjusted. Wooden beams, a pile of grain forgotten in the corner, and a grey sky peeking through holes in the walls.

The tithe barn.

Her blanket was damp from sweat or rainwater. Daciana exhaled a shaky breath, pushing the hair from her sweaty forehead. She shifted, trying to stand, but a weight held the blanket down. Kenna. Her mouth was slightly parted as she softly snored. Daciana gently peeled back her side of the covers—

A wail rang in the distance.

Daciana leapt from the straw-covered ground to listen through a hole in the barn wall. The storm had died down, the sky no longer openly weeping, but the roar of the wind was harsh and angry. The barn rattled against the rush of the fierce breeze.

Daciana turned away. She'd likely imagined the sound, as the last of her dream bled away. She pulled her clothes from the low hanging beam, yanking her leather leggings back into place and tugging her linen tunic over her head.

"Dac?" Kenna called out, voice muffled by sleep. Blinking through bleary eyes, she yawned and stretched. "Are you feeling better?"

Daciana nodded. Her skin was still clammy, and she'd need to wash the sweats from sickness away, but the room didn't spin when she stood.

They needed to get moving. They'd wasted hours here and needed to get to Emeraude Port before—

The sharp cry of an infant rang.

Kenna's eyes widened. She heard it, too.

Daciana lunged for the door, shoving it open. The wind ripped at the splintering wood, yanking it hard to slam against the outside of the structure. Her hair whipped against her face. The sky was a turbulent swirl of grey, deepening along the edges of the horizon in threat.

"Daciana, wait!"

She barely registered Kenna's words. She had to find that child.

The cry was distant as it carried on the wind as if it was floating away. Daciana would never let that happen. Ignoring Kenna's pleas, she headed straight for the sound. Stumbling against the harsh bite of the gale.

"Daciana!"

She paused, tying her thick hair back from her face and glancing in Kenna's direction.

Kenna hopped on one foot, laces undone and tunic askew as she tried to yank her other boot into place. "You can't—"

The wind swallowed whatever else she had to say. Daciana shook her head. If Kenna thought it a lost cause, she needn't follow.

The wail echoed, closer this time. Daciana sprinted toward the sound, across the barren field of wasted farmland. Forgotten land no one plowed yet somehow remained flat. Like the earth couldn't force growth. Not here. She ran, relying on the distant anguish of the helpless child to guide her.

The wind howled as if angry she pursued the cry.

Sweat trickled from her brow, and another gust dried it against her skin. The sting of salt seeped into her pores.

Daciana crashed into the edge of the forest, leaning against the damp trunk of an oak. Panting, she turned back to see the abandoned barn in the distance. A sharp cough rattled from her chest, the sound almost a bark. Clutching her side, she bent over to catch her breath. Under the cover of thick trees, the wind skirted around heavy branches, shaking leaves of fire and crimson to shiver. She waited, her heart pounding in her ears.

"Daciana!" Kenna's voice cut through the thicket as she shoved her way in. Her dark eyes were narrowed in anger, pale hands clenched into fists. "What in the fucking abyss was that?"

Daciana shook her head. "I won't leave a child to die."

Kenna's mouth parted, and her dark brows scrunched together. She curled her fingers as if she wanted to strangle her. "There is no child. That's what I'm trying to tell you."

The cry rang out, angry this time. As if the infant heard Kenna's doubt and needed to prove her wrong.

Daciana took off, leaving Kenna cursing at her speed. Kenna never could keep up with her.

The trees thinned, giving way to a clearing, and the cries grew louder, incessant now that she was so close. The lungs must have been strong to wail this loud for this long. Whoever this child might be, they were—

Daciana skidded to a halt, terror constricting her throat.

In the middle of the forest, mounted high enough she had to tilt her head to see its face, sat a scarecrow. A wide brim hat of muted grey hid most of its face. A long, rough-spun coat, riddled with holes, billowed in the breeze. Its limbs stretched out to the sides; gnarled bones twisted like roots. In its gloved hand was a rusted sickle. The stake it was mounted on, was no stake, but a spine too long to be human.

This wasn't a scarecrow.

This was a monster.

A Bubak.

Daciana backed away, never tearing her stare from the sinister creature. A Bubak could mimic a newborn's cry and lure unsuspecting victims to their death. How foolish was she to fall for its tricks?

The whistle of a blade hacking through thick shrubs sounded from nearby. Kenna emerged; the red hood of her cloak was up over her head. A sure signal she wasn't playing, she was hunting. She stilled when she caught sight of Daciana and the Bubak. "Daciana," she said, her voice slow and measured, "we need to go."

Daciana kept her stare trained on the Bubak as she edged back to where Kenna was waiting. She had made a careless mistake when she chased the deception. She left her weapons behind.

"Any point in running?" Daciana asked without turning.

"I've heard it's good for the heart."

"Kenna."

Kenna lifted a hand, placing it in front of Daciana protectively as she angled her longsword at the ready. "Save your strength. It'll follow us, regardless. Let's walk—quickly now."

It felt wrong not to run, to walk at a brisk pace that failed to match the beat of Daciana's pulse, but Kenna was right. They'd need their strength once it attacked.

And it would attack.

Bubaks were relentless once a victim fell prey to their deceits. Daciana had walked straight into its crosshairs, and the only remedy for that was death.

Well, it wouldn't be hers.

The trek back to the barn seemed twice as far. Daciana glanced over her shoulder—

The Bubak's grim mouth peeked beneath its large hat. The grisly creature was now mounted just beyond the edge of the forest. A silent and still pursuer.

"Don't look back. You know this." Kenna's voice was sharp.

Daciana pushed faster, boots sliding over the slick grass. When they were mere paces from the barn, she realized the wind had died down. Each breath, burdened with the sharp rattle of sickness, filled her ears. Did the storm answer to the creature?

Kenna hurried them along, a fine line pinching between her brows. A soft exhale of relief left her lips when they crossed the threshold and shut the door behind them. Heavy silence filled the musty barn.

Daciana snatched her sword belt from the floor and buckled it into place. Her sword and scabbard hung from her waist, home at last. She tucked her blades into place at her hips, giving a touch to the hilts in a familiar, soothing motion. She strapped her baldric over her shoulder and yanked her long sword from her back. It was heavy in her sweaty grip; her illness still rendered her weaker than normal, but it felt right in her hand.

Daciana gave a few practice swings. This was easy, preparing for a fight. It was everything else that was difficult.

"You remember how to kill it?" Kenna asked before she coated her sword with oil from a vial. Fire oil. A form of burning poison she covered her blades with when fire wasn't readily available. That was what she'd told Daciana once. That every monster had a weakness, and her job was to exploit it, by any means necessary.

The fire oil was her grandmother's recipe.

"Fire," Daciana said, finding her voice.

"Good. Get the flint and fire-steel from my pack. I'll keep it busy." Kenna made to move past her, but Daciana held her arm out.

"No, you build the fire. I'm not standing by while you face that thing alone." Fire oil wasn't the same as fire. Kenna was tossing herself into the fray as little more than a distraction.

"Come off it, this is what I'm trained for. Besides, you know damn well I'm not sending you out there sick." Kenna slid her hand down Daciana's arm, stopping to grip her wrist. "Be quick with the fire."

They could argue until the Bubak knocked on the damned door, and it wouldn't make a difference. Daciana's efforts would be better spent building the fire. Based on the set of Kenna's jaw, there was no winning this debate with her. Daciana gently pulled herself free, and set to work searching for dry material.

Kenna yanked the door open, revealing a mottled sky. Daciana knew the Bubak would follow them, but the sight beyond the splintered door tightened her throat.

There it waited in the middle of the field. Its wide-brim hat no longer hid its face. It stared at them with black, fathomless eyes, and a mouth stitched into a half-smile.

Kenna's red cloak billowed in her wake as she stepped out to greet the creature.

Daciana scrambled faster, searching. All the straw and tinder were damp from heavy rain and the state of the barn. She needed to find something that would catch. Perhaps Kenna had something her pack had shielded from the downpour. She snatched up the leather satchel and dumped it out. A bar of soap, her flint and fire-steel, a withered sketchbook, charcoals, and various vials spilled over the ground. Daciana grabbed the sketchbook, flipping through Kenna's bestiary, her drawings and written descriptions of every creature she'd hunted and killed. When she reached a blank page, she yanked some parchment free from the binding. If this could catch—

A sharp screech rang through the air, and Daciana clapped her hands over her ears. It rattled around her skull, blurring her vision and making her tremble. She glanced out the open door—

Swarms of crows beat their black wings, surrounding Kenna. She threw her arms up, covering her face. They circled mercilessly, cawing and pecking.

Daciana's stomach hollowed as the blood thrummed in her ears. Striking the flint, she cursed the spark that failed to cast an ember to the pile of crumpled parchments. She struck again and again.

"Light, damn you."

Another screech cut through the air. Daciana glared at the damp parchments, her anger stirring. This was her fault. She brought this upon them. And now she couldn't light a damn fire. Kenna was out there, and she was here.

"Light!"

The parchment burst into flames. Daciana fell back, her blood running cold. A warm, wet trickle seeped from her nose and over her lips. She wiped it away, refusing to look. She ripped a piece of cloth from Kenna's linen blanket and wrapped it around the end of a damp piece of tinder, lighting it with the flaming parchment.

It burned like a beacon, and Daciana held it high in her hand, her sword in the other. She sprinted out the door, running for Kenna. Gashes bled along Kenna's face, her neck, her hands. Every inch of exposed skin where talons could grip. The crows had dissipated, and Kenna was swinging her sword, a feral cry bursting from her lips. With each swipe, maggots and grubs rained down on her. Over her face and down her chest. The Bubak gave another screech and disappeared in a dark plume. A cloud of black wings surrounded Kenna once more, hiding her from view.

Daciana thrust her torch into the fray, and the sharp smell of burning feathers filled the air. The crows shrieked and flew off, leaving Kenna swaying on her feet.

"See?" Kenna was breathless. "I got the easy job."

A low rumble shook the earth.

It was coming.

Another high pitch screech—Daciana's ears rang.

The Bubak appeared, swinging its rusted sickle. It caught the edge of Kenna's sword, a sharp clang of steel. Daciana jabbed with her torch, pressing the fire into its midsection. Maggots spilled over the small flame. A few of them popped and sizzled as they snuffed out the fire.

The only weapon they had against it, gone.

Daciana looked into the face of the Bubak. She had never been this close to the creature. The pestilential scent of death and decay enveloped her. A wet, squirming sound of grubs and maggots filled her ears. Its skin was a patchwork of varying shades of grey.

That's when she realized it wasn't cloth stitched together, but human skin.

She sliced with her sword, aiming for its heart and trying not to gag when more pale wriggling bodies spilled out and over the hilt. It had no heart. It was a sack of human flesh sewn over worms and larvae. The Bubak raised its sickle, dead eyes fixed on Kenna—

An inhuman sound broke free from Daciana's chest. Her teeth hummed as the command tore through her veins.

Kenna's sword lit aflame, a burning red and orange licking up her steel without melting the blade. Her eyes widened, a shock of fear and warm light painted her features. She plunged the flaming sword deep into the Bubak. A thousand voices screeched. A shuddering cacophony of pain and anger. Its body erupted, immolating high into the sky.

Daciana pulled Kenna back, yanking her away from the scorching flames. They collapsed on the earth, still damp from the previous rain, and scooted away until their backs hit the wall of the old barn. Daciana glanced at Kenna. She was shaking, and claw marks marred her smooth skin—but that wasn't the sight that gave Daciana pause. A thin line of red ran from Kenna's nose and over her chin. Blood.

With a trembling hand, Daciana wiped it away.

Kenna's gaze finally broke free from the charred remains of the Bubak. Her dark eyes were wide with fear as she searched Daciana's face.

Daciana opened her mouth to speak. But what could she say? What

words would land softest? She shook her head and pressed her lips to
Kenna's forehead.

They didn't need words to know what she'd done.

Daciana had tapped into that forbidden well—called upon Kenna to
fuel her power.

Words were nothing when one was a monster.

CHAPTER THIRTY-TWO

LARK

Lark traced patterns against the damp earth as Gavriel changed her bandage. The forest floor was hard against her stomach, but her calf had needed stitching. Gavriel still refused to speak to her, but he was dedicated to preventing infection. He'd already wrapped her ribs in terse silence. The rest of her wounds were superficial.

Gavriel's leg had been the first injury they treated. His face didn't even flicker when she cleaned it out and stitched the gash closed. They'd cleared his wound of the beginning stage of infection. It could have been far worse.

Gavriel stilled, and Lark chanced a glance over her shoulder. He set his sharp jaw in stubborn determination. The shadows on his face had deepened in the low light of dusk. An autumn breeze skirted through the trees, ghosting a chill along Lark's skin. They'd made it through the mountains and into Arden Forest, where the harvest season claimed the land in a cool grip and chased the leaves from the trees. But Lark couldn't bring herself to miss the heat of the Desolates.

"Thank you," Lark said, knowing full well he wouldn't answer.

Gavriel wiped his hands and stood. Something cold had settled in

Lark's gut in that arena, a sinking feeling of dread that had yet to abate. Gavriel was hurting, and she didn't know what to do.

"Should be the last night we make camp before we hit the next town." Hazel's voice cut through the forest. Bridgebarrow couldn't be far off. And then they could be back on their way to Emeraude Port to meet the others.

Lark met Hazel's piercing gaze. The girl missed nothing, and by the frown she wore, Gavriel and Lark's distance was obvious. But she didn't say a word about it.

"That's good," Lark said. They still needed to halt the fall of the veil and rebuild it if need be. Inerys had told them the only hope was Vitas Conjuring, a practice that died out centuries ago. It seemed strange to refocus on the task at hand. She'd been so busy chasing Gavriel that it almost made this mission disappear. But it hadn't, and they needed to continue on their path.

Lark stared at Gavriel's back, at the firm line of tension in his shoulders. She bit the inside of her cheek. If they were going to face impossible odds, they needed to mend the rift between them.

Gavriel stalked off toward the river. It wasn't far, just through the thicket, but his refusal to grunt so much as a parting word before disappearing tugged at something in her hollow chest. Lark exhaled a tight breath and rose to her feet. She was done swallowing his silence.

Hazel blocked her path. "Lark," her voice was uncharacteristically soft, "I know it's hard, and if we're being honest, Gavriel is a right tit when he gets like this. But be gentle with him. I can't begin to explain why what happened back there was so fucked up."

Lark nodded. She understood as best she could. He had a different relationship with Hamlin than Lark did with Thanar. Had she been forced to kill her former master, she couldn't imagine grieving him.

"I'll keep that in mind."

Lark strode through the thicket, determined to make the man talk. Gently, as Hazel said.

Gavriel sat hunched over the stream. Lark crouched by his side, examining his face. His mouth was a grim line, and his forehead was creased with stern concentration. He made no move to acknowledge her as he cupped the water in his hands and slowly let it trickle through his fingers.

"Gavriel," Lark whispered, "I'm so sorry."

His throat bobbed as his eyes refused to meet hers, keeping vigil over the gentle rush of water. The last of the light bled through the trees, casting its farewell over his face. Soft gold peeked around the powerful line of his nose before dusk could give way to night. His silence was the darkest shadow of all.

"Gavriel, please talk to me."

"What do you wish to hear?" His voice was rough and thickened by time and grief. Finally, he turned those eyes to meet hers. They held impossible depths of green, like a forest of pine on a misty day. "What is it you need from me?"

His words landed harshly, like an accusation. Lark swallowed against the tightness in her throat. "I need nothing. I just wanted—"

"What?" Gavriel cut her off, angling his body toward her. Lark ignored the way her stomach flipped. "You wanted to hear me say thank you?"

"No, of course not. I just—"

"You wanted to hear my undying gratitude for coming to my rescue? Fuck, Lark!" Gavriel ran his wet hands into his hair, his voice lowering to a growl. "You weren't supposed to be there."

Something hardened in Lark's stomach. He couldn't blame her for this. Could he?

Lark wet her lips, desperately trying to keep her voice even. "You weren't supposed to be there, either." But they had taken him when she severed the bond without asking him. Sure, their consumption of the spelled wine was accidental, but it was her actions that set it in motion. Would she have awakened and prevented his capture were it not for the wine? Was this all her fault?

Gavriel released a sharp breath. He frowned, deepening his scar. "Forgive me," he said. "I'm not good company at the moment." He ran his thumb over the scar in his palm, suddenly miles away.

Lark wanted to reach out and take his hand. To grab his face and force him to look at her. But he needed time, and space, and—

"I met Hamlin when I was just a boy," Gavriel said, cutting off her thoughts.

Lark held her breath, not daring to make a sound.

"I didn't know we were destitute until my mother dropped me off on the steps of the Guild. I didn't understand how she could leave me like that. I thought we were happy. I thought—" He cleared his throat. "It took a long time for me to understand her sacrifice. Longer than I'm proud to admit. As a child, all I knew was she left me. She left me in the hands of the Crows. The Guild breaks you apart and welds you back together. Without Hamlin..."

Lark placed a hesitant hand on his arm. When Gavriel didn't flinch away from her touch, she followed the line of his arm down his palm to thread her fingers through his. He squeezed her hand.

"I would have lost myself. But he kept me centered. When my life was an endless series of punishments and brutality, when I couldn't bring myself to visit her in *that place*." Gavriel's grip tightened hard enough Lark's hand ached. He released her and stood, running his hands through his hair and pacing with short, jerky movements.

The ache in Lark's chest intensified. A fierce longing to wrap her arms around him and contain everything he was feeling.

But that wasn't what he needed.

Instead, she sat and watched him tread the same path of earth back and forth.

"She gave up everything to give me a chance, and took the only job near enough to still see me, despite how much it took from her... and I punished her with my anger." Gavriel swallowed audibly. "Eventually, I recognized the love in her actions, and vowed to be worthy of it. The morning after I completed my final training, I rushed out to see her. I thought if I could just grant her hope, that her sacrifice wasn't in vain and I would earn her freedom and mine..." A sound worked its way out of Gavriel's chest, caught somewhere between a laugh and a sob. "They told me it was an accident. Occupational hazard of a pleasure house with an unrestrictive policy. I hadn't even completed my first mark, and she was gone."

"Gavriel, I'm so sorry." To lose a mother, Lark did not know what that felt like. But if it felt anything like losing Hugo, it must have been unbearable.

He waved his hand dismissively. As if casually conversing on his grief was all he had patience for. "Connor, you remember him, yes?"

Lark remembered. The arrogant assassin and his band of cronies got the jump on her and Daciana. If they'd known Hazel and her brother Gregoir weren't really on Connor's side, they wouldn't have relinquished their weapons. But watching Gavriel kill Connor made it all worth it.

"Yes, I remember him."

Gavriel nodded and sucked on his teeth. "He offered a trade. My mark for his. We were both due to complete our first kill, and he suspected I'd prefer a change of assignment. You see, he claimed to have been assigned a man that frequented the brothel my mother lived in. That rumors circulated, naming that man as the reason she died."

"What did you do?"

"I took it to my superior, eager to trade but unwilling to break the rules. If he signed off on it, I'd relish killing the man who killed my mother." Gavriel shook his head. "I was young and angry. Reckless."

"What did Hamlin say?"

"Hamlin wasn't there. The Guild of Crows is dictated by three masters. Master Hamlin is who I trained with. There was Master Derwin and Master Eldridge." Gavriel leaned against a large oak tree and crossed his arms. "Master Eldridge confirmed the identity of the man as my mother's killer and granted me leave to trade assignments." His gaze dropped to the ground. "I found the man in his home. He lived on the other side of Arden Forest, and it never occurred to me how unlikely it was for a man that far to frequent an establishment on the edge of the wastes. I was out for blood, and I didn't care to question the details."

Dread pooled in Lark's gut. She could sense the regret in his words before he said them.

"He sat there on his bed, a lone candle burning on the table. Like he was waiting for me. I felt it in my bones. He was waiting for death, and I was the one to deliver it. It was his destiny—it was mine. Who was I to stand in the way of fate?" Gavriel ran a hand down his face. "He looked so surprised when I drew my blade across his throat. I—" He shook his head. In the absence of his words, the sounds of the forest intensified. A rustle in the underbrush drew a sharp crunch of dead leaves, and an owl's call trilled through the air. Gavriel cleared his throat. "I cleaved myself from an old ideal of who I might be, and I was free."

Lark stared up at the man who left his mark upon her soul lifetimes before they met. The man she wanted to sever the soul bond from. Now all she felt was an aching need to tether herself to him, to forge an unbreakable connection. It was tragic and strange, how much she longed for what she'd thrown away.

Gavriel appeared dazed for a moment, but he blinked and cleared his gaze. "Upon my return, Hamlin was furious with Master Eldridge. There was talk of banning him from the Guild. The man he'd sent me to kill, my first kill, was my own father. My father—he didn't even know I existed until Hamlin wrote to him. Evidently, the other masters didn't care for Hamlin's interference in my personal affairs and wished to rid me of the distraction. He was the only family I had left, and I killed him."

Lark's vision blurred, and a hot tear spilled down her cheek. How had she never known all the grief Gavriel carried?

"Nothing came of it. Both Connor and I completed our marks and moved on. What could I do? It was done, and I refused to dwell on it. The nickname followed me, though."

Father Slayer. Connor had taunted him with it as he held a blade to Lark's throat.

Gavriel rubbed his jaw. "He wasn't very clever, but there was a time when that nickname was enough to send me over the edge in a fight. Hamlin taught me to let go of my anger and focus. It was something I was proud to master." He gave Lark a pointed look. "Before a certain someone came along and disturbed my focus."

A small smile tugged at Lark's mouth even through the pain. If there was one thing she could not regret, it was crashing into Gavriel's life.

The corner of his mouth lifted before the smile was chased away by a frown. "And now, Hamlin is gone." Again, his thumb ran over the scar in his palm.

Taking a chance, Lark stood and stepped up to Gavriel. She came close enough to smell the lavender she'd used to treat his wounds. His gaze ran over her face, but he made no move to flinch away. She cupped his jaw, and he leaned into the touch.

"I'm so sorry."

Gavriel's throat bobbed, and he nodded. The short bristle along his jaw tickled her palm. She breathed in his scent, relishing being near enough to touch him. He exhaled, and his warm breath fanned against her mouth. Every nerve in her body over-fired, heat spreading over her skin. But this moment wasn't about her. It was about him. And it was about healing.

Lark pressed her forehead to his and sighed when his arms came around her.

For the first time in far too long, everything in her body resonated like the end of a sustained note, finally resolved.

CHAPTER THIRTY-THREE

LANGFORD

Langford hadn't set eyes on Princess Demetria since she was a child; since she was a hyperactive creature with a knack for mischief. The last time he saw her was at the Wintertide ball, where she and a small boy with red hair knocked over the tower of wine bottles and fled the banquet hall.

Now, Demetria stood before him, barely reaching his shoulder. Her dark eyes were hard and unyielding. Her black hair hung in small braids to frame her face, while the rest tangled loose and wild down her back. Light umber skin, elegant straight nose, and the slight cleft in her chin—there was no mistaking.

This was the Princess of Koval.

Princess Demetria surveyed him and Alistair with uncompromising judgment.

Langford wrung his hands, paralyzed between social decorum and proving he could maintain her secret.

Princess Demetria lifted her chin, as if finishing her assessment. "They're trustworthy?" Her voice had deepened over the years and settled into a clear dulcet tone.

Ingemar kicked off where she leaned on the wall and sauntered over. She had taken Alistair and Langford to a cabin they hadn't even known was on the ship. From the outside, the wall slipped into the grains of the wood, disappearing as if it never were. Inside was ample space and a princess pacing back and forth. Her bed was tucked in the corner, fastened to the wall. But above her mattress, the wall was adorned with sketches. Sketches of a rough sea, a waterfall in the forest, a boy with freckles.

Ingemar gave a nod toward Langford. "He is, and the other one isn't stupid enough to break his trust."

Langford's cheeks burned, and Alistair cleared his throat.

"I'm standing right here."

Princess Demetria sighed and shook her head. "Unfortunately, I don't have time to debate this. If Ingemar can trust you… I should, too. I need to venture as far south as possible once we dock. I can't risk any of my brother's supporters catching wind of my arrival."

Adler immediately sprung to mind. "Of course, your highness," Langford said. "Anything you need of us."

Alistair crossed his arms. "Anything? Langford, really. If she needed you to bleed yourself dry on an altar? If she needed you to drop your pants and sing the Kovalian canticle?" He scoffed. "You should be careful who you promise 'anything' too."

"Are you quite finished?" They'd already argued over the princess, and Alistair had made his position clear. Alistair harbored no love for Koval, and though Langford could go the rest of his life never setting foot on the continent again, he recognized a soul fleeing for their life when he saw one.

Alistair huffed an impatient noise before edging closer to Princess Demetria. "Let's get one thing straight. I am not your subject. This is not Koval, and once you step into my care, I expect you to hold your own. There will be no demands, and you follow my lead. If you've become accustomed to a certain standard of care, well, then adjust your expectations."

Princess Demetria raised her brows in surprise before a soft laugh escaped her mouth. Mirth warmed her eyes that had seemed so severe, and for a moment, she looked just like that little girl trying to pull the bottom bottle from the tower of wine.

"I think I would have liked you," she said quietly before the cool distance returned to her eyes. "But you have nothing to fear from me. I know where I'm going means my title is nothing apart from a bargaining chip. I'm decent enough in a fight, and I trained with Captain Ruslan Venier for three years. I expect nothing more than safe passage and discretion."

Something softened in Alistair's expression. He gave a quick nod before bustling over to the side of the room where Ingemar sipped from a brown bottle. With a gesture, he demanded a drink, and Ingemar rolled her eyes, passing it to him.

Langford addressed the princess. "We have matters to attend to, but unless something new has developed, there should be no reason we can't venture south immediately upon disembarking." Assuming Lark and Daciana were at the rendezvous on time, they could set out for the safer regions or even take to the forest. They'd have to purchase more supplies and gods knew he hadn't earned any extra coin.

"I don't want to be in your debt," Princess Demetria said. "So I will offer you what coin I have, and a promise to repay you when Zaire abdicates the throne."

A strangled cough sounded from the corner. Alistair's chin dripped with rum as he choked and sputtered into his fist. Ingemar reluctantly patted his back as he tried to breathe.

"You... said," he wheezed. "You think he'll abdicate the throne?"

Princess Demetria smiled, and gods above, she looked just like her mother. "Perhaps I was speaking too gently. I meant I will educate my brother about his inevitable future." Her smile vanished. "And it ends with me wearing the crown and him in exile."

Langford's head spun. He held no loyalty to the king and refused to regret aiding the princess, but this was sounding like a far more complex mission than mere transport and protection. Did she have any connections in Ardenas? She must, but how could she have sent word to them if her movements were watched in her kingdom? He was going to have to ensure her safety, that much was clear, but what about what she set out to accomplish? Was that his responsibility to help her achieve control of the throne? Gods above, and what about the veil?

Lark was counting on him to piece together a plan, and it was too much. Langford was just one man, and a fuck-up at that. He clenched his hands and ignored the space where his finger used to be.

Langford cleared his throat and straightened his shirt, choosing his next words carefully. "We promise to aid you in your escape, your majesty."

Princess Demetria's eyes flashed before she nodded. "Very well. I accept our temporary alliance."

CHAPTER THIRTY-FOUR

DACIANA

*E*meraude Port bustled with activity. Daciana and Kenna stood at the bottom of the sloping stretch of road, where merchants' carts waited beside the docks hoping to catch fresh trade off the ocean. No weapons cart, of course, so Daciana had quickly given up feigning interest in their wares in favor of keeping watch for Ingemar's Galleon.

A man in a blue feathered cap knocked into Kenna's elbow, grunting in distaste without so much as an apology. The chill off the water had most passersby clutching their cloaks as the grey sea churned, waves lapping against the shoreline. The sky was a muted cover above the town, and the imposing threat of rain hung heavy in the air. A gull's cry carried on the wind, along with shouts of merriment from sailors' return. Shops lined the square, buzzing with the energy of hundreds of patrons. The day hummed with conversations, and each time the door to the Maiden's Bear tavern swung open, the plucking of lute strings wafted across the street. Ships arriving at the docks brought more goods and bodies, and longshoremen ambled to offload them. Yet, there was no sight of the lion figurehead that marked Ingemar's ship.

And no sign of Lark.

Daciana thumbed the hilts of her daggers as the bracing sea air pulled dark strands of hair from her braid. Normally, she was the one returning to the warmth of Langford's fire, to Alistair's ale, to Hugo's kill, ready and waiting for her to gut and skin.

She wasn't accustomed to being the one waiting.

"They'll be here." Kenna's voice cut through Daciana's thoughts, carrying a soft tone. Of comfort. Of pity.

Daciana kept her gaze trained on the horizon, refusing to meet Kenna's probing stare. It wasn't worth arguing the point that any number of terrible things could have happened. Alistair could have pissed off the wrong people in Koval. Lark could have met a gruesome fate when Inerys sent her off with a drowsing tonic. The Guild could have found Gavriel.

But what good was breathing life into these thoughts? It wouldn't bring her friends safely to her side nor stem her unease.

And so she would wait. Wait and watch the expanse where grey sky met dark waters.

She and Kenna still hadn't spoken of what transpired with the Bubak. When she'd pulled from cursed power she never wanted to wield again. When she pulled from Kenna to achieve that end. She hadn't drawn from that forbidden well since that fateful day when she'd dragged Kenna's soul from its journey to the afterlife and stitched it back into her mortal body.

It was so blazing easy to slip up around her.

The wind swept harder, carrying Kenna's scent along with it. Daciana tightened her grip on the railing. She could never allow another mistake like that again. Kenna was lucky all she'd pulled from her was a nosebleed.

She could have taken more.

"Perhaps we should head inside while we wait?" Kenna bundled her red cloak tighter around her, hood drawn and black wisps hanging in her face. "We can sit near the windows so you can maintain your staring contest with the horizon." The hint of a smirk played on her mouth.

Everything was all fun and games, laughably ridiculous to her. But

Daciana was no fool. She knew what Kenna had lived through. What she continued to survive. If all the smiles and quips helped mask her pain, who was she to judge?

"I prefer this vantage point. Inside, I can't watch the road for Lark's return."

Kenna's face fell, and guilt sank into Daciana's gut. She had been cold to her since the Bubak. It was the only way. Letting her guard down the way she had in the barn only made it easier for her emotions to guide her hand.

She couldn't allow that to happen again.

The gentle groan of docked ships in the harbor and the sharp whistle of the breeze heightened Daciana's senses. Already, the next moon's call whispered in the back of her mind. Normally, she wouldn't feel the beckoning moon until three days before her turn. But this time it scratched her thoughts and skittered against her skull long before its call.

She could lie to herself and blame the worry over her friends' journeys, or the swarms of bodies crowding the streets. Or even Kenna's constant presence, an over-firing of every nerve with her proximity. But Daciana knew how little merit these lies held, even those of her own making.

This was penance for what she'd done in that field. When fear won out and she succumbed to her basest nature. The wolf wasn't the danger, but the blood that ran through her veins was. The power born of betrayal.

It had been a mistake leaving Lark to find Kenna. Here she thought she was protecting her, but she'd only put her at risk. Daciana was sure she'd learned this lesson long ago.

Kenna was safer far from her side.

A small shape appeared on the horizon. Kenna squinted. "Is that it? It's impossible to tell at this range."

But Daciana already knew what was coming. Every nerve in her body sang at the rightness of her instinct. A smile stole across her face, unrestrained and eager. A lightness she hadn't felt in weeks spread through her body, and for a moment she could let go of the terror she'd barely kept at bay.

The large ship sailed across the harbor, a fierce beacon of hope. As it grew closer, Daciana's joy only brightened. A great lion figurehead formed its bow. It was Ingemar's ship, *The Savage Jewel*.

Alistair and Langford were back.

CHAPTER THIRTY-FIVE

LARK

Lark elbowed her way through the crowd, too impatient to care. The ashen sky rivaled the dark sea, both a despairing grey. But nothing could dim her excitement. Towering buildings of brick and timber frames lined the town. More than one balcony carried the sound of boisterous voices from within. Unfamiliar songs sailed on the wind, beckoning for a moment or two by a warm hearth of the rowdy Maiden's Bear tavern. Hazel had suggested they stop to grab a meal, but Lark couldn't bear to wait another second. They'd finally, *finally* arrived at Emeraude Port. Daciana, Langford, and Alistair would be nearby. Lark could hardly believe she would see them again after all this time apart. It almost seemed like a trick, and at any moment, she'd stumble upon a fresh disaster, keeping her from reaching them.

A warm hand found Lark's shoulder. She glanced back to find the soft curve of a smile against a scarred mouth. *Gavriel.* He didn't try to slow her or give her pause. But his reassuring touch was enough to spread a glimmer of hope in her chest. Things between them had settled mostly, but it was near impossible to steal quiet moments alone with Hazel nearby. Gavriel remained somber most of the days, and losing Hamlin was an ache he still keenly felt if his withdrawal was any measure, but he always tried to find little ways to show he was there. That he wouldn't vanish again.

Lark turned back to the market vendors lining the street. The air was thick with the scent of brine and the catch of the day. Just beyond the herd of people, the docks awaited. They'd take up a spot to watch the road for Dac, and the sea for Alistair and Langford. Once they returned, then they could find a table for a hot meal to take the chill out of her bones. Perhaps they could even rent rooms—if any were available. It had been ages since Lark slept in a bed rather than on the forest floor.

In the distance, another ship approached the port. But from where Lark stood, she couldn't tell if it was Ingemar's ship. She squinted, willing the ship to sail faster.

A flutter of red caught Lark's eye. A red cloak, shrouding a slight form. And beside the hooded figure, the unmistakable posture of a familiar form leaned over the railing. A great sword strapped to her back, her long braid hanging over her shoulder as she stared out over the water.

Daciana.

Lark stumbled, knees buckling at the sight of her friend. She pushed through the crowd, uncaring if Gavriel and Hazel followed closely. Daciana stiffened and turned.

Her hazel eyes widened, and an unrestrained smile lit up her face. She pushed off the rail, striding toward Lark.

Lark's vision blurred with tears as she shoved a man in a blue feathered cap out of her way and ran. When she drew near, she threw herself at Daciana, wrapping her arms tight around her shoulders as the first sob broke free. Daciana hugged her back, huffing a quiet laugh. Lark tried to speak, tried to explain, but the words wouldn't come. Instead, she hugged her dearest friend, thanking the skies she was all right.

"You scared the shit out of me," Daciana said, still holding her close. "You couldn't leave a follow-up message stating you were alive?"

Lark sniffed and hoped her running nose didn't spill onto Daciana's shoulder. "There is much to tell."

Daciana pulled back to examine Lark. She ran her gaze over her face, searching. Had her scrapes and bruises healed? Lark's ribs ached from the tight embrace, but it was worth it.

"Were you hurt?" Daciana's question asked more than a simple answer could cover.

"It's a long story. One I fully intend on sharing after a meal and a bath."

Daciana nodded. "You look like you could use it."

"Food or a bath?"

"Both."

A laugh burst from Gavriel, which he quickly smothered with a cough.

Daciana grinned over at him. "Come here. We all smell like the road."

Fighting a smile, Gavriel allowed Daciana to pull him into a quick embrace.

A throat cleared behind them. The hooded girl stood, kicking the dirt with the toe of her boot, black fringe falling into her eyes. Shock swept through Lark like a fierce current. Daciana's unfinished business… it was Kenna? Lark hadn't seen the hunter since that day in the forest, when they met under the cloak of night and she gave Lark her hunter's talisman to show Inerys. But the memory of the conversation aboard Ingemar's ship came to mind, when Daciana told what little she could manage of her connection to the hunter.

"Sometimes, finding the person you'd burn the world for is the worst sort of curse."

Daciana stepped away. "It would appear we all have much to share."

Kenna grinned, dimpling her cheek, though her eyes remained tight. "That's a pretty way of putting it." She glanced over Gavriel's shoulder. "Whoever your travel companion was, she didn't stick around."

Lark turned to face the street. The milling crowd never ceased its trickle across cobblestones, bodies pressed tightly together trying to find an opening to their favored merchant. But where Hazel once stood, nothing but a filthy puddle splashing under the impatient trod of boots remained. She had pulled yet another vanishing act. "She's helped us enough," Lark finally said. Though a goodbye might have been nice.

Gavriel caught Lark's gaze and gave an almost imperceptible nod. "She'll be back again, eventually. She has a tendency to show up at the worst times, wouldn't you say?"

Despite herself, Lark smiled. "That's an accurate assessment."

A boyish grin pulled at the corner of his mouth, and an unbidden warmth curled in Lark's stomach. She'd missed his smiles.

"Well, you'll be pleased to know we'll still boast a large party, even without your third." Kenna tilted her head toward the ship sailing across the harbor. "Your friends are here."

Giddy excitement flashed through Lark's body. A flood of energy and boundless joy.

Daciana slung an arm around Lark's shoulders and steered her toward the rail to watch Ingemar's ship. The roaring lion stood proud against the slate water, a promise of hope and revival. Of fierce protection against any storm.

"What do you think Langford uncovered?" Lark had tasked him with researching. That brilliant mind could figure anything out if the answers they wished for truly existed. If they couldn't take down Nereida...

"I'd wager Langford discovered many things on their little mission." The corner of Daciana's mouth lifted. "*Many* things..."

A laugh burst from Lark's chest. "Skies, I hope so. For all our sakes. My pockets are empty, and I need Alistair to pay for food and drink. Not company."

"Let us hope the powers of Ingemar's ship work their magic again."

"What do you mean?"

Daciana eyed her with thinly veiled amusement. "You and Gavriel know the wonders of a locked door on a ship at sea..."

A hint of warmth bloomed on Lark's cheeks even as she laughed. "Oh, right! That's true. *Captain* Ingemar's ship has a seductive siren call. One can't help it."

Daciana rolled her eyes. "Yes, that's right. *Captain.*"

The Savage Jewel glided into port, claiming the prime spot by the dock. Lark thought she might vibrate right out of her skin; she was so excited. Daciana gave her shoulder a squeeze before releasing her hold.

"Come, Lark. Let's go get the boys."

CHAPTER THIRTY-SIX

LANGFORD

"Told you, didn't I?" Alistair slung an arm around Langford's shoulders. "There's a lesson in there, I'm sure. Never doubt my wisdom again." His crooked smirk sent bolts of heat through Langford's stomach, but there were more pressing matters at hand.

They'd made it to Emeraude Port. To where Lark and Daciana stood waiting.

Langford nearly leapt over the side of the ship when he saw them. Lark grinned up at him, her red hair unbound and whipping about her face in the wind. Daciana gave him a small smile and nodded, her apparent relief softening her jaw. For a moment, his uncertainty vanished. Whether he'd done enough, learned enough to be of any use, or if he'd invited more danger to their door by agreeing to aid the princess—all of it faded away. All that remained was the warmth in Daciana's eyes and Lark eagerly bouncing on her heels.

His friends.

His family.

His home.

When Langford's feet hit the wood planks, he dashed across the dock and gathered them into his arms, unsure he'd ever wish to let go.

IT TOOK the first flood of rain weeping from the sky to pry Langford away from Lark and Daciana long enough to scurry into the Maiden's Bear tavern. It was good to be in Ardenas again. He'd missed the rustic architecture of Ardenian construction. Langford ran his hand along the woodgrains, catching along the grooves. Considering the patrons that frequented this establishment, it was no surprise to find sturdy tables with thick, solid legs for the chairs. The windows were small and situated up high, a wise choice if a brawl broke out. What the tavern lacked in décor it made up for with spirits. Both the spirits of its patrons and the wide selection they offered. There was a buzz of excitement, of men and women, freshly docked and grateful for the solid ground beneath their feet.

Normally, the commotion would have brought on one of Langford's usual headaches, but there was no pain this night. He was where he belonged. It was almost as if no time had passed. Almost as if they'd never parted ways and were just finding a bed for the night while Alistair scrounged up work for them.

Almost.

Langford met Alistair's eye from across the crowded tavern while he and Daciana carried a tray of drinks back to the table. Alistair flashed him a grin and winked, the cad, and Langford's cheeks instantly warmed. They all sat in the corner, Lark, Gavriel, and Daciana's curious friend, away from prying eyes.

Princess Demetria stayed with Ingemar on her ship—until they could speak privately with the others. There would be no issue, of that Langford was certain, but they couldn't risk any of Zaire's men spotting the princess. Logic dictated the likelihood there were eyes on the ports. But first, they would catch up as old friends. They would share stories and laughter and whatever else they carried to the tavern on this night. Lark regaled them with her adventures across the country. Fighting an Undesirable, losing Gavriel only to find him at Aelcliff in the gauntlet. Gavriel's expression remained guarded as she spoke, giving nothing away.

Daciana's tale of the scholar and the beast was most curious. Langford was certain he needed to meet this person. Anyone who read as much as she and retained it all was worth sharing a lengthy conversation with. And a curse? Well, a season or two ago, Langford would have scoffed at the notion. But now, anything seemed possible.

The thought was both terrifying and exhilarating.

A soft kick to his shin under the table pulled Langford's attention to the redhead, whose smile was both teasing and affectionate.

"Did you hear me?" Lark asked. "I asked you what happened on Ingemar's ship."

Langford cleared his throat, unsure of how to answer. He couldn't imagine Alistair wished to keep them a secret, but it wasn't a conversation they'd had yet.

"Well," Langford began, "many developments transpired… of varying range in sensitivity and meaning."

As if summoned, Alistair's hand squeezed the back of Langford's neck as he placed a chalice of red wine on the table in front of him. "I don't think she's asking about that, darling, but if you wish to share our intimate details, I'm game." Alistair plopped in the chair beside him and traced the shell of his ear with his finger. Langford shivered and batted his hand away.

Alistair grinned. "Once we take to the forests again, I'm sure they'll hear more than I could adequately describe."

Langford's neck burned even as a smile fought its way across his mouth. Leave it to Alistair to embarrass and soothe him with the same breath.

Lark laughed, high and bright, and even leaned into Gavriel, who immediately pulled her closer. Though his expression remained carefully composed, like he was miles away in his thoughts.

Daciana returned with the rest of the tankards and passed them to Gavriel and Kenna, the girl with the red cloak and the dark gaze fixed on Daciana's movements. When Daciana took the seat beside Lark, Kenna's jaw tightened, and her eyebrow ticked. Langford recognized the tension on her face. It was a tightness he'd felt watching Alistair flaunt his dubious conquests. Though there was nothing between Daciana and Lark besides a fierce bond of friendship, and Daciana was nothing like Alistair. She would never flaunt her sexual exploits. A flicker of shame burned in his chest, but he quickly tucked it away and grabbed his wine. It was unworthy of him to think of Alistair that way. It wasn't Alistair's fault. He hadn't known the feelings Langford harbored for years. Again, he smothered his bitterness and examined the contents of his cup.

A quick waft of the chalice confirmed it was nothing to savor, so he took a tentative sip. It was sweet and sharp with a bite that would have been smoothed in a finer vintage.

Alistair's thumb ran gently along Langford's jaw. For a man so oblivious to his affections for years, he certainly seemed attuned to him now. Langford turned, caught in the impossible green of Alistair's eyes. Brighter than the nettle leaves he used to prescribe for Hugo's knee whenever it rained.

Alistair leaned in close enough to press his forehead to Langford's and exhaled a soft breath. "Do you need some air?"

"No... I only... I realized how strange it is to be here without Hugo." Hugo would have taken the seat against the wall, never one to leave his back unguarded, and surveyed the room while they ate and drank. He would have watched them all with a keen eye and a stern frown until Lark would have said something to soften the hard line of his mouth.

Yes, it was strange being back in Ardenas with someone so vital missing from their group.

Alistair nodded and pressed a kiss to Langford's temple, lingering against his hair. "I miss him too."

Across the table, both Lark and Daciana wore matching grins. Daciana whispered in Lark's ear, and Lark let out an undignified squeal. Her honey eyes crinkled as genuine mirth claimed her features once more.

"If something is funny, *wife,* please share. We could all do with a laugh." Langford waited to see if she recalled their affectionate nicknames for one another. The nicknames they'd earned after a horrible night at the ball and a few hours in the dungeon after they were captured.

Lark grinned, her lovely face lighting up with glee. "Why, husband, how could you ever accuse me of ridiculing you? We both know you're unmatched in vigor, and virility—"

"That bit actually is true," Alistair interjected.

Before Lark could respond with what Langford was sure would be far too personal a comment, a new bard took the stage. A disjointed round of applause rang from the drunken crowd, and they all turned in their seats to regard the entertainment. He looked vaguely familiar. His tanned face bore the smile lines of a happy life and his floppy emerald cap sat off-kilter, dark hair curling along his forehead. He wore a fine doublet of green velvet with silver thread detailing. When a broad grin stretched across his face, Langford met Lark's incredulous stare. It couldn't be. The chances were impossible even for this life.

"Good evening, gentle folks. I am Bartrand Rigglesby and I wrote this song for a remarkable soul I met on the road. I call it, 'The Songbird.' May she soar to great heights, wherever she is."

A choked noise escaped Lark's throat, and Daciana placed a hand over her mouth, trying to stifle her laughter. Gavriel's brow furrowed in confusion. Kenna stared at the table, rolling the bottom rim of her tankard against the wood.

Bartrand plucked the strings of his lute in a soft melody.

"There once was a bird, as fair as the sun
She flew as high as the sky would allow
But everyone knows, the time always comes
When the bird must come down. The bird must come down.

She sang a sweet song, a lost melody
And her wings spread so wide and proud as can be
But a songbird knows this terrible truth
She'll never be free. She'll never be free."

Langford chanced a glance in Lark's direction. Her mouth hung agape as she stared at the old bard. Her face caught between awe and chagrin.

"But caught in a cage, this little lark found
She no longer sang, could no longer fly
What could our little songbird do?
Bodies littered the ground. They littered the ground."

Another laugh burst from Daciana's chest, and Lark hid her face behind her hands.

Gavriel's frown melted into a grin, and he pressed his chin against Lark's shoulder. "He's singing about you, isn't he?"

Lark shook her head, refusing to lift her stare. "He could be singing about anyone," she said, her words muffled by her palms.

Alistair grinned and returned his attention to the bard. "Hush, everyone. I'll need to commit these lyrics to memory. It would be good to have a song to while away the hours on the road."

Lark dropped her hands. "You wouldn't…"

"The sweet songbird had a taste for blood.
A penchant for death and a call from above.
She slew her foes and set herself free
But a bird's song is never done. Her song is never done."

Bartrand ended on a conflictingly triumphant note before beginning his next song.

Lark wrinkled her nose and shifted in her seat. "Well… he said he needed to make some rewrites to my ballad."

CHAPTER THIRTY-SEVEN

DACIANA

Kenna had disappeared long ago, claiming fatigue. It was more than that, though Daciana wouldn't pry. She was giving Kenna space by remaining downstairs, listening to Bartrand's set, and laughing with Lark. When Bartrand finished, he even came over to greet Lark by kissing her hand and grabbing a nearby stool to catch up on her adventures. She indulged him with watered-down versions of her tales. Just enough that the glimmer of excitement shone in his eyes—the look of an artist mapping out his next creation.

Gavriel smirked at the exchange but said nothing. It was odd, really. He was there, his arm resting on the back of Lark's seat, and occasionally his hand found her shoulder. But his gaze fell far and wherever his mind went, it wasn't in this tavern. And where Gavriel was all distance, Alistair and Langford had grown closer. Alistair even ignored the private smile the barmaid gave him when they collected their drinks. The smile that normally would have resulted in Alistair's disappearance for the night. Now, he only had eyes for Langford. Daciana caught the touches and lingering looks long before Alistair had confirmed it, but it was good to see they had finally pulled their heads free of their asses and admitted their feelings. Every sign of affection warmed Daciana's heart and set Lark grinning with glee.

It was good to be with them. To be home.

When the drinks ran out, and Daciana's face was sore from smiling, she made her way up to the room Alistair had rented on her behalf. With a conspicuous wink, he'd paid the tab and shooed away their thanks, hauling Langford out the door with a firm grip on his backside.

Lark was reluctant to leave, and truthfully, Daciana was hesitant, too, but they would be on the road in the morning. They all needed a good night's rest, and now that she knew they were all safe, sleep would come easier.

Daciana climbed the sticky steps, limbs heavy with exhaustion despite the lightness of her mood. When she came to the door with the symbol of an albatross etched into the wood, she hesitated. She should knock, but if Kenna was already asleep, she didn't wish to wake her. Instead, Daciana listened, pressing her ear against the grain—only to be met by silence. Light spilled out from beneath the door. Kenna must have lit a candle and fallen asleep while it yet burned.

Daciana eased the door open, expecting to find her slumbering form hogging the bed—but the sight she uncovered left her breathless.

In the middle of the room sat a large bathing tub—a wooden barrel —and Kenna seated within. She had tied her long black hair up, a few strands stuck to her elegant neck, her narrow shoulders glistening in the soft candlelight. She turned, and her lovely face was unreadable.

Daciana choked on a thick throat, and scrambled in, shutting the door for Kenna's privacy as much as to have something solid to lean against. "How long have you been in there?" Her words came out even and composed, despite the rapid pace of her heart.

Kenna lifted her hands from the water, examining them. "Long enough." Without waiting for a response, she stood, water sluicing down her pale skin.

Daciana cleared her throat and drifted her gaze to the ceiling. If this was a bid to see if she would pick up where they left off in the tithe barn, Kenna would be sorely disappointed.

Even if Daciana was tempted.

"There, I'm decent." Kenna's voice was flat as she stood there, wrapped in a towel and dripping water on the floor.

Daciana shifted past her, dropping her pack on the floor by the window. She stared out at the town swathed by night. The rain had ceased, and the moon slipped out from behind the clouds. Ripples of silvery light covered the bay, and Daciana almost wished the moon was full, so she might have an excuse to slip into the forest and disappear for the night.

"So... your friends seem lovely," Kenna said. "Although Gavriel was even tighter wound than when I first met him. Naked. And being attacked by a vrykolaka."

Daciana scoffed, turning away from the window to find the hint of a smirk on Kenna's mouth. "You enjoyed reminding him of that."

Kenna shrugged, her bare shoulder immediately catching Daciana's attention. "I didn't think you heard a word I said tonight."

Daciana resisted the urge to sigh. So that was what vexed her. "You spoke often. With Gavriel, and Langford, and Alistair—"

"Alistair! Yes, I like him. Out of all your friends, I think he's best."

"Not Lark?"

Kenna scowled. Wrong question. "Yes," Kenna began, "I do like Lark. The Reaper who commands everyone's loyalty without question. No matter how many mistakes she makes, she's always forgiven. And doted on." Kenna turned her dark stare on Daciana. "Isn't that right?"

Daciana wet her lips, thumbing her daggers. "I have no interest in talking around the point. Speak your mind. You've never taken issue with that in the past."

Kenna's eyes flashed, and her jaw tightened. "Fine. For someone so determined to be alone, you show much allegiance to those people. And I can't, for the life of me, figure out why you can't be like that with me."

Daciana's head spun. "Like what?"

Kenna laughed. "Don't play dumb. You haven't been at ease with me since before..."

"Since before what?" Daciana clenched her hands into fists. "Say it, speak the words, and perhaps you'll answer your own question." To insinuate that this was easy for her. That she pushed Kenna away for anything less than necessity was madness.

"That isn't fair. We both suffered that day. We both lost everything." Kenna's face scrunched up, and something fractured in Daciana's chest. "Why do you still punish me?"

Daciana's throat constricted, and her pulse pounded in her head. She needed air. She needed to get away. "It's... not that." She forced each word from her lips. "Kenna... it's too difficult being around you."

"What is too difficult? You wanted me to speak plainly, and now I'll ask the same of you."

"I..." *I can't control myself around you. My power, my urges, my heart. I would burn the world for you.* Daciana shook her head. "You weren't even supposed to be here. You were supposed to alert the hunters and leave. That was the plan. Now you've forced your way into my life, and I didn't ask for any of it."

Kenna's brows furrowed, confusion stealing the pain from her face. She opened her mouth, but before she could speak, Daciana rushed to the door. She fled through the hall, down the stairs, and through the dimly lit tavern until the rush of fresh sea air blasted her in the face.

That went... poorly.

Daciana pressed the heels of her palms against her eyes. Kenna had a way of stealing any shred of control she possessed. It had always been this way, but years of practice in the art of self-regulation should have prevented Kenna from scaling those defenses so easily.

Daciana stalked down the road, over slick cobblestones glimmering in the moonlight. She couldn't let Kenna affect her so. She needed to rebuild that wall with iron, so she might never penetrate again.

In the years that passed in Kenna's absence, Daciana never slipped up and used that power. Not once. And now? She could feel it creeping along the edges of her mind, begging for release.

Why? Was it the nature of the curse? The blood she spilled was in answer to Kenna's death. Was this further punishment for what she stole that night?

Daciana kicked a nearby barrel, sending it careening into a brick wall, showering collected water across the uneven street.

She needed to calm down. To breathe. Kenna might be her undoing, but she'd lasted this long without calling to her power. She could tamp it down.

A grunt echoed from down the narrow alley. Daciana stilled, listening. A scuffle and the *crash* of a wooden crate rang through the night.

She charged to the dark passage, dual-edged haladie already in hand. She stepped over the puddle that promised a soaked boot and slipped soundlessly into the dark. The light of the burning lampposts failed to make it down the alley, but a sliver of moonlight carved into the space like the edge of a blade.

A group of men filled the alley, all facing one small hooded figure. At the sound of Daciana's approach, they all turned.

Even in the dark, she could make out their faces. The shadows offered no refuge from eyes meant for the night. One of the men groaned, a stream of blood trailing from his snub nose down to his chest. He wouldn't be much of a problem, judging by the way he held his ribs. Probably broken.

She caught the eye of a lean, twitchy man with sharp eyes and a sharper chin. He had yet to pull his bow or a single arrow from his back.

But one man, the sides of his head shaven to reveal Vallemerian tattoos on his scalp, held his weapon at the ready. The steel blade sliced through the dark, moonlight glinting against its metallic surface. Frozen in place at the tip of his sword was the small shape of a person beneath their hooded cloak. Their crouched, defensive posture was unmistakable.

"Evening, gentlemen," Daciana said, spinning her haladie, its familiar weight a welcome one. "Whatever your business, there are better places to conduct them than an empty alley."

The Vallemerian pressed his sword closer to the pulse point of his intended victim, the one who had yet to lower their hood. "Move along, lass. This isn't your concern."

"You're right, it isn't. Even so, I'm not leaving."

The man with the broken ribs groaned again, and the archer turned to him. "You all right, Davey? She got you good there."

She. Five men against one small girl. Daciana had no idea what the girl had done, but something about the way five men pursued one lone person left a bitter taste on her tongue.

One of the men pulled an Ardenian dirk from his belt, taking a deliberate step toward her. Daciana yanked her second haladie from her hip. She held no love for spilling blood, but if they wanted a fight, she would grant them one.

All at once, the air flattened. Something pulsed in the dark, like the steady thrum of a heart. Of life coursing through each body in the alley before her. It ran through the space like a ribbon she could wrap around her fist. Daciana could taste it. The tang of fear, of anger, of bright burning life. She could reach out—call to it. Just a nudge is all it would take—

No. Daciana stamped down on that urge, gripping her daggers tighter. No, she would never call upon that power, no matter how inviting. She had no control over where it took from. And whatever ruin she could bring upon them, she would do with her own hands. They were the only part of her she could trust.

The Vallemerian's eyes widened, as if he could sense the danger she posed, and he lowered his sword. "I'm not one for making enemies out of strangers. But watch your pockets around this one." He curled his lip and jerked his chin toward the hooded girl. "She's bound to make them lighter." With a nod to his companions, they all shuffled away.

A gentle stillness filled the air, and once more, Daciana could hear her own pulse in her ears. It slowed until the soft hush of night consumed the alley, gentle breezes whispering around tight corners. The damp scent of brick and dirt filled her senses, and a quiet calm spread through her body.

The hooded girl straightened, her hands clenching by her side. "You didn't have to do that." Her voice was a low rumble. "But I'm grateful for your interference."

"Interference? I quite like that. It implies you had a plan I interrupted."

A smile curved from just beyond the shadow of a hood, and an elegant hand lifted to yank the shroud from her face. She was barely out of childhood, with sharp eyes cutting from her youthful face. Her dark hair hung loosely down her back, save for the front section braided to frame her elegant cheekbones and dimpled chin. "Well, I hadn't quite formed it yet. But I'm fairly good at thinking on my feet." She flashed Daciana a wide smile, and something about it seemed familiar as it softened her eyes. "There's some loose brick over there, an abundance of ashes in the corner over here. I would have thought of something. And don't listen to what he said about my making your pockets lighter. Apparently my lack of interest in conversing with them was enough to warrant accusation."

Her accent wasn't Ardenian. It was softer, lilting, almost like Langford's.

A Kovalian girl, barely out of adolescence, all by herself in Emeraude Port? Her fine cloak and soft cadence boasted of a noble house. But which one?

"How old are you?"

The girl seemed surprised by the question. "Fifteen."

Daciana slipped her blades back into place, eyeing the girl with careful consideration. "Old enough to know the danger of walking these streets alone."

The girl's voice flattened. "You're out here alone." She sighed. "I wanted to stretch my legs is all, and now I have. Back to the ship before I'm missed."

Daciana didn't bother explaining that she was the most dangerous thing on these streets. "I can escort you to your ship." If the girl refused, she would leave her be. It was her life to gamble.

The girl nodded. "In case they come back."

Daciana left the alley, the girl following closely behind. They strode in silence, allowing the gentle lapping of water against the docks to fill the air. Daciana glanced over to find the girl once more lifting her shroud to cover her face. She was running from something, but she could keep her secrets. They weren't for Daciana to pry into.

When they reached the dock, the girl kept walking—straight toward *The Savage Jewel*. Daciana froze. The girl noticed.

"Thank you for your help, truly. I doubt I'd be standing here were it not for your aid." The girl patted her pockets, an expression of chagrin washing over her features. "I'm afraid I have nothing to offer as payment."

Daciana shook her head. "Your safety is payment enough."

The girl smiled and opened her mouth—

Shouts erupted from the ship. The girl winced before her expression hardened.

Langford appeared, hair wild and eyes burning with anger. Alistair followed closely behind, fastening his belt, and laughing. "Come, now, Langford. She couldn't have gone far."

Langford froze when he caught sight of them. His gaze slipping past to find Daciana before finding the girl again. "Where have you been?" Anger sharpened his tone into a very un-Langford sounding timbre. Daciana couldn't recall seeing him this angry. Not since the time Alistair used up his honey stores to lure a bear into a trap. It hadn't worked, but it had made Langford's tea bitter for the next week. "You snuck off on your own? Have you gone mad?"

The girl stiffened. "Where I go is my business, Langford. You'd do well to remember that."

Alistair grinned. "Wrong, Princess. You asked for our help, and I told you what that meant. You answer to me now." He cast a quick glance at Langford, who was still vibrating with anger. "And apparently you answer to Langford, too."

Princess. Of course, Langford and Alistair got caught up in Kovalian politics during their trip. A laugh burst from Daciana's chest, and then another.

Langford jolted as if he'd finally noticed her, and raked his fingers through his dark hair, trying to smooth his rumpled appearance. "Dac, I don't know how much you're aware of—"

"You brought the princess of Koval to Ardenas. What more do I need to know?"

The girl—the princess of Koval—turned to Daciana, clasping her hands before her like she was about to make a speech. And all at once, her youth bled away into something old and somber, like a life of wariness had added years to her eyes. "There's much more to share," she said evenly. "And you can call me Demetria."

CHAPTER THIRTY-EIGHT

LARK

Maiden's Bear had but one room left, which Lark was all too happy to leave for Daciana and Kenna. Langford had shoved his hands in Alistair's pockets and pulled out a small satchel of coins, insisting they check The Rusty Anchor Inn. Lark had protested, but Alistair echoed Langford's insistence and added that they would spend their night aboard Ingemar's ship because they hadn't even packed yet.

After bidding farewell, if only for the night, Lark and Gavriel made their way down the darkened street to the inn. The lampposts had been lit long ago, flickering flames carving against cobblestones. A companionable silence had descended between them. Like the quiet swath of night sky above.

This was the first time they'd been well and truly alone since… before.

Lark chanced a glance at Gavriel. His jaw was smoothed of some of the tension he'd bore during their travel. He caught her staring and let a small smile curve against his scarred mouth.

"Tonight was good," he said. "You're happy."

Lark yanked the hood of her cloak over her head, shivering. Already she missed the warmth of the tavern. The warmth of the others. It was hard to walk away from them, even knowing it was just until morning. "But you're not." The words slipped from her lips before she could catch them. Of course, he wasn't happy. It would take more than days of travel and an evening of drinking to lessen the loss of Hamlin.

Gavriel sighed. "Happy… if you mean in an immediate sense, I won't pretend I feel joyful lately." He frowned, and in the soft light of the burning lamp posts, his eyes were unreadable. "But if you're asking me if I'm grateful for this life, and happy in a sense that I'm where I wish to be"—he threaded his fingers through hers, tugging at something deep in her soul—"how could I not be?"

Lark swallowed against her thickened throat. "You don't need to do that, Gavriel. I know you're angry with me."

Gavriel stopped short. He yanked her against his chest, and the breath whooshed from her lungs. The warmth of his body flooded hers. "Why would I be angry with you?"

Lark's pulse thrummed in her neck, her limbs strangely tingling like they did before a fight. "Because if I hadn't—you said I wasn't supposed to be there!" What was she saying? The last thing he needed was for her to push him on this. He was grieving and needed time and —"You blame me for Hamlin's death."

Gavriel's eyes flashed dangerously as a sharp breath escaped his lips, ghosting against her own. "You think… I blame you?" His words were slow and deliberate. "You actually believe this?"

Lark pulled back, unable to think straight pressed against him like that. "That came out wrong." She was supposed to give him space to grieve. He told her what Hamlin meant to him. He didn't owe her another explanation. Not now, at least.

Gavriel sighed and ran his hand over his mouth, studying her with his unyielding stare. With a curt nod, he continued their trek to the inn. Whatever thoughts brewed in his head, he kept them to himself.

Lark huffed her hair from her face and maintained his pace. It would not do to press him on this… even if his silence burrowed something sharp in her gut. Maybe they needed the bond more than she thought. Needed the assurance of an invisible tug to bridge the divide their choices made.

But she would never regret searching for him. No matter the consequences.

THE INNKEEPER WAS ACCOMMODATING, and after prepping their room, returned with a large brass key. Lark pocketed it, grateful that Emeraude was a place that valued privacy.

A trip up the rickety stairs and down the hall, past the wilting flowers in the cracked vase, led them to their simple room. A dancing flame of a candle illuminated the melted wax dripping over the flat surface of the end table. The washbasin sat in the opposite corner with fresh water and linens, and a small window allowed the moon to spill its light across the pocked wood of the floor.

Lark crossed the room to the narrow bed, untying her cloak and draping it atop the comforter as another blanket. Without meeting Gavriel's eyes, she toed off her boots and peeled back her cloak, settling in beneath it and above the bedclothes. She didn't want to climb in fully without cleaning up, but the beckon of sleep was so inviting. She shivered as she nestled into the soft comfort of a bed rather than the forest floor.

Gavriel still stood by the closed door. Silent and waiting.

Lark chanced a glance over her shoulder. "Is this room not to your liking?"

A muscle feathered in his jaw. "I don't want to talk."

Well, then.

Lark pushed to sit up. "All right, so don't."

A low sound escaped his chest, and he stalked forward. "I don't want to talk… but I need you to know something." Gavriel stood over her, and Lark had to tilt her head to meet his eye.

"But that requires talking, which you don't want to do."

Gavriel huffed a laugh, and lowered to his knees, grabbing Lark's hands. "Just listen." His eyes bore into her, searching. "I don't blame you for Hamlin. He made his choice, and it was his to own. I only—" Gavriel's throat bobbed. "He died to save me, and a selfish part of me is glad."

Lark's lips parted, but no words surfaced.

"I'm glad I remain. That you yet live, and we can..." Gavriel's brow furrowed. "Death is inevitable, but I'm not ready to part from you. His death granted us time. Time I selfishly want, despite the sacrifices needed."

Lark's hand found the side of his face, and he leaned into her touch, his eyes falling closed. "It isn't selfish to want to live. And it doesn't mean it doesn't still hurt—"

"Perhaps not, but do you see how that might bring me incredible guilt?"

Lark leaned her forehead to his. Of course this weighed on him. She still grieved the loss of Hugo and felt the weight of his death with each breath she drew. And guilt? Guilt was the burden borne by the grieving, and a painful reminder that one lives on while another is lost. Guilt for the loss, for finding joy after such a loss. It was a tightening noose that gradually cut one off from the rest of the world. From joy. From life. Lark had witnessed many souls fall to the cycle of torment between grief and guilt.

"Without Hamlin," he continued, "without the Guild, I'm not sure what I am anymore. I know I wish to remain at your side, and selfishly, that's all I've decided on." He soothed his thumb over the back of her hand. "I suppose I'm a little lost, is all. And I can't help thinking my relief in the face of my freedom, of what it cost to gain us this chance, says more about me than all the marks I completed as a Crow."

Lark pressed her forehead to his, chest tightening at the pain he carried. "What if your relief was honoring his sacrifice rather than selfishness?"

Gavriel pulled away and opened his eyes, his gaze a deep plunge and a promise. "That sounds like a lovely thought." He inhaled, fixing Lark with a penetrating stare. "But right now, I don't want to think."

Lark's blood pounded in her ears as warmth flooded her cheeks. She wet her lips, weighing her response. "Then don't think."

Gavriel went wholly still, and for a moment Lark was sure she'd said the wrong thing. But when he crashed his lips to hers in a harsh, bruising kiss, she pulled him to her, and relief speared through her limbs. The tension in her body melted away, and she claimed his mouth just as roughly. Maybe she was angry. Maybe she resented how he turned from her when his pain was its worst, but right now all she could do was rake her fingers through the hair brushing the top of his neck and yank him, so his body covered hers.

There was nothing slow about their descent. His teeth grazed her lower lip, pulling a desperate noise from her throat. His touch was fire, and he burned his way up to her hair before gripping a fistful to angle her head back. He scorched his mouth down her neck—a sharp bite sent a shiver down her spine. His touch was rough but careful, avoiding all the injuries she sustained. The ones he had tended with a clenched jaw and terse silence. Now, his touch was possessive, consuming, and adept. Knowing every inch of her body in both pain and pleasure.

Lark untied his cloak, letting it fall away as she made quick work of the top ties of his tunic. She tugged it too quickly, and it caught on his head. A deep chuckle vibrated through his chest, the sound the most beautiful thing she'd heard in far too long.

"Patience, Demon. Before I lose an eye."

Lark grinned, hips wiggling in anticipation. "Well, then hurry it along, mortal. I haven't all day."

Gavriel extricated himself from the offending garment, a bright smile lighting up his face and crinkling his eyes. Lark let her hungry gaze rove over his body. Over every fight-hardened edge. She ran her hand over his powerful form, over old scars, and new ones.

Lark surged forward, kissing that smile. Oh, how she missed this. Missed him.

The rest of their clothes were tugged, ripped, and thrown across the room. There would be time for mending later.

When nothing was between them but skin and a soft huff of breath, they stilled. The candlelight caught his eyes, green with flecks of gold, and for the first time since the arena, Lark could see life in them once more.

Gavriel kissed her again, slower this time. His lips, languid against hers, as if the urgency had dissipated to something more. To something they had all the time in the world to explore. As if nothing else existed outside this moment, his heartbeat against hers, and the air they breathed.

Lark slid her hand down to line him up with where she needed him most. There would be countless nights to take her time with him, but she couldn't wait any longer.

Gavriel nodded as if he felt it, too, the need to join, and slowly sank in. The sharp stretching sting of being filled quickly gave way to liquid pleasure, and when he was flush against her, she shivered. Gavriel's brow furrowed. His mouth parted as he stared into her eyes and dragged out before sinking back in.

Lark cried out. It was too much and everything she needed. Her nails bit into his shoulders, needing something to hold on to as she unraveled with every thrust. He wasn't gentle, a fact she was grateful for. As they poured everything they had into each other. Every moment of anger, every ounce of strength, of fear, of all-consuming need, Lark's eyes blurred with unshed tears.

Gavriel froze. "Am I hurting you?"

"No," she gasped out. If he stopped, she wasn't sure she'd survive.

He groaned, whether in relief or something else, Lark wasn't certain. But he claimed her mouth once more, a violent kiss of power and strength before he lifted her hips and slammed into her hard enough to rattle her teeth. His grip, tight enough to leave marks. Lark tried to meet his thrusts, but each one was a force that shook through her.

Gavriel, Gavriel. Gavriel. His name was a litany in her mind until nothing else existed but him. Her eyes slid shut, and tears rolled down her cheeks as she clung to him. His lips found her closed eyes as he kissed away her tears and continued his punishing pace. Lark's skin tingled, and her stomach flipped. Like she was teetering on the edge, and the call of the void was beckoning.

Her eyes fluttered open to find Gavriel gazing down at her, something akin to wonder on his face as he slowed his rhythm, his hand sliding down to find the spot that sent stars through her vision. A firm circle of his thumb, and her vision blurred, her nerves over-firing as she shattered. Her limbs slackened, everything gone heavy and boneless. Gavriel kissed her, whispering against her hair as he pressed her hip back to the bed.

He pulled free, and it was like a tug on her heart.

"Wait," she said weakly.

Gavriel smirked, pulling her favorite scar taut. "I'm not done," he said in a rough voice. He stared down at her with hazy awe, before lining himself up and slowly sinking in. If before was a violent race to oblivion, this was a measured descent into madness. He held the back of her head in one hand, the other gripping her hip.

Lark tried to hold his stare, even as sharp pleasure stole her awareness.

"Lark," he growled. "You are *everything.*"

Her head spun, and a soft whimper escaped her lips.

With one last drive, he filled her deeper than she thought possible, finding his release. Lark slid her hand to his jaw, holding him in place as his eyes closed and pleasure flashed across his face. He was impossibly beautiful this way.

After a moment, an eternity, he pulled free of her and bundled her in his arms. His breath, wild and erratic as the pounding of her heart. His hand found her hair once more, but instead of gripping it possessively, his fingers threaded a soft path. Over and over.

Lark nestled in close, needing to speak and fearing she'd break whatever spell they were under.

"That was very nice."

Void take her treacherous tongue.

Gavriel only laughed, a ragged sound. "I'm pleased you enjoyed yourself." He kissed the top of her head, his lips lingering as he inhaled deeply. "I've missed you," he murmured.

Lark felt her lips curve as she sighed. There was an unspoken relief as the last of the tension fled her body. Gavriel was hers, and she wasn't letting him go. Deep down, she'd always known this, but some nagging fear always got in the way.

Never again.

Gavriel peered down at her, and Lark realized she hadn't responded yet.

"How many sailors have rattled this very headboard?"

Gavriel groaned, lifting a hand to cover her mouth. "Why do you say such things?"

Lark pushed his hand away. "Think about it. How often are these linens washed, do you think?"

Gavriel's finger found her uninjured ribs, and a fit of giggles erupted from her chest. She shoved and kicked against the onslaught until, finally, he relented.

"All right, you little demon," Gavriel said, pushing up to stand. He grinned and turned, giving her an eyeful of his sharply honed backside. When he faced her again, he held a rag in one hand and the pitcher from the washbasin in the other. "I'm washing you and that filthy mouth of yours before you have your way with me again."

Ebullience spread through Lark like a flame lighting a pile of tinder. "What if I enjoy being filthy?" she asked with a laugh. It was so good to laugh with Gavriel again.

His mouth twitched. "Then I'll have to force you to sit still, a task I assure you I will find no enjoyment in." He set the pitcher down on the end table and yanked her across the bed to him. Lark went willingly, offering no fight as she stared up at the man who owned her heart.

The first swipe of the rag was once more on her ribs since he'd discovered the weakness of her ticklish spot. She once again fell into a fit of laughter.

CHAPTER THIRTY-NINE

LANGFORD

Langford always considered himself a man of principles. Loyalty, honesty, and a refusal to make promises he couldn't keep. Ever since the promise he broke to Ryker, he'd endeavored to uphold these principles.

Demetria was testing his fortitude.

After berating her for her asinine stunt and receiving her nonplussed reaction, Langford gave up, storming off to his quarters. If she cared so little for her well-being, so be it. He wouldn't put her under guard.

The weight of shame landed hard in his stomach. He should remember what it felt like to run away from home, from duty and a life planned out. He'd once walked away from a future built on certainty, and if he'd been forced into hiding, with nothing but his thoughts, he'd have gone mad for want of distraction. Considering all she left behind, he couldn't fault her.

But she could have waited until they weren't at the port where King Zaire's spies would likely check first.

The door to his cabin opened, and Alistair strode in, eyes alight with excitement.

"That display was possibly the most attractive thing I've ever witnessed." Alistair theatrically arched against the door. "Take me now, you utter brute."

"Is she all right then?"

"She's in excellent hands." Alistair claimed the spot on the bed beside Langford. "Daciana will look after her tonight, so you needn't fret over our escape artist."

Langford groaned and laid back against the pillow, covering his eyes. "I yelled at the princess."

Alistair yanked his arm away to peer down at him. "Yes, you did. You scolded a young girl, you beautiful tyrant."

"It isn't funny." Langford was no fool, and he always remembered his place. To disregard her rank was something Alistair would do, not him.

"Now, now." Alistair's voice was gentle. His ability to switch from teasing to sincere was yet another thing that endeared him to the man. "You spoke out of concern, out of fear. I'd wager she understands this and even finds gratitude in it."

"You think she's grateful some disgraced nobody feels mighty enough to yell at her as if she's a child?"

"She is a child." Alistair ran a soft hand along Langford's jaw, and Langford couldn't help but lean into it. "And she's grateful someone is looking out for her. That she isn't alone."

How the same man who once played a game called "Guess What's In My Trousers" found the wisdom in moments such as this was beyond Langford's comprehension. But perhaps Langford didn't need to understand everything. Perhaps he could bask in the wonder of Alistair's heart and take solace in the fact that he was his.

Langford felt a smile pull at his mouth, and Alistair's answering expression of triumph was a thing of beauty.

"Ah, that's much better," Alistair said, his low voice rumbling as his hand lazily followed the path of Langford's collar. "Now… where were we before all this unpleasantness?"

With a laugh, Langford gripped Alistair by the back of the neck and drew him in for a hungry kiss.

LANGFORD BLEW against the steam curling from his third cup of tea. He knew better than to expect a decent brew, so he'd brought his own mixture of camellia sinensis and ginger, asking the barkeeper for hot water. His chamomile and sage were running criminally low, and he looked forward to harvesting more supplies once they took to the forests again. Daciana must be due for another of his lavender and wolfsbane brews. How had she fared without? And Lark? Had she kept up with the thistle and knotweed tonic he brewed for her to prevent pregnancy? It hadn't occurred to him to ask last night, but perhaps the first chance he got, he should speak to both of them privately.

Right after they discussed their findings. The tome in the leather satchel he wore slung across his chest was an ever-present weight.

"There you are." Alistair's voice carried across the empty tavern, his boots echoing against the freshly washed floors. "Imagine my surprise, waking up naked and alone. You used me for my body and left, you absolute scoundrel."

"You mean, I tried to wake you and you not only muttered the most colorful curses in all of Ardenas, but actually tried to kick me?"

"A technicality."

Alistair sat in the chair beside Langford, his boots finding their way to the top of the table. He had a way of being comfortable no matter where he was, and unapologetically so. Langford darted a glance around the tavern, expecting the barkeeper to yell at him for muddying up the freshly wiped tables. But the man with the red beard and glossy forehead continued polishing tankards and dutifully ignoring them.

Footsteps sounded from the stairs, and Daciana descended the last step. Alone.

"Where is… Ophelia?" Langford stumbled over the name Demetria had chosen last night. They'd agreed to call her something other than her title and given name, at least in public. One never knew the extent of Zaire's contacts. After Langford's disgraceful reprimanding of the princess, she'd immediately demanded a change in protection, naming Daciana as her guard. Though the girl's instincts weren't wrong,

Daciana was her best chance at remaining safe, the ease with which Demetria attached to a perfect stranger was troublesome.

Perhaps he should tell her as much.

Daciana rolled her eyes. "She and Kenna ordered everything off the menu to be delivered to the room." She cast a sympathetic glance toward the kitchens behind the bar. "The tab is still in your name, right, Alistair?"

Alistair gave a half-hearted growl. "I suppose that was my error." He angled the empty chair beside him, gesturing for her to sit.

With a grin, Daciana sat, smacking Alistair's legs and pointing to the floor.

It reminded Langford so much of Mrs. O'Connell and the last time they were all together at the Walden Inn, that his throat tightened. He drank another swill of tea and pushed the memory aside.

The echoes of soft laughter and the scuffing of boots against the poor barkeeper's floor interrupted Langford's thoughts. He glanced up to find Lark, her bright grin positively impish as Gavriel snaked a hand around her waist. Another fit of laughter broke free from her chest, and he softly shushed her, smiling with unbridled sincerity Langford hadn't seen from the former assassin in ages. Whatever troubles they'd had the evening before seemed to have melted away. One look at Alistair's knowing smirk confirmed he realized this, too.

"Good morning!" Lark said brightly. "I trust everyone is well-rested?"

"Not everyone," Alistair replied smoothly, grabbing Lark's hand and placing a quick kiss to her knuckle before pointing at Langford. "This one kept me up all night with his wicked appetite. Utterly insatiable, he is."

Langford's cheeks burned. Insufferable man.

"Hmm," Gavriel said as he somehow slid a chair over without making a sound. "That makes two of us."

"We have much to discuss. Let's not waste time." Lark fought valiantly to change the subject, even as her mouth twitched. "As you know, Gavriel and I sought Inerys."

Daciana folded her arms and nodded. She waited until the barkeeper disappeared into the kitchen to respond. "Yes, the witch shared with me what she'd offered as counsel. Some ancient form of magic that could restore the veil, should it fall. One that no longer exists." Her words were sharp and dismissive. Interesting.

Lark traced the woodgrains on the table with her finger. To the untrained eye, it might appear a random, thoughtless act, but Langford had known Lark long enough to recognize her nervous habits. "Yes," she said uneasily. "Vitas Conjuring. Life Magic. Evidently, the only thing strong enough to harness that much power and it was eradicated by Avalon. There aren't any true Life Wielders left." Lark wet her lips and folded her hands. "It's just as well. Apparently, it's far more dangerous than it once was and not worth the risk."

A shadow passed over Daciana's face, and an unfamiliar line of tension stiffened her shoulders.

Langford's hands itched to pull the tome from his satchel, but he resisted. For the moment. "Did she mention anything about a Reaper Blade?"

"No… and I've never heard of such a thing." Understanding stole across Lark's face, and her golden eyes lit up with excitement. "Would it work on Nereida?"

Something akin to satisfaction rushed through Langford's blood. He had been useful. He smiled, and he reached for the tome in his satchel. "Perhaps. It's written here. There is a weapon of great power." Langford delicately lifted the crumbling book onto the table and turned the pages with great care to the translation he'd memorized aboard Ingemar's ship.

"Messorum Ferrum. Forged by blood. Bound by fate. The only blade strong enough to kill any being, both living and dead. The stone of a dragon and the touch of a Reaper breathes life into its edge, and life it demands until enough have fallen to anoint with power strong enough to slay a god."

Langford looked up to find Lark's mouth slightly agape, and Daciana's frown only deepened. Alistair looked on with a smug sort of pride, and Gavriel's gaze was busy sweeping the room, even though he'd caught every word.

"What does this mean?" Lark's voice came out soft and breathless.

"It means," Langford began, "we might have a way to kill Nereida.

CHAPTER FORTY

DACIANA

Daciana absorbed the information Lark and Langford shared. She frowned, and nodded, and schooled her expression into feigned concentration when the moment called for it. She refused to acknowledge the unspoken truth of what they sought. The tightness in her chest, a breath not fully exhaled, kept her wound tight until finally it was time to be on their way.

When their bags were packed, and they'd traded for new canvases and supplies for camp, they trekked along the road until Emeraude Port was lost beneath the horizon. They would go to see the hedge witch, yet again, for answers Daciana hoped she could give. If they could craft a Reaper Blade, perhaps they stood a chance at halting Nereida's plan. Inerys' hut wasn't far, but they planned to stop by the Walden Inn to see Mrs. O'Connell and rest for a spell. Lark bounced on her heels at the mention of visiting Apple, and already Daciana could tell they'd have a hard time leaving the horse behind once more.

Every nerve in Daciana's body rejoiced at the loss of solid walls confining her. The forest was always a safe refuge, and the air thickened with the heavy scent of pine as they slipped deeper into the woods. The rest of the trees had shed their leaves already, leaving scattered remains of browns, reds, and golds on the forest floor. They plodded along, the steady crunch of dried leaves underfoot.

Kenna slipped a blade from the freshly stitched pocket of her cloak. She had complained of her belt growing tiresome under the weight of so many weapons. "And this is a silver dagger. You'll need one of these if we cross paths with all sorts of nasty baddies," she said with a grin as Demetria examined it with reverent care.

Kenna had taken an immediate liking to the princess. If Daciana had to guess, it was because Demetria was another outsider in their close-knit group. Lark, too, had found the girl fascinating and barraged her with endless questions for what seemed like hours until Alistair threatened to gag her. A threat Gavriel didn't take a liking to, but Lark had merely rolled her eyes and focused on examining Langford's hand and comparing cauterized scars.

Daciana took a deep breath, filling her lungs with fresh air sharpened by autumn. They found a decent clearing between the copse of trees, close enough to fresh water for all their needs. A nearby stream hurried over stones and carved its way along the bank, the gentle sound smoothing her tension. Her next breath felt easier than the last as she began the familiar act of setting up camp.

THE WARM LIGHT of the fire spilled across Daciana's now empty plate. The realization that Hugo had always been the pack grunt was swift and startling. He'd always carried the plates, utensils, and cups. He'd bring back a fresh kill, which Daciana would set to work on skinning and cleaning before he'd cook a simple, if hearty, meal. She glanced down at the plate that had held her roasted herb potato, courtesy of Langford's cooking.

A bottle was passed her way, and Daciana took a deep swill without examining its contents. A sharp and bitter rum, spiced and warm, hit the back of her throat. She couldn't afford to lose her wits this night, but she could dull the edge of her wary mind.

"It's a shame your fiddle was lost," Lark said, quietly. She sat between Gavriel's knees, closest to the fire. She held her hands out for warmth. "This seems a good night for music."

Gavriel hummed his agreement, resting his chin on the top of her head. "We'll get a new one in Brookhill. A shame your fellow, Bartrand, wasn't selling his wares at the port."

Lark nodded, absently staring into the fire. The flames danced in the gentle breeze, along with the fiery wisps of her hair.

"I need no accompaniment to sing," Alistair called from the log he'd sprawled across. "I'll sing a tune we all know!" He sat up with a devilish grin, clapping his thigh to a steady beat.

Lark glared at him. "By the skies, if you sing that blazing song from the tavern, I'll pour water all over your favorite silks."

"There once was a bird, with breasts like a goddess."

"That's not the words," Lark said through gritted teeth.

Alistair only sang louder.

"They sat as high as the sky would allow.

But everyone knows, the time always comes

When the breasts must be bound, they must be bound."

Langford snorted, and Lark threw a handful of dirt in Alistair's direction. He leapt up from his log and began dancing around the campfire. Dodging her attacks, which had quickly escalated to the launching of small rocks and sticks.

The intoxicating sound of a high laugh pulled Daciana's attention from the display. Kenna's mouth was parted, a laugh still poised on her perfect lips. Her dimples creased her cheeks, and her dark eyes were warm with mirth. The fire painted her in a soft glow and cast a shining sky of stars amidst her black hair. When Kenna caught Daciana staring, a comely blush crept up her cheeks. She lowered her chin, and her dark fringe fell in her eyes.

But she didn't turn away.

Blazing nethers. How strong was that rum?

Unwillingly, Daciana broke Kenna's stare to see what the princess made of all this. Demetria wore a soft smile but didn't appear scandalized. She was more preoccupied with whatever she was sketching in that book of hers.

Alistair was still jumping about like a fool and singing his interpretation of Bartrand's ballad.

"A taste for blood, has our sweet Lark.
Who knows what games she plays in the dark?
She makes Gavriel shriek like a frightened lass,
When with nimble fingers she plays with his—"

"That's it!" Lark tackled Alistair to the ground, pushing his cheek into the dirt as his rich laugh filled the air.

"No one appreciates my art!" Alistair called, spitting out a leaf. Lark sat on his back, his front firmly pressed into the earth. It was a half-hearted maneuver, one Alistair could have easily extricated himself from, but Daciana could tell he was having too much fun to spoil the game just yet.

Langford fell off the stump he'd been sitting on, shaking with silent laughter.

Gavriel shook his head, grinning, and tossed another log into the fire. The embers shot off into the night sky. "You know the life of an artist. You won't be appreciated until after your death."

Alistair laughed, his face still in the dirt. "I yield!"

Lark huffed, climbing off him and reclaiming her spot in front of Gavriel.

Gavriel leaned in to whisper, "Do you want me to hurt him? Only a little, for good measure."

Daciana was sure his words were meant for Lark's ears only, and no one else paid him any mind as if they hadn't heard him. There would be no discretion, not when her senses were heightened, as if the change was imminent. Daciana pretended not to hear, as she had done many times before.

"Only if he writes another verse," Lark whispered back with a grin.

Gavriel nodded his consent, kissing her forehead.

Their affection was so easy, almost second nature. Daciana glanced over at Kenna, only to find her watching Gavriel and Lark, her face twisted in an expression of fierce longing.

Just once, Daciana would love to know what it felt like. The unencumbered freedom of love freely given. Kenna gave her heart all too willingly, but Daciana couldn't bring herself to do the same.

She avoided Kenna's gaze for the rest of the evening.

DACIANA LEANED her head back against the thick oak, resting her elbows on her knees. She'd taken first watch so the others could get some rest. Alistair's distinct snore rumbled from his tent, and a smile fought its way across Daciana's mouth. It was hard to brood on her disappointments and failings when part of her, almost every part of her, was still so grateful to be with the others once more.

A soft rustle of movement came from the farthest tent, and Daciana rolled her eyes. Lark and Gavriel were trying to be quiet, and perhaps wholly human ears wouldn't detect their activities, but even if her change wasn't near, she'd have heard them. She'd have to tell Lark in the morning. Even if it would humiliate her, she'd appreciate knowing.

Daciana shook her head, ready to patrol the perimeter in favor of giving them privacy, when the flap to their tent opened. Lark's face popped out, a grin lighting up her features.

"Care for some company?" Lark whispered. Of course, she remembered Daciana's hearing. Within her tent, Gavriel groaned his displeasure at being awakened before his shift. Lark's grin only widened, and she shoved her way through, hastily tying the flaps closed for Gavriel.

Warmth filled Daciana's chest as the former Reaper crept her way over, and sat against the tree at her side.

"So," she began, "we've had little chance to catch up in private."

Daciana nodded. "You're right." And though she hadn't said it, she'd missed their chats. The ones meant for each other and no one else.

"Well..." Lark said, expectantly. "Tell me more about Kenna. I didn't want to pry, but you brought her here, so now you spill." Lark hugged her knees, leaning her head against Daciana's shoulder. "It's good manners, as my confidante, that you confide in me, too."

Daciana huffed a laugh, laying her head against Lark's. What point was there in hiding? She knew all of Lark's secrets, and for once, the prospect of laying her own bare was inviting. Safe. She was safe here in the dark woods with her dearest friend.

"Where do I begin?"

"Wherever your mind goes when you think of the beginning."

Daciana began long before the beginning. She told Lark of her mother, and her father. Of how she loved them more than the world. How proud she was to be their daughter, and how much her title meant to her. And after her mother was gone, she clung to her mantle that much tighter, for it was all she had left of her. She told her of how she fell for the hunter, and the hunter for her—for the wolf. How they promised each other forever, and how foolish they were to offer things that weren't theirs to give.

When she got to the story of her ascension, and how she'd slain her pack, including her beloved father, Daciana's voice never wavered. She never showed an ounce of that weakness her mother forbade. And she kept the depth of her truths to herself. She didn't tell her Kenna's soul was gone when she found her. Lark didn't need to know the power in her blood—fueled by death.

"And after all of that, everything we lost... all the pain I caused... I couldn't even look at her without feeling it all. Without remembering the horrors I brought upon her." Daciana said, a heavy silence descending over them. She had no right to claim a hold on Kenna. Not after what Kenna had suffered at the hands of her pack, and who she lost. Not after the destruction Daciana had wrought in the wake of Kenna's death. *Death.* Kenna had died, and Daciana drew the life force from an entire village, save for one lone babe, to bring her back.

She couldn't afford to love. Never again.

Lark studied her, red hair spilling over her shoulder. "Each day is its own journey—a new beginning. You don't have to carry yesterday —not if you don't want to."

Daciana hesitantly met Lark's unflinching gaze, finding both warmth and sadness mingling within her stare. Her skin held a darker tone from her time in the Desolates, but the raw, aching honesty in her eyes was the same.

Lark scooted forward, taking Daciana's hand. "You deserve to be happy."

Did she? And would Lark offer the same words of comfort if she told her the entire story? The truth danced on the tip of Daciana's tongue, begging for release.

She swallowed it down and offered a weak smile. "I quite like wise Lark. She offers sage counsel."

Lark grinned. "It's scary, isn't it? Now I feel all weird. Quick, remind me of my hypocritical nature and how I jeopardized mine and Gavriel's safety for the sake of severing a soul bond! Or how I can never take my own advice! Oh, I know! Let's recall the time I killed Talbot by tripping."

Daciana laughed, squeezing Lark's hand. "No, this suits you."

Lark's face lit up with a smile to rival the sun before her eyes turned mischievous. "You never said what happened in that barn when you and Kenna were caught in the rain."

Daciana opened her mouth, preparing to offer the explanation of her fever and sickness, when the flaps to Kenna's tent fluttered open. Kenna stood there, frozen, her eyes zeroing in on where Daciana and Lark's hands were clasped.

Kenna's face hardened, and she stormed off.

Lark jolted, shock and confusion claiming her features. Her gaze fell to their hands, and she groaned, pulling her hand free. "Really, Dac? You couldn't have shown her a little affection so she wouldn't find fault with our friendship?"

Daciana sighed, pulling herself to stand. "It's not that, it's—never mind. I have to take care of this." She veered in the direction of Kenna's anger, leaving Lark and camp behind. It was foolish, really. The way Kenna reacted in the face of baseless assumptions. They'd already had this discussion in the room at the tavern when—

Regret tightened Daciana's chest. They hadn't spoken of it, had they? Kenna tried, and Daciana had run away before she could explain. This time, it was Kenna fleeing the complication of their attachment.

Was this to be their cage? A pattern of always running and never finding common ground to stand on?

Daciana slowed her pace. She could let her go. If she turned back right now and let Kenna wander with whatever thoughts played in her head, that could be it. This was Daciana's chance to break whatever bound them, to end it and never worry after Kenna again. Never worry about what she would do to protect her. All she had to do was go back the way she came.

Daciana stilled, the sound of the stream louder now. A silvery ripple of moonlight broke through the branches, and sharp shadows cut through the light with every gust of the wind.

Daciana pushed forward, toward the sound of the stream, where Kenna's scent was the strongest. Her steps were sure and quickened. She thought she was ready to let Kenna go, but the way she propelled herself through the forest told her otherwise.

When Daciana reached the stream, she followed its winding path until the trees thinned and the ground flattened. A river stretched before her, stars and a thick slice of moon illuminating the dark water. Kenna's slight form was crouched on the bank, her hood up over her head as she stared into the water. Her red cloak and hood were her armor, but Daciana never wanted Kenna to feel she had to guard herself from her.

"My talisman senses you," Kenna said without looking up. "I've been tracking the moon, and your turn isn't due for my talisman to sense you, yet it does."

Daciana didn't have a response. She wasn't prepared to have that conversation. She'd steeled her nerves, and she would say what she came to say. "You asked me why I can't be a certain way with you. Why it's so easy with the others." Daciana edged forward, but Kenna made no move to stand or answer. She took her silence as permission to continue. "I care for them, I do. I love them like they're my kin."

Kenna turned, her hood still hiding her face. But even in the shadows, Daciana could see the pain flash in her eyes. In the furrow of her brow.

"But you," Daciana continued, "I... I burn for you. With everything I am. I always have. Every part of me yearns for you, even the parts I wish did not exist." Daciana's voice faltered, and she clenched her fist as her throat constricted around the truth. "It's not easy, feeling so helpless to my desires. I need control and without it..." She shook her head as her confession threatened to steal the breath from her lungs. "Without control, I'm terrified of what I'm capable of."

Kenna tossed her hood back, impatiently pushing her hair out of her widened eyes. A heart wrenching expression dawned on her beautiful face, the light of hope filling every shadow and curve. "What do you fear most?"

A ragged laugh broke free from Daciana's chest. "I fear how much I love you."

Kenna's eyes glimmered, and she bit her lip, but that smile kept breaking free. "I knew you still loved me."

A tight sound, almost like a laugh, escaped from Daciana's chest. She took a staggering step forward, knowing there was no going back, not after this. It was like a weight had lifted. Whatever had held fast in her stomach and burdened her legs was gone, and she could surge forward—

Before Daciana could feel the warmth of her touch, Kenna jerked toward the water. A stark look of shock painted her features right before she fell into the river. Her splash was the only sound as black water swallowed her whole, and the night was once again still.

Daciana scrambled, landing hard on her knees beside the riverbank, and peering into its depths. She plunged a hand in, and the icy water swallowed up to her shoulder. She didn't find the river bottom. It couldn't be that deep, could it? Kenna was a strong swimmer. Daciana knew this from summer months spent in the lake. But she hadn't fallen. She'd been yanked in.

Daciana unbuckled her belt, trying not to think too hard about removing her weapons before charging into danger. But she needed to lessen the weight, especially if she had to drag Kenna back to the surface.

Daciana toed off her boots, watching the surface of the water warily for any signs of bubbles or ripples.

The still, glassy surface sent fear sinking into the pit of her stomach.

Taking a deep breath, Daciana dove in. Icy silence and utter blackness engulfed her. But the dark was a welcome home to eyes meant for night.

The river was deeper than Daciana thought, but she found the murky bottom. A graveyard of bones, of armor and swords, adorned the muck and river plants of the river's floor. Leaves sprouted through the empty eye-socket of bone, the skull's mouth still wide in a silent scream. Movement in her periphery pulled her away from the skeletal remains of those unfortunate souls. A flash of red undulated in the dark.

Kenna.

Daciana kicked her legs, desperately swimming toward her. Kenna's head shook back and forth, black hair like ink pooling in front of her face. At each arm, a shadow held fast, and a third clung to her legs.

A shout absorbed by the river escaped Daciana's mouth in a torrent of bubbles. Three pairs of eyes turned on her, luminescent flashes of bright blue. Kenna's head slumped, the fight leaving her body. Daciana surged forward, fingers finding the slimy face of the creature holding Kenna's legs. She felt until she found its eyes, thumbs gouging in. A muffled, watery shriek sounded, and the creature fell away. The two holding Kenna's arms reached for Daciana—Daciana grabbed one by the throat and squeezed, feeling a tendon pop beneath her palm.

Its head slanted to the side at an unnatural angle, and the third creature swam off.

Daciana grabbed Kenna, wrapping an arm around her waist. The weight of them both slowed her ascent, and as Daciana felt the last of the air in her lungs shrivel away and tighten under the pressure of the water, she knew Kenna's air had gone long before.

The glimmer of light, of blessed air, beckoned from above. Daciana kicked harder, but something held them firm. Kenna's cloak had snagged on the gnarled branches of a fallen tree adorning the river's edge.

Daciana peeled Kenna's red cloak from her body, letting it remain in the muddy depths and kicking up toward the promise of moonlight dancing along the surface.

When they broke free, she gasped in a greedy lungful of air and pushed toward the riverbank. She'd hardly gotten them on dry land when she started pumping Kenna's chest, desperately trying to expel the water from her lungs. Kenna was so still, so pale in the moonlight. Like her soul had fled and left nothing but a too-perfect face behind. A mockery of the life that should shine behind her eyes.

"Breathe, damn you." Daciana covered Kenna's cold mouth with hers, forcing air into her lungs. Her chest expanded, but Kenna's eyes remained closed. Daciana pushed even harder. "Breathe!"

Kenna's eyes fluttered open, and she gasped, a wet ragged sound before river water streamed out of her mouth. Kenna gagged, coughing violently as more water spilled from her blue lips.

Thank the skies. Thank the skies and the earth and the stars and whatever else granted breath into Kenna's lungs.

Kenna rolled over, still coughing and gagging. Daciana rubbed her back, unable to form a coherent word.

"Dac," Kenna said, her voice cracking. "Were those vodníks?"

Vodníks were creatures of water, said to have drowned in their first life. They pulled unsuspecting victims to the depths, drowning them so they might have more company below the surface. They weren't so hard to kill, so much as dangerous if one was caught unawares, like Kenna had been.

It wouldn't happen again.

Daciana sighed, still rubbing her back. "I believe so."

Kenna groaned and sat up. "Any still alive?"

Daciana had taken care of two while the third swam away. And those were just the ones she had seen. She nodded.

Kenna stood, and Daciana followed, keeping a steady hand out and ready. Kenna staggered into her as she found her bearings. "All right, point me toward danger. I'm ready. Just… need my dagger." She reached for her cloak, panic gripping her features. "Where's my cloak?"

Daciana winced. "The bottom of the river."

Kenna's jaw clenched before she let out a stream of curses.

CHAPTER FORTY-ONE

LARK

"Gavriel," Lark hissed. She stood outside their tent, knowing he would wake at the slightest hint of sound.

Gavriel poked his head out. His hair had grown long enough that it stuck out at odd angles from sleep. Lark fought a smile at the sight. His eyes were already alert, and he darted his gaze about the camp. "Where's Daciana?"

"She went after Kenna. I need you to keep watch so I can go find them and explain." It was partially her fault that Kenna took off like that. Though it made little sense. She understood her friendship with Daciana was of a familial sort.

Perhaps that was why it stung.

Daciana had always been a private person. Respectful of everyone else's privacy while fiercely safeguarding her own. It must have been excruciating for Kenna to wish for more while Daciana kept her guard up. There was once a time when the walls between Lark and Gavriel had been a source of pain and confusion.

Not even that long ago…

"What do you have to explain?" Gavriel glided out of the tent, clad in only an unlaced black tunic and dark trousers. He slipped his boots and belt on, a short sword at his waist and a dagger in his hand. "Whatever you need to tell them can wait until they return, can't it?"

"No, it can't." Though she wished to tell him exactly why she wished to smooth things over as best she could, that would require sharing Daciana's business. Lark wouldn't betray her confidence, not even to Gavriel.

Gavriel shrugged. "All right, then. But you're not going alone."

"Someone needs to keep watch."

A harsh groan sounded from Alistair's tent. "With all that racket, I'm already awake." Alistair flung his tent flaps open, staggering out with a decidedly cross expression and bare feet. "Go. Just go. Find them and try your very best not to twist your ankle in the dark."

Somehow, Lark doubted he meant that last bit.

She and Gavriel pressed through the night, following the subtle signs of tracks. Daciana must have been in a hurry to leave any hint of her trek behind.

The barren branches of waning autumn creaked in the wind's call. It was almost like that first night Lark spent as a mortal in the Twisted Woods. Only this time, she had Gavriel by her side and a purpose beyond survival. Lark snuck a glance in his direction. The moon painted the side of his face with a soft glow. Even now, after all this time, his beauty took her breath away.

Gavriel caught her staring, and a wry smirk curved against his mouth. "Keep looking at me like that, Demon, and I might have to press you against a tree before we catch up to the others."

A shiver chased down her collar at his bold words, and she considered testing the truth of them. But she pushed forward, intent on finding Daciana and Kenna and making things right.

Something inside Lark shifted. A humming along her bones and between her teeth before a wave of dizziness sent her vision rolling. She staggered forward, bracing herself against a tree.

"What's wrong? What is it?" Gavriel's voice, laced with fear, ghosted against her ear.

Lark lifted her head, and the trees spun. Something wet trickled over her mouth and down her chin. Gavriel's thumb found her lip, and when he pulled it away, her blood coated his skin.

"What's happening?" Lark's voice was weak in her own ears, and she slipped. Gavriel's arms came around her, holding her up. Even in the haze of her increasingly dim vision, she could see terror twisting his features.

A sharp pain split through Lark's skull, like a current rippling from the top of her head through the bottom of her feet. Her dwindling strength fled her body as a searing flash tore through her and lit her veins on fire. Distantly, she could hear Gavriel saying her name.

And then darkness.

A cool, numbing sensation coursed through her. Soothing the blaze of pain that had threatened to boil the blood beneath her skin. Gradually, Lark's vision cleared, and once more, the forest remained a fixed point. Trees swayed in the whispering breeze rather than spinning her sight.

Gavriel's arms held strong while she found her bearings. On shaky legs, she stood and wiped the blood from her nose. The appearance of her own blood had long since stopped shocking her with how many wounds she'd sustained as a mortal, but the snaking trail of dark liquid along the top of her hand sent a faint echo of fear through her human heart. This was no wound, no visible hurt. Whatever this was, she couldn't guess.

Her muscles were weak, and her skin was sticky with sweat. Fatigue loosened any tension in her body, like when Hugo would make her run drills until the exhaustion sent her into a calm state. But there was no more pain.

"Lark," Gavriel repeated, concern tightening his brow and the scar across his mouth. "Are you well?"

Lark nodded numbly.

After a moment's rest and a dozen assurances she was all right, they continued their journey through the forest.

Once or twice, Lark caught Gavriel studying her with an unfamiliar expression. Unfamiliar to be directed at her, as of late. One of calculating rather than wanting. As if she were something to be studied and sorted out.

"You can stop looking at me like that," she said with a shaky smile. "I already told you, I'm fine."

Gavriel stepped into her path, halting her in her tracks. "I know, and I think you're overlooking something serious."

Lark made to push past him, but once again he stood in her way. Finally, she sighed. "I don't know what to think. Until new information comes to light, my only guide is how I feel. And I feel fine." It could have been a dozen different things. Nereida could be working some sort of spell from the Netherworld. Lark could have some sort of human ailment that causes dizzy spells and bleeds from the nose. What good was it to worry? One task at a time. Right now, that task was Daciana and Kenna. Next was traveling to Inerys, and so on and so forth. But to spend her time agonizing over a what if? If her time on this earth was limited, she would not spend it so.

Lark adjusted her tunic, and a chill shuddered down her back. It was sheer impatience that prevented her from bringing a cloak. "Now, step out of my way before I tie you to a tree."

A sharp shriek from up head interrupted any retort Gavriel may have had. They plunged through the forest, seeking the sound. A steady rush of a river carving along the bank reached Lark's ears. She broke through into a clearing, where Daciana stood poised before Kenna in a protective stance. Kenna stood half behind her, one hand out as if about to shove her out of the way.

A large form towered over them. Steady drips of water fell from its massive body. The creature turned. Its wide, unblinking eyes reflected and refracted in the pale glow of the moon. Muck and mottled green algae hung off its body. Its hair was a curtain of drenched vines, and white flowers sprouted along its arms and legs.

Vodník.

As a Reaper, Lark had slain such a creature before. An Undesirable who drowned in their mortal life, only to live out their days in the waters that had claimed them. These souls, when clawing their way back to the living, were transformed into something else. A creature of malice. Of loneliness. They dragged the living beneath the surface of their home, so they might join them in their eternal suffering. It was a cursed tragedy, really.

But no amount of pity for the dead could bring Lark to allow such a thing to live. Not when they threatened Daciana.

She surged forward just in time to see Daciana raise her blade and cut the creature down. Its body landed with a squelch on the riverbank. Not even so much as a twitch.

A pitiful end to a lonely soul.

Lark stepped around the vodník, careful not to track through the aquatic plant life adorning its person. "Are you both all right?"

Daciana nodded, adjusting the short sword in her grasp with a bend of her wrist. She glanced over at Kenna, awaiting her answer.

"I'm having the night of my life, can't you tell?" Kenna rasped out the words and winced. "My cloak is at the bottom of the river—"

"I am sorry for that," Daciana cut in. "You'd been without air too long and I couldn't swim fast enough."

Kenna waved her hand, dismissing the response. "I know," she said. "Thank you."

A weighty silence surrounded them, only the sound of the river filling the space. Its gentle current was almost a mockery of the gruesome scene.

Daciana sheathed her sword, her gaze finding Lark's face. Her brow pinched, and she touched a hand to Lark's chin. "Were you hurt?"

Lark had nearly forgotten about her strange dizzy spell. She wiped at her nose and mouth again. She must have missed some of the blood. "I'm fine. Just a nosebleed."

Behind them, Gavriel cleared his throat. "It wasn't, and you know it."

Daciana stiffened, her eyes darting to the ground. A flash of something Lark couldn't quite name stole across her face. One of fear... or was it guilt? But her face smoothed into a careful mask of neutrality.

Well, then. Whatever that was would have to wait, for Lark was on to an opportunity. An olive branch, even. She peered around Daciana to find Kenna ringing out her long black hair and muttering to herself.

"Your cloak," Lark said. "It's special, isn't it?"

Kenna pushed the wet locks from her face impatiently. "Yes. Irreplaceable even. At first light, I'm retrieving it."

"No need," Lark said with a grin. This was her chance to win her over and smooth whatever edge lay between them. She kicked off her boots and dove in.

CHAPTER FORTY-TWO

LANGFORD

angford studied the samples he'd taken from the water spirit, or the vodník, as Kenna had called it. It was extraordinary. Langford demanded to be shown its remains, and Gavriel had quickly brought him to the specimen. Lark had described the creature as covered in plant life, but Langford hadn't realized its very skin was made of watercress and lily pads. Even its hair hung in strands of tassel stonewort. Incredible!

He had the idea to test a newly formed theory regarding these monsters, these Undesirables. After collecting his samples, he stashed them for safekeeping. One of these days, he'd have a fixed point to call his own, where he might work in peace without fear of losing his findings. There was so much to learn. He'd spent years studying the human body and healing. But this was an entire world he was completely ignorant of. A thought that was both terrifying and exciting.

Alistair didn't share his enthusiasm. In fact, when the four of them had returned, he'd rolled his eyes and said, "Moonlight skinny dipping is best *without* clothing. And you could have invited us."

Their dripping clothes hung off low branches, and the campfire burned against the first rays of dawn.

There was a change in the air. One Langford picked up on almost immediately. A sort of tension that had lifted, while something new took its place. While Kenna and Lark seemed as if they were getting on swimmingly, it was Demetria who had fallen silent when she awoke. The princess kept her thick black hair braided away from her face, a face that revealed nothing, while she poked the fire with a long stick. She accepted her plate of bread and cheese from Alistair with a soft thank you and ate, meeting no one's eye. She ripped apart her bread with charcoal stained hands, her notebook at her side for her to sketch in as soon as she finished her meal. Something was off. Her warmth was gone, along with that stubborn determination that seemed to sharpen her jaw.

Langford scooted over to sit beside her and cleared his throat. "Princess—" At her blank stare, he quickly amended, "Demetria, I realize you're far from home—intentionally so—but if you ever wanted to talk about anything, really, anything at all, I'm always willing to listen."

"You were supposed to take me south."

Her flat and direct response surprised him, but he recovered quickly. "Yes, as soon as our business is sorted, and I intend to keep my word."

"How long will that take?" Her dark eyes had sharpened, a glimpse of that fire returning to her gaze.

It was an impossible question, with an even murkier answer. Langford hadn't dared hope he'd found anything substantial in his research. But with the information Lark and Daciana had gleaned from the witch, they had the beginnings of a plan, his research at its center.

"Who waits for you there?" Langford studied her carefully. "South is such a vague notion. Which town do you hope to reach?"

Demetria's brow creased, her mouth tightening. "When we begin our journey south I will reveal more." Her hands clutched her plate.

There it was. She had no one waiting for her, no connections, and no idea where to seek refuge.

Langford nodded, accepting her lie. "You could stay with us, if you wanted. Even if your southern contacts are worthy, you could stay with us for the foreseeable future."

Demetria stared into the fire, refusing to meet his gaze.

"Very well. Let's speak of other topics. Tell me more about your-self." Langford aimed to direct the conversation in a more comfortable direction and laughed at her dubious expression. "Come, now. There must be something you can tell me."

Demetria twisted the stick in her hand. "What do you wish to know?"

"It isn't what I wish to know. It's what you wish to share."

She shrugged. "I don't know what is worth sharing anymore."

Langford nodded. It was a precarious thing, knowing what to carry and what to leave behind. But he knew what it felt like to spend one's days running, only to realize you have nowhere to run. Perhaps he could work harder to make her feel at home. "I know we haven't shared much of our dealings with you." The truth was, he had no idea how to begin revealing everything to her.

"No, you haven't," Demetria said with a wry smile, "but that doesn't mean I don't know more than you think I do."

Langford stiffened. She couldn't possibly suspect what they hadn't told her. About Lark and Daciana. About the veil and chasing legends that were all too real. They'd been carefully discrete whenever they discussed certain delicate topics—

"It's easy to eavesdrop when no one thinks you're listening," she said, drawing shapes in the dirt with her stick. "I wish I'd realized it sooner, back home, how to pay attention to hidden whispers. Perhaps things would have turned out differently."

Langford considered several responses before settling on, "What do you know?"

"Enough." At his expectant expression, the princess sighed. "I know what Daciana is and how she studies the face of the moon each night. I know what Lark was before she decided a life of pain was a better option—can't say I agree with her on that. You're searching for a way to kill a goddess, whom I'd never heard of until this trip. Alistair is far more tender and affectionate with you than he lets on in public, and he can't sleep unless you're beside him. Kenna watches Daciana's movements as if she's about to take an arrow through the chest for her.

Gavriel has a secret stash of chocolate, and you put far too much honey in your tea."

Langford gaped at her, shock flooding his system at how accurately and astutely she assessed him and his companions. "Right, well," he laughed, threading a hand through his untidy hair. "If you know all this, why haven't you run screaming?"

Her eyes shuttered, and she cast her gaze to the ground. "My mother told me stories of monsters. Of beasts and demons. But she failed to prepare me for the monster that grows in the hearts of those we love." She snapped her stick in half, tossing it into the flames. "If you're the type of people who slay monsters, consider me on board until I'm ready to face down my own demon."

Langford studied the young princess. She had more strength in her than her brother would ever be able to stamp out.

"And," she added, "your tea preferences happen to mirror mine."

THE WALDEN INN and Tavern was the finest establishment in all of Ardenas. Not for its soggy biscuits or over-salted pork. Not even because of the apple pie Mrs. O'Connell was famous for. It was because she seemed to collect patrons like stray cats and turned her establishment into a home.

When Langford crossed the threshold into the familiar tavern, the scent of burnt sugar wafted over him. Stiff drinks and pastries. What more could one want?

Alistair's brilliant green eyes lit up in excitement as he all but dragged Langford toward the kitchens.

"She'll want to see me," he said, before Langford could ask what he was doing. Langford smothered his smile. Of course, Alistair would try to mask his eagerness to see Mrs. O'Connell.

They found her rolling out dough atop a large wooden counter. Flour coated her cheeks, hands, and apron, and her pale blonde hair peeked out from beneath a sage kerchief. Even beneath the white dusting atop her cheeks, a rosy color bloomed from warmth and exertion. Did the woman ever rest?

Alistair cleared his throat, fingers still laced with Langford's. Langford tried to pull his hand free, but Alistair only gripped him tighter.

Mrs. O'Connell looked up, a frown on her face that quickly melted into unbridled joy. "My boys!" She dusted her hands off and swept over to pull them both into a flour covered embrace. The scent of cinnamon and nutmeg washed over him, and he closed his eyes, hugging her back. It was awkward since Alistair still refused to let go of his hand. A fact Mrs. O'Connell seemed to realize as she stepped back. Her round face brightened in understanding.

"Oh!" she cried. "Avalon be praised! It's about time, you two. Do you know how many nights I watched your lovelorn glances across the tavern?" She smacked Alistair on the arm. "And you! Always stickin' your cock where it doesn't belong. I hope Langford made you beg his forgiveness for all the lost time."

Langford's cheeks burned. So everyone around them had been witness to his unrequited longing?

"Oh, he knows how to make me beg, all right," Alistair said.

Langford shook his head, fighting a smile even through his humiliation. "Don't be crass."

"It's all right," Mrs. O'Connell said. "Alistair can't shock me, much as he tries."

"Aye, but one of these days, you won't be able to resist my charms."

Mrs. O'Connell laughed, a rich and hearty sound, and returned to rolling her dough. "All right, boys. I need to get these in the oven and then I plan to stuff you full o' good food while you catch me up on your wanderings. Off you pop!"

Alistair steered Langford back toward the tavern, pausing in the hall to fix him with a heated stare.

Langford's stomach flipped, and a nervous laugh left his mouth. "What? Wanted to show off another conquest?" A shadow passed over Alistair's face, so Langford quickly amended. "I didn't mean that."

Alistair lifted a hand, and his thumb brushed against Langford's cheek, ever so slightly. Langford trembled at his touch.

"You had flour on your face." His words ghosted against Langford's mouth, and it took every shred of control he had not to lean forward to taste his lips. "And," Alistair continued, "maybe I did want to show you off a little. Is it so bad that I'm proud to call you mine?"

Langford's gaze ran over Alistair's face. Over the dark scruff along his jaw and upper lip. Over the faint scar above his eyebrow and his eyes now half hidden beneath the hair that hung in his face.

"No," Langford said, breathlessly. "That's not so bad."

TRUE TO HER WORD, Mrs. O'Connell stuffed them all full of roasted chicken, buttered potatoes, an apple pie Lark attempted to keep for herself, and a new hot drink of melted chocolate that Gavriel became obsessed with.

Langford adjusted in his saddle, uncomfortable from the enormous meal. It had been some time since he'd indulged in that much food in one sitting, and he would have rather fallen asleep after eating so much. But Lark was eager to travel and Inerys wasn't so far from the inn, supposedly. Langford was beginning to wonder if they'd lied just to get him to agree to travel before a decent respite.

Alistair had stayed behind, much to his displeasure, with Demetria. Gavriel, Daciana, Kenna, and Langford borrowed horses from Mrs. O'Connell's stables. Lark, of course, claimed her chestnut mare, Apple, and whispered things to the beast while they traveled.

"You'd better not be speaking about me," Gavriel called to her from the black Ardenian Charger he rode. "She and I bonded last we rode, and I won't have you driving a wedge between us."

"I have more important things to tell her, Gavriel," Lark said with a smile. "Not everything is about you."

Emerald Forest was in the throes of autumn. The trees were black against a grey sky, wind whistling between empty branches. Dead leaves and undergrowth overran the forest floor. Bracken and brambles replaced what once, Langford was sure, were lush, green shrubs. Besides the occasional call of a crow and the harsh wind, the woods were quiet.

"Last time we were here, it wasn't quite so... barren," Lark said. "It's nice, actually. Though I miss the green."

"The green will come back." Gavriel turned to give her an affectionate smile. "It always comes back."

"We're getting close," Daciana called from up ahead. Her first spoken words since they left the Walden Inn.

Before them stretched a large lake. Mist rose from the surface, and the surrounding trees hung low over its waters, branches leaning over the misty shore. Beyond that, a cottage encased with vines sat, steam billowing from its brick chimney.

A small boat rested on the shore waiting for rowing. That seemed ridiculous. The lake wasn't that large, so they could just ride around and tether their horses outside the cottage.

"Are we going around, then?" Langford asked.

Lark started laughing as she dismounted Apple. Even Daciana smirked and shook her head.

Whatever the joke was, Langford didn't get it.

Inerys' home was like the whispered fables of witches of the woods. Except in the children's stories, the witches were old and gnarled like the branches of the trees that rose above her house and touched the sky.

The comely girl with the dark hair and darker stare was not who Langford expected to answer the door. She took one look at Lark, winced, and stepped aside for them to enter.

She pulled off her knitted cowl and long mittens, both a chocolate brown to match her bodice, and tossed them on the low bench in the entryway. Mud splatters painted the hem of her grey skirt, as well as her boots.

"I hope we didn't interrupt anything," Langford said. Even if the world was ending, manners went a long way.

She offered an indulgent smile that creased the slightly flushed apples of her bronze cheeks. "You didn't. I thought I sensed you coming." Her gaze fell to Daciana, who didn't so much as blink. "It's good to see nothing unsavory has befallen you, Lark. Or you, Gavriel." Inerys almost seemed sheepish.

A tight laugh left Lark's chest. "Yes… I suspect we have much to catch up on. But we're short on time—"

"You're always short on time," Inerys said, rolling her eyes. "Come, help me put on the kettle and catch me up quickly. Then we can discuss why you're really here."

Lark nodded, following the witch through the parlor and into the kitchen. Langford took the opportunity to look around.

Her home was filled with herbs Langford had only seen in books. Withania somnifera, brahmi, feverfew—everywhere he turned was another marvel. They spilled across shelves, wrapping around stacks of books he was eager to flip through.

"It's a relief she fills her home with healing herbs." Gavriel's voice startled Langford. He hadn't realized he stood so close behind him. "If she cultivated dangerous plants, I might be worried."

Langford turned to study the former assassin. Gavriel's hands were behind his back, the picture of innocence. "You know these plants?"

Gavriel shrugged. "I'm familiar. Not by name, but I've studied their pictures enough to know by sight what to avoid. Poisons, especially, have been committed to memory. Ingredients, warning signs to look out for."

"If that's so, how did Waking Nightmare wind up in your system so easily?"

A broad grin spread across Gavriel's face. It dimpled his cheeks in an inviting way Langford rarely saw. He was handsome. Langford could appreciate that. But his smile was far too rare. Unlike a certain someone who stayed behind to keep an eye on the princess.

Inerys swept out of the kitchen, carrying a tray of chipped, mismatched teacups and saucers. Lark carried a steaming iron kettle with a towel wrapped around the handle. When the cups were poured and everyone was seated, besides Daciana, who paced the room with a restless energy, Inerys cleared her throat.

"Are you here for the locator spell?"

"Are you ready to prepare it?" Kenna responded before Langford could even question Inerys' meaning.

Inerys arched a brow. "You seem surprised? I've gathered what I need. There's still the matter of your contribution, but yes," she said with a nod, "I'm ready. I suspect that wasn't your aim, or at least not your only aim, in coming here today."

Kenna nodded emphatically, angling her head to meet Daciana's stare. A silent communication passed between them, and Langford caught the way Inerys' eyes narrowed.

Curious. An unspoken history, perhaps? Whatever they were searching for, it would have to wait. Though the tension between the three women was intriguing and begged further investigation.

Inerys swept her hand through the air impatiently. "One of you, explain what I can do for you this time."

Lark shot Langford an eager glance. He blew against the steam rising from his rose patterned cup. The scent of lavender and lemon filled his senses. He took a hesitant sip and sighed. Of course, the witch could brew the best bloody tea he'd ever tasted.

"We need to know everything you can tell us about the *Messorum Ferrum*."

Inerys froze mid-sip. After a moment of terse silence, she lowered her cup with an audible *clink*. "Tell me where you heard of this."

Langford swallowed against a dry throat. "I found records in the ancient archives in Koval."

Inerys' eyes seemed to pierce with the way she stared. A deep jab of a gaze that cut deep enough, he was sure she was sifting through his mind.

But that would be ridiculous.

"Wolf, if you don't sit, you'll be sent outside like a dog." The sharp slice of Inerys' voice and the audible groan of the floorboards beneath Daciana's feet almost drowned out the choking sound Lark made when she inhaled her tea. She held still for as long as she could, face red and mouth clamped shut, before the first cough broke free. Then another. Then a violent coughing fit that had Gavriel reaching over to pat her back.

Daciana stalked over to the hearth and leaned against the stone cladding. "Better?"

Inerys studied her with pursed lips. "Your change is close; I can sense that. But that's not what weighs on you, is it?"

Daciana folded her arms against her chest. "We're not here to talk about me."

Inerys' gaze hardened before she nodded. "Quite right. You wish to ask me about Reaper Blades, yes? Well, if you can't find a Life Wielder, you can't forge one. You need Dragon Stone—the rarest mineral only ever found in the mines of what you now call Koval—a skilled blacksmith, and most importantly, a Vitas Conjuror. Without all three things, you're just making common swords." She lifted her tea once more, as if to say 'that's that,' and took a deep sip. "Oh, and a passenger soul to wield the damn thing."

"Back up," Lark said, leaning toward her. "What was that last bit?"

"A passenger soul? Oh, someone whose soul has made journeys across planes. Typically, a Reaper." She patted Lark's knee. "At least you've got one of those things!"

"Two," Daciana said from where she stood by the hearth. "We have two of those things. A Reaper, and a skilled blacksmith."

The man whose daughter was living with a cursed beast. Langford recalled Daciana mentioning his name… what was it… oh right! Felix was the man.

"That means we're half-way there," Lark said, casting a side glance in Gavriel's direction.

He huffed a soft laugh and shook his head. "Yes, I suppose it does."

Though statistically that was true, Langford couldn't shake his unease. "Is there anything else you can tell us? Anything at all?"

Inerys nodded. "One more thing. Whatever you're planning, whatever you think you'll achieve, I urge you to consider the alternative. Brace yourself for a storm instead of running toward it."

Thinly veiled warnings didn't scare Langford half as much as unanswered questions. But at least they had a clear goal in mind. Gods only knew how they'd achieve it.

"What if… what if I used the lantern from Solana to find a Life Wielder?" Lark's golden gaze lit up with excitement. "That could work, couldn't it?"

Memories of the Forbidden Shrine, of following Lark by the azure glow of her lantern, flooded Langford's mind. Where shame used to tighten its grip in his chest, a soft warmth took its place. He could finally think back on the wish that ensnared him, the image of a life by Alistair's side, without cringing.

His wish could actually come true, and not by the work of an illusion.

Inerys' face drew up in pity. "You forget the Life Wielders were not granted peace in Avalon. They were hunted down, one-by-one, and slaughtered, the Netherworld created for the sole purpose of imprisoning them."

Lark's jaw formed a hard line. "Even if they're in the deepest pits of the Netherworld, I can find them."

Inerys shrugged, a dismissal and a refusal to weigh in on that notion. Lark's hands clenched against her knees, and after a moment she dropped her stare. Probably already planning to slip away and track down the soul of a Life Wielder.

Langford cleared his throat, eager to head off Lark's trail of thought. "Thank you for your time, Inerys. I'm certain we'll cross paths when we need you yet again."

Inerys flashed Langford a wolfish smile. "I suspect you're right." She turned her attention to Daciana, who was busy staring at the flames crackling in the hearth. "Daciana, I need a word with you before you leave. In private."

Langford expected Daciana to dismiss Inerys' demand. But she nodded and followed the witch into the kitchen.

Curious. Very curious, indeed.

CHAPTER FORTY-THREE

DACIANA

"You already know what I'm going to say." Inerys stormed ahead of Daciana, tray in hand. The hanging bundles of dried herbs swayed with her agitated movements. Inerys' home always gave Daciana an enclosed feeling of panic. Every surface was overcrowded, and even the ceilings and windows were overburdened. The sill above her kitchen basin was teeming with varying shapes and sizes of glass vials and crystals.

How the witch could find anything in her cluttered mess of a home was a wonder.

Inerys spun to face her, distaste curling her lip and furrowing her brow.

Daciana thumbed the daggers at her hips. "You sense much. Can you guess what my response will be?"

"Foolish girl!" Inerys slammed the tray of teacups on the wood counter, rattling the porcelain. "You know what you are. You might be coward enough not to say it, but I am not—"

Daciana's blade was at the witch's throat in a blink. How it had gotten there, she couldn't say with much certainty, but the way the blood pounded in her head signaled she needed to calm down. Now.

"Take care with the next words you choose," she seethed. "I am not myself."

Inerys' dark eyes widened, and a flicker of fear flashed across her face before that stubborn set of her jaw and the narrowing of her gaze stole her expression. "You know better than to threaten me in my home, wolf."

"As I said" —Daciana forced a slow breath to expand in her chest, to fill her with control before she exhaled— "I am not myself."

Understanding lit up Inerys' eyes, before her delicate hand enclosed around Daciana's knuckles. "Peace," she said. "I will not force your hand, so long as you can control your urges."

Trembling, Daciana pulled away and sheathed her dagger. What was happening to her? Her impending change always put her on edge, but this?

"I can practically hear your racing thoughts," Inerys said with a note of amusement. "If you promise to keep your murderous impulses to yourself, I'll explain."

Daciana nodded. She couldn't find it in her to speak.

"I know what you are. There's no use in pretending." Inerys braced her hands on either side of the tray, and leveled Daciana with a meaningful stare. "You shouldn't exist."

Daciana's throat squeezed. "No, I shouldn't." There were a lot of things that shouldn't have happened. "Not like this."

"That wasn't a judgment. You're a blooming miracle." Inerys suddenly appeared visibly uncomfortable with the words she'd just spoken, and quickly cleared her throat. Tendrils of black hair framed her bronze face. A challenge plainly written in her eyes. "Will you truly let your friends flounder in search of an answer, when it's right in front of them?"

Daciana bit down on her own tongue, hard enough for the salty taste of blood to fill her mouth. How dare she question her loyalty? If she understood. If she knew—

"You look about ready to break your promise to me." Inerys smirked. "I wouldn't advise that."

"You don't know what you ask of me."

"Don't I?" Inerys sauntered around the butcher-block until she stood close enough Daciana could smell the herbs and the earth she'd been tending when they arrived. "You don't know what you're capable of. If you would let me show you—"

Daciana recoiled, revulsion spooling in her gut. "No. I know what I'm capable of. I won't call on that power again."

Inerys tightened her lips, jaw clenching. "Have it your way."

Daciana turned to leave when Inerys' words followed.

"I wonder how you'll feel when you realize the consequences of your actions." Inerys paced over and gripped her by the arm. "When you learn the true meaning of sacrifice. For the sake of your senseless fear."

"I know what it means to sacrifice." Daciana shook off her hold and stormed out of the room. The ache of Inerys' words clung to her like a second skin. But she was used to shedding her form and pushed the warning from her mind.

BEFORE THEY COULD LEAVE, there was one more piece of unfinished business Daciana was loath to admit to because that meant she needed to tolerate more time in Inerys' presence.

But something had been stalking Stormfair, and Kenna would not rest until the beast was dealt with.

Inerys had brought Daciana and Kenna down into her workspace, her ingredients readied and prepped. The raven feather, the small bit of cloth found in the clutches of a dead child, and the rare wolf mushroom all sat in a large copper bowl. Inerys slugged a vial of green liquid and wiped her mouth with the back of her hand.

"All right, then. One of you needs to give me something of value."

Daciana glanced over at Kenna, only to find her frowning. Evidently, she hadn't known of this. "Is this payment?"

Inerys scoffed. "I'd never demand payment from Kenna. It's

required for the spell. Something must be lost for something to be found. The greater the value, the clearer the path."

Daciana's hand slipped into her pocket, finding the small stone she'd taken from Hugo's burial. Something swelled in her chest, angry and raw. If this was required to ensure no other child was harmed, it was an easy decision to make. This was a mere stone, not Hugo himself.

Kenna laughed, though it sounded forced. "Do you ever charge anyone? I maintain you are the surliest yet most charitable witch I've ever met." She quickly unclasped her hunter's talisman, holding it out to Inerys. The pendant hung from her fist, the image of a mountain beneath a living sky glowing in the dim room.

Daciana couldn't possibly allow her to trade her talisman. Not when she held a mere rock worthy of the exchange. Kenna needed it to sense monsters, to denote her place as a hunter, to honor her grandmother—

As if sensing her thoughts, Kenna spun around, giving Daciana a stern expression. "This is what we're trading. This is my responsibility and I won't hear another word about it."

Inerys grabbed the pendant before Daciana could protest and flung it into the copper bowl. It sizzled, steam billowing from the hidden depth, and the acrid stench of sulfur filled the room. Kenna blocked her nose with her sleeve, and Daciana's eyes watered.

Slowly, the steam dissipated, and the sharp sizzling sound lessened until, once again, silence filled the room. Inerys grabbed an oven mitt and lifted the bowl to pour its contents into the empty vial she'd just drunk from. She scrunched up her nose at the smell, and when she pushed the cork stopper into place, she took a deep breath.

"There we are. One locator spell. *Do not drink it.* Pour it out and follow its path. It will lead you to the one you seek."

Daciana grasped the vial with shaky fingers, nodding her thanks. She slipped the stone back into her pocket, a strange combination of queasy guilt and relief unfurling in her stomach. "Thank you."

Kenna nodded, her hand flexing at her side, and Inerys gave a dismissive wave of her hand.

Daciana climbed the rungs of the ladder with growing unease. Kenna had given much for this spell. She only hoped she wouldn't come to regret that choice.

CHAPTER FORTY-FOUR

LARK

Lark ran a gentle hand down Apple's mane. They maintained a steady trot, lacking urgency but not dawdling. The day had ceased its hold on the land. Another sun set as night approached, and the groan of the wind filled the air.

Dusk descended over the trees, a sky rapidly darkening behind barren branches. A faint hint of light still revealed the path. They would make it back before true night fell, but not even the shadows could hide the fact Langford had been giving her strange looks the entire ride through the forest. They were almost back to the Walden Inn, and she kept catching him watching her.

Blast the infernal man. He knew what she was thinking.

He'd likely never forgiven her for descending into the Netherworld to save Gavriel.

Langford knew her far too well, and he hadn't forgotten.

But if Lark were to traverse to the Netherworld and retrieve the soul of a Life Wielder…

How could she even find one? It wasn't as if she had an established tether to their soul, or even an inkling of where they'd gone when they died. The Netherworld was massive, endless, even. More circles of the afterlife than Lark could name. Her thoughts flitted to the lantern she'd obtained in the shrine. After completing their role in Yuri's game and fleeing the arena, she'd thankfully retrieved all of her possessions. Solana's lantern, the illuminator of paths, remained untouched in Lark's pack. But perhaps Nereida was expecting this and waited with a trap as soon as she entered the realm.

It was worth the risk if it meant forging a weapon to kill her, wasn't it?

Lark caught another narrowed-eyed look from Langford, and she quickly tucked her thoughts away. There would be plenty of time to form a plan without his watchful presence.

ALISTAIR PACED HIS ROOM, the one he'd insisted they all convene in following their return.

The lantern glowing beside the washbasin and the misshapen wax candle on the bedside table illuminated the room in a golden glow. Lark took another sip of her cider, delighting in the sweet yet tart flavor on her tongue. She drank so deeply, a drop missed her mouth and rolled down her chin, earning a soft huff of laughter from the shadowy corner where Gavriel was content to observe, with a wall against his back and a full view of the room. Some things never changed, did they? His gaze kept finding Lark's, and even in the dimly lit room, the warmth in his eyes was a beacon.

Kenna stood leaning against the wall, arms crossed, and an expectant expression on her face. Daciana sat on the bed with her back to Kenna, a deliberate position by Lark's guess, while Demetria claimed a spot on the floor, quietly sketching in her book with a bit of charcoal.

Langford sat at the small table that housed their meals and a pile of worn books and parchments. He sipped from his tea with a contented sigh while Alistair continued to prowl about the room. His leather boots thudded against the wood floor in a steady pass as his hand came to rub against his chin. It was a familiar posture—one Lark had witnessed many times by now. But the room, and all its inhabitants, felt different. Tighter. There was a tension that seemed to follow the group without abating.

Kenna and Daciana. Demetria and everyone. It was disorienting. Like being trapped in a space without windows and not enough air. Even Alistair and Langford, though their tension was an entirely different sort.

Lark stuffed the last of the bread into her mouth, savoring the taste of rosemary and thyme, and crossed the room to open the window wide. A fresh gust of air blew through the space, ruffling the wisps of hair from her forehead. Lark draped against the sill, wishing for Alistair to cease his pacing and say something.

He'd been eager for Langford's return, that much was obvious, but the look on his face when Langford recounted Inerys' information… Well, eagerness for his bedfellow had shifted into calculated planning. Bedfellow was the wrong word. Alistair always had a soft spot for the healer and for far longer than Lark had even been around for. Even before they confessed their affections, his gaze had always lingered on Langford and followed his movements.

Lark's skin prickled with the distinct sensation of being watched. Her eyes met Gavriel's from where he sat in the corner, and a soft smile tugged at his scarred mouth. Lark inhaled another deep breath of air.

Lark had yet to slip away long enough to attempt to use the lantern. It was worth a shot, and she couldn't just sit around waiting for a better idea. But one unsettling thought remained. However many traveled by lantern must return. Even if she wielded the artifact, she'd never be able to bring a soul back with her. Unless she brought a soul as an offering…

No. There had to be another way. Someone on the other side could help. All soul deaths passed through Leysa. If Lark could sneak away from the Walden Inn, and return to Inerys alone, she could communicate with Leysa again. She hadn't seen her since her search for Ferryn, when Inerys sent her soul to the in-between. And instead of Ferryn, she was met by Leysa, who gave her all the information she needed to contact him in Lacuna, a middle world and punishment for Reapers.

Ferryn.

The thought of him sent a pang through Lark's chest. She'd promised to stay out of his way as he sought to escape Lacuna, but that didn't mean she didn't miss him. Or that the memory of his shadowed smile didn't hurt.

Where was he now? Had he escaped?

"I got it," Alistair finally said. "We'll go to Koval, sneak into the mines masquerading as laborers, mine some dragonstone, find a discrete smithy, and be on our way."

"If dragonstone was that easy to attain," Gavriel cut in smoothly, "Koval wouldn't be flooding their mines with more and more indentures trying to find it. And besides" —he crossed his arms and canted his head to the side— "you're still forgetting the most important part. A Life Wielder. None of it matters if we can't find a proper magic source."

"He's right," Lark said. "Inerys said it would be an ordinary blade without one."

Alistair grunted and tugged his jacket straight. "Look, opportunities arise on the journey. We should form a plan for what we can control, and figure out the rest as we go, no?"

"We just returned from Koval," Langford said with a heavy sigh. "We barely made it out alive the first time. You want to go back?"

"What choice do we have?"

"I appreciate your willingness to spring to action, but we need a better lead than this. Sneak into the mines?" Langford's brow furrowed, pinching his forehead.

"Well, you think of something better!"

Silence.

"Alistair," Daciana began.

Alistair rounded on her where she sat on the bed and grabbed her hands. "Yes, my goddess? I always get the best ideas when you argue with me."

Daciana pried her hands free. "I was merely going to say, as much as I value the idea of this mythical Reaper Blade" —she arched an elegant brow— "I have to side with Langford on this.

You're talking about sailing across the ocean on a whim. That's not a plan."

"I think best on my feet, cannons firing and blades clashing," Alistair said with a grin. "We'll sort out the details on the ship. The important thing is we book passage before Ingemar is out of reach—"

"And what of Demetria?" Kenna cut in. Demetria stared at her drawing of a waterfall, refusing to meet anyone's eye. "Ingemar tasked you with protecting her. You would jeopardize her safety by bringing her back to her kingdom?"

"I never said she'd come. She'll need a private guard. Someone she trusts." Alistair's brilliant green eyes flashed with excitement.

Kenna rolled her eyes and settled into sharpening one of her daggers. Clearly done with the conversation.

Lark watched the exchange, all the while imagining how she would access the Netherworld. She'd need to sneak back to Inerys once the others were asleep, contact Leysa, find a Life Wielder... and what if they weren't granted peace or even afterlife? What if their souls were obliterated to prevent this very thing from happening?

Lark clamped down on that thought, unwilling to follow the thread into panic. Her gaze found Gavriel's again. When Inerys and she had prepared tea in the kitchen, they'd spoken of things she would need to catch him up on. Just... not yet.

"How else are we supposed to find dragonstone?"

The argument shifted back into Lark's awareness as she realized Daciana was now leaning against the wall, staring out the window into the night. Her change must be soon. They would have to wait for that to pass before making any travel arrangements anyway—

"What if there's another way?" Demetria's smooth, low voice cut through the room, and a hush fell over them.

"Another way for what?" Alistair asked.

"Getting your dragonstone. Depending on how much you need, I might have a solution." Demetria slowly stood, rising to her full height, which admittedly wasn't much. Despite this, she held herself with an air of authority that commanded the room.

"All right, Princess," Alistair said with a smirk. "Dazzle me."

She raised her chin, refusing to break his stare. "It would be very dangerous."

"Even better."

"My brother will still hold the All Soul's Ball. That means visiting nobles, landowners, and anyone of renown will be welcomed into the castle." Demetria offered Langford a nod. "You father is still highly regarded, thus, your family name will still be on the lists. You should have no trouble entering as a guest." She turned to Alistair. "You might be able to infiltrate the servants' hall. I can provide you with the right names and excuses as to why no one has seen you before." Her brows furrowed in concentration as she studied Gavriel. "You might be able to pass as a distant relative of someone who would surely be on the list though not in attendance. He had a scandalous spring and couldn't possibly be ready to face court again."

Alistair waved to catch her attention. "You still haven't explained why we'd go through all the trouble of sneaking into the most heavily guarded place in Koval."

Demetria straightened her skirt. "I have an heirloom in my chambers. I inherited a hand mirror when my parents died and when I fled, I didn't have the chance to grab it. There are these stones along the handle, as black as onyx but far stronger. Ruslan told me it was dragonstone, the rarest of Kovalian minerals." Her brow twitched. "He also told me not to tell my brother of its existence. I assume because of its value."

Alistair's eyes widened, and his smirk grew into a genuine smile. "You have dragonstone?"

"Yes."

"In a fortified palace, guarded by some of the best fighters, under the watch of your tyrannical brother? And you think infiltrating a revelatory ball is the only chance we have at getting our hands on it?"

Demetria didn't so much as flinch. "Yes."

"Well," Alistair said, taking a step closer and clapping her on the back hard enough, she swayed. "That sounds like the start of our most intriguing mission yet."

DACIANA AND KENNA were quick to promise to guard the princess while the others ventured back to Koval. Aboard Ingemar's ship, Lark had to admit Daciana was right: the magical wonders of a locked door at sea brought people together.

Warm and sated against Gavriel's bare chest, Lark snuggled closer, reveling in the afterglow of their intimacy. The room they shared aboard Ingemar's ship was as cramped as she recalled, but it perfectly suited their needs. Ingemar had been willing to ferry them across the sea to Koval, only because of a letter from the princess asking for her compliance. Alistair was eager to lock Langford away for the fortnight at sea, but Langford was insistent they all study the map of the castle Demetria had drawn for them. A wise use of their time, certainly. But Lark preferred to spend her time at sea enjoying privacy with Gavriel in a way they hadn't been fortunate enough to have in quite some time.

He ran his touch down the length of her back, returning to coil a tendril of red hair around his finger.

Lark shivered under his touch. Perhaps it was the drowsy comfort in his arms, or simply the fact that she felt so close to him, but the gentle search of his wandering hands eased whatever nervousness she felt. It was time to tell him what Inerys shared with her back in her kitchen. "Inerys and I talked."

Gavriel hummed, drawing lazy circles against her back. "I gathered as much."

"We spoke of the tonic."

"The one that severed the bond."

Lark nodded against his chest, a prickling heat crawling up her neck. Would she ever get used to human reactions? "She said what she gave us was a deep sleeping draught, nothing more."

He angled his head to regard her with incredulity. "She knocked us out?"

"Apparently."

Gavriel tightened his arms around her. "So... the bond remains. Is that so terrible?"

"No," Lark began, wetting her lips and reaching to clasp his hands in hers. "I told her everything Nereida said, about the ritual we completed that created the bond during my human life. And... Inerys seemed to understand a great deal about it."

"What did she say?"

That it was nothing more than a binding spell. That they would always be drawn together, but their feelings were their own. "She said it doesn't determine what we feel. Had I found you in another one of your lives, I might not have harbored any of these feelings."

"See? I told you as much." He pulled her up to face him, a brilliant smile lighting up his face before he planted a kiss on her nose.

"Inerys said she could restore our memories. My life, your lives, she could give it all to us." Lark dodged another kiss, sitting up so her legs bracketed his hips. At his heated gaze, she tucked the covers tighter around herself. "Is that something you would want?"

Gavriel's eyes softened, and he ran his thumb along her jaw. "I'm trying my best not to dwell on the past these days."

"And if I wish to remember?"

"I would not fault you for that."

"I don't know if I will," Lark said quickly. "I haven't decided."

"Let me know when you do. If you wish to remember, I do, too."

Lark lowered to place a gentle kiss against his lips. Gavriel's arms encircled her, and he deepened the kiss, heat already erupting across her skin. She pulled back before they could get carried away. "Just... not all of your lives. Not all at once. Inerys said it would be too much for you."

Gavriel shook his head, gazing up at her while he slowly ran his hands down her back. "Any life without you is hardly worth remembering."

A euphoric weightlessness spread through Lark at his words, and she placed a kiss against a raised scar on his chest before rolling to lie by his side. "We should enjoy this while we can. Once we dock, you and I can't be seen together."

"Mmm," he rumbled his reply as he climbed atop her, caging her body with his.

"And you'll have to pretend I'm a perfect stranger at the ball."

Gavriel glanced down at her. "You mean I'll meet you for the first time again? Can I redeem our first introduction?"

Lark bit him, earning a playful pinch. The memory of their first true encounter used to burn shame in her cheeks. The day she refused to guide his soul to the afterlife and instead saved him. When he lashed out at her for being what she was, for being the outlet of his grief over losing Emric. She once thought it made her a monster, but she knew better. Enough time had passed that the memory no longer churned her belly. She could not regret that day, for it led her here to this moment.

"What would you do differently?"

"For starters" —Gavriel leaned up, pulling her with him— "I'd check my teeth for blood."

"Naturally."

"Then," he continued, slowly tugging the covers away from her and revealing her body bit by bit. Her skin goose pebbled from the sudden chill. "I would worship every inch of you starting right... here." He yanked her thighs toward him so Lark was flat on her back, completely exposed. He rose over her, spreading her legs wider and leaning in close. With a whisper of a touch, he kissed the tip of her nose. He moved lower, a soft, gentle kiss ghosting along the seam of her lips. As chaste as his kisses were, the way his hips moved against her was anything but.

Lark laughed to cover her moan, and nipped at his mouth. "That's a poor way to make a first impression. I'd never let a perfect stranger take such liberties."

"We'll see, won't we, my lady?"

Gavriel buried his face in her neck, kissing and biting with enough force to make her laugh and squirm, shoving and pulling as they rolled off the tiny bed. She landed atop him, the triumphant victor, and lined his hard length up with her entrance. Slowly sinking over him, she hissed as his hands gripped her hips.

When they collapsed again, sweaty and sated, Gavriel pressed a kiss to her temple and hauled the two of them off the floor and back into the bed.

The ocean gently rolled beneath the ship, lulling Lark into a deep slumber.

LARK FLITTED ABOUT THE BALLROOM, her abundant skirts sparkling in the candlelight. Someone had tied ribbons far too tightly in her hair, and her scalp ached. She spun around, dizzy and flushed. Searching. Gavriel was nowhere to be seen. Only a swirl of sneering faces, all half-hidden behind their masks, dipped into view.

A woman with long golden hair slipped past, the only one not wearing a mask. Lark reached for her, wishing to see her face for some inexplicable reason, but she disappeared as quickly as she came.

It mattered not. Lark needed to find Gavriel, not some faceless woman.

But where was he? Where was Langford, or Alistair?

Lark spun again, searching.

They'd left her. They'd abandoned her and returned to Ingemar's ship without her. How would she ever get back? She had no coin for passage, her weapons were still aboard the ship. She was trapped in Koval with no connections. With no—

"Larkin," a familiar low voice, strained and weakened but familiar all the same, rang out. Thanar staggered through the crowd, slipping through revelers as if he was a mere illusion.

He had to be an illusion.

Lark glanced down at her gown. Shimmering blue threading adorned the white fabric of her fitted bodice, and followed the path of her wide skirt. This wasn't even the dress Demetria picked out for her. Relief flooded her chest in a lurching current. None of this was real.

"Thanar. I have nothing left to say to you."

His face had always been sharp, but now it was gaunt. Dark circles formed the space beneath his eyes and the hollow of his pronounced cheekbones. He looked so frail. So weak. Like at any moment he might break. Lark had always hated feeling weak compared to him, but seeing him like this...

Fear curdled in her belly. If someone such as he could fall so far, what hope did anyone have against Nereida? But it wasn't just Nereida, was it? Lark condemned him to his fate the minute she signed the contract that granted her mortality and gave the smallest piece of his power to Nereida.

"I cannot stay." Thanar crept into her space, whispering as if there were spies even in her dream.

Could Nyx and her shadows follow him?

"She will discover I've wandered, but I had to come. I had to warn you." His hand shook, and when he caught her staring, he clenched it into a fist.

"I don't understand—"

"Listen to me!" He grabbed her hands, tugging her close. "There is a betrayer in your midst. Someone is watching you. They're reporting on your movements. Whatever you have planned, she knows."

His fear was a palpable thing. But fear came in many forms, and it didn't guarantee his honesty.

"Nereida could have compelled you to say anything. You might be the very one betraying me to your mistress."

Thanar's dark brows pinched. "All I've ever done is seek to protect you. That will never change. No matter how much you hate me." He dropped her hands roughly. "Be careful who you trust, Larkin. That's all I know at present."

He stepped back, swallowed by the throng of ball gowns, feathers, and glitter. Lark reached out tentatively, needing to know more of his cryptic warning. She surged forward—

Lark fell onto the hard floor of the cabin, the breath rushing out of her. Gavriel leapt up, dagger in hand.

"Lark?" he called out.

Lark stood on unsteady feet, climbing back onto the bed. "Shhh… I had a nightmare is all."

Gavriel pulled her against his side, tucking the dagger away. "Want to speak of it?"

Lark kissed him and shook her head. "Perhaps in the morning."

CHAPTER FORTY-FIVE

LANGFORD

*L*angford could scarcely believe Captain Ingemar acquiesced to their request for transport *again*. She'd been murderous at the request, until they explained the reasoning behind their plan and assured her they were taking great care with Demetria's arrangements. The princess even had the forethought to send a message with them, so Ingemar would know she was safe. It bought her willingness but not her enthusiasm.

A fortnight at sea, and here he was again. Back in his home country, dressed in finery, and nursing a stomachache.

Langford tugged at the gloves pinching his wrists. Alistair was masterful at thinking of every detail, but these blasted gloves were too small. He'd stuffed the empty finger where his knuckle ended, and the sensation was entirely unpleasant. Better that than unwanted questions. Questions led to answers, which led to scrutiny and attention. All things they didn't want during a mission that included sneaking into the princess' chambers.

It could be worse. Word of their misdeeds at Adler's estate hadn't traveled, likely because the man would implicate himself. It was far more advantageous to collect debts through secrets and blackmail than to expose anyone outright. At least this time, when he and Lark donned their façade of Mr. and Mrs. Brenner, they would have backup within the walls.

Demetria had been thorough in her details of the castle—of which servants would be likely to help. Alistair was to contact someone on the list of Demetria's aforementioned allies and determine the best way to collect the mirror. Lark, Gavriel, and Langford were to await further instruction, watch King Zaire carefully for any signs of suspicion, all the while appearing to enjoy the ball, and thus remaining above reproach. Gavriel even slipped into the identity of the wealthy cousin of a recently disgraced lord whom Demetria was certain wouldn't show his face at court after the scandal he'd only just lived down.

It was merely a matter of sailing back to Koval for the only event that would open the castle doors to the public. One Kovalian tradition that had survived the ages was the All Souls Ball. It always took place after the harvest season in Ardenas. A masquerade, in true Kovalian fashion, and an invitation for revelry and mischief. King Efrain used to insist on many games during this event, always ending in a grand unmasking. But Langford hadn't any idea which traditions Zaire maintained.

The last ball they'd attended, another masquerade in favor of Kovalian traditions, he'd encountered more than he'd bargained for.

"Are you nervous?" Lark's voice cut through the silent carriage. Their arrival would be noted, another detail Alistair had thought of.

"I'm always nervous," Langford said, curving the corner of his mouth into a smile he hoped she believed. "It's part of my charm."

Lark huffed a laugh and ran her hand into her hair, wincing when her fingers snagged on the intricate plait Alistair had wrapped to form a crown. He'd taken great strides to not only to weave gold leaves through her braid, but to brush a dusting of gold along her cheekbones to pay homage to Koval. Even her mask shimmered with gold sparkles.

The carriage knocked over a large bump, and Langford peered out the window to keep his stomach from rolling. The trees shook with the force of a mighty gale. A magnificent sight… so long as it didn't upend the carriage.

Lark smoothed her hands down the skirt of her burgundy gown, over the gold threading and beading. "Do you think Gavriel has already arrived?"

Langford snorted, remembering the look on the assassin's face when Alistair revealed more of his role in their ruse. Demetria had shared the sordid details of the disgraced lord that was to be his peer and supposed cousin. Apparently, the man was caught with the wife of a fellow lord, and if that wasn't bad enough, he'd also dallied with said lord's sister. Demetria strongly advised Gavriel to act the part of the scoundrel. Gavriel insisted he'd had to slip into character many times to complete marks assigned by the Guild. Masking the scar across his lip was a simple task—nothing a little clay and powder couldn't hide. His hair had grown long enough to be combed into a refined style, something he grumbled over on Ingemar's ship as Alistair had artfully crafted his disguise. Lark had been curiously quiet while Alistair primped and prodded him, watching with careful fascination.

"I doubt it. He's under orders to arrive fashionably late. Though I'm sure Alistair is already wreaking havoc in the servants' halls." It was a shame they couldn't risk bringing Demetria back to Koval. She'd instructed them as best she could. Which servants would aid them, what to say to gain their trust, and which nobles to avoid. But even this wasn't enough to feel well and truly prepared for Kovalian's royal court. Langford's only solace was that his father had never been social and was certain not to be in attendance. Despite this small comfort, Langford tugged at the collar of his tunic that seemed unbearably tight against his rapid pulse.

"So, husband," Lark drawled with a smile that usually preceded mischief, "when will you slip away to help Alistair with his search?"

"We agreed if he needed help, you'd aid him." Langford gave another tug at his tunic before giving up on the notion that he'd be comfortable. "That was the plan."

Lark shrugged, the action at odds with the refined façade she wore; though Langford preferred her in green, the elegant shape of her burgundy gown complemented her figure most becomingly, and her glittering gold mask framed her amber eyes. "Does it matter who goes? I'd much rather watch Gavriel in character than traipse around the castle." A glint of amusement flashed in her gaze. "Maybe the two of you could find an empty room."

"Don't be crass." Langford's cheeks flooded with heat. As tempting an idea, it was a foolish one. There was far more at stake should they fail this mission, and an entire ocean between themselves and the help they would desperately need. "You can keep watch on Zaire. Perhaps even distract a few guards if it comes to that. But we aren't here to enjoy ourselves."

Lark gave a resolute nod. Perhaps this mission wouldn't be a complete disaster if they could all remain focused on the task at hand.

"Or," Lark said casually, "we could enjoy ourselves *and* keep out of the dungeons this time. Right? Can't it be both?"

Langford sighed. Gods help him.

Koval was a wealthy kingdom, and its crown jewel of the capital, the royal estate, was a testament to that.

The carriage pulled up the stairs. A footman dressed in burgundy livery with gold embroidery opened the door, and Langford sucked in a deep breath. The basalt columns stood tall as some of the trees in Arden Forest. How they carved stone this strong into ornate shapes with the intricate detailing of sunbursts, stars, and the moon in all its cycles, was a wonder. The front garden was a marvel of hedges, pruned rose bushes, and statues, though it paled in comparison to the inner gardens. Langford hadn't set foot in them in years. Perhaps he'd get the chance tonight.

He offered Lark his elbow, and they fell into their roles of Mr. and Mrs. Brenner. The balmy night was a far cry from the raw chill of autumn in Ardenas. Sweat broke out along the back of Langford's neck. Lark squeezed his arm.

When they reached the foyer, a great golden dragon loomed over the entryway. Its glittering emerald eyes watched them, as if judging all who passed. Lark eyed the textured scales of the ornate statue, an expression akin to restraint and longing twisting her features. Lark was always running her hands over everything she could reach. Touching, experiencing, learning.

She turned from the dragon, and tugged Langford away.

This time, when they gave their names to the overworked scribe assigned to announce each guest, he didn't even offer a second glance. He had the twitchy look of a man recounting all the ways he might fail, even as he performed his task.

The ballroom was a display of the finest metal workers and artists in the world. The walls were crafted with golden filigree, swirling and edging along the crown molding. Langford studied the ceiling. Stamped metal and intricate detailing of flowers reflected the candle-light of the chandelier, making it glow like a midday sun.

The windows were masterpieces spanning from floor to ceiling and overlooking the gardens. A few balconies were available for guests to stand in the night air and breathe in the floral perfume of Kovalian hyacinths.

Lark tightened her grip on his arm, giving him a bright smile, and nodding toward the crowd. Just as Demetria predicted, most of the gowns were of burgundy or gold.

Langford gave Lark a quick twirl, and her full skirt swirled about their feet. He leaned in to whisper, "Be seen enjoying yourself. Come find me later." He gave her a quick peck on the cheek, as a husband ought to, and released her hand.

Lark nodded and danced away toward the dessert tables.

Langford took up his post against one of the marble pillars along the outer perimeter, schooling his expression into one of boredom. Eventually, a server would appear with a tray of drinks, and then he could have something to occupy his hands. Unease scratched at the back of his mind—all the ways this could go wrong.

What if Zaire had already searched her room for the hand mirror? If he was desperately mining for dragonstone, wouldn't he seize any small trinket he could get his hands on? Demetria was certain he was ignorant of the item, as he'd hardly paid attention to her in the first place, and likely had no knowledge of the stone in its handle. But who's to say he didn't empty her quarters upon her disappearance?

A server in a golden dress-tunic and pants appeared, tray extended. Langford carefully selected a gleaming chalice and offered a nod of gratitude without even glancing at the man's face. One didn't address the servants directly. That was uncouth and conspicuous. Only secrets and scandals passed between nobles and servants at these events, and he would not draw unnecessary attention. No, interactions with any servants fell to Alistair. Hopefully, he gained their complicity.

Langford focused on the couples gracefully dancing their way across the glittering dance-floor. A man in a white mask with a long beak spun his partner so her satiny skirt billowed out in its full shape. He and Lark would have to make an appearance on the dance-floor at some point. Gods above, this had better be the last ball he was forced to attend. A headache gnawed at the edges of his temples.

Langford sipped his wine, letting his eyes slip closed for a moment. Imported Anquan Red, like the wine Ingemar served. Familiar notes of berry and a deep, musky plum slid over his tongue. There truly was no comparison to an excellent red wine. Perhaps Ingemar had raided the same ship that delivered this bottle. Langford snorted at the thought, nearly choking.

"Take another taste, only this time slower."

A familiar voice breathed against his ear, igniting a heated shiver down his spine. Langford turned to find Alistair in the golden servant's uniform, a white mask framing his brilliant-green eyes. Eyes that put the emeralds in the dragon statue to shame. A crooked smirk graced his face as he held the tray of wine with all the poise of a man trained to do so.

"You—you're supposed to be—"

"Right here, plying you with enough wine that I might convince you to let me ravish you out in the gardens." Alistair ran his hungry gaze over Langford, thorough and shameless in its pursuit.

Panic fluttered through Langford's body, his headache throbbing. "I can't be seen talking to you."

Alistair sniffed and adjusted the remaining chalices to a diamond formation. "That's awfully elitist."

"You must go." There wasn't time for Alistair's games or the way he found amusement in ruffling feathers. Langford had no desire to see the inside of a Kovalian dungeon.

"Calm yourself, love. I just need to speak with Lord Frown Lines." Alistair's gaze flicked over to where Gavriel casually leaned against a pillar, already drawing the eye of a few interested ladies. Alistair had coined the nickname while he was busy shaping and combing Gavriel's hair, a joke the assassin cared little for.

Langford made a show of dusting off his own jacket, as if bored by the exchange with the servant, hissing under his breath, "What do you need with him?"

"I have drinks to serve, sir." Alistair gave him a devilish wink, refusing to tell him any specifics.

"I need to know—"

"I have a plan. But since you can't be seen talking to me, just trust that it's well-formed and brilliant." Alistair gave Langford one last lingering look before sauntering away to bring Gavriel a drink. Gavriel never once acknowledged him, his stare far-off and bored as he took a sip of his wine. Alistair bowed and swept away to offer a group of ladies some refreshment. Langford ignored the unpleasant twist in his gut when Alistair leaned forward to utter something with a salacious grin at his rapt audience. The blonde fanned herself, tipped her head back, and laughed.

Langford's gaze found Gavriel once more, just in time to see him to push off the column and strut over to King Zaire. Zaire was unmistakable. He looked just like his father, if only with a severity King Efrain never bore. He dressed impeccably in a military jacket adorned with medals and honors Langford didn't recall the man earning. No crown graced his head. He would have found the item gauche and desperate outside of coronations and weddings. As much as Koval was worth, it was in poor taste to wear an abundance of jewels and refinement.

Gavriel flashed the king a disarming smile, bending in a bow. They'd practiced the Kovalian show of respect. Right hand over his chest, left hand sweeping away, and leaning back to sink into the bow. Zaire's gaze shifted past him, obviously bored, but Gavriel must have said something to gain his attention because the young king laughed.

The two men slipped into what appeared to be a friendly conversation. Gavriel's hand flashed between them, so quickly Langford couldn't be sure it happened. But the king continued speaking animatedly, even clapping Gavriel on the back as he gestured toward the gardens.

Langford pretended to sip his wine, casting his gaze in Alistair's direction. Alistair flashed his most devious smile, causing the blonde woman enraptured by him to take half a step forward, as if pulled by his charm.

The bloody fool. It would be all their necks if he didn't stop preening like a peacock. Langford gripped his chalice tighter and grit his teeth as the blonde, with an over-embellished décolletage, placed a hand on Alistair's arm.

His frustration with Alistair's carelessness swept over his skin in a heated sweat. That was why he was angry. Not the ardent look some woman was giving him. And certainly not the way Alistair bent forward to whisper in her ear.

Langford downed the rest of his wine and glared at the ridiculously ornate ceiling.

CHAPTER FORTY-SIX

DACIANA

The princess seemed at ease with Daciana and Kenna, a blessing since they were the ones protecting her. Kenna had a way of winning people over, so it wasn't a surprise when Demetria fell into an easy camaraderie with her. They filled their days with light sparring and their evenings with dinners at the Walden Inn and Tavern. They would have to wait until they were closer to Stormfair to try the locator spell. There was no reason to believe the monster was still nearby, but it was the last known location. After Daciana answered the moon's call, they would resume their search for the child-killer. She loathed the idea of bringing the princess—it seemed an unnecessary liability, but nor could she leave her unguarded.

Every nerve in Daciana's body sang of the impending change. The edge, the hint of wild power that heated in her blood when the witch questioned her days ago, was gone, and an itching restlessness remained. Once the sun slipped beneath the horizon, she would have a matter of hours. It was fortunate that the Emerald Woods sat so close to the inn. She would have no trouble seeking solitude as the wolf claimed her form.

She would have to remind Kenna of this, but for the moment, she allowed the easy distraction of tending her blades as they practiced.

"Again!" Kenna called, tossing the sword back to Demetria's outstretched hand. "This time, imagine leading with your arm."

"My arm will not fell my foes," Demetria said with a grin as she fell into her stance.

"No, but your weapon is an extension of you. You'll have more power and control if it feels as connected as your hand to your wrist." An impish smile crinkled Kenna's nose. "Have at it!"

Demetria lunged, laughing at Kenna's hoot of approval.

Daciana turned away from the sparring match, running her whetstone over her blade again. The metallic ring reverberated in her ears, blocking out the sound of laughter and the friendly clanging of swords. The princess was skilled—there was no doubt about that. Someone had taken the time to train her in proper form, but she lacked the discipline one could only learn in the face of battle. Sparring with Kenna was a good start, but Demetria wouldn't learn what it meant to trust her sword until it was the only thing standing in the way of a fatal blow. It was a fool's hope to wish that day would never come, and Daciana was no fool. Instead, she hoped Demetria's lessons would be enough to keep her alive.

"You're getting better! You nearly had me there." Kenna laughed as she spoke her words of praise.

"You're far kinder and, I suspect, far more dishonest than my last instructor." Demetria huffed and plopped down beside Daciana, disrupting the neat formation of sharpened blades. Sweat had the wisps of her hair curling away from her face. A soft wistfulness stole across her youthful features, instantly transforming them. "Ruslan... I only hope he's all right. He risked everything by helping me escape, and I never even thanked him."

"In my experience," Daciana said, straightening the row of blades once more, "people don't commit acts of kindness for a *thank you*. I'd wager he already knew whatever you didn't say." It was an easy thing to regret, but if she could convince the princess to let go of even one regret, it might do her some good. Daciana knew the ache of words unspoken. But just because a thought was without words, doesn't mean it wasn't written in every lingering glance, every touch, every pulse of her heart. She glanced over at Kenna where she rested on a fallen log nearby.

"That's oddly comforting," Demetria said. "Though I still wish I knew he was all right."

"The others will report on his well-being. I won't tell you not to fret until then. We both know that's shit advice, but you'll have your answer soon enough." Daciana focused on the blades. It was a simple thing to keep one's hands busy. She should buy more swords to keep from running out of things to sharpen.

The late autumn sun sat low on the horizon, and orange light cut its way across their makeshift practice ring. Supper would be soon, and then Daciana could excuse herself for the night and leave Kenna and Demetria to their smiles and laughter.

"Do you worry about the others?"

Daciana glanced up to find the princess' young, soulful eyes—eyes darker than sloe—observing her carefully. Assessing.

"I've learned not to worry about them." That was a lie, but it fell easily from her tongue. She loathed the fact she couldn't assist them in this. It was an aching reminder of how much she was letting them down lately. Inerys' words were never far from her thoughts. Perhaps the witch was right.

Daciana tightened her hold on her whetstone.

No. Inerys knew nothing of what she spoke. Her knowledge came from books and stories passed down through whispers around a dying hearth in a world of hypothetical. Daciana knew what her power was capable of.

"If we can wrap up Stormfair with time to spare, I should search the surrounding areas for any jobs while we await their return. However long that might take." Kenna tied her long black hair back, but her fringe hung in her eyes. As always. There was a restless energy about her. That she'd lasted this long without disappearing to hunt monsters was a miracle. Almost as if she was patiently waiting for a reason to stay.

"You've never been bound to us or our mission." *Ring.* The blade sang under the whetstone. "You're free to leave whenever you wish."

The audible sound of Kenna sucking on her teeth sent a ripple of tension through Daciana's body.

"Is that what you want?" Kenna's eyes held a challenge she so rarely showed.

Is it what she wanted? Blazing nethers, it was as if the night she'd laid her feelings bare never happened. Though, they'd had no privacy since—a choice, born of fear on Daciana's part—but in no way a rejection of Kenna's presence.

Demetria gave a nervous chuckle. "I'm going to practice with the staff." As if someone lit a flame beneath her, she jumped up and scurried to the end of the clearing.

"Well?" Kenna insisted.

Daciana placed her weapon down and faced Kenna fully. It would be far easier if Kenna went her own way. She was the only one who knew what Daciana really was—what she was capable of. Ever since that day at Inerys' hut, a heavy shroud of shame had weighed on Daciana, heavier in Kenna's presence.

So why should she ask her to stay?

A breeze carried Kenna's scent, washing over Daciana. Tart and sweet, like berries and rain. The itching restlessness beneath her skin returned with a vengeance. Daciana swallowed against a dry throat. "No," she finally said, "I don't want that."

Kenna nodded, her mouth twitching. "So… is it just being on babysitting duty that's prevented us from finishing where we left off?"

Skies above, this woman would be the death of her.

"No," Daciana said, fighting a smile even as something tightened in her chest. "That's not the only reason."

"Of course. Wouldn't want to miss a chance to self-flagellate. It's your favorite pastime." Kenna stood, stretching her arms high above her head. A thin stretch of skin peeked out from beneath her tunic. "Well, after the kid goes to sleep, I might wander tonight. Who knows where I'll end up?" With a suggestive smile, Kenna sauntered away, grabbing the second staff to continue her sparring lesson with Demetria.

Daciana ran a hand over her heated face, desperately trying to rein in her thoughts. She cast her gaze to the sky and its bloody sunset. The moon's call was already beckoning.

There once was a time where Kenna would track the wolf. It was almost a game to her. And when Daciana awoke, naked, with Kenna's warm body by her side, it was a joyous thing. A reminder that she wasn't a monster, but an untamed soul that finally found its mate.

The lies told to the mirror carried the most bitter taste.

EACH TURN of the moon was the same. There was comfort in that.

In the familiar.

In the predictability of it.

The moon's call was both a blessing and a curse. It was a tumultuous coupling of pain and relief as every nerve over-fired and buzzed beneath Daciana's skin as her blood called back.

It was a strange thing, the dichotomy of almost domestic normalcy mere hours earlier and the wild freedom of succumbing to the night. They dined early since dusk approached swifter with each passing day, giving her a chance to have her meal and chat and laugh, all the while pushing down the excited thrum in her blood. Daciana needed those moments more than she cared to admit. Those moments that seemed unimportant, but seared into memory like a brand.

There was always the fear that she would lose herself, that she wouldn't remember where the wolf ended and she began. So she tucked these thoughts in the pocket of her mind, until it became too much to bear both the memory and the pain—tucked away images of Kenna laughing, crinkling her freckled nose as Demetria grimaced into her first taste of cheap Ardenian ale.

Daciana tugged her clothes from her body and tossed them onto a nearby branch. The first chill against her skin raised gooseflesh. Lowering into a crouch, she dug her fingers into the cold ground, dirt and leaves grinding beneath her nails. A ripple of energy shivered down her spine. A building of anticipation before she plunged deep into the wolf's skin. This was the moment her power felt almost gifted

—a brief glimpse at what her legacy could have been had she become Alpha. A whisper of a broken promise.

Soon, the pain would come.

Like a crack of lightning, fire burned through her body. A flash of agony that twisted and subsided faster than the blink of an eye.

This was only the beginning.

Her shoulder gave a loud *pop*—a deep sound of something snapping out of place. A groan fell from her lips as cold sweat beaded her forehead and trickled down her sides. Another flare of heat scorched along her skin, and her bones cracked, fissuring before they broke and reformed.

Daciana lowered her head, arching her back as a scream threatened to loosen from her throat. She was alone in the Emerald Woods, but not far enough that the sound of a bellowing woman would go unnoticed.

Her skin ripped open, wet and raw, and Daciana screamed into the earth, soil and rocks filling her mouth. But her body was too strong for her mind to shut her off from the pain as she was shredded into bloody tatters.

A final howl tore through her chest as finally, *finally,* the agony melded into something else. Into a trembling force, humming between her teeth and along her marrow. Her eyes slid shut as her form shifted.

Rightness sang in her veins.

A howl slipped free, echoing against the dark sky. The moon shone harshly through the empty branches, basking her in its ever-watchful glow.

The snapping of a twig.

Her ears pricked at the sound.

She exploded in a sprint. The expanse of darkness claimed the forest, curling around silhouettes of trees, black against the night. Cool air ruffled her fur, blowing through her as she tore through bracken and skeletal leaves. Her senses came alive with each stride of her powerful legs.

Yes, it was a curse. But on a night like this? It was pure freedom.

This is what she imagined flying must feel like. The weightlessness of riding the tail of the wind.

The sharp, coppery scent of blood stopped her dead in her tracks. She lowered her snout to the ground, seeking where the trail was strongest. Human blood carried a bitter edge, either due to diet or emotions which carried a scent that sullied the veins. Either way, the scent she caught wasn't human. It was too rough. Too *other.*

Something was wounded nearby. It would be a kindness to snuff it out and end its suffering.

She filled her lungs with the scent, padding over decaying leaves and damp earth. This blood smelled familiar, yet unknown. Like two scents collided to form something new.

A low groan sounded from a distance. Something distinctly *human.*

It couldn't be. She would have sensed it. Unless...

Could it be like Lark? Another Reaper who tore through the veil to their world?

Lark still carried the scent of a human. She was just... more. Whatever this was... Daciana had never encountered its scent. Not in this form, at least.

Another moan seeped through the trees. She was running out of time. If someone was dying, she needed to find them.

Daciana dashed through the dark forest, leaping over roots, chasing the scent of blood and the sound of labored breathing. The odor grew stronger as she rounded the thick trunk of a leafless oak tree to find a large figure slumped against it. Daciana stilled as a low growl slid out from between her teeth.

The ground was wet with his blood. His head hung heavy against his chest, white hair shining silvery in the harsh moonlight. One black horn curled from the side of head, while the other had been crudely broken off at the base—jagged shards forming the edges. She'd know this face, this beast, in any life and in any form.

Balan.

Impossible.

It couldn't be.

The demon she swore she'd kill the next time she saw him. The one responsible for Hugo's death.

It wouldn't take much, judging by his weakened form. Daciana's mouth pooled with saliva at the prospect of sinking her teeth into his throat. But where was the justice without seeing the flash of understanding in his eyes as she ended his existence?

Another growl escaped her chest.

The demon lifted his head, blood dribbling from his gaping mouth. His once silver eyes now appeared grey as they widened. A wet cough bubbled from his lips.

"Well," he rasped, "I suppose the gods really do have a sense of humor." And with that, he slid off the tree, unconscious.

CHAPTER FORTY-SEVEN

LARK

Lark sucked on another candied kumquat. The sharp sweetness and gritty coating were a delectable combination. She'd already inhaled two of the honey-preserved plums, a roasted fig with notes of vanilla, and a bite-sized apricot tartlet. This might have been her favorite mission yet. Excitement pulsed through her as she snagged a chalice from a servant hovering nearby. This time, she didn't have to fret over searching rooms and blindly trailing a vague lead. The last time she'd embarked on an undertaking such as this, she'd still been new to her humanity, and found the entire ordeal to be overwhelming. Now, she'd mastered an emotion or two. Including giddy eagerness to sample every delicacy offered.

"Careful, you'll get a stomachache." The rich timbre of a familiar yet foreign voice ghosted down her neck, leaving a chill in its wake.

Lark turned to find forest green eyes framed with a simple gold mask, dark hair styled back from his face, and the curve of amusement against a smooth lip.

Gavriel.

Alistair had really outdone himself with his disguise, but Lark would know his face anywhere, even under the mask, makeup, and clay that filled in some of her favorite features and a too-smooth jaw, freshly shaven. Also, his voice. He'd softened his r's, reflecting a Kovalian accent, similar to Alistair and Langford, but the edge he maintained. The way her body immediately responded to it...

"Perhaps that's my plan," Lark answered with a smile of her own. "Eat until I'm too sick to dance. It might soften the blow to my pride that no one has asked me yet."

Gavriel tilted his head in feigned confusion. "A beauty such as you? I find that hard to believe."

Lark stuffed another kumquat into her cheek. "It's true," she said around the fruit. "Will you save me from further embarrassment?"

Something akin to affection softened his eyes. "I fear, should I take you in my arms, I might never let go." His thumb caressed the inside of her wrist, and it took every ounce of restraint not to step into the warmth of his body.

She was, after all, Mrs. Brenner tonight.

"We wouldn't want that, would we?" Lark's words sounded soft and breathy in her ears.

So much for mastering her emotions.

Hesitantly, Gavriel removed his touch. "Perhaps later." His gaze darted in Alistair's direction, just as the man disappeared through the servant's entrance, tugging a laughing blonde woman with him. "Unfortunately, I must be detained by odious company." He gave her a wry smile, and made to step by, whispering in her ear, "But know this. I shall be watching and imagining when I rip that dress off and taste every inch of you."

Heat flared across Lark's skin, and she shivered at the way his breath fanned against the side of her neck. When she recovered, he'd taken up his position by the outer column, eyes glittering with thinly veiled lust as he watched her. She grabbed a few more kumquats and stuffed them in her mouth. Gavriel shook his head, his gaze shifting to amusement.

Already, a pair of ladies were approaching him. Their arms entwined in friendly kinship and both wearing gowns of burgundy and gold in different styles and shapes. The one with long waves of dark hair wore a tightly fitted bodice that flared to a ballgown gliding across the floor. Her golden gown was adorned with crimson beading. Her companion wore a form-fitting blood-red gown, smooth as silk, with golden appliqués sparkling with every movement. Lark bit her lip against a smile. Demetria was right about the popularity of dressing patriotically.

The brunette in the form-fitting bodice pressed an assertive touch to Gavriel's arm. His hand smoothly shifted to clasp hers, bringing her knuckles to his lips. The woman leaned in and ran her hand up the center of his chest while her friend laughed behind her accordion fan.

Gavriel flashed her a crooked smile, letting the woman run her hands all over him as if public groping was a common affair. He tugged her close, pulling her out onto the dance floor.

Lark's vision spotted as every muscle tensed in her body. Yes, he was playing a part, but did he have to play it so convincingly? If that woman didn't get her hands off him—

"Wife," Langford's voice cut through her awareness, intruding on the satisfying mental image of gripping the woman by the hair. "You've been unattended too long. Come, let me hold you."

Lark ripped her gaze from Gavriel's dedication to the role of the flirtatious cad and found Langford's grey stare, softened in a look of almost pity. He took the chalice from her grasp, a difficult task since she'd white knuckled it hard enough her hand shook.

Once the wine was safely removed, Langford led her onto the dance floor, rubbing soothing circles against her back.

"You're going to crack a tooth," he murmured against her hair.

"What?"

"Your jaw," he said. "Relax."

Lark forced her face to relax, and a sharp twinge through her jaw and cheeks proved just how hard she'd been grinding her teeth. "I don't know what's wrong with me," she said, leaning her head against his shoulder and trying desperately not to look in Gavriel's direction.

"Nothing," he said sharply. Behind his black mask, his eyes flashed. "There is *nothing* wrong with it paining you to see him with someone else."

"It's all for show." It wasn't like he was truly *with* someone. They had agreed, save for Lark and Langford, for minimum contact between each other in case any of them drew unwanted attention and suspicion. Gavriel had a particular identity that would avail him of all sorts of gossip and secrets while keeping his attention firmly placed on the king. Lark still hadn't spotted the king, but he had to be hard to miss.

Still, the sight of Gavriel, smiling at the pretty brunette as he spun her around the ballroom, made Lark seethe, squeezing Langford's hand, and imagining ten different acts of violence.

Langford let out a quiet huff of pain and shrugged, keeping her close as if she might fall without his support. "The heart is unencumbered by logic. You can feel what you feel. I won't pass judgment on the validity of that."

Lark loosened her hold on Langford's poor hand and leaned up to press a kiss to his cheek. "I really don't deserve you, husband."

Langford grinned, his boyish face all mischief and youth. "Hush now, and let us show these other couples how it's done." And with that, Langford spun her wide, nearly sending her into another pair of dancers.

Lark laughed, the buoyancy in her chest making her feel lighter than air. He spun her again, faster this time. He was certainly in quite the mood to make such a ruckus. Last time, she practically had to force him to dance.

"Do you think Alistair actually has a plan?"

"We'll know when we know." He dipped her with a rough jerk of his arms, nearly sending her to the floor. Lark laughed again, and he spun her faster.

Too wide.

Lark stumbled and tripped over someone, nearly landing on her skirts, but a powerful grip stopped her short. Dazed, and head spinning from Langford's questionable dance form, she glanced up to find a handsome face staring back at her curiously. Beneath his gold filigree mask, he had deep golden skin, and dark eyes narrowed in a familiar expression she swore she'd seen on another face.

"Should I call for a medic? Perhaps you need some air after

sampling too much of the wine?" He arched a brow as he gently helped her to her feet.

Lark fought for even breaths as her pulse pounded in her ears. "That isn't necessary! My partner got a little carried away…" She gestured toward Langford, who had moved on to another dance partner.

Ugh. The traitor.

The man studied her, assessing, before he finally sighed. "I understand. Perhaps a less adventurous dance partner would be a pleasant change of pace?" He extended his hand.

Cheeks still heated from the humiliation and unwilling to spend the evening watching Gavriel twirl his lovely partner and flirt the small-clothes off every available woman in the ballroom, Lark took his hand and allowed him to lead her back to the center of the floor.

She reached up to rest her hand against his broad shoulder. He was a fluid dancer, smooth and assured of every step. Even when it seemed they might collide with another couple, they magically found clear footing without remaining to their narrow square of dance space. Lark caught the image of Gavriel, tightness feathering a muscle in his jaw. His partner seemed oblivious to his discomfort as she pressed herself against his chest in a manner that was decidedly not the fashionable style of dance—

"You're quiet. Have I done something wrong?"

Lark nearly startled at the voice of the stranger whisking her around the ballroom. She needed to stop worrying about Gavriel and stay focused on the task at hand. "Not at all. Are your partners usually quite chatty?"

He laughed, revealing a dimple and a flash of white teeth. "You could say that. People offer their praise too freely. Without constant flattery, I find myself wondering what people normally talk of."

Lark laughed before she could help it. Was arrogance meant to be charming? It was amusing, if a little ridiculous, but she could appreciate the moment of levity amidst an otherwise tense night. "Praise is unwelcome?"

He shrugged, lifting her hand with the motion. "Not unwelcome, unnecessary. Though I'm finding your lack of complimentary nature a tad distressing. Quick, soothe my bruised ego before anyone takes notice."

Lark grinned, not at all needing to fake it. "You have very nice ears."

"Ears? My word, woman, you know how to make a man feel wanted."

"You also have a very fine set of shoulders. I should like to hang my sturdiest cloak upon you."

He laughed, pulling her in close. "You're terrible at flattery. Perhaps instead of pretty words, you are merely meant to be ornamental."

Lark bit the side of her cheek to keep from spewing a barb in retort. No, this was decidedly less fun than she thought, and she had half a mind to trip him as he spun them around the room. But she had a part to play, Langford's empty-headed wife. "You'll have to ask my husband of my uses. In any case, I'm sure you have no shortage of admirers to flatter your vanity in my stead."

Something in his smile hardened. "Too right, but if I needed the opinions of others to feel secure in my decisions, I'd make for a terrible king."

Ice speared through Lark's veins, hardening her legs, and making her step falter. If King Zaire caught her reaction, he didn't let on. She and Langford were supposed to blend in. To be seen but not noticed, and here she was dancing with the very man they were stealing from.

Lark schooled her expression into polite confusion. "You're King Zaire? But you're so young." She swallowed the fear that crept up her throat as she forced herself to add, "And handsome."

Zaire grinned, a practiced smile that reeked of disarming charisma and falsehood. As if he hadn't ordered the beheading of his little sister's friend close enough for the blood to soak the bottoms of her shoes for merely *questioning* his choices.

Oh yes, Demetria told them exactly what kind of man he was.

Despite his alluring features, complete with a full-lipped mouth that promised mischief and sensuality, his eyes gave him away. The steely hardness offered no mercy and hinted at his swift anger.

"So, I've heard," he said. "But not usually from one of my subjects." His hand tightened ever so slightly, and Lark fought the urge to pull free from his hold. "Where are you from?"

"Anquan, your majesty," Lark said, allowing her gaze to fall to his chest—as if she possessed a demure bone in her body. Anquan was a small island off the coast of the Permafrosts. A mountainous region whose flatlands consisted mainly of port cities. Kenna had told Lark she sometimes visited the island for 'old time's sake.' Lark would like to see the region at some point.

Kenna spoke of its many beauties, from waterfalls to ocean-side bluffs to feast days when the whole of each city gathered for food, drinking, and dancing. Perhaps one day she'd travel the world for leisure.

"My husband hails from Koval. I met him when he was passing through the port and the rest, as they say, is history." She laughed, scanning the ballroom for signs of Langford.

Zaire studied her. "They say Anquan harbors stowaways and thieves. I prefer to think of it as a place of rebirth."

Lark still hadn't exhaled a complete breath, and her head pounded. "Quite right, your majesty."

She still needed to slip away to help Alistair search Demetria's room. What if Zaire occupied her all night?

He gave her another crooked grin that failed to meet his eyes. "I haven't asked you your name. Are you offended by this?"

"No. Is it a terrible offense? I can feign hurt if it pleases you." The words flew off her tongue quicker than she could halt them, and she cringed at her own lack of restraint.

He laughed, a soft puff of breath that sounded more surprised than amused. "Not at all. I merely hope my intent is clear. You are the wife of one of my subjects."

Former subject. "I am."

"Though I can admire a woman with principles and loyalty to her husband, I will not insult your sensibility with flattery and falsehoods.

Your name doesn't matter anymore, for it isn't your own. It is your husband's."

Lark ground her teeth. "That's not the way things are done anymore."

"No?" Zaire leaned in, the scent of evergreen overwhelming her. "I learned something from my father when I was a boy. Would you care to hear it?"

Lark plastered a false smile on her face, ignoring the sinking in her stomach. The sooner she could put distance between this man and her, the better. "Anything you're willing to share I am eager to hear."

"A man's sins are carried by his sons, his daughters" —Zaire wet his lips— "and his wife."

Lark nodded, a frown fighting its way across her mouth. It was better than baring her teeth at him. "A wise lesson for a future king."

"A wise lesson for any man. I wonder what sins you bear for your husband." He pulled back, glancing around the ballroom. "What is his name?"

Lark's throat tightened. They had rehearsed their story dozens of times. Practiced reciting facts about one another. But she hadn't been prepared for this.

"Lord Brenner."

Zaire's brow furrowed in confusion. "Wystan has never and will never remarry."

"No, his son." Lark waited. Breath catching in her throat and pulse pounding in her ears, she waited. For his condemnation, for him to call her a fraud, for the guards to file in with Alistair in tow, and for it all to go belly up. A disaster of epic proportions with the punishment of death.

Instead, Zaire laughed.

"You're Langford's wife. I cannot say I would have pegged him as the marrying type, but time can change a man. I haven't seen him since my eighteenth nameday party. We didn't travel in the same circles, you understand, but his father is a good man." Zaire nodded as if that said it all.

Langford and his father weren't on speaking terms because the man was an utter ass and deserved to be set on fire.

The song ended, and Zaire quickly released her, taking a step back. Waiting.

Lark lowered in a deep bow, studying the floor so she wouldn't dwell on how her skin still crawled in his proximity.

"Bring Langford over to see me before the night is spent."

Lark froze, unsure of what to say. He left no room for argument.

"Of course, your majesty."

She rose to find his dark eyes cutting and disapproving. Perhaps he could sense how little reverence she felt toward him.

"I'm sure his father would love to see him again."

With that, he turned and left Lark alone on the dance floor. Horror tightening her chest.

CHAPTER FORTY-EIGHT

LANGFORD

angford wiped the sweat from his brow, pushing the curling edges of his hair back from his face. The steady hum of conversation made his temples throb, but he was determined to enjoy himself. Or at least distract himself. He wouldn't allow his thoughts to dwell on how Alistair whispered in that woman's ear or the salacious grin she responded with. Nor the gentle touches as he whisked her out of the ballroom—

Langford pressed his fingers against the pulse point of his forehead. It was for the mission and nothing more. A servant seen wandering the halls without purpose was suspicious. But if he was entertaining a lady of distinction… well, anyone would consider her gossip fodder and call him a good party favor. Langford was no fool, despite his heart's foolhardy desire to follow Alistair and his companion. He trusted him. He had to. Despite the countless times he seemed to lead cock first into trouble.

Langford craned his neck to see over the throng of guests. Off to the side, near the entrance to the outer gardens, Lark was wringing her hands and biting her lip. What had her so vexed? She'd been dancing with Zaire, and Langford had swiftly abandoned her to that fate. It wasn't out of unkindness, but he had no desire to speak to the man.

And if Zaire suspected them of anything, he wouldn't have left her unattended. From what Langford recalled, Zaire was many things, but subtle and tactful were not among them. No, he'd have detained her. Publicly. Whatever had her glancing about the room with unease was personal.

Gavriel? Last Langford had seen, he'd barely interacted with his dance partner and had taken to glowering at Lark's back while King Zaire twirled her around the ballroom. Where had he gone?

Langford needed to speak with her and sort out whatever was troubling her, and perhaps send her off to find Alistair. The man claimed to have a plan, but Langford had his doubts. They needed to hurry things along. The sooner they obtained Demetria's mirror, the better.

Langford let his gaze travel unhurriedly along the crowd. Gavriel had moved onto another partner, an unfamiliar blonde in his arms.

Blasted damnation. That was sure to set Lark off again. Langford began to push his way through the mass of tawdry perfume and taffeta.

"Wystan."

The commanding tone of authority, sharp like the crack of a hand across his face, paralyzed Langford where he stood. Unwillingly, he turned to find the face of a man he tried not to think about. The same blue-grey eyes that shone with disappointment each time he'd looked upon him were now widened in shock. His dark hair had receded from his pale forehead, his brow puckered in permanent distaste.

"Father," Langford ground out between his teeth.

Lord Brenner wore no mask. He'd always found games of merriment beneath him.

"How long have you been back?" No apology. No inquiry as to his well-being. Just a question that sounded more like a demand.

"I'm not really back," Langford said, calmer than he felt. "I only came for the wine." A tight chuckle rasped in his dry throat. He'd rather drink the wine on Ingemar's ship, regardless of the nefarious means by which she attained it.

His father recovered first and narrowed his steely gaze. "Five years. You've been gone five years with nary a word, and you stand here posturing?" He took a lazy sip from his chalice, dragging out his response. "I'd have thought you came back for your inheritance."

Langford's jaw clenched. *Inheritance?* Of course, he thought him little better than a parasite. His father's good opinion always remained just out of reach. Never mind the fact that Langford had fought for his place at the university, studying in a field that would win him no favor amongst the nobles. Or that he gave up his title to avoid a loveless marriage and chose a life in the woods traveling the dusty road over shallow comforts.

Heat flooded Langford's cheeks as he clenched his fist hard enough to crush the faux finger stuffed in his glove. "I never wanted your money."

"Wystan," his father said sharply. "You react without thought. Put your anger away before you pop a blood vessel."

Langford exhaled a shaky breath through his teeth. "Do not call me that."

His father snorted. "Why ever not? It's your name."

"No. It's your name, and I won't answer to it."

Langford had always preferred to go by his middle name. His mother, his friends, his peers, they all knew him as Langford. Wystan was the name he had never earned. It always seemed too big to fit. Only his father had ever taken to calling him that. The name he inherited from the man, along with his features. But it was the name of a stranger.

His father's inscrutable gaze traveled over his face. Again and again. As if searching for the boy who ran away from home. A familiar sinking took root in Langford's stomach, but he stood tall. He'd let his father bear the weight of the shame stretching between them. He was done carrying it.

"I see you are in good health. I wish you no misfortune, but I must take my leave," Langford said, choosing to fill the silence, not out of weakness, but a willingness to bid farewell to a past he thought would hound his steps—a memory he'd expected to haunt him to the last of his days. Only up close, it was nothing more than a tired, misguided man.

Langford almost pitied him.

Almost.

He turned to leave when a hand closed over his arm.

"This is not what family does to one another."

"Family?" Langford laughed. What family? The entire charade had dissolved into thin air the moment his mother died. Whatever had remained between them was nothing more than a shared bloodline and a sense of obligation. Both of which were insignificant compared to what he found with Alistair and the others.

"Family doesn't shut each other out" —his father shook him for emphasis— "no matter how convenient it might be."

Langford swallowed against the tight space in his throat. Now was not the time for this conversation.

Would there ever be a time for it?

"Darling."

Lark's voice rang from behind, as her hands soothed against his back until she came to stand at his side. His father dropped his arm as if burned and stared at her with incredulity. Langford wrapped his arm around her waist, clenching the fabric of her dress.

"Sweetheart," he said fondly, true relief shooting through his tense body. Though, if he were being honest, it would be far more satisfying to have Alistair draped on his arm. "Father, meet Sereia. My wife."

His father's gaze darkened, his frown deepening.

Lark ducked her head in the barest form of acknowledgment.

"I heard the rumors, but I didn't think them true." He leveled her with blatant disgust. "I know my son" —he stepped closer, peering down at her over his nose— "and he does not have a wife."

If his father drew more unwanted attention to them, it had the potential to compromise Alistair's position. Even Gavriel's.

Lark laughed lightly, running her hand up Langford's arm. "I assure you, I am his wife. I imagine you'd be less surprised if you had any contact with Langford."

Langford pinched her even as he fought hard against a smile. She could have her fun, but goading his father in the middle of a blasted ballroom mid-mission was too far.

Although… her loyalty and protectiveness were appreciated. A little.

His father's eye twitched, the only tell that he was edging closer to rage. "What a charming creature."

Lark grinned, a wide and uninhibited smile of triumph. "Thank you, Father. I should call you Father, shouldn't I?"

Langford intervened before Lord Brenner could offer a retort. "Sweetheart, why don't you sample the banquet table?" He pressed a kiss to her hand and silently pleaded with his eyes. "I'll find you in a moment for that dance, I promised you."

Lark darted a glance at where his father glared right back at her. "You are sure?"

She would never leave him without his signal. Something in Langford's chest swelled at the thought. "I am."

With a nod and another meaningful glance in his father's direction, Lark took her leave, layers of burgundy and gold sweeping along the floor.

Now was the time. He couldn't afford to delay any longer. But he couldn't rely on discretion with the watchful eyes of his father upon him. He doubted any move he made would go unnoticed.

"A wife? Really, Wystan," his father said with a scoff. "Was it all some misguided, stubborn attempt at independence? You destroyed our family legacy. For what? Pride?"

"No, Father."

He'd spent years rehearsing what he might say should he ever encounter the man again. Mostly, he'd practiced yelling every angry thought he'd ever had. Every counterpoint to his father's insults. Every word he'd bit down on when he was made to feel small and insignificant. But now? All he wanted was to walk away. Walk away and find the person who mattered. Because this? It mattered nothing. Nothing at all. Langford would cleave himself from the idea that he had to make his father understand. He didn't.

And that was freeing.

Langford gave him a gentle pat on the shoulder as he stepped by, done with the conversation, and done with his old life. "I just couldn't spend another day trying to be you."

Each step that drew him further from the man who'd raised him felt lighter. It wasn't running away, as he'd done years ago, when shame fueled his journey—it was power. Power over his own choices, over who he allowed room for in his life, and he owed this man nothing. A smile threatened to pull at Langford's mouth as an overwhelming sense of relief flooded his chest.

Someone stepped into his path, nearly knocking right into him.

Langford smoothed a hand over his doublet. He glanced up to find Gavriel blocking his way, a dangerous glint in his eye. The tension in his jaw hardened his mouth to a fine line. Alistair really had done well with covering up those scars.

"Excuse me, sir." Langford tried to push past him, but Gavriel once again prevented his departure. "What are you doing?" he hissed. Their contact should be kept to a minimum on the off chance anyone was paying close attention, and they needed to find Lark to rendezvous with Alistair—

"We have a complication." The grim set of Gavriel's mouth stalled Langford's thought.

"What sort of complication?"

Gavriel gestured over to where Lark stood by the dessert table. It took Langford a moment to recognize the frozen posture she adopted, along with the royal guard positioned far too closely. The tall, broad man towered over her, leaning in close to whisper in her ear. When she made to pull away, his hand closed around her arm. She glanced around wildly, locking her amber stare on Langford's. A quick shake of her head was the only signal she gave before being ushered toward the main hall, the guard's hand flat against her back. Lark threw one last look of desperation over her shoulder before she disappeared from the ballroom.

"I swiped the key off Zaire," Gavriel hissed, his eyes murderous. "Alistair was supposed to be discreet."

Langford's head spun. "What key?"

Gavriel glowered, a snarl forming against his mouth. "The rutting key to the princess' room. I've endured mindless conversation and unwanted advances all night because *he* was supposed to have it well in hand." He took a steadying breath. "So help me, if anything happens to Lark, I *will* kill him."

"Easy," Langford said, glancing back toward the doors where she disappeared. "If Zaire was on to us, he would have made a scene. Lark can handle herself, especially against one guard. Smile, yes, smile, and go back to your partner so nothing seems amiss." He was surprised by the steadiness of his own voice, since his heart was trying to bludgeon its way through his chest. "Lark will be fine, I promise."

"She fucking better be. Count to two hundred, and then follow them. I'll leave as soon as I can." Gavriel made a show of glancing over his shoulder at the blonde, who eagerly waved back at him. He took lazy strides toward her as if he had all the time in the world. But the fist clenching at his side told a different story.

Langford sucked in a sharp breath and began counting.

CHAPTER FORTY-NINE

DACIANA

Daciana had many attributes. Resourcefulness, loyalty, even ruthlessness when the occasion called for it. But above all things, she was patient.

In human form once more, she'd collected her clothes and now sat calmly waiting for Balan to rouse from his unconsciousness. The air had a chill to it, and the threat of frost hung heavy in each wet breath drawn. Dawn bled across the sky, spilling through the trees. Red and orange light tumbled through bare branches and across the ropes encircling his shoulders and torso to the tree, along with the binding around his wrists.

Weak or not, the demon couldn't be trusted.

Daciana studied his slumped form: The sweat and dirt that matted his white hair against his forehead and neck, the blistering marks on his forearms and the purple bruising scattered along his neck. Gone were his pristine black leathers. His filthy tunic hung open enough to reveal crisscrossed cuts along his chest that appeared to be festering.

What happened to him?

It didn't matter. It wasn't nearly enough, not after Hugo. He deserved to have every finger cut from his body. His skin flayed from his muscles. A slow and painful death until all he knew was never-ceasing torment.

But mortal weapons did not harm demons.

Daciana glanced at the blood caked to his skin and the earth beneath him. Red. Human blood. She sniffed. Not entirely human, but close enough. Perhaps her blade could grant him the punishment he so justly deserved. Even if she couldn't kill him, she could delight in showing him all the clever ways the body can hurt.

Her hand found the small stone in her pocket, and she smoothed her thumb along its surface. They hadn't even been able to give Hugo a proper burial rite because of him.

A low groan rumbled in Balan's chest, and his head swayed. His dark lashes fluttered as he wriggled against his bindings. Finally, he cracked an eye, his lip curling.

"I suppose I've woken up in worse situations." His voice was like the rough scrape of metal against granite. "Is this the part where you explore the boundaries of seduction through dubious consent? I find nothing tempting about the human form, apart from how easily it bleeds, but you're welcome to try." He attempted a sultry chuckle, which led to a deep coughing fit. Wet and thick.

"Do you remember my face?"

Balan opened his mouth to speak, but she continued.

"Because I remember yours. I remember every disgusting detail. I've imagined this moment for months." She leaned in close, looming over him like the predator she was. She swore she saw a flash of fear in his silvery-grey eyes. There would be time for fear. And pain. "Now, answer me."

Balan arched a brow, his mouth curving. "I've met many mortals. They all start to look the same."

"Don't lie." Daciana whipped a small dagger from her boot, angling it between the webbing of his first and second finger. "You recognized me last night."

Balan rolled his eyes, but Daciana caught sight of the jumping pulse in his neck. "Yes, yes, I remember you. Now take me to the others so we can come to an accord."

"Tell me how you know me."

The smirk slowly faded from his face. "You're the Reaper's protector." He wet his dry, split lip.

Daciana clenched her teeth hard enough her jaw ached. "You took someone very dear to me. Tell me his name."

Balan's brows furrowed, and he fought against his ropes. "I don't remember."

Wrong answer. She sliced the blade through his delicate skin, reveling in the muffled grunt of pain he bit out.

"Tell me who I left in that gods-forsaken shrine."

Balan shook his head. "I don't remember his name."

Daciana brought her blade to his lip, slicing through the thickest part. His dry skin rasped against the steel.

A sharp shriek gurgled in his throat. "Fuck, I don't know his name. I didn't kill him! Stop!"

"No. You don't get to make demands anymore. You'll tell me the name of the man we buried behind stone." Her eyes swam with tears, and she frantically blinked them away. "Tell me who I never said goodbye to." Memories of her and Hugo staying up to tend the fire while Alistair and Langford slumbered in their tents snuck through her mind. Of silently working side by side, gutting and cleaning his kills for future meals. Of things said and unsaid, an unspoken understanding they shared. The burden of heavy losses and even weightier guilt. On a quiet, unremarkable night, he extended a future request. A task he entrusted to her and her alone. That she bring him back to his home-land when he died—back to Vallemer for his final resting place to reside with his wife and daughter. She'd regarded him with the rever-ence his entreaty deserved and swore she would.

She'd failed to keep her word.

It was too much. She would never find satisfaction with torturing this demon. She would never find peace in his pain because Hugo couldn't find peace without his last wishes honored. Better to kill the demon now and be done with it.

Daciana angled her blade at his throat. "You bleed like a human. Let's see if you die like one." A tiny press of her wrist, and fire sang in her veins. Just a touch more, and his blood would paint the front of his dingy tunic.

Just a—

"Daciana!"

A panicked voice stole her from her revelry. Kenna stood near, dark eyes widened in alarm. Her hair was still mussed from sleep—it hung over her shoulders, unbound, as if she'd fled her room searching for her.

Demetria sprinted up behind her, gasping at the sight. She recovered quickly, but the muscle flexing in her jaw appeared to be holding a gag at bay.

Daciana had nothing to apologize for. But it wouldn't do to murder him without explaining. She could be patient a bit longer.

"He's a demon."

Kenna scoffed, crossing her arms. Her stance exuded casual ease, though the panic in her eyes remained. "I can see that. What are you doing to him?"

"Look at the color of his blood." Daciana angled the tip of her blade. "I think he can die."

"Well, of course I can die, you mongrel! But would you really kill an unarmed opponent?" Balan set his sights on Kenna, his eyes wide, silently pleading for her support.

Kenna ignored him, instead turning to Daciana. "A word?" Without waiting for a response, she yanked Daciana to her feet and dragged her several paces away. "Demetria," she called out, "watch him. But don't get too close."

Demetria nodded and tucked a loose tendril of black hair behind her ear, lowering into a crouch a safe distance away from the bound demon.

Kenna pinned Daciana in place with the force of her stare. "All right, out with it."

"It's a demon. Why are we even debating—"

"This reeks of personal vendetta. Who is he, and what did he do?"

Daciana thumbed the dagger in her hand, twisting the handle against her palm. "He killed someone I cared about." It was more complicated than that. Or was it? The demon abandoned Hugo in the shrine, leaving him to face certain death. But did Balan command the horde or was it a stroke of misfortune that led to Hugo and Gavriel being trapped, facing their foes alone?

Blame was a tricky thing, fluid in its placement, and sometimes the truth got lost in the shuffle.

But this demon was responsible for Hugo's death.

Kenna nodded. "Fair enough. Is there a reason you're drawing it out?"

Guilt threatened to curdle in Daciana's stomach, but she had nothing to feel ashamed of. "I'm not sure if he'll die, and I'd hate for his suffering to end too quickly." Did that make her a monster? Perhaps, but it could punctuate a long list of reasons preceding it.

Kenna studied her carefully, her expression curiously blank. "I see," she said, glancing over her shoulder. "Well, then… have at him." She jerked her head in their direction, where Demetria was speaking low enough, they couldn't hear.

Good. That was good. Kenna wouldn't fight her on this. Nor should she. A demon in any shape wasn't worth keeping alive. The hunter understood this.

Daciana approached his bleeding form just in time to catch Demetria reaching out to touch his broken horn. She froze mid-reach and scurried back out of the way.

Balan's gaze lifted, and panic widened his eyes. "Wait! Wait! You don't want to do this!"

"Oh, but I do." It wouldn't bring Hugo back, but it sure as shit felt like a good way to honor him.

"You need me!" Balan twisted against his ropes, sitting up straight and huffing against the edges of white hair that hung in his eyes. "I know what Nereida is planning."

Daciana froze, her blood cooling from the rage she'd felt only moments ago. "Explain."

Balan licked his ruined lip, a flash of red smearing against his tongue. "I know what comes for you." The smug arrogance returned to his features, smoothing them of any lingering fear. "And I can help."

"If he mentions his aching feet again, I'll kill himself."

Kenna repeated her sentiment for the hundredth time.

They'd been traveling to Stormfair—the four of them. The journey would have been a day's ride, but they were forced to walk, dragging a whining demon.

Daciana still couldn't decide what to do with Balan. If he was telling the truth… she couldn't kill him. Not yet. And if he was lying? She couldn't risk whatever destruction he could rain on them.

But it seemed as though he'd fallen into their laps at the most fortuitous time. Whether it was a trick, or simply impeccable timing, Daciana couldn't be sure. Inerys' words still scratched in the back of her mind.

"I wonder how you'll feel when you realize the consequences of your actions. When you learn the true meaning of sacrifice. For the sake of your senseless fear."

She'd dismissed the witch, too angry to examine how her words made her feel. But now, Daciana couldn't overlook this chance at an advantage. This possibility they might turn the blade, and cut Nereida off from her plan.

In the meantime…

Though Daciana was a patient sort, she couldn't stand being useless. They'd decided to deal with whatever monster stalked the citizens of Stormfair—the monster stealing and murdering their children, and by the blazing nethers, they were going to see it through. Even if it meant keeping the demon under constant watch and tying him to a tree when they made camp the night before. To his credit, he never complained about the measures they took to keep him from betraying them. However, everything else was a terrible burden to the bastard.

Demetria was the only one who seemed at ease in his presence. Probably because she was a curious sort who'd never witnessed a demon firsthand. She'd peppered him with endless questions, delighting in his cantankerous responses, all delivered with that rough scrape of a voice.

"How old are you?"

Balan groaned, rubbing his boot, an awkward movement with his hands bound. Demetria held his tether like he was a leashed pet. "Old enough to know it's rude to ask about one's age."

"So, really old, huh?"

He curled his lip in distaste, pushing off the tree with a moan. "Is it much farther?"

Kenna held her dagger aloft as if she was about to throw it at him.

"We're probably close enough to begin," Daciana said before Kenna could spill blood, as entertaining as that might be. It wasn't as if they knew the beast was still near Stormfair, so keeping to the outer woods wasn't a bad idea.

Kenna nodded, lowering to one knee to pull the vial with the locator spell from her pack, and stood with a somber expression. "We need to sort out what we do when we find the trail."

It was risky to balance protecting the princess, guarding Balan, and hunting a monster all in one go. "We can't leave Demetria alone with him. They'll have to come."

The demon growled at that, plopping on the ground with an exasperated hiss. "You will give me leave to rest. If I die, I can't help you halt Nereida's plan."

Kenna's eyes narrowed. "You keep saying that, and I'm beginning to think you have no way to help. Perhaps we can take our chances—"

"We'll take a brief rest before we begin," Daciana quickly intervened before turning on Balan. "You have no room to object to our conditions. I still think it would be easier to slit your throat and leave you to your fate."

Balan winced, tugging his boots off and flexing his feet. "You are most magnanimous."

"Ready?" Daciana asked as Kenna uncorked the vial.

Kenna nodded in response. "I don't know what we'll find or how far we'll have to venture, but it's time." She poured the vial's contents from Inerys' locator spell onto the ground, steam hissing from where it seeped into the dirt. A blue mist rose, hovering above the skeletal leaves and desiccated earth. Slowly, it wound its way through the trees, creating a clearly marked path to follow.

Oh, Inerys was a clever witch.

The four of them plodded along, following the wispy trail. It carved through the undergrowth, over the carpet of fallen leaves. Balan tripped over his own feet, but Demetria caught him by the elbow, helping him stand.

Gradually, the sounds of the forest dissipated until only their footfalls snapping twigs and disturbing the earth remained. The cold air was damp with the threat of rain, and a muted sky of dark grey loomed above.

Daciana thumbed the hilts of her daggers, hoping whatever they faced would fall to steel or silver. Memories of fighting the bubak lingered along the edge of her mind, taunting her with questions. What if this monster was beyond their knowledge? What if her cursed power called? What if Kenna paid the price?

She tucked her thoughts away, refusing to let them cloud her focus. Kenna kept her under a watchful eye, searching her expression for signs of what she was thinking.

When the wispy trail led them into a clearing, a small cabin came into view. The sweet scent of a burning hearth filled with hickory thickened the air. The blue mist encircled the home, hugging tightly to the fastened lumber of its outer walls before it evaporated as if it had never existed.

Daciana pulled her daggers free. In her periphery, Kenna patted down her weapons, taking stock of what she carried.

Casting a sharp glance at the princess, Daciana said, "If things go badly, tie him to a tree and run."

Demetria gave a little start, opening her mouth as if to argue, but Balan gave a little tug on his tether. "It's all right, mortal. At least I'll get to rest without your incessant pestering." The two of them dipped out of sight behind a trio of trees all growing out of the same round stump. A soft rustling filled the air as Demetria tied his leash to a thick trunk, and then quiet fell.

Before Daciana and Kenna could signal to one another, the door to the shack thrust open revealing a woman in a filthy apron and dark linen dress. A loose handkerchief tied her pale hair back. She held a basket of laundry, wearing a befuddled expression on her plain face.

This was… unexpected. But Daciana had long learned never to trust anything as it appeared.

The woman propped her basket on one hip, darting a confused glance at each of them. "Can I help you?"

Kenna's brow furrowed, a scowl claiming her lovely face. "You can tell me what you are. That would be an immense help."

Never let it be said that Kenna was one to mince words.

"What I—" The woman shook her head, more blonde tendrils escaping her kerchief. "I'm afraid I don't understand."

"Don't lie." Kenna edged a step closer, yanking her sword from its sheath. "Are you a witch? Something else?"

The woman's eyes lit up with fear, the basket beginning to shake.

Daciana turned to Kenna. "I don't think—"

"The trail led here! Inerys' spells never fail." Kenna lifted her sword, pointing it at the frightened woman. "I'm going to ask you again. What are you?"

Whether it was Kenna's frustration at not having her hunter's talisman to confirm her suspicions, or the brutal truth of how many children had fallen to a monster they couldn't name, there was a hardened edge to Kenna's words. A desperate determination to understand. To hunt and kill without uncertainty.

Daciana reached out to Kenna, trying to calm the hunter—when she caught sight of it. The faint glimmer, a step or two closer to where the woman stood frozen in fear. The faint scent of burning hickory slowly transformed, turning both sweet and acrid, like burnt honey.

Daciana approached, waving her hand through the glimmering veil.

"It's an illusion." Kenna's words echoed Daciana's thoughts.

The cabin transformed into a burrow, a tree hollow adorned with roots and deep purple mushrooms, so dark they almost appeared black.

Daciana's eyes watered as the cloying scent of magic became over-powering. But where the woman balancing a wicker basket on her apron-clad hip had once stood—something new took her place.

A twisted crone with eyes like the moon, full and milky with a sheen catching the light, crouched before her den. Her limbs were like gnarled roots, and her skin like the forest floor, dotted with moss and lichen. Her mouth parted to reveal black teeth, and a hacking laugh ripped free from her terrible lips.

"Is your curiosity sated, little one?" She directed her question at Kenna, awaiting her answer with ravenous anticipation.

Kenna sighed in relief, her shoulders relaxing. "I would have borne the weight of regret, you know," she said, "if you'd managed to hide your true form. But this is so much easier."

Daciana almost laughed. There weren't many ways Kenna could still surprise her, after all this time, but witnessing her staggering relief in the face of a grotesque monster—

The girl was incredible.

The forest crone growled. "You needn't die today. Collect your woman and return to your life. Your grief is stale and holds no interest of mine."

A grief eater. That was why she left the bodies of the children behind. The immeasurable pain of the town as more of their young fell prey to horrible deaths was the only consistency in the attacks. It wasn't children she was after, but the potent woe of their families.

"You remain close to Stormfair, though you haven't hunted its children in months," Kenna said, ignoring the assessment of the crone. "Why?"

"I am savoring after the feast. It will be some time before the town overcomes their losses, and in the meantime" —she licked her black teeth with a moss-covered tongue— "I'm appreciating the aftertaste."

A sharp cry rang out from behind them as Demetria tore her way through the trees. "You are a wretched, loathsome monster! I cannot listen to your poison a moment longer!"

Blazing nethers, take this reckless girl. "Demetria, stop!"

The crone lifted her head, interest lighting in her too-round eyes.

"You… you smell fresh in your sorrow. A loss you relive each day." She gave a pointed sniff, mouth and lichen-covered hands curling. "Guilt seasons your anguish, a flavorful morsel to be sipped slowly. Oh, child, if you would allow me a taste, I can take the pain away. Wouldn't you rather sleep dreamlessly, instead of reliving his death night after night?"

Demetria's face crumpled before she quickly smoothed it away. Her hands fisted by her sides, and she clamped her mouth shut. Either fighting the words or trying not to cry. "I would rather watch you die for your crimes."

Daciana cut a glance Kenna's way, assessing. Kenna watched the exchange with curious fascination, her head slightly tilted, but made no move to intervene.

"Oh, but what of your crimes?" The crone licked her black teeth. "Your naivety caused his death. I can hear the way his neck fought against the blade. Had they not even sharpened it? So many cuts to sever the boy's head from his body."

Demetria's hand flew to her chest, her knees buckling. But the grief-eater continued, "You may as well have held the sword yourself."

"Enough!" Balan's rough voice echoed through the dormant forest. He edged around the tree, hands still bound by fraying rope, but the tether lay in tatters where he must have chewed his way free. "You will not speak another word to her, you pathetic, weak, bottom-dwelling insect."

The crone startled, stiffening her crooked spine. For the space of a moment, all was silent. Then the woman howled out her thick, rasping laugh. "You aren't nearly as formidable as you once were. In fact" — she inhaled deeply, eyes rolling back— "you're too weak to mask your scent, even to one as low as me. You *reek* of lifetimes of grief. Oh, the loss you still yet carry as if it was yesterday rather than centuries ago. And now you have nothing! You are nothing but an empty vessel, sagging under the weight of useless disappointment. Was it worth it? Was everything you gave, the monster you became, worth being stripped of every ounce of power you bled for?"

Balan's jaw tightened, his silvery eyes narrowing. "I'll cut you open, you worthless hag!"

Another rasping cough filled the air. "You can kill me, but you'll never atone for what you've done. I am a mere bit of mischief compared to the destruction you've wrought—"

A metallic ring, and Kenna's silver blade was at the crone's throat. Her brow pinched in annoyance, her delicate nose wrinkling. "I grow impatient."

"Wait! There are others. Little bodies they haven't found. Don't their families deserve to mourn properly?"

Kenna hesitated, indecision transforming her features.

"She's lying," Balan hissed. "Do not fall for her schemes. Even if such a thing were true, she'd never reveal where she hid them."

There was a telltale sign of a quaver in his voice. Whatever the crone spoke of, it rattled him. Daciana tucked that detail away with the mental note to assess it later. He was right about one thing, trusting her now would be a mistake. Whatever she could share—and she wouldn't share—wasn't worth the risk of falling into her trap.

"Kenna," Daciana said, gently, "let's end this."

Round milky-white eyes flicked over, studying her with increasing interest. "How did I miss your scent? You might be the sweetest I've had in many moons. If you come a step closer, lovely wolf, I can numb the pain you try to forget. I can—"

A thick gurgling sound erupted from her bleeding throat, as Kenna sank her blade in deep. Black blood oozed over the silver dagger, like sap from a tree, and the eerie glow in the crone's eyes dimmed to grey. When she slumped over, falling to the forest floor, roots eagerly snapped open to pull her corpse deep beneath the ground. The sharp scent of her enchantment dissolved until all that remained was the smell of rotting leaves and freshly dug earth.

Daciana cut a questioning glance Kenna's way.

Kenna shrugged, yanking a cloth from her pocket, and wiping black blood from her blade. "She talked too much."

CHAPTER FIFTY

LARK

The unrelenting hand at the small of Lark's back ushered her down the empty corridor. Her pulse pounded in her ears, filling the silence with the rapid pace of her heart. No sooner had she left Langford's side, one of Zaire's guards had demanded a private audience and escorted her out of the ballroom. Not wanting to make a scene and compromise Alistair's position somewhere in the castle, she'd gone willingly.

But she'd met Gavriel's terrified gaze across the crowded hall before she was shoved through the doorway. She would deal with this quietly, and out of earshot of any guests. She couldn't afford for word to reach King Zaire.

The silent guard pushed her harder, and she tripped over the hem of her gown.

"I'm complying. You needn't be so rough."

He arched a dark brow dusted with grey and met her with a disapproving stare, as if this was all a mild annoyance. But he still hadn't explained his purpose.

"Apologies, my lady." He lowered his hand, but maintained his proximity. Hounding her steps, shepherding her to whatever fate she would meet. That he wanted discretion gave her hope they could get out of this unscathed. This guard hadn't alerted his king as far as she could tell, and if Alistair was caught, he'd never give her up. He'd never give any of them up. He was far too loyal. Perhaps this guard was acting on his own—a rather chilling thought, but it was better than being named a traitor to the crown. Or perhaps Langford's father requested a private audience.

She would bide her time until no one could accidentally stumble upon them, then she would take care of him.

Lark dragged her feet ever so slightly. If only to track what he'd do with the hindrance. It would determine what measure of incapacitation he deserved.

A deep sigh of exasperation sounded behind her, and she almost laughed at the absurdity of it.

"Where are you taking me?"

The guard was amenable enough to answer. "To your accomplice."

Lark startled, stalling her steps. He stopped just short of running into her, but his hands found her arms and steered her to the remaining steps. To the heavy wooden door at the end of the hall. Stairs and lower levels leading to dungeons were usually behind such heavy doors, in her experience.

"There must be some mistake—"

"No mistake. He named you as his contact. The one with the red hair, the gold and burgundy dress, and an insatiable appetite for sweets, he said."

Alistair, you son of a bitch.

So much for loyalty. Lark schooled her expression into one of bewilderment. "This is an outrage! I'll have you know my husband is in the ballroom right now looking for me. I demand you return me at once!"

The guard ignored her tirade, silently ushering her down into the darkness. If Alistair betrayed her position, he must be in grave danger. She would assess the situation, maintain her innocence as a lady of distinction until she could properly deal with this guard, and get them out of there. She only hoped Gavriel and Langford took their first opportunity to flee rather than mount a rescue mission.

A foolish hope. Gavriel would sooner storm the castle than bide his time, waiting to discover if she had a plan.

"I'll have your job for this," she said sullenly. She could have sworn his mouth twitched.

They rounded the corner and stepped through the narrow door. A faint glow illuminated the back of a figure perched on a stool.

Alistair.

What had he done to him? His bowed head hid his face from view, revealing the back of his neck glistening with sweat in the candlelight.

Lark took a steadying breath, bracing herself for discomfort. The guard was, after all, wearing armor. Spinning on her heel, she slammed her elbow into his jaw—one of the few places unprotected. He huffed a deep grunt, leaping out of the way before she could land a blow to his nose. She struck low between his legs with deft precision before grabbing the hilt of his sword. A large hand closed over hers, preventing her from pulling the blade free. Another hand gripped her throat, squeezing hard enough black spots dotted her vision.

"That's enough!" Alistair's voice.

Lark yanked her dagger free from her thigh, sinking the blade into the hand at her throat, and immediately the pressure released, flooding the air into her lungs. The sound of metal ringing from its sheath sent a shiver down her spine.

She would not fall to some nameless guard.

Lark spun the dagger and fell into her stance. By the skies, she'd spill his blood before he spilled hers.

"Lark!" Alistair's face filled her vision. He gently pulled her arm down to her side. "I thought you'd be the most reasonable of the three, but perhaps I should have called for Gavriel."

Confusion loosened Hugo's blade in her hand. Lark's gaze fell to the corner of the stone room, where she expected to find irons and chains or whatever they used to keep their prisoners. There were no bars or cells... perhaps they didn't keep prisoners long enough to house them. A stack of crates and sacks came into view as her eyes adjusted to the dim lighting. Was that... flour?

Alistair grinned at her, taking a bite of what appeared to be a loaf of bread she hadn't noticed he was holding.

"Where are we?" Lark asked.

Alistair looked at her like she'd gone mad. "Have you never seen a larder before?" He dusted his hands on his pants. "This handsome creature over here found me rifling through our princess' belongings. I showed him I had the key and everything."

"And you still haven't answered how you got that key. King Zaire keeps it—"

"In his left pocket alongside his father's old pocket watch. Yes, I know. Maya told me, lovely girl, who deserves far more than her betrothed will offer. If he can't surround her with enough affection to remove all doubt of his feelings, then he doesn't deserve such a treasure."

Lark's head spun as she fought to keep up with the revelation that Alistair was not, in fact, in danger. "Which one is Maya?"

"Demetria's handmaiden." Alistair grinned.

"And the key…?" Understanding dawned on Lark. "Gavriel?"

Alistair nodded. "I was the obvious choice for such an endeavor, but we all know Zaire wouldn't let someone like me anywhere near him in front of an audience. Gavriel got the key and discreetly slipped it to me, and while I was respectfully searching—"

The guard growled. "You were traipsing about the room wearing one of her evening robes."

"I do love a fine fabric."

"Alistair, focus!" Lark wanted this night to be over, and they needed to return to the ballroom before Langford and Gavriel could do anything to compromise their positions.

"Apologies. Where are my manners?" Alistair gestured to the scowling guard who stood by their only exit. "The man you nearly maimed is Ruslan. Ruslan, this is Lark. She really is a darling girl once you get over her affinity for violence."

Ruslan's name clicked into place. Demetria had told Lark of the Captain of the Guard, her father's oldest friend and her trainer. If there was anyone left in this castle they could trust, it was him.

Relief flooded Lark in a staggering current.

"Did you lie to me?" Ruslan wrapped his bleeding hand with a scowl, his sword tucked safely back in its sheath.

Alistair sighed. "Of course, not. How else would I know the princess favors honeyed rolls to cakes? Or that she's constantly sketching on any parchment she can get her hands on? Or that she sounds like a strangled cat when she sings?"

"It's true," Lark cut in before Alistair could say anything to make the situation worse. "Demetria sent us. She's the one who swore we could trust you."

The aged warrior spared her a brief glance before he crept dangerously close to Alistair. "If any harm befell her, I'll cut your sack from between your legs and feed it to the dogs."

"Now, now. Is that any way to speak to a new friend? I expect an apology before this insult festers and ruins our relationship." Alistair frowned at Lark. "You should probably apologize, too."

"I am sorry about the hand," Lark said. Ruslan shrugged off her apology, so she turned her attention back to Alistair. "I thought you'd been captured."

"Ah! Yes!" Alistair strode over and slung an arm around Ruslan's broad shoulders. At the warrior's glower, he extricated himself. "I thought the mission had gone tits up when our new friend here caught me searching Demetria's room. Luckily for me, she told me all about the grumpy captain and how to convince him she was safe and our ally." He eyed Lark meaningfully. "How all she wanted was a precious keepsake of her mother's that she hadn't had the chance to grab when she fled the castle."

She nodded her understanding. Better not to explain the real reason they needed the mirror. Or more importantly, the dragonstones adorning its handle.

Ruslan snorted. "Demetria is a smart girl. She'd never risk an ally for a trinket. No matter how sentimental it was. Tell me why you want the princess' heirloom." Doubt worked its way through the shadows across his face. Now that Lark's human eyes had adjusted to the darkness, she could appreciate the concern tightening his features.

Demetria was right. He cared for her. More than an assigned guard had to.

"You seem a logical man," Lark said. "Why would we steal a mirror when we could search for something of greater value? Her crown or her jewels, perhaps? You believe us, or else you would have told your king of our trespassing."

Ruslan's lip curled in disgust. "My allegiance is to the princess."

Lark stepped closer, tilting her head to meet his eye. "So is ours. There's a reason you told her not to reveal that mirror to Zaire, isn't there? She knew it was worth the risk to get it away from him." Several heartbeats passed in silence.

Even in the dim light, his stare bore down on her, critical and assessing. A muscle feathered in his jaw before a soft huff of breath escaped his lips. "I won't speak of my suspicions with strange thieves, but answer me one question." A vulnerability shone on his face, softening his features, and making something tighten in Lark's chest. "Is she safe?"

"Yes. She's safe with the most honorable person I know, and none of us will let anything happen to her. That's why she isn't even on this continent—so Zaire can't hurt her."

Ruslan barked a humorless laugh. "He's already hurt her. I failed her in that."

Lark wanted nothing more than to bring the captain with them, across the sea, to Ardenas. To Demetria. It seemed Ruslan had nothing tying him here. He was already a traitor to the crown in his heart. Perhaps he could join their crew and she could bring a piece of home back to Demetria.

"Have we all made up yet?" Alistair's voice cut through her thoughts. "Because there's a handsome gentleman in the ballroom I'd love nothing more than to ravish indelicately in the gardens."

"Do you have the mirror?"

Ruslan pulled it out of his pocket. Swirling filigree adorned the golden mirror, and the glass face sat no larger than Lark's palm. Black stones decorated the handle in a row. *Dragonstones.* "I'm not some daft sod. I know the value of this piece, but I need to believe Demetria is all right." Reluctantly, he handed it over to Alistair, who swiftly pocketed it. "And... I do. At least she's where that bastard can't get to her."

An invisible weight lessened in Lark's chest. But they were far from done. The true task would be to find their way back to the ballroom without suspicion. Sooner rather than later, so Gavriel and Langford wouldn't cause further complications.

"Zaire saw us leave together. Is it safe for you to escort me back?"

"*Safe.* I can promise no safety to anyone so long as he's on the throne. But we'll give him no reason to distrust us. So long as you're convincing." He reached over and pulled a few tendrils of hair loose from her style before running his thumb roughly across her lips a few times. The scrape of his callouses left her mouth sensitive. So, it was to be the ruse of a tryst.

Lark could play at that. She unbuckled his chest plate, letting it hang slightly off-kilter from his shoulder.

Ruslan frowned. "I would never allow my armor to fall into such a poor state."

"Hush and let me leave my mark." She dug her nails into the back of his neck, earning another scowl.

"Oh, Gavriel is going to love that."

"Shut up, Alistair."

THE HALLWAY GREETED them once more, a blessed reprieve from that dank larder. It made no difference. Dungeon, cavern, food storage space—anything beneath the ground made Lark's chest tight. A quick glance at Ruslan, and she found the man's stern expression. His hardened brow and clenched jaw, along with the fist by his side as he staunched the bleeding from her attack, would give them away.

"You don't have the look of a man who just slipped away for alone time with a lady," Lark said, fighting a smile.

"She couldn't have been a disappointment," Alistair said with a rakish grin.

"I look like a man who is trying to get you and your friends to safety."

"Right. Look less like that. It's rather obvious." Despite Alistair's typical demeanor, there was a frantic urgency to his gait, and Lark had a hard time keeping up.

He was just as eager to return to Langford, but they all needed to tread with caution to remain above reproach. Didn't Alistair understand this? He seemed to play his part well with the lady he escorted from the ballroom.

"Whatever happened to the woman you left with?" If she was a loose end, they needed to deal with it.

"Ah. She might be waiting for me in the gardens."

A grin tugged at Lark's mouth, the memory of pulling the same stunt the last time she attended a ball resurfacing. "And you wanted to seduce Langford in front of the poor girl? Utterly indecorous!"

"I thought the lass might appreciate the view. It's the least I could do."

Lark's laughter flittered from her chest, echoing in the cavernous hall. A sharp look from Ruslan reminded her they needed to be more careful. "Alistair, you go on ahead. Be as discreet as possible. I'll follow with Ruslan." She turned to him. "After we collect the others, can you see us out?"

He nodded. "I give you my word. Even if this is the worst plan I've ever born witness to."

Alistair glared at him. "You try scheming from across the ocean, with only four people actively participating, breaching the most protected castle on the continent, and without the advantage of someone on the inside."

Finally, Ruslan spoke. "Fair enough."

Alistair gave a short nod and slipped the mirror into Lark's pocket. "In case anyone gets handsy with me," he said and scurried off, disappearing around the corner, leaving Lark and Ruslan alone.

Lark took the opportunity to study him. His light brown eyes were tinged with gold and narrowed in suspicion at her perusal. A frown creased his deep bronze skin, and his dark brow arched in silent question.

"Demetria shared with me what you did for her, how you helped her escape." Lark watched his expression. "You care deeply for her."

Ruslan's mouth tightened. "I never had a family of my own. My role as captain was enough. But when King Efrain and Queen Zibhia had Demetria, I could see the value of becoming a father." He sighed. "It isn't right, losing her parents so young and getting saddled with someone like me. She's meant for more than this. More than hiding from her brother."

Lark placed a hand on his arm. "She's very lucky to have you. Don't diminish how much you matter to her." She turned away before he could dismiss her words.

Voices and music fluttered down the hall. It was time to return to the ballroom.

Ruslan offered his arm, keeping his injured hand tucked away at his side. Lark linked her arm through his and allowed him to lead her toward the doors. The mirror pressed against her thigh in the pocket of her skirt, and she took a deep breath.

The job was almost done.

Lark smiled at the memory of Hazel telling her to think of perilous situations as a job, nothing more, to keep the panic from setting in. It seemed like ages ago.

Lark was actually starting to miss her.

A commotion broke her from her thoughts before they could make it to the ballroom. Alistair, Langford, and Gavriel burst into view, rushing toward them.

Alistair motioned for them to hurry. "My, my, look at the time! We best be off. Quickly now."

Lark and Ruslan spun around and kept pace with them. "What did you do?"

"Apparently," Langford said, "Alistair offended the wrong lady."

Alistair winced. "There's no way we won't draw attention now. She already told all of her friends, and they're all watching us like blood-thirsty hawks."

Lark laughed, shaking her head. "What about the two of you?"

Langford grimaced. "I was intercepted whilst trying to come to your rescue. My father tried to arrange a private audience with the king, and I refused."

"And Gavriel?"

He shook his head, sighing. "Supposedly, I'm betrothed to two different women now. I had to leave before their fathers could negotiate their dowries."

Lark rolled her eyes, shooting Ruslan a look that silently voiced all of her frustrations with the group. Ruslan's mouth twitched.

They fell into step—a hastened pace filled with intention. Carving their way through the castle and further from the straining notes of music from the ballroom. Two more turns, and they reached a wide hallway. Moonlight filtered through open archways, painting the marble floor in bright silver. It was a shame they would once again flee Koval before Lark got a chance to explore some of its accomplishments. The features of the castle seemed to allow nature to creep through open doors and windows, and she longed to see more of the land and human dwellings.

Alas, it wasn't meant to be. Perhaps when everything was over, her and Gavriel could travel the world. Anquan, Vallemer, even the Permafrosts. Venture everywhere and see everything this world had to offer.

First, they needed to escape the castle with their heads still attached to their necks.

"What will happen if someone spots us?" she asked.

They rounded a corner, and before Ruslan could answer, Lark walked straight into a wall. No, not a wall. A broad armored chest. She glanced up to find the man's face flash with surprise.

"Captain? What are you doing?" the guard said.

"Stand aside," Ruslan growled, a sharp, commanding edge to his tone.

The guard reached for his sword.

"Bastian," Ruslan said, sorrow claiming his expression. "Stand down."

Bastian shook his head, his eyes narrowing at his captain. "I'm afraid I cannot." Before he could free his sword from its sheath, Ruslan advanced, aiming a forceful blow to the young guard's face, before knocking his head against the wall hard enough the man slipped to the floor, unconscious.

Panic tightened Lark's throat. They couldn't stay, and neither could Ruslan. Not after this. A resigned look came over him. He'd effectively destroyed whatever standing he had here, ending his career and putting his life in danger for openly aiding them. "There's a secret tunnel only the family and I know about, just through here."

If the family knew, that meant Zaire knew, but Lark followed without question.

They rounded the corner—

Running straight into two armored guards.

Ruslan growled. "I'll handle this." He pulled his sword from its sheath. Before he could cut down his men, each guard seemed to stiffen, bringing a hand to their necks, before crumpling to the floor unconscious.

"Well... that seems either very lucky or oddly foreboding," Alistair said.

"Whatever that was, we need to move quickly." Ruslan tossed one last frown at his unconscious men before taking off down the hallway.

Lark studied their necks as they passed, recognizing a needlepoint dart in each one. She spun around in time to see a flutter of black fabric disappear around the corner. It couldn't be...

"I know what you're thinking," Gavriel said, hurrying her along, "and I'm inclined to agree with you."

They trailed after Ruslan, taking a sharp turn where they found a heavy oak door. Ruslan unlocked it swiftly, pocketing the large iron key once more. A dark stairwell greeted them as they descended into the dungeon and moved through the darkness with efficient ease. Each door they passed, he shut and locked with methodical precision, as if shutting each door on the life he was now forced to flee.

A tug on her Lark's arm brought her back to reality. A certain man's hand burned against her skin, and his forest green eyes studied her with an unspoken relief. "Gavriel," his name left her lips with the force of a sigh.

He smiled, an unrestrained boyish smile, and yanked her into his chest. "Glad you're safe, my lovely demon. You had me worried."

Lark breathed in his familiar scent, content to steal this moment before they continued on their way. "It sounds as though you suffered a far worse fate. Two betrothals in one night? Skies above, what a cad you've turned out to be."

Gavriel groaned. "Don't remind me. I pledged nothing of the sort, and I'm convinced they concocted a plan to entrap me into marriage. All I could think was how much I wanted you in my arms." He pressed a kiss to her temple. "I believe I still owe you that dance."

She leaned into his touch. "My biggest regret was not dancing with you when I had the chance and missing the opportunity to sample the chocolates. Did you see the platters? I heard they were imported from Anquan."

Gavriel rumbled a laugh. "I swear we'll dance, and it won't be at some ridiculous ball. As for the chocolate…" He pulled a cloth from his pocket, unwrapping it carefully to reveal a secret hoard of sweets.

"You stole these!"

"It was my recompense for enduring incessant prattling all night."

"You're a cad and a thief!"

"Do you want some or not?"

Lark grinned, sighing into the safety of his warmth, before gently extricating herself. "Later, after you deliver on all the promises you made me tonight." The memory of how he whispered his plan to rip her dress off and taste her *everywhere* burned in her blood.

Based on his heated expression, he recalled the same thing. "I eagerly await the opportunity."

They took off running after the others. Their footsteps were swallowed within the darkness of the wide tunnel. Ruslan had lit a torch, and the light bobbed ahead of them.

"Ruslan" —her voice echoed off the cavernous walls— "what will happen to you now?" There's no way Bastian hadn't come to and alerted the others by now.

Ruslan said nothing up ahead, maintaining his pace.

"Ardenas is lovely this time of year," Alistair said.

"We have access to a seaworthy vessel," Langford said.

"And Demetria would want you to come," Lark added, hoping it was enough to sway his decision.

Another beat of silence before finally his voice scraped out with a note of resignation, "I hate the cold."

A broad grin stretched across Lark's face. They could commission him warmer clothes until he acclimated, and there was plenty of time before winter arrived. Come to think of it, she hadn't experienced winter in her mortal form yet, either.

They could face their first snowfall together, and Demetria would be pleased. Lark had assumed the young princess would have a delicate sensibility, but she took everything in stride: travel, less than luxurious accommodations, the cold she wasn't accustomed to. But for all her strength and bluster, she was little more than a child. A young girl who had lost more than anyone should, and if they could deliver the person she cared for, bring her a piece of home, they would—they owed her that much.

After a few more turns, the flutter of a breeze made its way to Lark's face. When patches of grass peppered the dirt floor, relief filled her chest. The tunnel let out beneath a steep hill; a night sky full of stars greeting them. She sucked in a deep breath of floral, perfumed air and sagged against Gavriel. They still needed to hurry to the docks to meet Ingemar, but at least they were free from the castle.

Langford ripped his gloves off and tossed them away with a haughty glare.

"Well," Alistair said, "that was one of the better parties I've been to."

Lark huffed a laugh, preparing a retort, when a *whooshing* sound reached her ears.

Thwack. It landed with a wet thud, but she couldn't track its entry. The ground was soft and wet, likely it landed—

Ruslan turned, revealing the arrow had pierced his left eye, blood trickling down his cheek. He opened his mouth a few times before slumping to his knees.

"No," she whispered, reaching for him. Her stomach sank like a stone. It couldn't end like this, not when they were so close.

The whistle of arrows started raining down on them. Gavriel yanked her away with a harsh shout. Lark turned and sprinted down the hill, legs screaming with every step. Gavriel's grip was bruising on her hand as he pulled her away from the sound of Ruslan's last choking breath.

She cast one last glance over her shoulder, where he lay prone on the grass, arrow still lodged in his eye.

Lark broke her gaze and didn't look back again as she and the others disappeared into the night.

CHAPTER FIFTY-ONE

LANGFORD

angford stared out over the dark waters, bright stars reflecting upon their surface. The air carried the scent of brine, and a southern breeze blew soft and warm through his hair. His legs still ached from sprinting through those tunnels beneath the castle.

The rip in his trousers and the sting of his bloodied knee were painful reminders of how sloppy their escape had been. Perhaps it was time to retire the notion that undercover missions in fortified castles were part of their gambit. It always seemed to end badly.

The image of the arrow piercing Ruslan's skull, the bloodied tip sticking out through his cranial orbit, flashed in Langford's mind.

No one had volunteered to deliver the news to Demetria.

Perhaps if Langford's father hadn't been there, his and Lark's moves would have gone unnoticed. But from what Demetria shared about Ruslan's allegiance… a man like Zaire had to sense the absence of loyalty. It was likely Ruslan was already under scrutiny. Perhaps Zaire was itching for a reason to dispose of the captain.

Langford only hoped his death was worth it.

They accomplished their mission in its entirety and retrieved the mirror, but it didn't feel like victory.

The warmth of a familiar hand slid up his spine. Langford shivered and leaned into Alistair's touch.

"Are you well?"

Gone was his usual preening and posturing, the carefree demeanor he so desperately clung to. No, after a tough job, this was when Alistair's soul was laid bare—the guilt that ate away at him until he lost himself at the bottom of a bottle or in the arms of another. Langford had witnessed this phenomenon enough times to recognize the signs.

"Quite well," Langford said with a tight smile. "I didn't lose any appendages or extremities."

Alistair responded with a crooked grin that failed to meet his eyes. "Our truest measure of success." He brought a brown bottle to his lips and drank deeply.

Langford gently took the bottle from his hand. At his questioning look, he said, "It's a lonely business, drinking alone." Langford tipped the bottle against his lips. He was unprepared for the burn of the bitter, vaporous substance, and he cringed. "You could have offered to share."

Alistair huffed a laugh, prying the abominable drink free from Langford's grasp. He lightly kissed him on the nose. "Aye, that's not all I wish to share with you tonight."

Was he a placeholder for all the nights that blurred together in a sea of bodies and drink? Would Alistair seek him for comfort until it stopped working? Langford pressed a hand against his forehead, willing away the images that seemed determined to remain perfectly preserved; images of Alistair disappearing with strange women, men, professionals, amateurs. It was foolish to dwell on the past, but was it still the past? "Were you as generous with the blonde you escorted from the ballroom?"

Shock splashed across Alistair's handsome face, and Langford inwardly winced at his careless questioning.

"That was just for appearances." Alistair spoke slowly, a slight tremble in his voice. "You know that, don't you?"

Shame churned in Langford's stomach and heat pricked the back of his neck and the tops of his ears. Sure, he knew it was an act. But how many times had he witnessed Alistair disappear with a new companion for the hour or for the night? How many times had the space behind his ribs ached as he watched him seek the comforting warmth of a body? And Langford was expected to forget all that—forget years of anguish and hiding behind friendly smiles and poor jokes?

"Langford," Alistair's soft voice cut through his thoughts, and Langford blinked back the moisture clouding his vision. "What's happened?"

"Forgive me, it's just a headache. Tonight drained me is all." Langford tried to push past him, eagerly seeking the safety of a solid door and a sliding lock, but Alistair stepped in his way. Langford couldn't bring himself to meet his gaze. "I'm poor company tonight. I wouldn't subject you to my mood."

A firm grip found his bicep, and a gentle touch lifted his chin, forcing his eyes to meet the unyielding stare of the man crowding his space. His impossibly bright eyes, even in the dim light of the nearby lantern, bore into him, stripping him bare.

"You, in any form, is the only company I'll ever desire." Alistair's voice had gone rough. His touch softened before it traveled up the length of his shoulder, resting against his pulse point. "There was something I should have mentioned earlier, about the job with Ingemar. Actually about the woman I sold her out for."

Langford swallowed. "What about her?"

"Though I stand by what I said, none of my people are expendable, she wasn't just a member of my crew." Alistair's eyes tightened as the old hurt flashed across his gaze. "She was my sister."

His sister. Alistair had a sister—a sister who was murdered in a Vallemerian village after he helped her escape Koval. "Oh, Alistair…"

"No. I've made peace with it all. That isn't why I told you. I just" —he lowered his stare— "wanted you to know more of me than anyone else. Well, you already do. I just meant, I want you to know how much I trust you. I know I don't deserve you, that much is clear. But I hope one day to be the man worthy of you and earn your trust. Because nothing, *nothing* in this world matters as much as you—"

Something fractured in Langford's chest, and a dam broke. He surged forward, claiming Alistair's mouth. His familiar taste of vanilla and spices was intoxicating, and any semblance of finesse was lost as their kiss turned brutal. Their teeth knocked, and the scrape of Alistair's whiskers sent a shiver down Langford's neck. He fisted his hand in Alistair's hair, harsh and ruthless.

"Fuck," Alistair murmured, biting into Langford's lip, and backing him away from the rail and toward the stairs. He broke the kiss to say, "We need a door and a lock, now."

Alistair's mouth was upon him once more, his greedy hands already tugging at his tunic. A few stumbles, and nearly succumbing to their passions against the wall in the very public hallway, and they were finally in their room. They shed their clothes with alacrity, and when Alistair laid him down on the bed and loomed over him, time stood still. He brushed a few strands of hair from his face, gazing down at him with yearning and reverence. "I love you."

There was no laughter this time. Nothing to hush the clarity of those three simple words. But they were anything but simple, weren't they? They were an offering. A promise.

An oath.

Langford stared up at the man who'd owned his heart longer than he dared to examine. The one who filled his days with joy and laughter at a time when he didn't think he'd ever smile again. The one who spent years numbing a guilt Langford couldn't comprehend.

And it was simple. It was the simplest, most natural thing in the world to whisper back, "I love you, always."

"How did your little mission go?"

Ingemar had kicked her feet up onto her desk, crumpling maps and parchments under fine Kovalian leather. Her worn hat sat low over her eyes, hiding her from view. She picked her nails with the tip of her dagger, cool and nonchalant.

When they first boarded her ship in Ardenas, embarking on a trip to attend Koval's event of the season, their initial greeting hadn't gone well. It included a colorful berating that slipped into Anquanian, a language Langford was familiar enough with to recognize her descriptive knowledge of human anatomy. She'd been furious they were leaving Demetria behind when she specifically charged them with protecting her. After she came around to the plan, she kept her distance, too angry to entertain them in her captain's quarters.

It would seem now that she was returning them to the princess, her mood had softened. At least toward Langford. Nor did she take issue with Lark and Gavriel. But Alistair... he still wasn't permitted in her quarters. Alistair had made Langford promise to slip one of her bottles of Anquan Red out with him, but he doubted he could sneak anything past her.

"We achieved that which we set out to do," Langford said cheerfully, taking a sip of his wine. "That counts for something."

She nodded absently. "What was the damage?"

Langford took a deep breath. "No servants were lost that I know of."

"*That you know of,*" she mocked with a sharp laugh.

"However, the captain of the guard aided our escape."

Ingemar stilled, pushing her hat up to reveal her lovely face. Her dark eyes narrowed, cool anger returning. "Ruslan?"

Langford nodded, the wine in his stomach threatening to turn on him. "He's dead."

"Shit." She slammed her dagger through the maps and into the wood, leaving it jutted from the top of her desk. "He didn't deserve that."

"You knew him well?" Langford eyed the upright dagger. At least she aimed for the desk instead of him. It was a good thing Alistair wasn't present. It appeared she was itching for something to stab.

"He was a good man. Saved many people with his help. He brought the princess to me because he knew I'd get her out. But he was a bleeding fool for staying behind. I told him as much." Ingemar reached into a drawer and pulled out a crystal decanter of dark liquid. "And now he's dead."

She didn't bother with a glass, drinking straight off the bottle.

Langford hadn't known they worked so closely with one another. If

Ruslan was smuggling slaves to freedom, he'd had a target on his back long before they arrived. He must have known the risk, not only to himself, but to the continuation of their operation.

"I'm tired," Ingemar said softly enough it could have been meant for her ears alone. "I'm tired of fighting the tide. The current is always stronger."

Langford set his chalice on the edge of her desk. "You have been invaluable to us, and your work is vital. You can't measure against the loss. But each life you save is a victory brighter than death."

She stared at him, searching for something he couldn't identify, until she snorted and took a deep drink from her private stash. "You possess a silver tongue, my friend."

"They aren't just words. My work might not align with yours at the moment, but if I am successful, if we are to stop this world from falling..." Langford stood, unable to sit a moment longer. "I trust you to ensure this is a world worth saving."

A brief flash of emotion crossed Ingemar's face, her eyes widening with alarm before she recovered. "That's a tall order, sweet talker. But you needn't fret. I won't stop sailing, not until the end of eternity." She gazed out at the sea through her large windows. The sun glinted off the surface of the calm waters. The streaming sunlight refracted through the crystal decanter, sending beams of colored light across the desk. Ingemar gently twisted the bottle, and the light danced. "If I can save a few souls on my journey, that's what I'll do."

She was downplaying her achievements again, but Langford held his tongue, sipping from his wine as the distracted captain watched the light in silence.

THEY ARRIVED at Emeraude Port and immediately set off to meet the others. In the weeks at sea, autumn had nearly passed into winter in Ardenas. Frost covered the ground each morning, and the sun seemed to retreat further in the sky. Langford shivered and blew into his hands.

They were nearly to the Walden Inn, and no one seemed eager to arrive.

Instead of excitement, a nervous energy filled the air, a frenetic tension like a rippling current. Lark fiddled with her cloak, constantly shifting and readjusting. Gavriel would reach out a hand to calm her, which worked for a moment or two before she'd start fidgeting again.

Thick clouds hovered over the sprawling hills as the bend in the road finally revealed the town of Oakbury in the distance. They plodded along, their breath ghosting in front of their faces in the cold air. Langford wrapped a bit of cloth around the bottom of his face when his nose started to sting, much to Alistair's amusement. He'd always laughed at Langford's intolerance for the cold, but this time his smile felt kind, adoring even. Langford smiled back behind the cloth. It was damp and warm against his mouth, but better than the bite of winter's impending arrival.

When, finally, they stood outside The Walden Inn, Lark stilled, leaning against the stone cladding. "So," she began, "how do we want to handle this?"

"Delicately," Langford said, his response muffled by the fabric. Impatiently, he tugged it off to let it hang around his neck. "There's no easy way to tell Demetria, but we can't lie to her." Only fools thought hiding the truth was protection. It wasn't. It was cowardice and delaying the inevitable.

Lark nodded. She reached into her pocket and pulled out the mirror, examining it with a somber expression. "I'll tell her, but I don't want to be cruel about it. I hardly think she'll find this mirror worth Ruslan's death, so it's best if we deal with this first and then, after she's calmed down, we can move forward with the plan." She tucked the mirror away.

"Right," Alistair said, rolling his eyes. "Let's coddle the child, *then* resume saving the world. Because priorities."

Langford winced.

Alistair wasn't wrong. But he didn't need to be an ass about it.

"That's not what I'm saying," Lark bit out through clenched teeth.

"No, of course not. When have you ever let personal sentiment come in the way of the bigger picture?"

Gavriel stepped between them, his jaw tight and expression dark. "That's more than enough, Alistair. I will not take lectures on *priorities* from the whoremonger and drunkard."

Langford's stomach sank.

Alistair snarled and stepped into Gavriel's space so the men were nose-to-nose. "You don't know a fucking thing about me."

Lark squeezed between them and forced them apart. "We've been stuck on a boat and traveling through the cold without enough gear. We're all on edge." She shot Langford a pleading glance.

He cleared his throat. "She's right. Let's get a hot meal and a strong drink in us, and then you two can go at it."

Gavriel laced his fingers through Lark's, glaring at Alistair as he tugged her away.

Alistair's chest heaved with each breath until Gavriel and Lark disappeared through the door and into the inn. He turned to face Langford, a pained look on his face.

"I'm sorry."

Langford gave him what he hoped was a convincing smile and shook his head. "There's nothing to apologize for."

Alistair didn't look convinced, but he let Langford pull him toward the door.

Before he could reach the handle, the door swung wide, nearly knocking into them. Kenna appeared with Lark and Gavriel in tow.

"There you are! Daciana said you'd arrive any day," she said with a bright smile. She shivered and yanked her red hood up. "Sargon's balls! It's freezing. No matter, she was insistent I bring you to her upon your arrival."

Daciana wasn't here? "What about Demetria?" Langford stumbled to keep pace with the hunter as she led them back into the forest. He cast one last longing look over his shoulder at the fire burning in the warm hearth before the door closed.

Kenna laughed. "She's with Dac. I couldn't tear her away, if you can believe that. Not even with the temptation of a hot bath."

For some reason, Daciana and Demetria were camped out in the forest, awaiting their arrival. Hope spread through Langford's chest. "Has she found a Life Wielder?"

"Not exactly…"

"Daciana would want you to tell us," Lark said. "She would never leave us in the dark."

Kenna scoffed. "I'm not leaving you in the dark. I'm leading you to her because she wanted to show you herself." She stopped, turning to find Lark's gaze. "It isn't mine to share. We'll leave it at that for now."

Lark opened her mouth, but quickly closed it, and gave her a hesitant nod.

Dead branches and frost-claimed leaves crunched underfoot. Langford resisted the urge to loop his cloth around his face again. The sky lost the sun in the early evening, slipping into night all too early. But a faint orange glow shifted through the trees. Fire.

Kenna glanced over her shoulder. "I only ask that you keep an open mind. You especially, Lark."

"Why me especially? Daciana knows she can trust me with anything, and I trust her judgment."

"Eh… better hold on to that mindset."

They broke through the clearing to find Daciana sharpening her many blades and Demetria kneeling before a tree. Lark dropped her pack and started running, only to stop short, paralyzed where she stood.

"Daciana," she began, a quaver in her voice.

Demetria stood, turning to face them, wringing her hands with an unreadable expression on her face.

Leaning against the tree sat a man dressed in warm furs and thick wool. His gleaming white hair shone in the firelight, and a single black horn curled from his head. On the opposite side, where once there was a matching horn, a jagged, round mass of black bone jutted out.

Langford's stomach sank, his intestines tightening in a knotted tangle. He recognized this man, only he was no mere man, but a demon. The demon who taunted them with news of Hugo's death.

When the demon's silvery eyes landed on Lark. He smiled, revealing sharp teeth. "Hello, meat sack."

CHAPTER FIFTY-TWO

DACIANA

*L*ark snarled, yanking Hugo's knife from a leather sheath at her side.

Daciana held out a hand, adopting slow, careful movements. "Lark, wait."

The rage on Lark's face was a palpable warning. She lunged—

Daciana leapt in her way, blocking her from cutting down the demon from where he sat. "All is not what it seems. He's weakened, and his blood almost smells human."

"All the more reason to kill him!" Lark tried to shove past, but she held her firm. Daciana recognized this drive, this need to spill blood without thinking. It was an impulse to protect the mind from examining anything too closely. But she needed Lark to see, to understand.

Finally, Lark's gaze found her face, and amid the rage, the blood-thirsty fury, there was hurt. "Dac," she said, shaking her head as if she already knew what she would say.

"Trust me." The words were ash in her mouth. "I'll tell you everything when I'm certain you won't attack."

A deep laugh slithered out behind them. "Look at you, meat sack. You'd sooner carve out my eyes than listen to reason."

Daciana growled. "Still your tongue, or I might slip and let her pass me."

He laughed again, unconcerned. Of course he wasn't afraid. He knew they couldn't kill him.

Yet.

Lark's nostrils flared, anger staining her cheeks. Even as she vibrated with rage, her voice wavered. "Why are you protecting him?"

The accusation hit its mark, and Daciana resisted the urge to wince. "I'm not protecting him."

This would seem the greatest betrayal to Lark. To allow the creature who killed Hugo to break bread with them and share camp. But if she could get her to understand how difficult this decision was, how she'd nearly killed him herself, perhaps she would stop looking at her like she'd just spat on Hugo's memory.

"Please," Daciana said, "trust me once more, as you always have."

Lark's eyes glimmered, and her brows drew together. She wiped the back of her hand across her nose, the hand clutching Hugo's dagger. She took a step back, retreating from Daciana and toward Gavriel, who seemed to draw her to him on instinct.

Daciana waited until everyone sat down. Langford and Alistair didn't openly glare, thank the skies, but poorly concealed anger permeated the camp. Everyone took their place across the fire while Demetria claimed the spot by Balan's side, a clear divide. Kenna hovered nearby with a hand on the hilt of her sword.

"I've been lying to you—to all of you." Daciana wet her lips, drawing strength from the bottom of her well. "When Inerys told us of how to make a Reaper Blade, how even if we attained dragonstone and found a blacksmith skilled enough to forge the ancient weapon, it still wouldn't bear the mark of a Life Wielder."

"Right," Alistair's smooth voice cut in, the first she'd heard of him. "We tackled what was in reach. Now we set our sights on the impossible." He wore a smirk that felt like an apology for not greeting her warmly. "We got the stones. Show her, Lark."

"I'd prefer to hear the rest of what she has to say." Lark was looking toward her, though failing to meet her eyes.

Langford held his hands over the fire, a calculating frown on his face. Gavriel kept his sights on Balan, adopting the stillness of an assassin waiting to spring.

This was going about as well as Daciana had predicted. "There's an incantation that needs to be spoken over the forge before the blade is formed. Words to make the fire hot enough to cleanse the dragonstone. Words Balan knows."

Lark's eyes flicked up to meet Daciana's. "And you believe this? He'd say anything to twist the world to his purpose. He's a snake."

"A snake I may be, but we share a common goal. Nereida's death." Balan sat up taller, abandoning his casual posture.

"Why should you want that?" Lark spat.

"Some of us like the mortal realm as it is. It's so much more fun to entice a soul into bargaining than it is to pick from the scraps. I only aimed to lessen the scope of her destruction so we might enjoy our indulgences still." A strange look of disgust crossed his face. "After she discovered my *treachery* she punished me greatly. Now, I desire old-fashioned petty revenge."

Lark scoffed, flipping the dagger in her hand. "All that proves is how your allegiance shifts with the wind."

"If my motives don't convince you, perhaps this will," Balan said. "I know someone hunts you. She has been watching you this entire journey. I gain nothing by sharing this with you. It proves nothing of my innocence apart from my willingness to help." He ran a hand through his hair, wincing when his fingers grazed his broken horn.

Lark tensed at his words, a strange ripple of fear crossing her features. Her arms crossed over her chest, and she locked her gaze on the ground. Demetria tried to hand her a sack containing bread and apples, as if this were nothing more than dinner conversation. It occurred to Daciana they hadn't even given them a chance to bathe and eat after their journey. They must be starving. But Lark shook her head, keeping Hugo's blade balanced across her knee.

"He knows the witch queen's plan," Kenna called out from where she leaned against a tree, her hand finally relaxing from the hilt of her sword. "He knows where she intends to drop the veil."

Lark's brow rose. "And he's divulged this?"

Balan sighed. "I will when I'm certain I won't get your knife in my back."

"You're worried about my honor?" A humorless laugh burst from Lark's chest as she focused on Daciana. "Nereida promised to give my soul to him, for him to torment for all of eternity. He's her pet."

"Actually, the bitch lied to me about that," Balan said, rage twisting his sharp features, "among other things. You wish to know why I'm helping. As I said, I wish to see her punished for her crimes. I can't begin to list the horrors she's caused. She's loyal to no one but herself, and I grow tired of her tyranny. I'll align myself with you if it means bringing her down."

"How noble. And what of your crimes?" Lark stood, balling her hands into fists. "He killed Hugo, or have you forgotten that as well?"

"I have forgotten nothing." Slowly, Daciana stood. "I have not forgotten all that we've lost, that the entire world hangs in the balance, that we face a foe we cannot hope to defeat." She lifted her chin. "Until now."

For a moment, only silence and the occasional crackle of the fire filled the air. Lark had stilled, holding Daciana's gaze with a ferocity she'd come to know and love. That bleeding heart she wore permanently stitched to her sleeve. That fearless abandon with which she approached all things as she sized up her opponent. Finally, her voice rang out, even and clear. "What's changed?"

Daciana exhaled, the tension gripping her chest. "We have a Life Wielder."

A WANING MOON, bright and lonely, lit up the night sky. Daciana and Lark huddled in the nearby field, watching the vapors of their breath. After finally sharing everything, *everything,* with the others, Daciana had hoped their reunion would smooth over. But Lark had said little. Langford had immediately jumped into theorizing and planning mode, excited at the prospect that they had found the final missing piece of the puzzle. Alistair was eager to return to the inn for food and rest, a desire all those who traveled seemed to share.

Except Lark.

Kenna and Demetria took watch over Balan. There weren't enough rooms at the inn, and they were more than happy to offer theirs to Alistair and Langford, while Gavriel snagged the last room for himself and Lark.

While everyone had their fill, Lark took distracted bites. She didn't appear angry, or saddened, or even hungry. More unfocused. After they finished dining, Lark finally asked to speak with Daciana in private.

And that was how they came to be sitting in a field in the middle of the night, shivering in silence.

"I'm sorry," Lark finally said.

Daciana wasn't expecting those to be the first words Lark breathed into the stillness of an uncertain night. She didn't dare respond, not yet.

Lark continued. "I'm sorry you were alone in this for so long. I'm sorry you felt you couldn't tell me."

"It wasn't that I couldn't tell you," Daciana interjected. "It's that I couldn't face this. Knowing what I've done, what I could still do. I knew if you asked me to use that power, I would. In a heartbeat, without thought. But I couldn't promise I wouldn't hurt anyone. I couldn't risk—" The words got lodged in her throat.

Slowly, Lark turned to face her. Her expression, achingly ragged. "But now you can? Because of *him*?"

Daciana cringed. "I nearly tortured the bastard to death before I realized he could be of use." Inerys' words had hit their mark, and guilt over withholding the truth of her power had festered. When Balan came along, claiming to know enough about forging a Reaper Blade to guide her, it was guilt that fueled her trust. And he promised to show her how to control the reach of her power. It still left a bitter taste in her mouth to trust the demon, but one thing he couldn't lie about was his humanity. "He's vulnerable, Lark. Nereida cast him out. He has no loyalty to her."

"Nor us," Lark said, turning back to face the inky black sky touching the tops of the trees across the way. "We don't know his motives, nor his allegiances, but we do know they aren't to us."

Daciana thumbed the hilt of her dagger. "If the world existed in such stark hues of certainty, decisions would be nothing but easy to make."

Lark huffed a soft laugh, gently pushing her affectionately. "Ever the philosopher."

Daciana couldn't help but grin. "Yes, and where did my idealistic Reaper go?" It seemed like ages ago, Lark was begging them all to trust the assassin determined to kill her. Seeking a way to redeem a lost soul she felt personally responsible for.

"Perhaps ideals are easy to have when you don't know any better." She leaned her head onto Daciana's shoulder, the easy affection settling the last shred of discomfort between them. "I feel the weight of my choices more and more with each passing day."

"What happened?"

They sat in silence for a moment or two before Lark answered. "A good man aided us in fleeing the castle after retrieving the mirror." She pulled away, hugging her knees to her chest. "Perhaps we could have escaped without his help. We didn't even try, we merely pulled him into our schemes. When I thought we still had no way to forge the weapon, not without a Life Wielder, his demise felt so… needless. But now that we do, does that justify his death?"

Daciana nodded. There was that gentle-hearted Reaper. "It's hard to measure the worth of a life. But his choices were his own, and we can't let that sacrifice be in vain."

Lark sighed, plucking the dead grass beside her. "I suppose you're right. Don't listen to me—I'm weary from traveling." She bit her lip. "I just thought my mortality would mean I'd fill my days with less death."

If anything, mortality guaranteed death. Daciana rubbed her arm for warmth. They'd need to head inside soon. But a few more moments wouldn't hurt. Who knew how many nights like this they had left? "What would you fill your days with if you had the choice?"

Lark hummed thoughtfully. "Pie. Rides through the forest with Apple. Oh! Gavriel naked!"

Daciana groaned. "I do not need that image right before I go to sleep."

"I haven't even explained what I'd do with him. He knows this trick with his tongue—"

"Lark!" Daciana shrieked, a laugh slipping from her lips. However impossible it seemed hours ago, there was a lightness in her chest she hadn't felt in ages. This was a far cry from the demure, blushing Lark the last time they spoke of Gavriel in this light.

"All right, what else? Oh, Langford's cooked apples!"

"Naturally."

Lark laughed, and suddenly it was as if they were on Ingemar's ship again. Drinking her reserves and laughing as if they hadn't a care in the world.

"Dac?" Lark's voice had sobered, a quiet sincerity stealing her tone. "Something Balan said… it troubles me." She shifted, running a hand through her hair. "He said someone has been watching our journey. Hunting us."

Daciana nodded, staring out over the dark field. "Nereida?"

"That's the thing," Lark said, wiping her hand on her trousers. "I've been having strange dreams. At first I thought they were nothing, merely a byproduct of my subconscious and my fear. But now… I can't shake this feeling it was a warning."

Daciana listened patiently. "What were the dreams?"

Lark's brow furrowed, the corners of her mouth turning down. An unfamiliar expression stole across her face. One suspiciously close to shame. "I've dreamt of Thanar coming to me. He's warned me of loss, and of repeating his mistakes, but the last time I dreamt of him he told me there's a betrayer in our midst."

Daciana prevented several responses from taking shape on her tongue. One seemed almost dismissive, another accusatory. She let her thoughts settle so she might respond with the least amount of damage. "You think Balan is the betrayer? Or do you think he speaks true of another?"

Lark shook her head, unusually somber. "I don't know."

Perhaps that was the scariest part of all. This helpless burden of the unknown.

Lark spoke again, quieter this time. "After we forge the blade… what do we do with Balan?"

Daciana eyed that lonely moon in the sky, shining down on them with harsh scrutiny. She was many things, and long ago, honorable might have been one of them. But there was scarcely room for honor in a world that demanded sacrifices like a gluttonous beast. "After we no longer need him," she began, "I'll kill him myself."

NIGHTS WERE LONGER, while days held a brief slash of warmth before returning to the chill of autumn's end. Traveling in their group almost felt like the old days. The days when Hugo would keep watch after dark. Back then, their biggest concern had been keeping to Daciana's moon cycles.

Since her change had passed, they could bring horses without scaring them. Lark was delighted at the prospect of bringing Apple, riding with Gavriel, and taking turns walking to give her precious horse a break. Alistair and Langford doubled up, and Kenna took charge of Balan, much to Demetria's dismay.

Daciana walked beside their horse, glancing up at Demetria. Ever since their run-in with the forest crone, her attachment to the demon had grown. Whether it sprung from pity or gratitude for how he stepped in to silence the crone's taunts, it left Daciana rattled.

"Do we really need to overshoot Felix's place?" Kenna called from where she walked beside her horse. Balan complained incessantly, resulting in his near constant turn riding. Kenna took it in stride, reins firmly planted in her hand. Probably because she didn't want the demon to have an easy getaway. "Do we need Amara to ask him? Or can we just save time?"

"Felix charged us with rescuing his daughter," Daciana said. "We failed him in that."

"Because she didn't need rescuing."

"Not the point." The man was unstable, but according to Amara, he was once the greatest blacksmith in Koval. If they were to approach him, asking for both his skill and discretion, it would do them well to bring his daughter for the trip. "I'd rather skip the part where he turns us away, and we have to collect her to earn his acquiescence."

"I could just threaten him," Kenna said with a shrug.

Daciana laughed and shook her head. They hadn't had the chance to continue their much-needed conversation, but it was a welcome comfort to slip into an easy truce. A truce of denial, which entailed ignoring the way her body responded to Kenna's voice, her scent, or the sight of her pink tongue wetting her lips—

Daciana cleared her throat and the unwanted images of Kenna from her mind. That trail of thought was not part of the truce.

"A willing partner is far more valuable than a prisoner under threat," Lark said.

"I don't know," Gavriel called out, gazing up at Lark with a private smile. "It worked on me."

Lark kicked at him, but Gavriel dodged in time, catching her boot and placing a kiss to the leather.

"I'm inclined to agree with Daciana," Alistair said from where he led the group. That was a refreshing change of pace. Normally, he argued with her on everything. "She is our capable, fearless, ravishing goddess—"

"Ugh, enough." Daciana scrunched her nose in discomfort. The sound of his laugh brought an unwilling smile to her face.

Yes, it was almost like old times.

DACIANA AND KENNA kicked the snow off their boots in the atrium of the massive castle. The shivers wracking their bodies had their teeth chattering, and the violent gales of the warding storm were muffled behind the heavy doors.

It was easier to leave the others behind. Once the branches overhead thickened, and the chilled air turned blistering cold, they sent them back a way to sit tight while they retrieved Amara.

Hopefully, the beast was in good humor this day. Overprotective wasn't strong enough of a word to describe his demeanor toward the girl.

Kenna grabbed the small brass candelabra by the door. But instead of the three flickering flames serving as the only source of light, candles lit the entire entryway, illuminating the deep crimson walls. Candlelight gilded a warm glow across gold-framed mirrors, portraits of untamed oceans and flower-spotted meadows.

"Looks like they spruced the place up," Kenna said with a shrug.

"Hello!" Daciana called out. "Amara!"

She listened intently, but no answer came. She and Kenna shared a glance and crept down the hall toward the dining room.

It wasn't fear that quieted Daciana's steps, but a discomfort in making herself comfortable in someone else's abode without their knowledge. Though some of that discomfort could have been the warding spell.

Distantly, soft notes floated down the hall. A gentle melody nearly lost to the spacious home. Wordlessly, they followed the sound, leading them to the closed doors of Amara's private library.

Under Daciana's gentle touch, the doors swung open to reveal Amara reclining on a chaise, nose in a book. A plum-colored velvet gown wrapped around her generous curves. One dainty finger played with an errant curl as her eyes greedily devoured the book she held. Seated at the piano, was... *the beast?* He'd combed and styled his mane into a low-sitting queue with a blue ribbon tied into a bow. He sported a fine jacket of white and blue, threads of gold glimmering against the fabric. When he caught sight of them, he stilled, chagrin stealing his expression.

"Daciana!" Amara closed her book and swept up to her, wrapping her arms around her in an affectionate embrace. She stepped back, a radiant smile lighting up her face and setting her dark skin glowing. "How good it is to see you! And Kenna!" She tucked her book into her chest, hugging it.

"Amara," Daciana began, "we really need—"

"Oh!" Amara's face lit up with excitement. "I have to share my findings! I couldn't find anything on the death of a divine deity, could you believe that? But I did find a great deal of speculation on the existence of a veil between planes of existence." She bustled over to the stack of books on the ornately carved end table, grabbing an aged and worn brown leather book. "This is the journal of Edwin Prewett. He claimed the existence of the veil is the only reason we can't see the dead all around us. He goes into great detail about life force energy, and that energy needing to go somewhere, and likely never being destroyed even after death." She flipped through the book, rousing a dust cloud and sneezing. "He says all energy needs a tether, and this veil must be tethered to something." She rushed back over, pointing to the passage she referenced. "Whatever, or whomever, the tether might be, that is how to protect the veil. That is how to keep it from falling."

Daciana carefully took the book from Amara, running her gaze down the handwritten page. It was an interesting theory, especially from what Lark shared regarding her life before humanity. She would file the information away for safekeeping. Maybe even ask to borrow the book for Langford to read over.

"Thank you," Daciana said, carefully closing the book and tucking it under her arm. "That's not actually why we came, but this is very helpful."

Amara's cheeks bloomed with chagrin. "Here I am, dreadfully out of practice using my manners. We don't get many visitors, do we, Aidan?"

"Fortunately, no." He huffed a gentle laugh. "But it is good to see friends."

Genteel manners and a proclamation of friendship? Last time, they were considered intruders. Daciana hoped the shock numbing her face didn't show in her expression. Kenna didn't seem to have the same concern.

She narrowed her eyes at him, scanning him from head to toe. "You're different."

The beast smiled shyly, such a strange sight, and Amara laughed into her hand. "Shall I brew us some tea? I'm sure you've had a long journey."

"We can't stay," Daciana said. "Actually, we were hoping you could come with us." She glanced over at the beast, who was frowning. "Only temporarily, but we need your help."

Amara tilted her head, brows drawing together in confusion. "Where do you wish me to go?"

Daciana inhaled a deep breath, suddenly realizing she held no certainty of Amara's answer.

"We need you to speak with your father."

CHAPTER FIFTY-THREE

LARK

The branches groaned overhead, spindly limbs clawing against a swath of dark-grey clouds. A harsh wind whipped through the forest, whistling its call. They stood waiting in the skeletal forest for Daciana and Kenna to return. Lark dismounted and bundled her cloak tighter. Reaching up, she ran a gentle hand down Apple's auburn mane. The hair was soft—a calming distraction Lark sorely needed.

Whatever it took to refrain from stabbing Balan.

Though she and Daciana had come to an accord, and it made perfect sense why they needed him alive... for now. But Lark couldn't shake the flare of anger that burned in her belly. Each time she remembered that the demon still drew air, a coil tightened in her stomach, threatening to spring loose.

Balan was their temporary ally... and Daciana was a Life Wielder. It was a lot to take in. Lark understood why Daciana hadn't told them sooner, as much as it stung. But Lark couldn't begrudge that decision, especially when she'd harbored her own secrets for as long as she could. She'd waited to tell Daciana about the dreams—when Thanar would warn her of things he had no business knowing.

And she still hadn't told Gavriel.

Whether it was a trick, a trap, or her mortal mind conjuring her fears and worries, she hadn't wanted to draw unwarranted attention to the phenomenon. Daciana would not betray her confidence, but keeping it from Gavriel was beginning to feel like a betrayal.

Lark chanced a glance in Gavriel's direction. He was chatting with Langford, a broad smile gracing his handsome face. Just the sight of it was enough to send a flutter of warmth through her. Almost enough to banish the ice in her veins, but the memory of her dreams, of Thanar and his poisonous words, refused to abate. Her subconscious still wrestled with the fear of his control, even after he'd become Nereida's pet.

He had no power over her any longer. His words were just that, words. He couldn't breathe life into them. She would not lose Gavriel simply because Thanar dictated it so.

Even reminding herself of this fell short of comfort.

"Reaper," Balan's grating voice called out, "I'm rather parched. Could I drink from your waterskin?"

Removing her hand from Apple's mane, Lark clenched her fist tight enough her nails bit into her palm. "I care nothing for your thirst."

"It would be inconvenient for me to perish before I can be of use to you."

Lark stalked toward him. "Your death would be useful enough. It would be the least you could do after everything you caused."

Balan's eyes narrowed into silver slits. "You wish me to atone for your friend's death? Fine. I apologize for his unfortunate end. But I didn't kill him, you know. I merely chose to leave without him. Can you claim you did any differently?"

Heat erupted in Lark's blood, and a steady pounding filled her ears. How dare he? *How dare he?* She yanked Hugo's dagger from its sheath. He would know pain by the time she was through. First she would cut out his tongue, and then she'd carve out as many pieces she could before she ended whatever life flowed through his veins.

Gavriel appeared in front of her, his eyes alight with anger. "He only means to goad you." He aimed his words over his shoulder. "A foolish endeavor from someone who wishes to live."

"It's working." She tried her best not to think of the pile of rocks they left outside that skies forsaken shrine. The stone wall that Hugo never emerged from. She'd fled the shrine, so sure that Hugo would grab Gavriel and follow. As soon as they'd crossed the threshold, the door sealed shut. The demon was right about one thing. She'd left him. Left Gavriel. Hugo died, sealed in that tomb, while she pounded against the stone.

Balan was merely exploiting her human penchant for guilt and self-blame in the face of loss.

And yet, the truth of his words burrowed deep in her gut, filling her with a queasy shame.

It would be so easy, so *satisfying* to kill him. It wouldn't change what happened in that shrine, and it wouldn't lessen the ache in her chest, but it would be easy.

Acid coated her tongue, and she swallowed it down. Taking a deep breath, she tried desperately to calm her racing heart.

"Lark, look at me." Gavriel's deep voice called her out of her thoughts. Her gaze snapped to his face, and those forest-green eyes with specks of gold appraised her in slow sweeps. "Let's take a walk."

Blade still shaking in her hand, she nodded. He led her down the path until the others were almost out of sight. Warm hands cupped her face, calluses against her jaw, drawing a shiver from her.

"Tell me your thoughts."

"He breathes. I wish to remedy that."

Gavriel huffed a laugh, pressing his lips to her forehead. "You are an excellent problem solver. But I wish to know your plan." He pulled back to watch her reaction. "If you kill him, then what? How do we forge the blade?" His voice wasn't cruel, but soft in its questioning.

Lark blew a stray lock of hair out of her face. "I don't know."

Gavriel nodded, remaining silent.

She took it as an invitation to continue. "The promises he's sold Daciana feel too convenient. It's a mistake to trust him and a mistake to keep him alive. He's going to betray us—I feel it in my gut." *There is a betrayer in your midst.* Thanar's warning formed in her mind. "Why would he help us? What does he stand to gain? It's too convenient for him to show up right when we need his knowledge, and trusting him is a mistake. Someone is going to get hurt, and whose fault will that be?"

Lark's words fell in rapid succession, and she could scarcely keep up. "We have the dragonstone, we have Daciana, and we're about to have the blacksmith. Why do we need him?"

Her breath grew ragged, and tears pricked her eyes. Gavriel's hands tightened on her shoulders, but she didn't give into the urge to throw herself against his chest. "And I still haven't told Demetria about Ruslan, and all I can think is, what if I'd never learned of Hugo's death and I never knew to mourn him? I've taken that away from her, and the longer I wait, the harder it becomes to give it back."

A carefully built wall had crumbled, and she couldn't halt her confession. "I've been having dreams of Thanar. He comes to me and tells me terrible things. I don't know if it's real, if his warnings are true, or if part of him has forever altered my mind, taunting me. He said I would lose you. You would slip through my fingers and there was nothing I could do. I didn't tell you because I didn't want you to worry or think the shadow he casts means something it doesn't. But now I fear his warnings were real and Balan will betray us. He will! And what will be the price of our trust?"

Her throat constricted on a sob, and Gavriel pulled her to him, threading his fingers through her hair as he held her close. "Oh, Lark." He breathed against the top of her head, a low rumble of a sound leaving his lips. "I'm sorry you couldn't share this with me. I know I haven't been... well, ever since Master Hamlin... I'm here now, and nothing could take me from your side. I understand why you didn't tell me sooner, but I hate that I made you feel you couldn't." His hand traced a gentle path through her hair and along her neck. "You've taken nothing from Demetria. It's no easy thing, bearing painful news, but it should not be yours alone to deliver. There is no good time to tell her, and as much as I hate to say it, we do have more pressing matters. No one can fault you for waiting."

Lark pressed her face against Gavriel's chest as the tears finally fell. The familiar scent of burning embers, leather, and dark chocolate surrounded her. The scent she knew as him, as home. What a fool she was to hide any of this from him.

"As for Balan" —his voice hardened— "nothing would please me more than watching you gut him. But you needn't worry about his movements. I've observed the others around him. Alistair won't let him anywhere near Langford, and Kenna keeps a close watch. No one trusts him as much as you think they do, so he'll never go unattended."

"Demetria trusts him. What's to stop her from untying him and letting him slaughter us all in our sleep?"

A low laugh rumbled in Gavriel's chest against Lark's ear. "The princess… I think her fascination has less to do with him and more to do with her own losses. I do not think her foolish, or at least, not so foolish to free a demon. But rest assured, one of us, Daciana or I, is always watching. I won't let him harm you or anyone you care about ever again."

His lips brushed against her hair. She tightened her grip on him, needing to hide in the safety of his warmth for a moment longer.

"But if he can offer an advantage to end this, put this ghost to rest and start a new life—" Gavriel pulled back, and Lark groaned her displeasure. He wiped the tears from her cheeks, and a soft smile tugged at the corner of his mouth. "I would grant him the air he breathes so I might finally be free with you."

Starting a life, one that didn't include racing across the land and living in constant fear, seemed the impossible dream. Having that life with Gavriel? It had been ages since she'd dared wish for such a human thing. "You're not sick of me yet?"

It was meant to disarm the discomfort of the heightened conversation. To dismiss her tears that tightened the skin on her cheeks and stained the front of his fighting leathers.

But Gavriel's brows drew together as he answered, "No. I will never tire of you. Of your smiles and your warmth. Of your fearless heart and the way you love things without measure or limitation. I'll never tire of you because I spent my entire life wishing for you. I may not have known your name or your face, but I spent my nights wishing for home."

Something deep in her chest finally settled. The last jagged shard of something unnamed, smoothed. Her mouth found his, parting his lips. She pressed her body against his hard enough, she nearly knocked them off balance, but Gavriel found his footing.

She backed him behind a large tree, gasping through breathless kisses as she fumbled with his leathers. She might not have the words to profess how she wished for him, too. How he changed everything with the depths of his fire, his loyalty and love for his friend, Emric, those many months ago. How his pain revealed the last piece of what she needed, what she was missing as a Reaper.

How he brought her to life.

She might not have the words as he stole the breath from her lungs with each deepening kiss, but she could show him.

If she could just get those blasted leathers off.

Just as she was starting to work the laces, Gavriel broke the kiss and stilled her eager hands. His chest rose and fell with each harsh inhale. His eyes burned into hers. "Why didn't we stay at the inn?"

Lark laughed, the fire that had just threatened to light her ablaze, settling to a quiet smolder. For now. "Poor planning."

"That it was." He kissed her again. "We should head back."

This moment was far too enjoyable to ruin with reality. But he was right. Daciana would be back soon, and they would be underway to see the blacksmith.

"Fine. But each time Balan opens his mouth and I'm feeling murderous..." Lark trailed off, hoping Gavriel caught on to her demand.

The corner of his mouth lifted in a crooked smirk. "I shall distract you in this manner."

She nodded, pleased with this plan.

LARK ARCHED HER ACHING BACK. It had been a long time since she'd ridden this much, and although she'd missed Apple, it reminded her of riding through The Wastes on a sand horse with Hazel. Their mission to rescue Gavriel now seemed like a lifetime ago. She glanced down at him, missing the familiar warmth of his chest when he rode behind her. Not just the warmth, the back support.

But they were nearly to their destination, and he'd given Apple frequent breaks to relieve the horse of their combined weight. It made little sense to complain now.

Whitebridge crested at the brow of the hill, bending the road to its shape. The sounds of civilization, of business, of laughter, of life, gradually carried over the wind as they drew near the center square. Amara stiffened atop Daciana's horse, a line of tension snapping her posture upright and silencing her previous conversation with Langford—a conversation that included philosophical debates and quoting names and books Lark had never heard of. But Langford seemed delighted, if the way his eyes lit up and the speed of his hand gestures were any indication.

But as they crossed into town, the change in Amara was near palpable, and even Langford seemed to eye her quizzically. She'd tucked her raven black hair into a neat chignon at the nape of her elegant neck, dark eyes trained on the horizon as if nothing could distract her from her purpose.

Lark's gaze fell to the girl's hands where they tightened on the reins.

Villagers seemed to freeze as they passed, all eyes on Amara who dutifully ignored them. A small boy covered in sawdust came running out in front of their group, his father chasing after him. He plucked him out of their path, holding him to his chest as if guarding against great danger. Amara didn't spare him a glance as she loped past.

Lark slid down, offering a comforting pat to Apple's head and handing Gavriel the reins and smiled at the boy and his father. The boy answered with a gap-toothed grin and the father gave a terse nod.

"What a charming village," Alistair said, before halting Langford's mount to allow him to dismount.

Kenna laughed, abruptly yanking Balan off his mount. He tugged his hood tighter over his head as he glared at her with no real malice behind it. Almost as if they were friends.

Lark swallowed the sharp anger that rose in her throat at the thought.

They brought their horses to the hitching post outside the local inn. Daciana and Gavriel entered the establishment to work things out with the innkeeper and pay for lodging for the night. Amara stayed behind with Lark, helping to tie the horses in silence.

Lark glanced across the square. Demetria, Kenna, and Balan stood before a noticeboard, reading over parchments and ads. Beneath the dark hood hiding his horns, Balan's lips moved. Lark couldn't make out his words. But Demetria gave a startled laugh before recovering and yanking her own hood tighter over her face. It was unlikely that anyone would recognize the princess here, but her paranoia made sense. Especially after Lark witnessed just how ruthless her brother was.

Alistair and Langford wandered over to a cart filled with books. Lark laughed as Langford handed him book after book until the stack reached the bottom of his chin. Alistair gazed at him with a soft smile that made Lark's throat tight and filled her chest with warmth.

"Not very practical," Amara's smooth voice called out beside her. She also watched them with an unreadable expression. "Books make for heavy packs. I would have brought a volume or two were that not so."

"Or ten, in Langford's case. Though if you had a personal book carrier, you might have changed your mind." Lark didn't bother telling her that Langford would probably read as many as he could while they remained in town, and before they left, barter them with someone else for more useful items, Alistair aiding in the trade so they'd always make out with more. Instead, she watched as Alistair allowed him this impractical custom.

Amara laughed. "True enough." Her smile grew wistful, and her gaze fell distant. "No one seems to mind his hunger for learning."

Lark knew Langford well enough to assume there would be scholarly pursuits amongst his stack, but he read for pleasure as well. "It's better this way. Without books to occupy him, we might get an earful we haven't bargained for when he baffles us with theoretical debates."

Amara smiled, though it dimmed as soon as it dawned. "It's strange being back here. Different, smaller, yet completely unchanged."

Lark couldn't imagine how peculiar it must be. If she ever ventured back to the Otherworld, how unbearably small would her former home feel? Just the thought was enough to make her skin itch as if the walls were closing in.

Daciana and Gavriel emerged from the inn. Gavriel wore an eager grin as he strode up to Lark. Pulling her close to him, and pressing his mouth against her ear, he murmured, "Guess who charmed his way into getting the most private room?"

Lark shivered, laughing at the way his breath tickled. "Aren't all the rooms private?"

"Ours has its own entrance. Formerly the innkeeper's room, but they've expanded enough to sleep off site."

Warmth bloomed in her belly, but she quickly smothered it as the weight of the mirror in her pocket reminded her of why they came.

"So long as we have walls and a door, I'm utilizing this privacy you're so pleased with procuring. Make sure you're ready for tonight," Lark said.

Gavriel's smile turned wicked. Reluctantly, he let Lark disentangle herself. The others had all gathered outside the inn. Alistair tucked the stack of Langford's books beneath his chin, and Kenna kept a hand on Balan's shoulder. Demetria hid beneath her shroud.

They weren't all going to see the blacksmith. A decision Lark and Daciana had come to when they spoke that night in the field.

Daciana nodded to Lark as if reading her thoughts. "Alistair, Demetria, and Gavriel will stay here."

"What?" The volumes of leather and parchment muffled Alistair's indignation.

"Absolutely not," Gavriel said, giving Lark a cutting glare.

"We can't leave her undefended." Lark gestured to Demetria. "And the rest of us are apparently vital." This, she aimed at Balan who, for once, didn't spoil the air with his voice.

Gavriel frowned, and Alistair tried to glare over Langford's books.

"This is more of an errand than anything else," Lark said with what she hoped was a reassuring smile. There was no need for all of them to go traipsing through the blacksmith's home. And truthfully, Lark couldn't stand the idea of Demetria witnessing Balan's death. Not when she seemed so fond of the bastard.

Not when she still hadn't told her of Ruslan.

As soon as the blade was forged, and he shared all he knew, his use would run out. Daciana would kill him or she would. It was inevitable.

The demon in question cleared his throat. "It would be wise if all parties involved attended the forging." His voice was rough, deep, and gravelly, but it lacked his usual brand of arrogance.

Still, Lark glared at him. "You suggest this merely to disagree with me?"

His silver eyes found her gaze, a challenge written in them. "No. You're so quick to distrust me." Balan stepped closer, and even though they were in public, Lark noted in her periphery the way Gavriel's hand found the hilt of his sword. "I do not wish to explain the nature of the spell in the middle of a town that smells like horse, but we need as many bodies as we can get within a close vicinity of where Daciana will work."

Work. Not conjure. Not summon. It was a simple thing to assign an innocuous word to the task that lay before them. But that he would think to offer that simple comfort to Daciana was... unexpected.

At his words, Daciana stiffened. Lark broke his stare to find her face, searching for the certainty they'd come to when they formed to the plan to dispatch him after forging the blade. But all she found was indecision.

"Dac," Lark said.

Daciana shook her head, a pained expression on her face. "I'm sorry, Lark. He's right."

Lark bit the inside of her cheek. It would seem Balan's counsel held more sway with Daciana than hers. Didn't Gavriel mention distracting her whenever she felt murderous toward the demon? But the way her stomach rolled with the truth that Daciana trusted Balan's judgment over hers, Gavriel's distraction was the last thing on her mind.

"Fine." Lark pushed her way past, uncaring that she didn't know where to find the blacksmith. All she knew was she needed to get away from Daciana's guilty stare.

INSTEAD OF A SMITHY in the square, the blacksmith's little cottage was set apart from the rest of the town. Amara knocked on his door, faded flowers and chipped paint adorning its face. The man who greeted them had vacant eyes and frizzed hair, as if he'd been struck by lightning and the charge lived permanently in his head. When his gaze focused on Amara, his eyes widened before the tears rolled down his cheeks.

"It's you," he breathed.

"Hello, Papa," she murmured.

He yanked her into his arms, tucking her shoulder beneath his chin, and stroking her hair. "My darling girl. You're finally free."

Daciana and Kenna exchanged a knowing glance, one Lark didn't understand.

Amara pulled away and gestured behind her. "These are my friends."

Felix startled. "Dear me, I didn't realize you brought so many guests." He stepped aside, patting down his pockets as if he'd lost something important. "Please, come in. I can put on tea."

"Not a social call, Felix!" Kenna called out with a broad grin. Daciana gave her a chiding look before they all filed into the home that was likely too small to house so many.

Lark stepped through the low doorway and froze.

Suspended from the ceilings and adorning every surface were sculptures of glass and metal. Butterflies, an intricately crafted dragon, and some unidentifiable shapes but still beautiful. A gentle chime of tinkling glass filled the air, as the northern wind snuck through the open door.

"Did you make these?" Lark couldn't hide the wonder in her voice.

"Oh, those?" Felix waved his hand dismissively. "Just a hobby."

These did not look like the work of a hobbyist. They were crafted with care, with intention. The way the glass complimented the woven metal like entwining ribbons was a song personified.

Gavriel prodded a hummingbird hanging from the ceiling with the tip of his finger, grinning when it swung and refracted the light. There was something about witnessing his awestruck expression, delight and appreciation mingling on his obscenely handsome face and tugging on each scar, that made Lark's heart give a lurch.

Balan's voice dragged Lark from her revelry. "We should make haste."

Daciana nodded and gave Amara a pointed look.

Smoothing her fine velvet gown, Amara cleared her throat. "Papa, we need your help."

"Anything," he called as he fiddled with the iron kettle, pumping water from a basin.

"We need you to reopen the forge."

He stilled, staring at the water pouring from the spout but failing to catch it in his kettle. "Why do you ask this of me?" He turned to regard them—each of them—his eyes traveling from one face to the next with a wary expression.

"Your daughter claims you were once one of the foremost sought-after blacksmiths in Koval."

Felix rubbed his jaw, the harsh scratch of bristles against dry skin filling the air. "That was a long time ago."

Lark pulled the mirror from her pocket and placed it on the table. "Can you forge a blade using these stones?" She pointed to the handle.

He scoffed. "That's barely enough to make a knife. I don't even know what mineral that is. I'll make us some tea, and we'll forget this nonsense."

"That's dragonstone," Lark said. Felix's eyes widened, and he stared at the mirror with newfound interest. "We need someone with the skills to forge a blade from these stones."

"Please, Papa."

Hesitantly, he lifted the mirror from the table, running a finger over the handle and each stone.

Demetria seemed to take a step forward, whether to snatch the mirror from his hand or to ask him to treat it with care. But she did neither of those things. Instead, she gripped the back of the chair, and Balan placed a hand on her shoulder. Lark had the sudden and intense urge to yank Hugo's dagger free and bury it in the demon's hand. Soon enough, he'd no longer be her problem. Or he'd betray them all.

"I meant it when I said this isn't enough to forge a true weapon." Felix's gaze fell to Lark's face. "What do you need this for?"

"To kill something unkillable."

If this shocked the aging smithy, he didn't show it. He narrowed his eyes at the mirror, as if working through a puzzle.

"I have the schematics here." Langford laid a bit of parchment on the table, nodding once to Demetria. She must have helped him sketch it from his books.

"I don't know anything about that unkillable nonsense." Felix snatched it up, running his gaze over the parchment before humming. "But as I said," he looked up at them over the page, "this isn't enough for a blade." He sighed, frowning at the mirror. "What if… will it work if this isn't the only mineral within the blade's edge?"

Lark cast a puzzled look to Daciana, who lifted her chin to Langford in silent question.

Langford's face screwed up in confusion, before understanding dawned in his widening eyes. He laughed. "You mean to weave the metals?"

Felix smirked and shrugged. "It's worth a shot." He eyed the mirror once more before tucking it into the pocket of his apron and rolling up the schematics. "All right, girl," he said to Amara as he started toward the door, "let's fire up the forge."

CHAPTER FIFTY-FOUR

LANGFORD

angford blinked the stinging sweat from his eyes and debated the necessity of his tunic. Felix's forge was scorching enough to melt the propriety right off him. That, and the heat of ten bodies crammed in a small hut.

Felix had quickly led them to what appeared to be a garden shed. Once they'd all squeezed in, he set to work uncovering his forge, workspace, and anvil. It was a sight to behold. A low table ran along the wall, a small set of blades and an iron chain atop its surface. Anchored to the wall was a shelf littered with twisted and bent metal. One piece caught Langford's eye in particular. A single rose in a dull coppery color with sharp edges, rested across the shelf. Ribbons of bronze formed each delicate petal, and even the stem was shaped with tiny thorns he was sure could draw blood.

The forge blazed with burning coals. Amara blew the hair from her face and continued bellowing the fire.

Felix extracted the stones from the handle, passing the mirror to Demetria's eager grasp.

He'd placed an iron ingot into the forge and all the raw pieces of dragonstone into a crucible. Before he could shove the crucible into the forge, Balan held up a hand.

"This is where she comes in." He nodded to Daciana. "Otherwise, you'll never get the flames hot enough."

Felix gave a soft hum and waved for her to get on with it.

Daciana stepped toward where Amara was dutifully pumping the bellows. She cast one last look at Lark before squaring her shoulders and facing Balan. "What now?"

"Let your mind stretch—reach. Whatever you do, do not fight the flow of power. When you feel each tug, push it out as far as you can. Understand? Do not hold it in."

Daciana nodded, uncertainty etched along the crease in her brow.

"Your power will respond to your intention," Balan continued. "Do not fear or reject it. Now, repeat the words:

Ignis aeternus

Per sanguinem

Per vitam

Per mortem

Ignis aeternus

Ignus aeternus."

Daciana arched a brow before letting her eyes slip closed.

"*Ignus aeternus.*"

Amara let out a small gasp.

"Focus, Daciana." Balan's voice was low and steady.

"*Per sanguinem.*"

Langford coughed, a sharp bitter taste filling his mouth. Beside him, Demetria stumbled, but she grabbed a hold of his cloak for support.

"*Per vitam.*"

Lark let out a cough, covering her mouth with her fist. Red bloomed between her fingers. Blood. Balan whipped his head to regard her, before calling to Daciana, "You feel it, don't you? Low in your belly? Push it away, push it as far away from you as you can. Don't hold on to it, Daciana. Speak the words, but let the fire go."

Daciana cracked an eye, but Balan shouted once more, "Quickly now!"

"*Per mortem.*"

Pressure built in Langford's head. His gaze found that rose on the shelf, both delicate and sharp in its casting, and utterly out of place here. He covered his ears, his pulse pounding against his hands. When he pulled them away, his palms were wet with blood. Alistair's hand found his, and he gently squeezed.

"Ignus aeternus."

Kenna let out a grunt, knees buckling. Gavriel caught her before she hit the ground. Sweat poured down Langford's face, his back, his neck. Like the very skin was melting off his body. His head spun, and he clung to Alistair's hand to remain upright.

"Ignus aeternus."

A harsh breeze blew through the space, tousling Langford's hair and evaporating the sweat from his slicked body. The forge blazed, blasting the space with a bright orange light. Felix didn't waste a moment and shoved the crucible into the flames.

Demetria slumped to the ground, and Balan rushed over to lift her into his arms. He studied her face with a wariness that didn't belong with his features. "She needs air," he said. "We don't need to be in here for this part." And without another word, he carried her through the door and out into the daylight.

Kenna groaned and gestured to the door. Daciana nodded, and Kenna took off after them.

Amara had dropped the bellows. When she bent to pick it up, she whimpered.

"Fire's more than hot enough. Go get some air while I finish up." Felix pointed to the door with his hammer before using his tongs to pull the ingot and crucible from the forge with practiced efficiency.

Lark and Gavriel whispered to each other, too quiet for Langford to hear, but Gavriel placed a gentle kiss to her head before disappearing out the door.

For a moment, all was quiet, save for the crackling fire in the forge. Felix brought his softened ingot to the anvil and poured the molten dragonstone atop it. Raising his hammer, he struck with deft and precision. Each *clang* of the hammer served to punctuate the unanswered question.

"Is everyone all right?" Daciana's voice was hoarse.

"Yes, we're all fine." Lark's automatic response carried all the force of a whisper. A reassurance.

Alistair squeezed his hand again, and Langford squeezed back.

Silence fell once more, as Felix's blows came quicker, hammering the metal into a shape vaguely resembling a short sword.

"Shaping and treating the metal takes time," he said. "You can go join the others while I work."

No one answered. They all stood in his workroom in silence. Listening to steady blows against iron and dragonstone as he shaped its edges and forged their only advantage against a god.

Minutes or hours dragged at a pace stretched out by the infernal heat. But at last, he quenched the blade for a final time in the brine before holding it close to his face for inspection. He hummed, a pleased sound, before laying it atop his workstation.

"I'll craft the hilt tomorrow. I need food and rest." He eyed Daciana warily. "So do you all. You need a place to sleep?"

"Only some of us. Most of us paid for rooms at the inn."

He nodded and mopped the back of his neck and brow with a rag. "All right, then. Off you go. We'll pick this up in the morning."

Langford stepped out of the cramped, overheated shed and cool night air blasted him in the face. He shivered, and his sweat-soaked clothes hardened against the cold. Up ahead, Lark pulled Daciana into an embrace, whispering something in her ear. Daciana nodded before pulling away and disappearing into the cottage.

Things would be better by morning. They all needed to shake the last remnants of a taxing day from their exhausted shoulders. Langford stretched, willing life into his aching muscles.

As if on cue, gentle fingers found the nape of his neck, and Alistair's shameless grin swung into view. The man was incapable of keeping his hands to himself.

Not that Langford was complaining.

"So… what say we order dinner at the tavern and have them bring it up to the room?"

"Do they do that?"

"Fine, let's order food and I'll carry it up to the room. Same effect."

Langford laughed. "As you command."

MORNING CAME EARLY, streaming through the window. Langford blinked, eyes bleary. He moved to sit up, but Alistair's body held him firm to the bed, his arm and leg thrown over Langford's hips and chest. The man seemed keen to sleep with as much skin-touching-skin as humanly possible, not that Langford minded in the least. He'd kept his stack of books on the bedside table, reading a third of a dissertation on the Avalonion Pantheon, and when that became too dry for his tired mind, he'd switched to a romance about a pirate and the wench who stole his heart. It was silly, really. But there was something transcendent about losing himself in the safety of a story. The way a captivating tale could spin his emotions as if those characters and their trials were real. It was a true testament to the mind's limitless capacity for imagination.

And a far more inviting distraction than the worries they currently faced.

Langford stretched as much as his range of motion beneath Alistair's inferno of a body could allow and rubbed the sleep from his eyes.

A low grumble vibrated against his neck.

"It's early." Alistair's voice, roughened by sleep, was the greatest sound Langford had ever heard. If he could bottle that sound and carry it with him, he would. He'd have to settle for waking each morning with the aggressive cuddler.

"We have much to do." Langford sighed as Alistair pressed lazy kisses to his jaw.

They needed to retrieve the Reaper Blade from Felix and see Amara back to the castle. There would be no way of knowing if the blade worked unless they used it on a being of the Otherworld or Netherworld.

Understanding dawned on Langford, rushing through his limbs and jolting him into hyperawareness.

"Do you think Dac and Lark intend to try the blade on the demon?" Would that even prove anything? From what Langford observed, his speedy healing rate had been suspended. The bruising and cuts he bore on the night they met him appeared weeks old, only just fading. If memory served, his healing should have been immediate. Not to mention the broken horn, his partaking of food and drink. He'd even disappeared for privacy, well, as much privacy as Kenna allowed to relieve his bladder and bowels. If he had mortal mechanisms of the body, was he even still a demon?

Alistair leaned up, his dark hair a tumbled mess. "I haven't the faintest idea."

"Well, if they are, I'd recommend a larger sample. I doubt he can give us certainty in his current state." Should they perform a summoning? He'd read of such a practice in his research on the veil. If they bound the demon before summoning, it would be far safer should the blade fail. But the whole process was archaic, and scholars couldn't agree on the safety measures needed to ensure the summoner was protected. One text cited a ritualistic sacrifice to protect the summoner, painting sigils in their blood. Another claimed it was unnecessary, and the use of blood was an ancient practice steeped in misguided tradition.

In either case, it was foolish to confront Nereida without testing the mettle of this new weapon. But he couldn't justify performing a summoning without more research.

Langford ran a hand into his hair, yanking against the roots as his thoughts spun in never ceasing circles. It was one thing to honor the warriors of Avalon and paragons of virtue. But this entire mission challenged some long-held beliefs he wasn't ready to examine.

Alistair's hand slid up his bare stomach, leaving gooseflesh in its wake. Teeth grazed his ear, and Langford's nerves fired.

"You give too much of yourself to everyone else." Alistair's baritone voice filled his ear. "Allow me to command your attention until you leave this bed."

Langford shivered. "I'm leaving this bed right now, and so are you."

Alistair's low chuckle sent warmth through his limbs. "Care to make a wager?" His hand snaked lower, and Langford cursed the needy noise that escaped his lips in response. Alistair swallowed the sound, the roughness of his unshaven jaw scraping against Langford's cheek.

They never agreed on the terms of the wager, and even though Langford didn't make it out of their room for another hour, it still felt like he won.

CHAPTER FIFTY-FIVE

DACIANA

"You're up early."

At Amara's gentle voice, Daciana lifted her head. The girl wore a thick robe over her nightdress, her black curls loose over her shoulders. She padded into the kitchen, shivering as she set to work filling the kettle. Her knees were dusted with soot. When she caught Daciana staring, she let out an embarrassed laugh.

"It took me a few tries to get the hearth burning. I guess I've grown spoiled living with Aidan."

Daciana smiled, though it felt strange on her face. Like stretching new muscles. "Does he do most of the housework?"

Amara hummed, dripping water onto the floor beside her bare feet. "Not exactly. It's more like… the castle anticipates his needs. His mood affects the state of things. It's remarkable." She slipped out of the kitchen, into the sitting room, and placed the kettle on the crane. Holding her hands out, she warmed them by the hearth.

Daciana crept into the sitting room, careful not to wake the others. Kenna had stayed up almost all night. For once, she didn't fill the silence with idle chit-chat. She seemed content to share the space with nothing more than her presence while Demetria slumbered. It was a quiet night, spent breathing the same air yet offering no words of comfort or confession. It wasn't until the sky lightened with the impending morning that Kenna finally fell asleep.

Realizing she had yet to respond, Daciana asked, "How does it work?"

Amara shrugged. "I still don't understand it fully. But whatever he wants… whatever he feels he *deserves* is provided. When I first began my research, the house was crawling with spiders and covered in dust. But now… it's truly a home."

The library, the new furnishings, and decorative touches. Was she saying they resulted from magic? "Is that part of the curse?"

Amara nodded. "I believe so. It's hard for him. He carries such a significant burden—so much guilt."

"What has he done?"

Amara pursed her lips, as if choosing her words with care. "He doesn't remember why, or how. Only that this is his punishment. He can't venture off the grounds—he's trapped. Trapped in the body of a beast in a ceaseless winter. If you hurt long enough, you begin to think you deserve the pain."

Daciana's stomach burned, and her throat tightened. She shoved the feeling away before she could dwell on it. "Are you any closer to a solution?"

"I'm not sure. I don't have any clear answers, but" —a small smile played on her mouth— "each day he's less the beast and more the man. Perhaps it wouldn't feel like such a curse if his form wasn't a prison."

"You think his curse is more of a state of mind?" It was a lovely thought, this idea of control. Daciana sorely missed the feeling of control over her own life—over her own mind. Memories of the previous day, by Felix's forge, stole her thoughts. She'd felt every heartbeat in that room and tasted something in the words she spoke.

Something forbidden.

Something sweet.

Death. Or Life. Who could be certain anymore? But the overwhelming chaos of a power she couldn't control was a terrifying thing. She couldn't choose where she pulled from. Or who she pulled from.

She'd done her part, drawn from the well she swore she'd never draw from. Now it was time to cleave herself from this power, or forever be a risk to those around her.

Amara sighed, pulling Daciana back to the crackling hearth. "The mind can be an impenetrable cage. If you're trapped up here" —she tapped against her temple— "you'll never know freedom."

The kettle whistled, ending the conversation.

HOURS PASSED. Morning bled into late afternoon. The day was spent in a veiled unease. Kenna took Demetria to the market for a distraction. The others had stopped by, but Felix shooed them off, citing his need for quiet and concentration to finish the hilt before nightfall. Alistair dragged Langford off with a determined stride, nearly bringing a smile to Daciana's face. They deserved all the time in the world. Lark was hesitant to leave, but Gavriel enticed her with a day of training and practicing. Lark used to combat nervous energy by training with Hugo. From the gleam in her eyes, Lark must have remembered that fact.

Amara spent her time cleaning and puttering around the house. The wayward daughter trying to bridge the divide between her father's wishes and her own. As if a little dusting and sweeping might fix what would break when she left again.

Daciana remained seated at the kitchen table, while Balan prowled the rooms like a cat waiting for someone to open the door. It was midday before he finally ceased his movements, claiming the bench seat by the picture window.

He spoke first. "You did well yesterday."

She didn't flinch, but her heart kicked up its pace. "What would have happened if I did poorly?"

Balan studied her with an unreadable expression. His silver eyes were thorough, though passionless. "You would have killed one of them. Maybe more."

Daciana clenched her fists as he spoke her fears aloud. For some reason, she knew he spoke true. Perhaps it was easiest to believe the worst thoughts she could conjure. Like hearing them aloud gave her a sense of validation.

"Why are you helping us, really? I know what you said about Nereida and wanting to see her punished. But that can't be the only reason."

Balan exhaled a weighty sigh, his expression unreadable. "Do you know how demons came to be?"

With a frown, Daciana searched her memory for tales of demon origins.

"My breed is called *renatus*." He leaned his forehead against the window pane, the jagged shape of his broken horn scratching the glass. "It means I was once human. I was weak, and foolish. I paid the price for someone else's mistake." He blew against the glass, fogging its surface. "Knowing I was trapped, I made the best of it. I became strong. I became more than I had ever been." With a swipe of his hand, he wiped the glass clear once more. "I've done more than you could possibly fathom in all the lifetimes I've been in the Netherworld, and Nereida thinks she's going to dump me back in my weakest form?" A snarl formed against his mouth. "You might question my reasons, but know this: I am a vengeful entity, and once I set my sights on the object of my ire, I do not yield. Nereida will fall, if it's the last thing I do."

Daciana studied the demon carefully. He wasn't exactly expressing regret, but it was the closest someone like him might ever come. She could press him for more, but she wouldn't. Not yet. She doubted there was anything he could say to truly convince her of his reasons. But there was another matter of concern she needed to raise.

"Your fascination with Demetria—"

"The princess," he sneered, but the expression rang hollow. Forced.

"What is your intention with her? I've watched you carefully. The way you are with her… you are not like that with the others."

He shrugged, the movement oddly human. "Can you blame me? She's the only one who doesn't wish to slit my throat in my sleep. I did nothing to stop your companion's death, sure. But it seems ironic the least of my offenses would warrant such vitriol."

Shaking her head, Daciana fought to temper the sudden rise of heat in her cheeks at the callousness of his words. "There's more you're not telling me. Why do you fawn over her?" If he thought to worm his way into a position of power while he was trapped in human weaknesses—

"She reminds me of someone. Someone I'd almost forgotten." His brows drew together and his expression darkened. "Satisfied with my answer?"

Daciana eyed him cautiously. It was easy to spin lies out of truth. But one thing she couldn't deny was the accuracy of Demetria being the only one without a personal stake in his demise. Maybe she even reminded him of his humanity. And he was helping them. They couldn't have crafted the blade without the words. It was enough for now.

"Why do you have so much knowledge about something that isn't supposed to exist anymore?"

Balan let out a harsh chuckle, cold and brittle. "My memory surpasses your human libraries."

"That didn't answer my question."

He turned his eyes on her, a dangerous glint in his glare. "I've lived long enough for the privilege of not having to explain myself."

Daciana met him with unyielding focus. He might not want to share his past, and perhaps that was his right, but he possessed knowledge of a power she wielded. A power she still didn't fully understand. "Why didn't I kill anyone yesterday?"

His shoulders relaxed, and the grim set of his jaw eased its tension. "You pulled evenly. It was why I wanted everyone in the room. Without enough life to draw from, you would have brought death."

"Is that my power? Death?"

Balan tilted his head, considering. His remaining horn glinted in the sunlight. "Your power is balance."

"Can I master it?" She didn't wish to know the answer, but still she asked.

He turned to face the window. Amara had painstakingly scrubbed the filmy grime from its surface, giving them a clear view of the broken bird bath. "No one can master balance without failure. The scales always tip, and they always right themselves."

It was the answer she already knew, but hearing it was like daring the sky to storm. A foolish challenge, and a plea for punishment.

They didn't speak after that.

WHEN THE SUN hovered above the horizon, the front door flew open.

"It's done!" Felix emerged, sweat shining against his dark forehead. His grin almost made him appear youthful, a buoyant energy to his step. He held a long thin shape of a sword, wrapped in cloth. He struggled under the weight of it, groaning as he thrust it onto the kitchen table. "I've finished."

Daciana joined him where he stood, admiring his handiwork. Even in the dwindling light of the day's end, its beauty and craftsmanship shone.

At the end of the hilt was a simple round pommel, a firm leather grip for its handle. The blade was a river of black bleeding into steel. The design almost danced like fire. This weapon was the answer to their problems, the key to all that was locked away. Their chance at defeating Nereida.

"What do I owe you?"

Felix beamed, a proud artist, as he quickly tucked it into its leather sheath. "Your satisfaction is my payment." He leaned closer. "Consider it an incentive to speed up my last request."

There it was. He still wanted them to slay the beast. Daciana shook her head. "I'm afraid it isn't possible."

His face soured. "I would have my daughter back."

"She isn't gone. If you could only see that, you'd already have her."

Felix ran a hand down his face. A wary expression aging him again before her very eyes. "You don't understand, and how could you? You are but young and naïve to the way years slip by. She wastes her life in that castle, shackled to a beast who would let her rot away so he wasn't lonely." He shook his head. "She's meant for more than that."

Before Daciana could respond, he gave one more pat to the weapon he crafted, the sword they all bled for, and shuffled out of the room.

Daciana sighed, reaching to lift it from the table. Her muscles strained with the effort as she strapped it onto her belt. It was heavier than it looked. Already, she could feel the leather sagging with the weight. Amara's soft footsteps carried through the house, and Balan still sat by the window with a far-off look on his sharp face. The others were at the inn, waiting. They didn't have to say it, but it was clear they desired a wide berth. Distance from the one who could pull from their blood like ripping petals from a flower. Perhaps after all this she could lock this power away, never letting it surface. But a sinking feeling in her gut told her there would be no going back.

"You've been quieter than usual." Kenna kept her voice low, her words for Daciana alone.

Daciana ignored the passing comment, aiming her sights up ahead. Lark had strapped the Reaper Blade to her back, and occasionally her hand would tentatively reach for the hilt.

When Daciana had met them at the inn, and passed the weapon to Lark, it was like a weight lifted. Until she saw Lark's face darken at Balan's presence. A stark tension tightened in her shoulders, and she hadn't relaxed since.

They needed to speak. Perhaps after Amara was home safe, she could explain why she couldn't bring herself to kill him. They still needed the location of where Nereida would destroy the veil, and he claimed to know where. Lark would argue he couldn't be trusted, but it was more than that. There was anger—there always would be—he lived while Hugo was dead, a fact Daciana could never truly forgive. But there was something in the way he carried himself. A sort of defeated look of a man with nothing left to lose. He wasn't even human, but he wore his weariness like a person who'd seen too many winters.

Daciana was a monster, but this small mercy gave her hope. For what? Redemption? It seemed an idyllic notion, but whatever the reason, she trusted the demon enough not to cut him down. She couldn't be certain it wasn't a terrible mistake. While she'd once trusted her instincts so implicitly, now she was utterly lost in doubt.

Lark would never forgive her. Perhaps she didn't deserve it, anyway.

Kenna stepped in her way, halting her path. Anger tightened her pale face, sharpening her jaw, and forming a line with her perfect mouth. "Say something."

What could she say? She needed to know nothing had changed? That no one feared her? That she could live her life without worrying she'd kill someone with the power she didn't understand? Daciana wanted to scream, to weep, to press Kenna against a tree and lose herself in her soft skin. There were too many thoughts fighting for dominance in the cluttered tangle of her mind. Something was twisting like a sharp blade in her belly, and it was too much. All of it was too much.

Daciana inhaled deeply, exhaling with purpose. The knife in her gut softened. She would not break. Not today.

"I'm just tired." It was a weak response, but enough to reserve this conversation for a later time. "I slept little."

Kenna narrowed her dark eyes, unconvinced, but let it go. As Daciana passed, Kenna's soft touch ghosted against her cheek. It was a simple touch, but a promise. She was here.

After all this was over, would Kenna return to her solitary life as a hunter? Or would she stay with their crew? When they defeated Nereida, could they return to the simple life of collecting jobs and coin, sleeping under stars and trees? Perhaps it was madness, but Daciana was tired. Tired of fighting, of pretending, of hiding. She wanted something all her own, for once.

Up ahead, Amara chatted with Langford, both atop their mounts.

She couldn't catch what they said, but Langford's smile bore all the eagerness of topics he loved discussing. Alistair led Langford's horse by the reins, debating swordplay study with Gavriel. Their conversation wasn't so quiet.

"No, no. You're all wrong. Mouvin's method is far superior to Godwin's."

"You're mad!" Gavriel shook his head. "Mouvin's is all style. Godwin's is adaptive."

"I think the word you mean is boring."

It seemed as if things could go back to normal. They could work through all that had happened without losing the effortless camaraderie.

Lark's hand flashed again, touching the hilt of the Reaper Blade. Either reminding herself it was still there, or what she planned to do with it.

Perhaps normal was too lofty a goal.

Balan stilled, the sound of his steps faltering. His eyes flashed, and his head tilted as if sensing the air. Demetria froze by his side, watching his face with a crease between her brows.

"What is it?" she asked.

"Something's wrong."

Daciana felt it. The path should have been overladen with ice and frost by now. The beginning edges of the wards unsettling her stomach and whispering along her blood. Instead, there was only silence.

Daciana met Lark's gaze. Her eyes widened. She felt it, too. The gaping void. Lark darted a glance in Amara's direction.

It was all the confirmation Amara needed to kick her horse into a gallop, rushing headlong to the beast's castle.

Lark leapt onto Apple, reaching out to Daciana.

Daciana gripped her arm, swinging in behind her as they raced to catch Amara.

The snow had melted away, leaving dead grass and earth behind. The castle gates hung open, bent and distorted, as if something had fought its way in.

Not out.

They reached the courtyard, sliding from their mounts and onto hard, dry ground. If the snow had thawed, the earth would be soft. But it was firm and unforgiving, almost like ice, when Daciana sprinted to the front doors. They hung ajar, forgotten by Amara in her haste.

Lark yanked the Reaper Blade from her back. Dragonstone and steel bleeding together to form a sword that whirled in the light.

The first thing that hit Daciana was the smell. Like death and rot. She had smelled nothing like it since she stumbled upon a sulfuric marsh.

A sharp, keening wail froze her blood to ice. She ran toward the sound, Lark on her heels. Through the atrium down the hall… to the library.

The doors had been ripped from their hinges, hanging askew. She stepped through. A river of blood greeted her. Too much blood. In the center of the room, on the chaise Amara loved to read on, was the body of a man. Amara clutched him to her chest, smearing blood all over her dress and face. Another bone chilling cry strangled from her throat.

Daciana slowly approached.

Amara's face was matted with tears and blood. Her lips smeared with it. A sob broke free from her bloody lips before she pressed them against the lips of the unfamiliar corpse.

Daciana knelt down, trusting Lark to keep her wits should whoever did this return. She carefully examined the man in Amara's arms. His pale skin was white as the moon, mouth parted and dripping with blood. His red hair was tied at the nape of his neck, messy and loose from the struggle. A deep angry gut wound marred his white and blue jacket with the gold detailing.

Realization sank in her gut like stone. "Is this…?"

"Aidan," Amara cried, hugging his lifeless body to her chest. "Who would do this?"

The painting behind the piano sharpened into view. The visage of the austere man with red hair and a frown on his pale face.

Amara kissed him again, like the children's stories that boasted of true love conquering all. She kissed his lifeless, bloody lips with a violence that must have made her teeth ache.

But no magic answered her plea.

The curse had been lifted, and he was free from his earthly prison.

He was gone.

CHAPTER FIFTY-SIX

LARK

The weight of the Reaper Blade in her hand was a strange phenomenon. It felt light as air, like at any minute it might float away. How it would stand against Nereida, Lark wasn't sure, but she gripped it tighter, surveying the giant library for any hidden threats. All was quiet, save for the sounds of Amara's anguish. As a Reaper, Lark had witnessed thousands of deaths. Guided thousands of souls. She'd observed the pain of grief, and the way sorrow clutches at those left behind. But she hadn't understood the way mortals mourned, not until she'd found her heart once more. Now Amara's staggering sobs speared through Lark's chest as her eyes burned with the potent grief.

Daciana placed a gentle hand on Amara's shoulder.

Lark's gaze fell to the bookcases lining the walls. A gauzy curtain caught the breeze from an open window, billowing against the countless tomes and volumes. She shivered, raising the featherlight weapon higher.

"Is that the special sword?"

Lark jumped at the familiar voice, swinging around to face its owner.

Hazel crept out of the shadows, wearing her fighting leathers. Dark circles filled the space beneath her striking blue eyes. Her hands flexed —blood coated her fingers.

Something slippery coiled in Lark's gut as Thanar's warning echoed in her mind. *There is a betrayer in your midst.*

"Hazel, what did you do?"

Amara still clung to Aidan's lifeless body.

Hazel's brows drew together before her expression smoothed into cold neutrality. "What I had to." She eyed Daciana, who had unsheathed her sword.

A sickening flutter churned Lark's stomach, and the warmth was snatched from her blood. She forced herself to speak, "I'm afraid I'll need more of an explanation."

For once, Hazel's gaze lacked its icy challenge. Her eyes dipped to the floor, her dark brows drawing together before she glanced at the body Amara was cradling. When her stare once more found Lark, brittle anger had returned. "There's a lot of old magic here. Of all your stops, this was most fortuitous. It was easier to draw from so I wouldn't bleed myself out."

Silent tears trailed down Amara's face, and Daciana angled her stance to block her.

They hadn't seen any signs of Hazel since she'd disappeared in Emeraude Port without so much as a parting word. She wouldn't have even known where they were.

Unless she had been tracking them.

The guards... the attacker from the shadows as they fled the castle...

Realization struck Lark, the ground falling away from where she stood. If she'd followed them, watched them... "What do you know of the Reaper Blade?"

Hazel smirked, but it was more a curve of her mouth than an actual smile. "I know enough. I just needed to make sure you focused on your goal. Killing the witch queen of the Netherworld, right?"

Lark had never spoken of their plans. She never told her of the blade, of anything having to do with her world.

Gavriel burst through the doorway, short sword and dagger in his hands. Upon taking in the scene, his expression twisted in confusion and then sharp anger. "Hazel? What are you doing here?"

Hazel's stare never strayed from Lark's face. She never even turned to Gavriel when he spoke. "I need you to know," she began, "I never wanted it to be this way."

Hazel had appeared and disappeared many times. She'd always been there right when Lark needed her, asking nothing in return—it was almost too good to be true. And Lark had been too blind to recognize it for what it was.

An act. A trap.

As if she'd learned nothing from that contract she'd signed with Nereida.

Hazel strode forward, and Lark raised her sword to keep her at bay. "I was a desperate kid when I made a deal. I didn't know what I was doing. All I knew was I needed to get us out of there. My brother and I... we didn't have any other choice."

"You made a deal with a demon," Balan drawled as he crept into the room with a predatory grace. "That was foolish of you."

Alistair and Langford appeared, followed closely by Kenna and Demetria. Kenna brandished her short sword, her murderous glare aimed at Hazel. When her gaze fell to Amara, her throat bobbed.

"I had no choice." Hazel's jaw tightened. "You know nothing of what we faced. What we suffered. So I made sacrifices I didn't understand, and Gregoir paid the price. When I saw a chance to forge a new deal, one with better terms... what would you have done?" she spat the words like an accusation.

Balan snarled. "You're weak. Anyone who sells someone else to avoid paying their debt deserves the deepest pit of the Netherworld."

Hazel shook her head, focusing on Lark. "It's done. I've done my part. And now Gregoir will be free." She nodded, as if convincing herself. "He'll be free."

Where was Gregoir? Was he held in the bowels of the Netherworld, waiting for his sister's rescue? The memory of Gavriel stolen away to Nereida's domain flooded her mind. Lark would have sacrificed everything, given all she possessed.

But never would she have bled that sacrifice from someone else's skin.

Hazel had lied and betrayed them. Amara and Aidan had paid the price.

Hazel continued. "I kept you on your path. My contract holder came to me and told me to make sure you continued your work in finding a way to kill the witch queen. To help you save Gavriel so you'd follow your thread. And again in Koval… I had to make sure you'd have a way out once you got the dragonstone." She cast a glance at Demetria. "I'm sorry about your mentor. That wasn't part of the plan."

Demetria froze. "What do you mean? What is she saying?"

Lark winced as her stomach dropped. Shit. Demetria didn't need to find out like this. The memory of Ruslan, an arrow jutting from his eye as he slumped forward, filled Lark's mind. She'd needed more time to explain. To break the news gently.

"They didn't tell you?" Hazel almost looked regretful, but it didn't halt the next words from spilling from her treacherous tongue. "Ruslan was one of your trusted allies left in Koval, yes? He died helping them escape with your mirror."

Pressing a fist against her stomach, Demetria shook her head. "No… they would have told me."

Lark's vision spotted as the heavy weight of regret filled her over-crowded chest. This was all her fault. She should have told her sooner. She should have told her as soon as they got back. "Demetria, I'm so sorry."

The princess staggered, turning to flee the library. Balan caught her before she could slip through the doorway, shaking his head with an unnervingly human expression of pity.

Hazel continued as if she hadn't just launched a tempest grenade into the room. "She didn't come to me for a time… until she said you were going to craft a weapon strong enough to kill an Other-worldly being. Said to wait here for you, and make sure we weren't alone. It's been a long time since such a weapon was forged, and she couldn't risk it failing." Her brow furrowed as she regarded the dead man in Amara's arms. "Finding him was an unexpected advantage."

"You killed him!" Amara cried, her voice catching on a sob. "You butchered him!"

With a sigh, Hazel spread her hands out in a defeated posture. "I had to. Blood of the cursed for protection" —she marched over to the throw rug, yanking it back to reveal a series of symbols and runes painted in red— "and summoning."

"Gods above," Langford murmured, "you actually performed a summoning."

Lark recognized those symbols. Once, what felt like lifetimes ago, she'd scribed the same symbols on the floor of her chambers, falling into the Netherworld to meet the witch queen. "You summoned Nereida?"

"She summoned her dogs." Balan let out a growl.

Thanar's warning. He told her of this betrayal. He didn't say whom, but sure as the steel vibrating in Lark's hand, he had come to her and promised the sting of treachery.

"If you think to take the Reaper Blade," Lark said dangerously, "you'll find yourself at the wrong end of my sword. It won't work for you, anyway. You can't command any of its power." It would only work for a passenger soul, as Inerys said. Someone whose soul had crossed multiple planes. That left Lark and possibly Balan as the only ones capable of wielding it.

"I don't want it, nor do I need it." Hazel lifted her chin. "I needed only to ensure you created it. And now, I am done." Her voice softened on a note of finality.

Hazel had always seemed to appear and disappear out of thin air. She always seemed to know when Lark needed her most. In the forest, when she searched for Gavriel. In the arena, right before the assured fatal blow, the guards in Koval when they fled the castle—

Hazel had been playing them all along. Edging them closer to her master's plan. If she'd only told her of her deal, they could have worked together to free her and Gregoir. Lark would have helped, would have found a way.

Lark's anger became a living thing, a turbulent storm in her chest. Her skin burned, blood boiling beneath the surface, as the thrumming in her ears grew deafening. She could never trust Hazel, never again, and losing the friendship was like a visceral wound. There was nothing left to say besides, "Who commands you? Are you bound by silence?"

Hazel shook her head. "I can speak of her, but I can't say her name. My contract forbids it. Just know, whatever you think Nereida is capable of… whatever you fear the witch queen might do" —her face paled— "you haven't seen true destruction yet. She is a ripple compared to the maelstrom that's coming."

"What does she want?" Why did she seek answers from an unreliable source? Was it merely to stay her hand for another moment before the inevitable fight?

It ached somewhere deep to admit it. She would cut Hazel down for this.

Hazel laughed, a harsh, humorless sound. "Fuck if I know." She fixed her gaze on Lark, her forehead creasing as if in pain. "For what it's worth, I am sorry."

Maybe she meant it. Maybe she truly believed there was no other path to take.

Lark blinked away any hesitation. It was time to end this. "So am I."

Crash!

The shattering of every glass window erupted in the space, sending Lark to the floor. Books tumbled from the walls, pages scattering along a violent wind. Sharp bursts of pain bit into her hands and knees. She pushed herself to stand on unsteady legs.

Five unfamiliar figures stood at the edge of the room. Horns curled from their heads in varying shape and positioning.

Somewhere beneath the debris, Langford let out a cough.

Once again, Hazel was nowhere to be found.

She'd summoned these demons and fled like a coward.

Lark yanked a piece of glass out of her palm, hand trembling as she ripped a strip off her tunic and wrapped it as quickly as she could. They only had one weapon to kill a demon and five demons to slay.

Tightening her grip on the Reaper Blade, she took a steadying breath, and lunged before the fear could set in.

Her blade swung wide, shimmers of black and steel slicing through the air and through the chest of the nearest demon, the one with low-pointing horns and black hair. His face was unremarkable, save for the shock that splashed across his features, which immediately dimmed. His head slumped before his body crumpled to the floor. Black blood oozed across the rug, like spilled ink.

For a moment, nobody moved. Nobody even breathed.

And then chaos erupted.

Kenna leapt over the chaise, aiming her silver blades at the demon with round gold horns curling on either side of his head parting his long white hair.

Langford started throwing books as Alistair dueled a demon with long golden hair and four small spikes jutting from her forehead. One of the heavy books knocked into the back of her head, sending her careening to the floor. She hissed, surging toward Langford.

Positioning himself in front of Demetria, Balan yanked the sword from her leather belt.

Gavriel ripped one of his daggers free, leaping over a pile of debris and charging toward the opposite side of the room. He began scrawling a sigil on the floor, one Lark faintly recalled from Kenna's bestiary. Skies above, was he drawing a binding ward?

With a spin of her haladies, Daciana sank the blade into the throat of a demon with greyish skin and giant horns. But as soon as she pulled her blade free, his flesh rejoined.

None of it mattered. Not without the Reaper Blade.

Lark swung her sword in a circle, the way she'd seen Daciana prepare for a fight. And then she lunged for the massive demon. She struck without mercy, cutting through bone and sinew. A sickening squelch, and more black blood painted the room. The floor. Her skin. Its rank scent nearly gagged her. But she couldn't dwell on it, not when three still stood and she wielded the only weapon that could kill them.

Lark took off and aimed for Kenna's snowy-haired demon. His gilded horns glimmered as he began to turn at Lark's approach. She sank her blade deep in its back before twisting. The demon slumped to the ground, only two more remained. Lark fought for breath and her muscles screamed.

But she couldn't afford to rest. Not yet.

A howl ripped from Langford's throat as the golden-haired demon raked her claws down his face. Alistair's roar of fury followed, and Lark sprinted, tripping over stacks of books and parchments. She landed at the demon's feet, slicing anything she could reach. A calf, a thigh, before she sat up and swiped her blade across its gut. More blood. More putrid, black ichor coated her hands, her face. Snarls of rage filled her ears, and it was too much, all too much. Too much death. Too much anger.

"Lark! The blade!" Balan's voice called out, and she whipped her head in search of Gavriel. He'd been successful in his binding, even grinning as the last demon, his long black horns carving their path through long raven hair, entered the circle. As soon as he crossed, he realized his mistake, he roared in anger—

But Gavriel was trapped, too.

He had little space to move, slashing and slicing with his short sword and dagger, but the demon bore his blades as if they were nothing, and blocked him from escape.

She'd never make it in time. She had the only skies-forsaken weapon, and she was across the room. If Gavriel fell—if she couldn't save him—

She did the only thing she could think of.

She threw the blade to Balan.

Balan caught it, and with a flick of his wrist, he opened the throat of the final demon.

It slumped to the floor, quietly bleeding out while Gavriel exhaled ragged breaths.

Staggering relief flooded Lark's body in a violent rush. Only after her body sagged with the solace that Gavriel was all right did Lark realize how risky her decision was. Balan could have chosen to let him die. He could have taken the blade and fled. But in the span of a heartbeat, she was sure he would help him. It was strange, the way the body committed to a decision before the mind had time to doubt. How fortunate she hadn't had the chance to think.

Lark limped over to Gavriel, throwing her arms around his neck and kissing his filthy face. "That was," she said between kisses, "incredibly stupid."

Gavriel grunted his offense. "It took me longer than I'm proud of to remember all the symbols."

Lark laughed, pressing her face against the sweaty crook of his neck, allowing her heart to slow its rapid pace. Broken glass, ruined books, and tattered pages covered the floor. The breeze from the shattered windows disturbed the parchments, and they fluttered gently in the wake of the library's destruction. Alistair tended Langford's cheek with a rag, whispering to him. Demetria leaned against a bookcase, short sword in one hand and the other gripping the wooden shelf. Her eyebrow was torn, a glistening trickle of blood seeping down the side of her face.

Lark glanced over her shoulder where Balan stood, white hair a mess and Reaper Blade loose in his grasp. "Thank you," she whispered.

"Be thankful these were mongrels. I don't think we'd have had nearly as much luck with a high demon."

Across the room, Kenna laughed, sheathing her daggers. She and Daciana seemed drawn to one another's side, though their gazes remained fixed anywhere else.

"Do you count yourself among the highest?"

Balan sniffed. "Once, yes. Now I'm afraid I'm little better than a meat sack." He smirked at Lark.

"No," Lark said, "too soon."

"The next time your pet is trapped between death and a hard place, don't expect me to help."

Before Lark could respond, the door blasted open, breaking off the hinges completely. A powerful force shot through her, straight through her blood, and bones, and marrow. The mortal sense of preservation she'd come to know responded in kind, hairs on the back of her neck standing on end as instinctive fear took hold.

A man with two short horns, blacker than a raven's wing and jutting out from his bald head, strode into the room. His gait was smooth, unhurried, and a broad grin stretched across his face.

He glanced around, taking in the scene. "This is quite the mess." His voice was smooth and deep.

This wasn't a demon who once bore mortality—a soul who chose to inflict punishment rather than face it. No, he was something else, something far older. Every instinct in Lark's mortal body bellowed this truth.

Lark fell into a defensive stance, angling herself toward Balan so she might retrieve her weapon quickly. She hoped to use the Reaper Blade on Nereida. Perhaps this being was good practice. She held out her hand, but Balan ignored her silent instruction, and edged toward him, Reaper Blade raised.

"Valac," he said through gritted teeth.

The demon called Valac angled his head, amusement spreading over his sharp features. "Do I know you?" He swatted the air as if batting a fly, and a pulse sent Balan careening back against the bookcases, too far for her to snatch up the sword. He slumped to the floor and didn't move.

Valac clapped his hands, and another pulse of energy shot through the space. Lark landed on her back, groaning against the pain and stabbing against her ribs. As if tugged by an invisible tether, she was yanked upright, and pulled toward the demon. She tried to hold on to Gavriel's hand, but another violent tug and her hand slipped free. She dropped to her stomach, vaguely registering a series of sharp splinters piercing her belly. He curled his hand into her hair. The first yank brought tears to her eyes as he dragged her toward the door.

She fought, kicking and yanking Hugo's knife free of her boot, but the powerful demon dragged her without difficulty.

A kick to her gut and she gasped, choking as the air was ripped from her lungs.

"Don't fucking touch her!" Gavriel's voice rang out, but the ringing in her ears muffled the sound.

"How endearing," Valac said. "But I think it best all of you *stay down.*" His voice rippled in a menacing growl over the last words, and the unmistakable pressure of his influence fell over the room.

Lark curled on her side, blinking through blurred vision. Just out of reach, lay the Reaper Blade. She crawled toward it, pain lancing every movement. A firm boot pushed between her shoulder blades, pressing her into the floor and making her undoubtedly broken rib scream. A strangled cry of pain burst from between her bloodied lips, and distantly she heard Gavriel shouting her name.

Lark flipped onto her back, her hazy vision finding the face of the demon. His smile stretched too wide, and inky black devoured the whites of his eyes.

He sat on her ribs, and the pain was a sharp burst as her vision spotted. "Do you have any idea what you've started?"

She couldn't breathe. Darkness threatened to steal her awareness, and the pounding in her head intensified.

"I wonder where you'll go without a Reaper to guide you. Will you twist into something new? Once the veil falls, there is no governing the souls in the pits, no telling what monsters might find their way to the light. Is it a kindness to kill you now?"

The edges of Lark's vision blackened, blurring the demon taunting her.

"She'll be disappointed by your loss," he continued, his black eyes depthless and merciless. "But in the end, does someone so insignificant really matter?"

Lark scratched at his chest, trying and failing to find purchase. He gripped her wrists and slammed them to the floor.

Someone was shouting. Her name? A warning? It mattered little without the breath in her lungs to answer back. Valac's face started to fade.

A choking sound rattled above, and blessed relief filled Lark's lungs. The weight lifted, and air filled her aching chest. She blinked, staring up at her tormentor.

But Valac was gone, and standing above her was a new face. It shifted into focus, long blonde hair and large green eyes staring down at her. A face she hadn't seen as a mortal, but one she'd never forget, as it had set her on the path leading her to this moment. A face that represented everything she'd ever wanted—joy, love, pain, sorrow, hope.

Aislinn.

She extended a hand, and Lark weakly took it, allowing her to pull her to sit up.

"I told you I'd send you a sign, didn't I?" Aislinn's voice was soft and musical, as it had been the day she guided her soul to the afterlife.

Was Lark dead? Had she died and ventured to where Aislinn's soul rested?

Lark's gaze found the Reaper Blade in Aislinn's grasp. Fresh black blood dripped from its edge. At their feet, the bald demon lay motionless, throat gaping open.

She wasn't dead. But how could Aislinn be here? And how could she wield the Reaper Blade?

"Lark?"

A voice she hadn't thought she'd hear again rang out in its perfect clarity. The voice that used to serve as her only comfort in the Otherworld. The voice belonging to her oldest friend.

Lark turned to find Ferryn, his long blond hair bound at the nape of his neck and his turquoise eyes shining with unshed tears. His angular face crumpled, and he surged forward, lifting her up from the ground and crushing her against his chest.

She wheezed, a burst of pain searing her ribs, but she hugged him back, breathing him in. He was here. He was here. She blinked away tears as she buried her face against his tunic.

"I told you the next time I held you, I'd be able to feel it."

Lark's sob broke into a laugh, and the tears finally rolled down her cheeks.

CHAPTER FIFTY-SEVEN

FERRYN

he sun was bright, blinding, even. Ferryn had felt the phantom warmth of the sun against his skin, but never had it burned his eyes. He squinted, tugging Aislinn the rest of the way out of the hut.

They'd actually escaped Lacuna. He almost couldn't believe it. Any moment he'd wake up and realize this was all a dream.

But Reapers didn't dream.

A man tipped his wide-brimmed hat at them. "Good morning."

Aislinn squeezed Ferryn's hand tighter, and he gasped at the sensation. "He saw us. He actually saw us."

As a Reaper, Ferryn shouldn't have appeared to anyone. Not without him willing it. What was happening? Had something dimmed his power? Perhaps passing through Lacuna had altered his abilities.

A sharp stabbing pain in his stomach flared, as if answering the unasked question.

Aislinn wrapped her arm around her waist, letting out a soft groan. "I'm starving," she said and then laughed. "Starving, Ferryn! I haven't felt hunger since…"

Since her mortal life. So this sharp pain in his gut was hunger? The weakness in his limbs and the fogginess of his head? It was wildly inconvenient. They had nothing to barter with. How would they find food?

Aislinn tugged his hand. "Come, I'll find us something."

She ended up trading an afternoon of helping wash dishes at the tavern for a meal for the two of them. Ferryn wasn't eager to help scrub plates clean, but the heavenly aromas of mortal food wafted from the dining area. His stomach growled.

Finally, at the day's end, he had his first meal prepared by human hands. A thick stew of unfamiliar meat, carrots, and potatoes. He licked his bowl clean, savoring the hearty taste. Even if he burned his mouth and bit his tongue a few times. Aislinn offered him an apple, and he took a bite. It was all right, but nothing compared to the warmth of the steaming bowl of meat and vegetables.

Hunger wasn't the only thing Ferryn experienced. The heat of the sun burned and blistered his skin. The cool nights left him shivering and huddling against Aislinn for warmth. It had been a week of these newfound sensations—once only half-felt but now fully experienced. In the Otherworld, everything felt dimmer. His memory would fill in the gaps, but it was always just shy of genuine pleasure. Physical touch and taste and smell were muffled. And then in Lacuna... nothing.

If that's how Lark felt as a Reaper, he couldn't fault her for desiring another life. But he still wished they could go back to the way things were. When he could prod at Ceto, delighting in the way their animosity translated to the best fuck of his existence. When he could spend his days with his best friend in comfort and luxury.

From here, he couldn't do much of anything.

The first night, when Aislinn had awoken with a gasp, he'd known something was wrong.

"I saw Lark," she'd whispered between sharp breaths. "I spoke to her."

Ferryn nodded. His dreams had been strange, too. He had to be careful how close he rested to Aislinn, especially when dreams of Ceto plagued him. His mortal body was very responsive. Especially when he dreamt of unbuckling her endless armor...

"I know where she is." Aislinn stood, packing her bedroll as if they were about to go traipsing through the night.

"What do you mean?" Ferryn rubbed his eyes, cursing his newfound need for sleep.

"I can't explain it... but I was with her. We were in some sort of throne room, and she was frightened. She couldn't hear me, but it was her, and I was there." Her green eyes had burned brightly against the darkness in the abandoned barn they'd crashed in. "I know it was real."

That had been the first time Aislinn's soul traveled while she slept. But it wouldn't be the last.

FERRYN PULLED BACK and ran his thumbs against Lark's cheek, wiping away her tears. "I've missed you, little bird."

A stormy face appeared over her shoulder. His expression murderous and his scarred mouth tightening.

"Ah, you must be Gavriel!" Ferryn shoved Lark out of the way. "Let me get a look at you. I paid little attention when I was tethered to Emric."

Gavriel's face softened into understanding, his eyes widening. "You're Ferryn."

He sketched a bow. "The one and only. And you are exactly what I remembered from observing you and Lark. Hmm... well, done. I'm glad I gave your mark to her."

Leysa was right. Lark and this mortal were a matched pair. Leysa had come to him before he'd even won the mark in that card game, spouting off about fate and destiny, while Ferryn's eyes glazed over at how dull and tedious the conversation was. But when she mentioned Lark's longing, and the way the mortal's thread of fate glimmered when she was near, it made everything so clear.

Her counsel had been invaluable.

Aislinn placed the small sword in Lark's hand, a sheepish smile stealing across her mouth. "I believe this is yours."

With a stunned nod, Lark accepted the blade, eying her with incredulity. "How… how are you here?"

"It's a long story. But the short of it is, I dreamt of you. I found your dreams, and I felt a pull toward you."

"Like a tether," Lark said softly.

"Somniavi," a voice croaked. A beautiful woman huddled over a broken body, dark ringlets hanging around her shoulders. She stared with unseeing eyes. Nearly catatonic. "The one who walks the planes while they slumber." She blinked, and a hint of lucidity broke through. "I read about it, once."

Aislinn frowned but said nothing.

Ferryn felt a phantom tug within the room. He scanned Lark's companions. Two men huddled close, a hand gently stroking the other's hair. A young girl helping a man with white hair to his feet… not a man! Another demon. "You missed one."

Lark glanced over her shoulder. "No. He's not… don't worry about him." Something in her expression made Ferryn think she was sore about his survival. But no matter.

Ferryn's gaze landed on a girl wearing the familiar red cloak. Her black hair hung in her face, but her penetrating gaze shot through him like a bolt of lightning.

He stepped toward her, disbelief hollowing his stomach. "Don't I know you?"

CHAPTER FIFTY-EIGHT

LANGFORD

The destruction of this once-glorious library was a sin in itself. Langford resisted the urge to wince at the blood staining the pages of abused books. There was far more ruin contained in the walls of this room, but it was safer to focus on the books.

Or it was, until Lark's friend suddenly took an interest in Kenna.

Langford snapped up his gaze just in time to witness the hunter's reaction. The little color on her face paled, and she approached the blond man, Ferryn, as if she crept up on a sleeping giant.

"It's you..."

Ferryn laughed and clapped his hands with a solid *crack*. "This is splendid! Here, I thought your soul was lost for eternity!" He turned to Lark, waving her over. "Look! Remember that soul I lost?"

"You've lost a lot of souls..."

"I know, but this one was different. She didn't refuse to go, she disappeared mid trek! Absolutely astounding." He frowned. "But I saw your death... I waited until your soul cleaved from your body before I guided you." He stepped closer, angling his head with curiosity. "How did you make it back?"

Langford watched as Kenna darted a weighty expression in Daciana's direction.

Daciana sighed, running a hand over her face and smearing black blood along her temple. "It was me... I called her back."

Ferryn blinked. "You... called her soul back into her body?" He turned to Lark with a bewildered expression. "How do you collect the most fascinating people? My word, you're like the flame all the special little moths flock to."

Lark's nose crinkled. "I don't like that analogy."

Their banter settled into background noise as Langford turned the new information over in his head. Examining with precision. Daciana physically pulled Kenna's soul from her journey to the afterlife and stitched it back into her body. That sounded dangerously close to necromancy, a topic of magic study he'd quickly dismissed. Perhaps Kenna was merely close to death and Daciana revived her. It was easy to miss a faint heartbeat, especially if one wasn't trained to search for it. But if this Ferryn was a Reaper like Lark, and he remembered guiding Kenna's soul...

Langford massaged his temples, wondering how, yet again, he was entertaining impossible thoughts.

Something about this information troubled him. If using Daciana's power to craft a weapon pulled from the energy of a roomful of people, what would raising the dead cost?

Did it matter? Perhaps not. But nothing itched like an unanswered question.

"What was the price?"

Even lost in the din of conversation, Daciana snapped her gaze to his. As if she'd been waiting for someone to ask this.

"It cost a village of lives."

"Dead?" She couldn't mean it. That would be... utter madness. Unless she did not know the range of destruction when she performed the resurrection.

Balan appeared at his side, red and black blood mingling along his hairline. "She can't control where her power pulls from. It pulls from the life essence of those nearest. The strongest first, until it seeks the next. Sometimes, she might spread the force of impact, as she did with all of you. But it isn't perfect, and the more fuel it needs, the more unstable it becomes. This type of magic is a living thing, and what the balance calls for, the balance gets."

Daciana's expression revealed no hint of what she was feeling. Even as the demon calmly explained murdering an entire village for one person.

Langford glanced over at Alistair, and something tightened in his chest. What if it was Alistair? Would he make the same choice?

"We need to sort out where to go next." Lark's voice cut through his thoughts. She limped over to them, and Langford wrapped an arm around her waist, bearing some of her weight.

Balan nodded, a resolute expression tightening his angular features. "I know where Nereida plans to drop the veil. Now that her little spy is probably scurrying off to tell her we made the blade, she'll be ready and waiting for us." He sneered. "You know how much she loves a rapt audience."

That didn't explain why she worked to keep Lark on her path. Why would the witch queen ensure Lark found a way to kill her?

"Where do we go?" Langford asked. It seemed the easiest question to answer at the moment.

"Where it all started. In the heart of the Twisted Woods. Where the first tear was made."

Lark's eyes widened, and she glanced over at Gavriel, who met her stare with a grim expression. "Where I crawled out when I was first remade."

They had a location, they had the weapon, and they'd added to their numbers. Why did that settle like bad indigestion?

"You have all the knowledge I possess," Balan said bitterly. "I'm of no use to you." There was a challenge in his voice.

Lark pulled herself free from Langford's arm and stepped closer to the demon. Her grip tightened on the blade. This was the moment he'd suspected was coming. The moment Lark sought her vengeance for Hugo. But Langford doubted it would quell their grief. He debated calling out to her, asking her if she was certain, but the assured steps of her approach and her razor-sharp focus on the demon silenced his tongue.

Demetria flung herself between them. "What are you doing?"

"Get out of the way, foolish human." Balan's rough voice held the faintest tremble. "I don't need you."

"You can't kill him," Demetria insisted. "I know you want to. I've seen the way you watch him. If it weren't for Gavriel, you'd have killed him before you even crafted the blade."

"Demetria, move." Lark's voice held no room for argument.

"Ruslan was a father to me!" Demetria's face twisted in fury. "He died for your safety. I demand that you leave Balan be."

Lark's brows drew together as if she was bracing against a physical blow. "I'm truly sorry. But you need to step out of the way."

"Oh, for fuck's sake." Balan shoved the girl away and stood waiting unflinchingly.

Lark stepped into his space, staring up at him. She handed the Reaper Blade to Daciana and yanked out a familiar knife covered with runes and symbols. Langford's heart squeezed at the sight of Hugo's craftsmanship. "This is for Hugo," she whispered. She thrust her knife in, low and aiming for the side beneath his liver.

Balan gasped when she pulled it free, his trembling hand covering the wound.

Lark immediately pulled a wrap from her pack, urging him to lie down on the floor. "Now, I keep you alive. We're even." She shot a glance at Gavriel, and set to work treating the stab wound.

Langford knelt beside her, replacing her hands with his. "Allow me," he said. "It won't kill him, but we need him fit to travel, and I can clean this and stitch him up." Leave it to Lark to dole out personal justice at the least convenient of times. But a thick cord of tension evaporated from the air, as Lark knelt beside the demon.

Balan coughed, a raspy laugh breaking loose from his chest. "Is this how you make friends?"

Lark didn't even glance at him as she responded. "We're not friends."

Langford didn't scold her for wasting medical supplies, though it was well within his right to. After all this was over, he'd air his grievances and give them all a good verbal lashing. But for now, a familiar efficiency took over as he treated the wound.

LANGFORD HAD NEVER VENTURED into the Twisted Woods. It was the place Daciana would go when they camped on the outskirts of Arden Forest, so she might shift in peace. He'd never questioned why she didn't ask them to camp closer—he'd always assumed it was to protect her privacy.

Now, he suspected there was more to it than that.

Most of Ardenian forestry was in hibernation mode from the cold, the preparation of winter hardening tree trunks and emptying branches. But this forest was dead. Rigor mortis had set in on the branches, and the floor was an obstacle of sharp bracken and roots. A hushed quiet filled the air—not even the sound of a breeze penetrated.

Of course, this was where Lark had crawled out of the Netherworld. Memories of the first day he met her flooded his mind. She had seemed to curl inward, clutching her stomach as if fearing that an unknown blade might strike. Her filthy face and bare feet had made his chest expand with pity for the girl. She hadn't spoken, not at first—her silence filling the campsite. And the way she'd experienced every sensation… it was eerie. Langford recalled the powerful urge he'd had to wrap her in a blanket and promise her safety. He hadn't done those things, naturally. Instead, he'd yelled at her for picking the wrong herb. To be fair, it was hemlock. No one needed coddling where poison was concerned.

Langford glanced over at her. At the bright determination in her amber eyes. That hadn't changed. But each time she glanced over at the princess, her face fell. Demetria hadn't spoken since they left the cursed castle, falling into a somber silence instead. He couldn't blame her. They'd all made a terrible mess of things. How much longer would she deign to stay with them now?

Langford's foot caught on something, sending him to the forest floor. He cursed, standing, and wiping off his trousers. When he examined the ground, he found a series of broken grey stones in long slabs, each stacked atop one another, like low stairs.

"Gavriel!" Lark's voice called from up ahead.

Langford hurried to catch up with the others. Up ahead were a series of stone steps leading to nowhere. Like a builder began constructing a way to reach the sky and gave up. Age had worn away some of its shape, but the man-made construction couldn't be mistaken for anything else.

This was a ruin.

Lark ran her hand along the stone. "Is this…" Her gaze found Gavriel's face.

He knelt beside her, tentatively touching where her hand had just been. "I don't remember."

Lark stood, abandoning the stone steps. With each footfall, the mysterious stairs in the dead forest diminished until they vanished from view.

When they reached the ancient yew, Langford stared up at it in awe. Never had he seen a tree of this size. Some of its roots were wider than him. "This is where you came from?"

Lark nodded, gazing at the tree with an unreadable expression. "It seems like lifetimes ago," she murmured.

Langford hung back, observing the former Reaper. The familiar weight of Alistair's arm draped around his neck.

"We haven't had time to ourselves this entire journey," he growled in his ear.

"Is that all you can think of?" Langford's ears burned, even as a more pleasurable fire stoked in his belly. "You're utterly indecorous."

Alistair laughed. "Aye, but you knew this about me. In fact, you love it."

Damn him and the truth of his words.

Though Alistair was… a physical person, Langford had learned it wasn't as it seemed. Alistair craved connection. Every touch, every kiss, was a promise he spoke with his body. He needed that reassurance more than he could ever say.

Langford was more than happy to provide that. When they weren't in a dead forest with their companions, that is.

He sighed, leaning his head against Alistair's shoulder. "Tell me something lovely." It was a game they used to play, back when Alistair's answers consisted mainly of pleasures Langford had no interest in. But it was a way to find levity in a moment of weighty dread.

Alistair's hot breath fanned against his ear. "When all of this is over, I'm going to lock us in a room and make you scream until you lose your voice." Langford shivered, turning to reprimand him, but the intensity in his eyes stole the words from his tongue. "And then," Alistair continued, "I'm going to take you to all the best libraries in all the world. I'm going to follow you to the ends of the earth and spend every day until my last dying breath carrying all your damned books and making you forget your headaches."

Langford's throat thickened. He'd made peace with the fact that Alistair had been wholly oblivious to his feelings for years, and never meant to hurt him by flaunting his sexual appetite, but it was an altogether different truth he was swallowing now. The truth, that Alistair was perhaps the best thing that had ever happened to him, as mad as that seemed. That all the nights he'd spent hurting, nursing wounded pride, with an ache of his heart, weren't all for naught. They'd found their way to each other, against all odds, and by the gods, he would never let this man go.

Before he could respond, the tree pulsed. The ancient, unyielding tree actually shifted.

Lark jumped back, pulling the Reaper Blade free. Daciana, too, yanked her daggers from her hips.

The others stood still, waiting.

Something shimmered in the air, a glimmering veil of sorts, and a pale hand snaked through. A lean arm, draped in black, and then the body of a man appeared. He had the blackest hair Langford had ever seen. It hung in his face, hiding his eyes. The man stiffened when he saw Lark, taking a hesitant step in her direction before he froze. Paralyzed to the spot.

Another person appeared, a woman. She was outfitted with armor and more weapons than even Daciana carried. Her elegant face was hard and severe as she surveyed them with distaste.

"Ceto." Ferryn staggered toward her.

A muscle jumped in her jaw, but she remained firmly in place. Waiting.

Dark shadows curled in on themselves, and a woman with a blunt cut of sable-black hair and a sharp gaze stepped through. Her form fitting leather armor glittered with blades of varying sizes. She took one look at Lark and a malicious smile curved against her lips.

"Nyx," Lark spat. Nyx hissed back at her.

A fourth figure appeared, a full-figured woman with long tendrils of white hair. Her lips were painted black, and as they parted to reveal white teeth, something dark shifted on her inhumanly beautiful face.

"Well, well," her melodious voice crooned, "this is quite the reunion."

Langford didn't recognize any of these people, but he acknowledged the instinctive fear that ran cold through his limbs. His body's response, a keen alertness, before his mind could catch up.

He didn't need to hear Lark address her, to sense who this must be. But Lark's face hardened, and she angled the sword in her battle-ready stance. "Nereida," she said, "you have a lot to answer for."

The witch queen grinned, a broad smile that was all teeth and sharp edges. "How I've missed your spirit, sweet thing."

CHAPTER FIFTY-NINE

DACIANA

"Everyone seems on edge. Nyx, help them relax," Nereida said.

Black shadows crawled across the ground, covering their feet and circling their legs. The acrid scent of magic filled the air, and the wrongness of it climbed up Daciana's thighs. Lark fought against Nyx's shadows, a note of panic entering her voice as she grunted with the effort.

Daciana refused to flinch—refused to give them the satisfaction of knowing how much it curdled her stomach.

"That's better. Oh, Lark, you brought your man! I always rooted for you two. No offense, Thanar." The one called Nereida wore her hair, white as snow, loose in thick waves. The breeze never stirred even a wisp, as if she wasn't really there. She sauntered over to where Gavriel stood and ran a finger down his throat. "I loved your work in the arena. It was utterly titillating to watch." She shivered as if overcome by the memory. "Your master says hello."

Gavriel's mouth tightened as he held perfectly still against the shadows. "Are you here to torment us or to fight? I've never had much patience for games."

A chuckle slithered out of her chest like a poisonous snake. "Both.

But don't fret. I'm nearly done." She glanced at Lark. "You, my dear, have been utterly fascinating. First, you reject the bond I so lovingly revealed to you. Then, you forgive the man who killed your friend. Mortals are such complex and contradictory beings, are they not?"

Lark continued to fight her magical bindings as she glared at her, fingers tightening around the hilt of the blade. "You've always had a penchant for rambling. Let us be done with this and finish what we started."

Nereida shook her head. "You're wrong. You mortals are always in such a rush. Stop and enjoy the scenery occasionally. As for the point of my visit, we'll get to that in due time." She turned her violet gaze on Daciana. A chill swept over her as if her stare held the force of a touch. Nereida's stare was hungry in its pursuit, communicating enough to raise heat on Daciana's cheeks.

This was the witch queen, the ruler of the Netherworld. The one who now commanded death. She wore the face of a beautiful woman, her body soft with ample curves. It was meant to distract and entice, and perhaps in Daciana's impulsive youth she would have fallen prey to such temptations. But beneath the inviting facade, a steady pulse of danger warned of her venom.

Every instinct in Daciana's body recoiled at her proximity.

"Little wolf, at last we meet." The witch cocked her head, eying her with interest. "You are a rare commodity these days. Almost makes me wish you lived during my mortality. We might have even been friends."

"I doubt that," Daciana said as bitterness coated her tongue.

Nereida's eyes darkened. "I, too, would rain down destruction to protect that which I love. We are more alike than you think." She set her sights on Kenna. "And the hunter who claimed the wolf's heart. You played an important part in all of this, my dear. Tell me, do you enjoy the hunt? Does chasing monsters drown out the memory of your grandmother's screams when she roasted alive on a spit? I see you, little hunter. I see you at night when you think no one is watching. When you believe the dark shrouds your pain."

Kenna gripped her silver blades tighter, but offered a tight smile.

"Hunters have cut down many witches who fell prey to their greed, to their most base desires. This will be no different."

Nereida's smile vanished. "Perhaps you would choose your words more wisely if you knew your grandmother dwelled in my domain." At Kenna's horrified expression, she continued. "Oh, yes. Did it comfort you to pretend she'd found peace? There is no peace for hunters in the afterlife. Not for her, not for your parents, and not for you when your sand runs out."

"Sounds like someone needs a hobby. I've heard holding grudges causes premature wrinkles." Kenna's voice wavered, along with the forced laugh she gave as she trembled with barely restrained anger. Daciana wanted to reach out to her, but beneath the binding shadows, her hands stayed firmly curled around her weapons.

Nereida's gaze fell to Balan. "Hello, traitor. Enjoying mortality?"

At her words, Balan stiffened, a sharp line of tension elongating his spine. "The only treachery here lies with you. If you betray every weapon you wield, soon you'll find yourself empty-handed."

She laughed, waving a delicate hand through the air. "I love it when lesser men dispense wisdom. I don't even have it in me to be angry. I find it utterly adorable." She shifted past him, already done with the exchange. Her eyes lit up when she spotted Demetria. "The beloved princess!" She bent in a mocking bow. "Your fate is one I eagerly await. How bloody is your righteous path to rule? Will you have the stomach for what needs to be done, or is your appetite merely whetted by the death that follows you?"

Demetria lifted her chin, possessing more strength than her young years warranted, and refused to rise to the witch queen's taunts.

Nereida laughed, running her nails down the princess' arm as her hungry gaze fell on Ferryn. A wicked smirk curved her darkened lips. "Look, Ceto! Your little plaything."

Ferryn only had eyes for the one called Ceto, his expression earnest and hopeful.

"You poor, sweet thing." Nereida placed her hands on his shoulders, gazing up into his face. She spoke slowly, enunciating every word. "You were but a means to an end for her. You know, her heart always belonged to Priamos."

Ceto's expression darkened, but she refused to meet Ferryn's hopeful stare.

"Don't fret. You've been invaluable to my cause. I'll grant you a place at my side and we can put all this nastiness behind us."

Ferryn gently pulled her hands from him. "I'll never stand with you."

Nereida laughed, offering a playful but loud slap to his cheek. When she set her sights on Langford, a sort of hunger overtook her eyes.

"You, there, darling bookworm. Step forward." She waved her hand, and the shadows clinging to Langford and Alistair dissipated.

Eying his now unguarded sword, Daciana tracked his movement, hoping he'd gain the opening to strike. He'd have to be quick, calling no attention to the action if he were to have a chance at disrupting the shadow Reaper long enough to free them.

Langford took an unwilling step, as if pulled. Alistair remained at his side, refusing to stay back.

Nereida dusted her hand across his cheek, healing the claw marks until only a faded blush remained. Langford cringed at the contact. "You've been most rewarding to watch. As much as I love a slow burn, there's something so deliciously heartbreaking about unrequited longing. Tell me, do you ever wonder if your man is imagining you were someone else? That he uses your body to calm the storm in his soul?"

A flash of pain crossed Langford's face, as if she'd uncovered a shameful secret.

Stepping between them, Alistair pushed Langford behind him. "Shut your fucking mouth, witch."

Nereida's nostrils flared, and her jaw clenched. "Mind your manners, or your man will mourn your loss."

"I've grown tired of your incessant talking. It seems you're determined to bore us to death."

"Alistair, stop," Lark hissed.

"Listen to your friend, mortal. Or are you afraid I'll tell him something you wish to hide?"

Alistair yanked his sword from its sheath. "I only wish to cut your tongue from your mouth."

Nereida's smile vanished, a cold hardness claiming her features. Her eyes narrowed and her jaw tightened.

Daciana felt it. The shift in the air. Like Nereida had been playing with them and this was the step too far. Alistair always pushed too far.

"Thanar, take the man's voice."

Thanar held out a hand, curling his fingers.

With a gasp, Alistair dropped his sword, gripping his throat. Langford reached for him, holding his gambeson tight enough to whiten his knuckles.

"Now take his breath." Nereida's voice was a gentle caress, a wicked glint gleaming in her violet eyes.

Thanar's brows drew together, as if fighting against the compulsion. His hand formed a fist, and he shut his eyes, turning away.

Alistair choked, his face blooming bright red. He clawed at his throat, desperation widening his eyes. Langford cried out. "Stop! You're killing him!"

Daciana broke free of the shadows, ignoring the way they burned her skin, and rushed to his side, checking his throat for blockages. She found none, but the air was locked out. Quiet noises escaped his mouth, but there was no intake of breath. He was suffocating, as if his windpipe had been crushed.

"One thing you can rest assured of, little mortal" —Nereida lifted her chin— "I always keep my promises."

"Let him breathe, please!" Langford's voice grew frantic. His hands framed Alistair's face as tears streamed down his cheeks. Swiftly, he pushed Alistair to lie flat on the ground and whipped a quill from his pack, snapping it so the vane was separated from the hollow shaft. With expert deftness, he yanked a dagger from Alistair's belt. He carved an incision in the hollow of his throat, blood trickling from the wound. He aligned the shaft, and pressed it in without hesitation. "Please, please, please." Langford murmured the words to either himself or to Alistair. Daciana waited, dangerous hope flooding her chest that they'd hear the first rasp of a breath. If anyone knew how to bypass a closed windpipe, it was Langford.

But only Alistair's ragged search for air was heard. His eyes widened in panic, his hands clutching at Langford's shoulders.

Lark clawed at her shadows, a guttural cry filling the space until she finally broke free. She raced toward Nereida, blade raised—Ceto blocked the blow, spinning her weapon away and knocking her to the ground. Lark sank her dagger into Nyx's thigh, distracting her long enough for her shadows to flee. Like breaking through the surface of water, the pressure ruptured as the spell holding the others in place scattered.

Daciana stood over Langford and Alistair, unable to decide if she should fight or try to help him breathe.

There was nothing she could do.

She was trapped in her own helplessness.

Nyx kept Lark on her knees before them, fisting her hand in her hair, and holding a dagger to her throat. Lark lifted her gaze to the man killing their friend. "Thanar."

At the sound, he opened his eyes. His dark stare bore into Lark's, his expression one of pleading, of anguish. "I'm sorry," he said.

"No, no, no. Daciana, do something!" Langford shouted, his voice breaking on her name.

Alistair's face turned purple, and then he went far too still. His hands loosened their grip on Langford's shoulders, falling to the earth.

Langford's wail of anguish broke through the silence.

CHAPTER SIXTY

LARK

The air ripped from Lark's lungs.

Alistair.

Alistair.

He couldn't be gone. Couldn't be dead. He was too bright, too loud, too much to snuff out, like the flame of a candle.

But his body lay motionless against the earth.

Langford's sobs echoed in the forest, his pain swallowing the space.

"Next time, I won't stop." Nyx's unused voice rasped in her ear. She kicked Lark to lay flat on the ground.

Lark scrambled to her feet, legs shaking. She half expected Ceto or Nyx to knock her down again, but they merely watched, contempt marring their unearthly beautiful faces. Thanar reached out as if to comfort, and Lark stumbled out of reach, backing away until she hit the firm safety of Gavriel's chest. His arms automatically came around her, and a hot tear trailed down her cheek.

Alistair. She would never hear his laugh or his filthy jokes. She would never feel his fierce loyalty or the swell in her chest every time he watched Langford with a dazed expression.

Nereida hummed. "I hope I've earned some trust by now."

"You fucking monster!" The words broke free from Lark's chest without thought.

"Now, now. Deep breaths. Deep breaths." Nereida glanced back at Thanar with a wicked smirk, and Lark wanted to cut the lips from her mouth. "Besides, he's the one who killed him."

Langford finally glanced up, his eyes glazed over in the force of his grief. "Please." His voice was a feeble whisper. "Dac, please."

An expression of sorrow stole across her face, and she shook her head. "Langford... I can't."

Lark pulled out of Gavriel's arms to fit herself by Langford's side. The ground bit into her knees, and more tears filled her eyes as Langford gently brushed Alistair's dark hair off his brow.

"Please, Daciana." Langford's bloodshot eyes burned with such fire as he begged. "Please, give him back."

Exhaling a shaky breath, a tear slipped down Daciana's cheek. Lark couldn't ever recall seeing her cry, not in all their time together. Not even when they lost Hugo. She'd always shouldered her grief, carrying it with her iron strength.

Another tear trailed down Daciana's face as she shook her head.

Langford scrubbed a hand over his face, spreading dirt across his cheek. His eyes were glazed and unfocused as he gently arranged Alistair's arms and wiped away the blood from the incision he'd made.

Wiping her nose on her sleeve, Kenna called out, "Dac, do it."

"You don't know what you're asking."

Kenna stepped over to her and wiped away her tears. "It'll be all right. Just... do it." She pressed her forehead to hers, a silent communication passing between them.

Daciana gently pulled away to kneel on the ground beside Langford. "If I do this," she began, "I have no way of controlling where it goes. Who it takes from."

Langford glanced around with unseeing eyes. "Please."

With a nod, Daciana pressed her hands into Alistair's chest. A wind picked up, tearing through the stillness of the trees. The smell of overturned earth and blood swept over Lark. She stood against the gale, searching each of their companions for signs of injury.

Aislinn kept darting glances at the Reaper Blade where it sat in the dirt, her fists opening and closing as if itching to grab it. Ferryn remained at Aislinn's side, tucking in close and lightly grasping her arm.

Balan held himself in a defensive stance, shielding Demetria from Thanar. No. Not from Thanar. He was nothing more than a weapon in Nereida's arsenal. She was the real threat.

But besides bracing themselves against the harsh wind, no one bled, no one slumped over. Perhaps she was pulling from far away.

Lark set her stare on Gavriel, refusing to look away. He met her gaze as they waited to see who might be caught in Daciana's power. If she could command it the way Balan showed her in Felix's forge, perhaps she could control it and take a little from everyone. But so far, no one seemed weakened by the pull. No one was affected. It was as if—

A groan came from nearby. Lark whipped her head around, searching for the sound.

Thanar fell to his knees, bracing his hands against the earth. He lifted his head, and his dark eyes met hers. His gaze glimmered with fear and longing so fierce, Lark wanted to weep. His sharp face tightened as he braced himself against the pain, and his eyes began to dim.

Nereida stood over him, her expression wiped of any concern. Only a hint of amusement.

Thanar reached for Lark.

Part of her wanted to reach back. For what purpose? She wasn't certain. But she almost stretched out her hand to meet his.

His lips parted, as if he was going to speak—

He collapsed on the ground. Utterly still. His body disintegrated into dust, and the last swell of the wind swept it away. A harsh pulse shook the earth, rattling through Lark and sending a chill down her spine.

Thanar was gone. The final death of a god who couldn't die. Somewhere in the darkest corners of Lark's heart she knew it. She sensed it. He was well and truly gone.

A sharp gasp sounded behind her. Lark spun to see Alistair gripping Langford's hand and flailing. Langford cried out, pressing his lips to every surface of Alistair's face and pulling him into his arms.

Daciana had done it. She had brought Alistair back and Thanar had fallen.

So why did Lark's stomach hollow at the thought?

Nereida clapped, a slow ringing sound. "Well, done," she said, nodding to Daciana appreciatively. "You are… quite formidable. It's a shame we didn't meet sooner." Her violet eyes glimmered with excitement. "We could have had all sorts of *fun* together. I thank you for all your help, but dear me, I have so much work to do. Ceto?" She wrapped a hand around Ceto's wrist, tugging her.

"Wait!" Lark called out. "We're not finished here."

Nereida laughed. "Oh, yes, we are. And I couldn't have done it without Daciana! See? I knew we'd work well together."

A look of abject horror widened Daciana's eyes. She shook her head, staggering back with the force of Nereida's words.

Nereida wanted Thanar to die? For what purpose? Wasn't she supposed to drop the veil?

Horror struck sharp and deep, plunging Lark's heart to the pit of her stomach. A quick glance at Balan and the terror of his expression confirmed her fears.

"Thanar… the veil…"

"Yes!" Nereida nodded emphatically. "Keep turning those wheels, sweet thing. You'll catch on."

"He was the source of balance… the keeper." Lark's stomach churned, her vision spinning. "The veil was—"

"Tethered to Thanar," Daciana finished, a bleak expression of grim acceptance on her face.

Nereida grinned, all gleaming white teeth on display. "The veil was tethered to Thanar, yes. I needed a Reaper Blade" —she winked at Aislinn— "or a wielder to take him out." She set her sights on Daciana. "You just destroyed the veil, and I didn't even have to lift a finger."

Lark swallowed the bile that rose in her throat, threatening to spill over. She lifted her gaze, searching for Gavriel—she needed him to keep her grounded when it felt like the earth was falling away. He met her stare, and the sharpest edge of the blade in her belly smoothed.

After everything, Nereida was still right here, as was the Reaper Blade. They might not have halted the fall of the veil, but they could take down the goddess responsible for it all. Lark met Aislinn's eye, praying to the skies she could sense what she planned.

Aislinn gave an almost imperceptible dip of her chin.

Lark lunged for Ceto, hoping the element of surprise was enough to level the field between her and the ancient warrior. Ceto's dark eyes widened as Lark tackled her to the ground. That familiar anger and disgust curled her lip.

Some things never changed.

Jolting into action, Aislinn threw herself toward the Reaper Blade laying innocuously on the forest floor.

Lark rolled, trying to free herself of Ceto's form, when the warrior gripped her wrist, keeping her firmly in place. "You weak fool," Ceto whispered, closing her hand around Lark's throat. She bashed her head against Lark's and shoved her off. The world spun, and something warm and wet trickled from Lark's throbbing nose. Ceto left her defeated on the forest floor. Dazed, Lark stood on shaky feet, taking a staggering step forward.

Why hadn't she killed her? It would have been all too easy.

Aislinn held the Reaper Blade, angling it in a defensive stance against Nereida.

Why wasn't she striking?

What was she waiting for?

Lark caught the black glimmer of Nyx's shadows curling around her arm, keeping the blade frozen in the air. Aislinn trembled against Nyx's hold, fighting to break free.

The witch queen smiled indulgently, shaking her head. "My dear girls, you forget the stakes when you act so rashly." With a snap of her fingers, she appeared out of Aislinn's range. "Without the veil, there's so much more freedom of movement." She snapped her fingers again, appearing directly in front of Gavriel. "Instead of punishment, how about I offer you a gift?"

"No," Lark's voice strangled in her throat as she charged toward them.

Nereida touched a finger to Gavriel's forehead, sparking a soft glow. His eyes slid shut, and a tremor shuddered through him.

No. No. Not him.

Nereida vanished in time for Lark to crash into the solid weight of Gavriel's body. He caught her in his arms, holding her close. "It's all right," he murmured. "I'm all right."

Staggering relief coursed through her body as she clung to him. His eyes tightened as if in pain, and he pinched the bridge of his nose.

Nyx released Aislinn from her shadows, and Aislinn nearly crumpled to the ground. Ferryn ran to her, grabbing her hand and tugging her back to him. Ceto's gaze flickered over the sight, a new crease forming between her brows.

Lark studied Gavriel and the mounting tension in his expression. "What did she do to you?"

"I'm not sure." His mouth tightened as he placed his hand on the side of his head.

Nereida reappeared behind Ceto and offered them an exaggerated wink. "I gave him his memories back."

Gavriel winced. "It's burning." A grunt of pain left his lips as he struggled to stay upright. Lark watched in horror, fear clamping tight in her chest as she held on to him for dear life. Inerys said giving him his memories too quickly could break his mind…

"Take them back!" she pleaded. "You've already won!" At Nereida's impassive smile, she screamed, "You're killing him!"

"Sorry, sweetness. Like I said, I'm on a tight schedule. I'd be on my way, if I were you," Nereida called out, lifting her hand. "There's a target on your back, and no veil to stop all the souls dying for a chance to roam." She pursed her lips, gazing at Aislinn, as if weighing her choices. "Keep the blade. I rather think I enjoy having the barest threat of death to motivate me."

With a snap of her fingers, she, Nyx, and Ceto vanished.

Gavriel fell to his knees, howling in pain and gripping his temples between both hands. Lark sank to the ground with him, holding his shoulders as he gritted his teeth against the pain. He was heavy in her arms, his head landing in her lap in a vicious mockery of the way she'd held him all the months ago when she saved him from his fate.

This is why Reapers do not love. This is why your mortal shall fall and the pain will consume you.

Terror ran icy cold through Lark's blood, as all she could do was watch and cradle his head as he fell unconscious.

CHAPTER SIXTY-ONE

LANGFORD

*L*angford jolted awake, his sweat-soaked body trembling and throat hoarse from screaming. The blackness of the room surrounded him, pressing against his feverish skin as the sound of his own labored breathing filled the silence.

"Langford?" Alistair's voice, roughened by sleep, cut through the space. "Was it another nightmare?"

Langford nodded into the darkness, not trusting his voice to hold steady. Alistair pulled him hard against his chest, wrapping himself around Langford, and crushing him beneath the weight of his embrace. "I'm here," he whispered against the shell of his ear. "I'm all right."

A strangled sob escaped Langford's chest. Despite each passing day proving the truth of Alistair's existence, his continuous survival, Langford couldn't force the memory from his mind. The memory of him dying in his arms. The panic written on his face as he gasped for air.

Daciana had saved him, had stitched his soul back into his body, but his death hounded Langford's dreams. Each night brought the same incessant reminder: he had lost Alistair once. He could lose him again.

This ache that plagued him felt like a loss—the loss of blissful ignorance. He'd just been getting used to the idea that he and Alistair might finally have the happy ending he'd never dared hope for. And reality had to remind him of how precarious his happiness was.

It could have been worse. At least Alistair was here and whole, both body and mind occupying the same space. The same couldn't be said about Gavriel.

Nereida did something to the poor man's mind, but that didn't explain what happened next. One moment, he was fine, and the next he was screaming on the forest floor. Until he went still.

He didn't move again after that.

Langford kept tabs on vitals. He maintained his body temperature, and apart from a curiously slow heart rate, the man seemed otherwise in perfect health, unconsciousness notwithstanding. Lark was beside herself, and what could Langford offer as comfort? Gavriel was alive, but still he would not wake.

After the witch queen vanished along with her lackeys, they'd fled the Twisted Woods as fast as they could, holing up in the small village of Green Mills until they could sort out where to go next. Aislinn didn't dare venture into town, fearing she might see those who knew her as dead. The others kept to the forest. Langford was prepared to camp with them, but Alistair insisted they find the inn. Said since he died, he got to choose where he slept for at least a few days.

Langford didn't find that joke funny.

He didn't find many things funny these days.

"Langford?" Alistair's voice was a balm. He ran his hands down Langford's back, nuzzling into his neck. "Sweetheart, I'm here," he murmured.

Langford nodded again, even as the tears streamed down his face.

CHAPTER SIXTY-TWO

DACIANA

With a final swipe of her sword, Daciana hacked the head from a harpy's body. Blood and feathers coated her arms from the scuffle. Kenna panted through a wry smirk as she, too, stood over her felled foe.

Between the trees, the first hint of daylight, cold and pale, slipped through to illuminate the frost-coated ground, now marred with black blood.

"We should venture to Anquan."

Daciana peered at Kenna, wiping her sword against the feathered wings of the dead harpy. "Why?"

Kenna shrugged. "I have some contacts there. It might be good to connect with the other hunters."

"To what end?" The veil had fallen, thanks to her, and Undesirables were free to roam unchecked. For the first few days, all seemed quiet. Daciana almost believed Nereida was bluffing. But she'd felt the truth in her blood, in her bones, when her power pulled from Thanar—snuffing his life force and restitching Alistair back into his body.

Then came the reports. Stories of death, of blood, of children carried off from their beds and corpses found in the barns. People disappeared; curfews were enacted. But it didn't stop the flow of bloodshed. They'd seen it firsthand.

Monsters were free to roam.

"We could bolster our numbers, try to organize against our common enemy," Kenna said. "It might not make a difference, but it seems the logical step, doesn't it?" Her mouth twisted to the side, an expression of consideration on her face. "But before we rally the hunters, we should go see Inerys."

Daciana stilled. "We're not having this conversation again."

"Fearing this power put you at risk in the first place."

She had to concede that point. "Balan said—"

"I don't give a fuck what Balan said. I never want to see that fear in your eyes again. I never want to *feel* that helpless." Kenna took her chin in her hand. "We're going to see Inerys, and we'll figure it out. Together." She punctuated her point with a harsh kiss.

Daciana resisted the urge to run her fingers through Kenna's hair and hold her in place, she was still covered in blood and feathers, but she deepened the kiss.

Perhaps Kenna was right. Perhaps it was time to face the past.

Kenna broke away, her breathing ragged. "Tell Lark we leave at daybreak. I'll head into town and see if the others wish to come."

The others would come, there was no doubt about that. Lark was still reeling over whatever Nereida had done to Gavriel. Langford monitored him, assuring her his body showed no signs of distress. But he still hadn't awakened. Heading to Inerys was a sound plan, despite Daciana's misgivings.

The witch would know what to do.

Daciana smiled, despite the constant burning in her stomach. "Deal."

CHAPTER SIXTY-THREE

LARK

There wasn't any time to mourn their failure. No time to fall into grief over bringing destruction to the mortal world. It was a time for action, a plan.

When Daciana told Lark of her aims to train with Inerys, a newfound determination clicked into place. This was the focus they needed. Lark never would have pushed, but the only way to rebuild the veil was with Daciana.

When they first arrived on the witch's doorstep, she barred the door, refusing them entry. But once they camped outside her home, showing no signs of leaving, Inerys let them in and grumbled her acquiescence.

It was fortunate she was, yet again, willing to help. They could use a safely warded place to prepare, to train.

Undesirables were free, and they needed every advantage they could get. Kenna could teach everyone their strengths and weaknesses. Gavriel could help train Aislinn to fight—

The air smothered in Lark's throat as she glanced over at where he still slept. It was too easy to forget, especially upon waking, when dreams were still fresh in her mind. Lovely, tortuous dreams, the pain only ripping anew with the realization they weren't real.

She slid her hand into his, running her thumb along his knuckle. What she wouldn't give to see that scarred mouth pull into a smirk. To hear his deep voice call her 'demon' as he teased her for being so worried. But his face remained slack with sleep in the silence of Inerys' herb-filled room.

Lark gently pulled her hand away and rose to her feet. She splashed her face with water from the basin. The smell of dried lavender filled the space, and Lark stared up at the bundles of herbs hanging from the ceiling.

The fall of the veil, and whatever spell-induced slumber Gavriel had succumbed to, wasn't the only loss they'd suffered that day. She'd failed Demetria when she withheld the death of her mentor, and in all the commotion, the girl had fled with Balan. Lark released a tight breath that offered relief to the crushing weight in her chest. She couldn't blame the girl for hating her, but running off with a demon in a foreign country when she was labeled an enemy to the crown in Koval was a stupid risk. A stupid, impetuous risk she'd pushed her into taking. Just like Thanar's decision to sign himself over to Nereida to free Lark from her contract.

Lark didn't let herself remember the look on Thanar's face as he drew his last breath. Nor did she dwell on the way her stomach dropped at the sight of it.

She needed to worry about the immediate problems at her door or she'd spiral under the weight of it all. Find a way to wake Gavriel. Prepare for the fight ahead. There would be no exchange of words the next time she crossed paths with Nereida. No long-winded speeches or attempts to understand. There would only be blood and the death of the witch queen.

There was a comfort to forming goals when all else fell to chaos.

"So," Daciana said at the end of a long day, "care for a game of Paragons and Sinners?"

Lark huffed her best approximation of a laugh, shaking her head.

"No. I shot so many arrows I doubt I could hold the cards up." It had been ages since she'd trained this hard. Without Hugo, training had fallen by the wayside, a fact Lark was determined to remedy.

"Suit yourself." She offered Lark a spot beneath her quilt, and Lark huddled beside her.

Winter whispered through the Emerald Woods, freezing the pond and glittering the trees with ice that shone like crystal. They hadn't been with Inerys long, but Aislinn was settling in nicely. Ferryn was still quiet after everything.

She'd have to make more of an effort to connect with him. It wasn't easy, being human for the first time. Ferryn laughed when she suggested it, and then he realized she was right. Somehow, he had been made human. After that, his smiles were softer, restrained. Lark would do anything to bring back his careless abandon.

Langford and Alistair had grown even closer, if that was possible. Lark could already envision that cottage Langford dreamt of, the one from the Shrine. Someday, it might be reality.

And Gavriel. Lark drew up her knees, wishing to forget the way his unconsciousness held a stillness akin to death. Inerys had set to work, mixing concoctions she said would help her search his mind without harming him. She kept Aislinn close, demanding detailed explanations of how she entered Lark's dreams and what she used as a tether. Lark sat by Gavriel's side as they worked, swaying with exhaustion, until they shooed her away.

She still spent time each day whispering to him, just in case he heard her. Assuring him he wasn't alone. That they would find a way back to each other.

Lark gazed out over the frozen pond. So much had changed, and yet she still felt like she was treading water. The first few days after the veil fell, Lark thought Hugo might appear. That one good thing might come of lowering the barriers between planes. No farewells, not even in death.

He never came.

Daciana shivered, and Lark leaned her head against her shoulder. "Should we head inside?"

"All right, but if Inerys tries to make me cook again, I'm dousing her food with drowsing tonic."

A grin tugged at Lark's mouth, and even though her chest was a constant ache of burden, it was easy to fall into easy chatter with Daciana. "It's only fair, after what she did to me and Gavriel."

"That's right!" Daciana kept the quilt around them as they staggered toward the house, their movements restricted. "We owe her one good night's sleep."

Lark laughed, feeling a lightness she knew would dim, but reveling in it while it lasted. "We do at that."

As they walked, they bumped into each other, the result of numb legs, when Inerys' door burst open. Aislinn stood, panting, the light from the cottage silhouetting her rumpled clothes and messy wisps of hair. "Lark," she breathed, "it's Gavriel."

Panic slammed into Lark's chest, hollowing her out. "What's happened?"

Aislinn shook her head, giving a small laugh. "I was able to reach him."

Confusion numbed the weight in Lark's chest until a slow trickle of understanding spread through her. Aislinn was working alongside Inerys, and though they never mentioned trying it, not in front of Lark, Inerys was deeply fascinated by her somniavi abilities. Of course, they would try on Gavriel. "You entered his dreams."

"Yes." Aislinn nodded, a small sob escaping her mouth. "I can help you talk to him."

EPILOGUE

Merikh drummed his fingers against the war table. Its surface was littered with maps of mortal lands and silly little markers. All of it was a waste of time. Let the petty humans squabble and deal with the mess the witch made. It was below his rank.

Achar swept into the room, his billowing robes untied, and his dark hair mussed where it hung above his shoulders. Someone wasn't prepared for this impromptu meeting.

"Called away from something important?"

Achar glowered, annoyance tightening his face. "I was in the middle of answering a rather fervent prayer."

Meaning he was fucking a mortal.

Merikh laughed, cringing. "Humans are so filthy. Why do you debase yourself?"

Achar smoothed out his hair and straightened his clothes. *Such a vain creature.* "You don't know what you're missing. Their worship is so… *passionate.*"

"I'm not interested in fraternizing with cattle."

"One day, curiosity will overtake you, and you'll understand."

Before Merikh could respond, Basilius strode into the war room. His golden armor was blinding beneath the sun streaming through the windows. The sun in Avalon set when he bid it to, which was never. He enjoyed shining like a beacon far too much.

"There have been troubling developments." His stern voice cracked like a whip. "And we can ignore them no longer."

"What sort of developments?" Merikh was already bored. They knew the power-hungry witch was determined to bring destruction to the world. It made no difference. Mortals prayed even harder under duress.

"The veil has been lowered."

Merikh jolted, and Achar let out a breath. "How?"

"Not the witch?" Achar asked.

Basilius tucked his arms behind his back, taking slow, deliberate steps around the room. "She enlisted the help of a *Vitas Conjuror*."

"They were eradicated centuries ago!" Achar cried. "It isn't possible."

"Apparently, they weren't. Thanar is no more."

They fell silent. It had been eons since Thanar had been considered one of their comrades, but the news of his demise still sucked the air from the room. If someone such as he could be wiped from existence, they were all vulnerable.

They should close the crossing. Let the Otherworld and the Netherworld stew in their failures. If mortal souls were to fester, they should cut off any and all paths to Avalon. Not even the few who merited entrance were worth getting involved in this mess.

Basilius leveled Merikh with his implacable stare. "There's more. Reports have been brought to me of a mortal somniavi. Sargon wants it dealt with."

Somniavi were dream walkers. They could cleave their souls at will and venture into any plane, even into the mind of another. There was no greater threat than the ease with which one could slip into dreams and extort their influence. The very foundation of Avalon depended on avoiding these disturbances, for the place the warriors and paragons were most vulnerable was in their slumber. One clever somniavi could infiltrate their ranks and cause unspeakable harm.

It must be destroyed.

Merikh picked up one of the markers, a depiction of a Warrior. The marker that represented him. "Where must I go?"

Basilius pointed to one of the forests on the map. "Venture here and bring it to me."

Merikh placed his marker over the Emerald Woods. "By your leave, Commander."

ACKNOWLEDGMENTS

Writing the second installment of this series has been an adventure. Where Songs of the Wicked felt like a public journey, Lament of the Wolf was more of a quiet, closed door mission. I would be remiss if I didn't first and foremost thank my ever loving and supportive husband, Lance, who celebrated every win, helped me work through every plot hole, and kept me sane when I spent my nights retreating to my writing cave.

My daughters, both the wildling who reminds me that magic is real and monsters are worth slaying, and the wee wildling who is due to make her appearance in the world any day now. I love you both more than I could ever say.

My amazing editor, Friel Black, at Grey Moth Editing. Without whom this book would be a hot mess and still living on my Word Document, hiding from the public.

My writing soul mate, my sister, my best friend, Friel. I love you and I love that I can share my story with you when it's all vibes, and you're still excited for me. You've done so much for me, offered a shoulder to cry on when imposter syndrome makes me want to hide, talked me through plot holes, chased my plot bunnies with me, and you always believed in me, even when I couldn't.

Elle, my writing sister in blood and gore, every star in my sky. I miss you so much. But I know you're always with me.

Brit, I can't even begin to articulate how much you mean to me. I'm so lucky to have found you. One day, we shall feast on all the apple treats this world has to offer together.

My beta readers, Freya, Stella, Emmalee, Devon, and Brit. I forever appreciate you and all your help.

Fran at @coverdungeonrabbit once again, you've made magic of my book cover. Thank you so much for your brilliance.

My family for always being excited for another book of mine to release, (and for keeping the heckling to a healthy level. Just enough to remind me where I stand in the family, but not too much to shatter my confidence. The sweet spot.)

All the readers, writers, bookworms, cosplayers, magical creatures in our amazing community on Instagram. Each and every one of you inspires me, and though I wish I could list you each by name, this would quickly become the longest book I've ever written if I did.

Jaime, thank you once again for forgiving me for the sword in the eye bit all those years ago. You chose to remain my friend out of either loyalty or fear of a repeat offense. Whatever the reason, I'm grateful.

And you, dear reader. Every time you put faith in my story and step into my world, you bring a rare bit of magic to my life by making my dreams come true. Thank you, and know how much I appreciate you.

ABOUT THE AUTHOR

C. A. Farran is an emerging author of fantasy. She's addicted to video games, KitKats, and energy drinks.

Farran grew up by the sea on a steady intake of fairytales, renaissance fairs, and mythology. She's always felt a profound connection to horror and dark fantasy, spending her childhood searching the woods for monsters and magic.

Now, she spends her days photographing nature in Maine with her three cats; Commander, Demon, and River, her husband, and their two wildlings.

This is her second novel in the Dreamer's Misfortune series.

To stay updated on her shenanigans, check out cafarran.com